The Many Adventures of Donnie Malone

Paul E. Doutrich

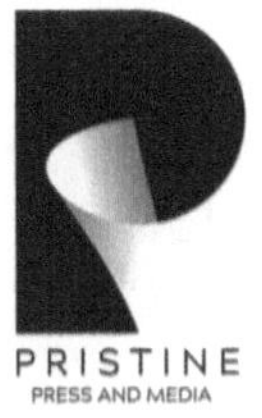

PRISTINE
PRESS AND MEDIA

ISBN
978-1-964804-58-3 (Paperback)
978-1-964804-57-6 (eBook)
978-1-964804-59-0 (Hardcover)

*For my wife, Cindy Brooks Doutrich,
whose enthusiastic support and
help made this possible.*

Table of Contents

The
Many
Adventures of
Donnie Malone
PAUL E. DOUTRICH

Chapter 1

LIFE ON THE FARM

My Uncle Don Malone was a born storyteller. When I was growing up, my favorite part of an Uncle Don visit was the new story that he always brought with him. He delivered his packages via an easygoing, clear speaking voice that he would modulate for a little dramatic emphasis. He was an unassuming, quiet man who disappeared into his stories and let his words and images carry a listener through the day's adventures. He was also a keen observer of his world and had an exceptional memory for details. And he usually mixed a little mischief into his stories because there was usually a little mischief mixed into him. Uncle Don was really a great storyteller.

Even after I had children of my own, I'd eavesdrop whenever he told them his stories. I had heard most of them before, but they felt just as good when I was an adult as they did when I was a boy. Sometimes he'd tell one about a friend or neighbor or somebody he had met along the way, but the best stories, the ones I liked most, were about his own adventures. Of course, like any good storyteller, he'd sprinkle his tales with a little bit of imagination, but from all I can tell, the important parts were true.

Uncle Don died twenty years ago, and I've missed him and his stories ever since. So about ten years ago I began stitching together as many of his tales as I could remember. I also read through my mother's diaries looking for "Donnie." She was a lifelong diarist who clearly adored her big brother. Add to that a little research at the county historical society to fill in some of the gaps. What I found is what follows.

My Uncle Don's adventures began on the second day of the twentieth century, January 2, 1901. Looking at my notes, I can hear him now....

As you already know, there were four of us. I was the oldest and bounced into this world right along with the new century. Then came your Uncle Pat who was born two years later. Your Uncle Ray was four years younger, and Mary Ann, your mother, was an unexpected package that was delivered seventeen years after I was. She was born after we had moved to Harrisburg. She was always special to all of us. I suspect you know that my dad, your grandpa, ran a men's clothing store in Middletown. What you probably didn't know was that when I was growing up, we lived on a small farm about two miles outside of Middletown. Dad hired a neighbor, Mr. Schultz, from up the road to work the farm for him. Mr. Schultz and his wife had immigrated from somewhere in southern Germany before I was born. He was the one who taught me about building things and growing things and fixing things, and Dad taught me just about everything else. Mrs. Schultz helped Mom once in a while. She also made the best pies and cakes I ever ate.

We had fun growing up on the farm. There were always places to explore, hills to conquer, and something or other to chase. My brothers and I knew every inch of that farm. We had so many secret hiding places. I think we could have disappeared for a month before anyone found us. Sometimes those hiding places came in handy when Mr. Schultz wanted us to do a chore or two that we didn't want to do. We usually helped out, but there were times when a tree needed to be climbed more than a stack of hay needed to be pitched or wood needed to be piled.

Considering there were three of us, my brothers and I were pretty well behaved, but every now and then we did get into a little trouble. I remember one summer day Mr. Schultz wanted us to whitewash the fence between our backyard and the cornfield. Whitewashing the fence was something my brothers and I enjoyed doing every summer. There were few farm chores better than slopping whitewash onto our dingy fence. I remember a time though when the job included more than just brushing paint onto the fence.

One year when I was about nine or ten, our annual whitewashing required a little extra paint. I can still hear Mr. Schultz's thick, German-splattered instructions:

"Ere you go boys, I got tree new brushes for yous und two gallons of da vitevash. If you need more a da vitevash come und git me from da house."

As always, I was the leader of our little work crew. We took the brushes and paint and got started. Mr. Schultz watched us work for a while, and once he saw we were doing it the way he wanted it done, he left.

Like most farms back then, there were always a few stray cats that lived in our barn. Most were friendly cats—we called them mousers and gave each one an unofficial name. We considered them as almost pets. Just about anytime we were in the yard those cats were rubbing up against a leg or begging to be petted. Every now and then, especially during the winter, we even added a few table scraps to their mouse meals.

As we were working on the fence that day, two of the cats, I forget their names, came over to get petted. To us three boys those cats looked especially scraggly and dirty and in need of some sprucing up. So, my brothers and I decided that a fresh coat of whitewash would do them both just right. Pat and I picked them up and held them while Ray painted them. He didn't paint them all over just on their backs and tails, but they were pretty soaked when he got done. About the time that Ray was putting the final touches onto our two models, Mr. Schultz came back to inspect our fence work. When he saw what we were doing to those cats he shouted at us to stop immediately. I don't know if it was his shouts or our surprise that scared those two cats, but in a flash, they were headed across the yard directly toward the laundry my mother had hung out to dry. A few seconds later two pairs of Dad's pants, a tablecloth, and some towels had dirty white stripes across them.

I don't remember exactly what happened when Dad got home that night, but our painting days were over for the year. As for the cats, we found them hiding in the barn with sawdust and straw stuck to them. A real ugly sight! Mr. Schultz sheared most of the paint off and Mom gave them some milk and table scraps special and put a blanket down for them in the barn. It didn't take long before they were back on mouse patrol.

A year or two later, Pat and I had another little caper. Ray was doing something with Mom that afternoon, so Pat and I decided to do some heavy labor stuff. Out in the far corner of the backyard, Mr. Schultz had stacked old bricks on top of each other to make a fire pit. It was about four feet long and about three feet wide, stood about three feet high, and had a heavy iron frame that held a thick screen over the top of it. We used it to burn trash and debris from around the farm. In the autumn we burned lots of leaves there. You could do that back then.

On this day, Pat and I decided that the pit was a bit crooked and needed some fixing, so we pulled the frame off the bricks, then took the pit apart. It didn't take long before every brick had been laid on the yard. Then for the next hour or so we tried to reassemble it. Along the way, we discovered that we weren't such good engineers. No matter how we tried to arrange the bricks, they just didn't fit together again. We also discovered that it was a lot easier pulling the screen and frame down than it was lifting it back up. As we were trying to figure out how to get the pit back together again, Mr. Schultz, who had been out in the fields, came over to see what we were doing. I never saw him angrier than he was that day.

Mr. Schultz was not a demonstrative man. Nor was he a particularly imposing figure: about five feet seven with broad, round shoulders that sloped down onto a thick frame. From watching him doing chores around the farm we knew he was strong, and once in a while he'd show off a couple of impressive arm muscles. He was also a quiet man who almost never raised his voice and only spoke when he had to. Maybe he was self-conscious about his German accent. Once in a while, we saw him smile, but most of the time, he seemed almost emotionless.

That day Pat and I discovered that when he was angry, Mr. Schultz could be scary. Stomping over to us, he pushed his head forward, scrunched up his mouth, and squinted his eyes into two narrow slits. The middle part of his face turned red, and his chin and cheeks turned white. He hunched his shoulders forward a bit and picked up his pace as he approached us. He looked like a miniature bull ready to defend his territory.

Never taking his eyes off the pit, he marched over to where we were standing. When he got to about ten feet from us, he growled "git." We didn't need more than that. We ran back to the house.

The next morning Pat and I snuck back to the fire pit. We wanted to see if Mr. Schultz had done anything to it. To our surprise, the pit was just as it had been before Pat and I took it apart. The bricks were neatly stacked, and the screen and frame rested on top. The only change was that the sooty side of some of the bricks faced out.

For the next week, Pat and I avoided Mr. Schultz, but when we did see him again, he didn't say anything about the fire pit, and I am sure he never told Dad what we had done. When we got old enough, we'd walk into Middletown. We used to walk everywhere. A couple miles was nothing. The biggest building in Middletown was the town hall right in the center of town where our road intersected the town's other paved road. Down our road just a bit farther at the other end of town was a railroad station. Several trains came into Middletown every day. Most came from Philadelphia or Harrisburg, but there were also locals to smaller places like Lancaster, Reading, or York. My dad's store was a pretty big building two doors up our road from the town hall. In addition to Dad's store, there were two churches, the Middletown Five Cent Bank, a grocery, a hardware store, three diners, a pharmacy, and a dime store. Middletown also had a movie theater; they called them nickelodeons back then. The nickelodeon became one of our favorite places, especially when it was too cold to be outside. It got so that just about every Saturday during the winter, Pat, Ray, and I would walk into town and watch a film. I liked Charlie Chaplin and Douglas Fairbanks movies best. Pat liked Fatty Arbuckle. Ray just liked being with Pat and me.

We also had a bunch of friends from school who lived in town. We'd go in and play sports with them almost every day when the weather was good. I loved baseball and was pretty good. I played center field and could catch anything hit near me. I was a good hitter too, but most of all I loved chasing fly balls. All three years in high school I was the starting center fielder and the leadoff batter. Pat was better at football. He was a rugged kid. Average height and weight, but pound for pound, the strongest guy I knew. Ray never got to play sports with us much because he was younger and smaller. Instead, he'd go into town and do things for Dad in the store.

Aside from baseball and movies, my passion in those days was my dad's 1910 Premier touring car. I fell in love with it the first time I saw it. We got it in the middle of the spring when I was eleven. I remember Dad driving it home the first time. I guess Mom knew, but Dad didn't tell any of us boys that he had bought it. He just said he was bringing home a surprise. There weren't many automobiles in Middletown at that point so when we saw one rolling up the road, we watched it pretty carefully. It didn't take long to recognize Dad in the driver's seat. After he got home, he took us for a ride up the road a couple of miles. It was the first time that Ray had ever ridden in an automobile. Boy, that was a great day!

Our Premier was a beauty too! Forty horsepower, four cylinders, three manual speeds with shifts on the steering wheel, and a crank starter—really exciting. It sat three in the back and two in the front, perfect for our family before Mary Ann was born. It was dark red, had a thick, tan-colored canvas top and bouncy leather seats, but the engine was what fascinated me. The first time Dad pulled up the hood and I saw the pistons pumping, I was hooked. I wanted to know all about how the car worked. Instantly I decided to become the family's mechanic, and with some help from Mr. Schultz, I did. It didn't take long before I could take that car apart and put it back together again with no problem.

I was fourteen the first time Dad let me drive the Premier. It took a few weeks before I completely mastered the gear shifts, clutch, and gas pedals. The brakes were hand brakes, which added to the ordeal. You had to be alert and coordinated to drive back in those days. You also had to be careful about where you drove. For a while, there were only two paved roads going through the town. There were also a bunch of dirt and gravel roads, but driving on any of them could be risky, especially in the spring when the dirt turned to mud. If you got stuck, you needed a team of horses to pull you out. Those roads also had ruts and rocks that could instantly blow out a tire. I blew out a couple, but we always had at least one spare, and no one could change a tire faster than I could.

Once I got to know how the Premier worked and how all the parts fit together, I started hanging out at the place where Dad bought the car. Until after World War I, Mr. Davidson operated the town's only gas station and was the only one who sold and serviced cars. For a while, he was also the town blacksmith. There was something about the smell of gas, the feel of grease on my fingers, and the sight of those engines that mesmerized me. I was there so often the summer before I started high school, in 1915, that Mr. Davidson let me help work on engines. By the next summer, I had become his chief (and only) mechanic, which gave him more time to sell cars. Throughout high school, I'd help him whenever I had time. I got to know how all sorts of engines worked. Model Ts, the Maxwell, Buicks, and more. My favorite was a Simplex Coupe. Little did I know then how important to me that engine would be. With a little time and the right parts, I could get any of them running. Occasionally, when he got busy, Mr. Davidson even let me borrow a car so that I could spend more time working at his station.

The Premier changed our family's daily life, especially Mom's. Before we had the car, she didn't leave the farm very often. Instead, Dad did the household errands and shopping. Since the grocery store was across the street from Dad's store, he'd get a list of things we needed from Mom and give it to Mr. Smith in the morning and then pick up the order on his way home in the evening. Mom never learned to drive the Premier, but after we got the car, she went along to work with Dad at least once a week. She did the shopping herself, did other errands, and then Dad drove her home at lunchtime. She also got involved with a couple of women's organizations in town and went to meetings during the week. I'm pretty sure Dad didn't know it, but one of the places where Mom helped out was at the women's suffrage office. It didn't take long before Mom was spending several afternoons a week in town. After I started driving, I became her part-time chauffeur. In fact, one of the reasons that Dad taught me to drive was so that I could take her places.

I was surprised when I found out about Mom volunteering at the suffrage office. It seemed out of character. At home, Mom wasn't very political. She was a quiet, discreet woman who preferred being behind the curtain rather than in the spotlight. I knew she was smart and that she was really good at organizing things. It didn't matter whether it was arranging shelves in the pantry or coordinating the annual church picnic, which she did every year. She was a great organizer. At home, Dad was clearly the authority, but Mom was the one who kept the house running smoothly. When they did disagree about how or when something should be done, she knew how to subtly lead Dad to decisions she had already made. For instance, it was Mom who convinced Dad to teach me to drive so that I could drop her off in town. She said it would make life easier for Dad. Mom was also a tolerant person who had a keen sense of right and wrong but rarely criticized anyone. On the other hand, if she thought someone was taking advantage of her, she tactfully but assertively let them know it. Driving her around town, I got to see a side of her that I didn't know existed.

The Premier was great for my brothers and me too. Occasionally Dad let me drive to school. I'd drop him off at the store, then drive my brothers and me to school. During baseball season I often drove Pat and a couple of teammates to our games. As I had for Mom, I also became Dad's part-time chauffeur. Sometimes that meant picking up things for the store or making a delivery to a special customer. Sometimes it meant driving Dad to Harrisburg, which was only about twenty miles away. The round trip usually took a couple of hours. I liked the time alone with Dad on those drives. We'd talk about everything from life in Middletown to baseball and school to what I wanted to do after school. Dad made it clear that I would go to college. He liked a couple of local schools, which was fine with me.

It was also clear that Dad wanted me to join him at the store once I graduated from college. That part I wasn't too sure about. I didn't know what I wanted to do, but a life working at his store didn't appeal to me.

Education was important to Dad. He was only the second in his family to graduate from high school and the first to go to college. He graduated from Lafayette College, then worked as a Pennsylvania Railroad station manager, saved his money, and started his own men's clothing store in Middletown. Image was important to Dad. You couldn't be a success if you didn't look like a success, and he looked like a success. He was a fastidious dresser. He always wore a suit, usually a three-piece suit, and a fashionable bowler hat. A wrinkled dress shirt was unacceptable to him. His shirts had to be starched and freshly pressed. He had dozens of ties that he coordinated with his suits. Dad was a shade under six feet tall, had perfect posture, a carefully trimmed mustache, and when he walked anywhere it was clear that he had a purpose. With him, there was never any question about where he stood on an issue. Politically he was a Teddy Roosevelt imperialist but not a Roosevelt reformer. When he made a decision about something, he was committed to it. Integrity was especially important to Dad. He told me many times that the two things you truly own are your integrity and your education. It was part of the reason he was so well respected in Middletown.

Dad's edict that I go to college was OK with me. I liked school and got good grades—better than Pat but not as good as Ray. Nobody got grades better than Ray! My favorite subject was American history. I liked both math and science but had a hard time learning them from a book. I was a hands-on, practical application person. I was also a project person. I always did well when a teacher assigned a class project. I liked gathering information, figuring out how to put it all together, and then getting completely wrapped up in making it into something that was mine. The standard method of sitting with the rest of the class going over stuff together was boring to me.

One of the nice things about growing up in a small town was that I had the same classmates all through school. The elementary school had only one classroom per grade with about twenty students in each. The junior high school and high school were bigger but not that much bigger. There were only forty-one in my graduating class, so we all got to know each other pretty well. Pat had only forty-four in his class, and Ray's graduating class was about the same size.

Baseball was my favorite thing about high school. Back then we played after school against our own schoolmates; they called them intramural games. Each class played the other two or three times. My class lost to the seniors my sophomore year but beat both classes the next two years. At the end of the intramural season, we had a school allstar team that played two games against the two city high schools from Harrisburg and teams from nearby towns, Steelton and Lawton. Unlike the intramural games, we got uniforms and went to the all-star games on the local train. It was special. I started in the outfield on the all-star teams all three years. Twice we went undefeated. During my junior year, the team from Harrisburg Tech beat us both times but we won the rest of our games.

The only time I ever got in trouble at school was one afternoon during my sophomore year when Charlie Snyder, who was the shortstop on our baseball team and the class troublemaker, locked the class and our English teacher out of her classroom. We had a big test scheduled that day and Charlie wasn't ready for it. Usually when he did his pranks, he did them by himself, but this time I got pulled into it. Before class, while Miss Robinson was down the hall, Charlie snuck up to her desk, opened the top drawer, took out the key, went out into the hall, and locked the classroom door behind him. As he left, he passed by me and slipped the key into my pants pocket. Since he was my teammate and a friend for almost ten years, I didn't say anything.

To get the door opened Miss Robinson had to get a passkey from the front office. When she came back, she brought the principal, Mr. Walker, with her. I am sure he had seen the scheme before and had it all figured out. He opened the door, and as each one of us went back in, he made us turn our pockets inside out. Of course, when it was my turn, the key popped out. That's when the interrogation began.

"How'd that key get into your pocket, Don?" I just shrugged my shoulders and didn't answer.

"Did you find it somewhere?" I didn't answer.

"Let's go to my office and figure this out." I followed him down the hall and into his office.

"Look Don, I know your mother and father well, and I know you're not a troublemaker. I also know you are doing well in English so I don't think that you would take the key from your teacher's desk and then lock everyone outside the classroom just so you could avoid a test. Miss Robinson also has a pretty good idea who the real culprit is."

"Who does she think did it?"

"I'll just say that it's one thing to be a good teammate and another to let a teammate take advantage of you. So, do you want to tell me what happened?"

"No sir, I'll just take the punishment."

"What if I call your parents and tell them what happened? Would that get you to tell us who took the key? I am sure you'd get a second punishment at home."

"No sir. You found the key in my pocket, so I helped even if I didn't take the key. I'm not going to get someone else in trouble too."

"Well then, you'll have to pay for the crime all by yourself. I hope that if someone else was involved that he is a good friend and that he appreciates what you're doing, though I suspect he doesn't."

For a week Mr. Walker made me stay for an hour after school and help the janitor clean up. He never called my parents. And he was right about Charlie. He didn't even say thanks. Afterward, our friendship withered. We still played ball together, but I avoided him whenever I could.

There was one other school-related escapade that could have been a lot worse than it turned out to be. In high school during the last week of school every year, the junior class spent a day on a dairy farm. Since most of us lived on farms, the educational part of the event was not particularly educational. Toward the end of the day that my class went to the farm, three of us drifted away and went exploring on our own. The class had been sternly told that there were dangerous things on the farm, so we should all stay together with our teacher, but my friends and I were bored.

Out in a side barnyard, there were four cows, and the three of us took turns being matadors. We'd pick out a cow, then one of us would use an old, faded red towel we'd found while the other two herded the cow from behind. Amid our fun, we neglected to notice that one of the gates to the cornfield was open. We figured it out when three cows disappeared. Matador panic followed. The corn was just a bit taller than the cows, so we had no idea where they were and worried that before we could find them, they would trample down stalks and eat their way through the field. We were also worried that we wouldn't be able to find them before we had to go back to school with our classmates.

Quickly we devised a plan. One of us ran up the first row close to the far end of the field, which was about one hundred yards away. I hurried off to the middle of the same row, and the third matador stayed at the barn end of the field. Then we started at one end and went looking row to row.

The first two cows weren't too hard to find and herd back into the barnyard. The third one was a different story. She had wandered all the way to a distant corner of the field. When we found her, as we expected, she was eating an ear of corn and enjoying her new freedom. She was also a bit belligerent about returning to her safe barnyard. It took a while, but we finally coaxed her back where she belonged just in time to rejoin our classmates and head back to school. We were lucky. I can only imagine our punishment had we not found those cows in time.

Looking back, I had a very happy boyhood. I had a good family. There were rarely disagreements between my brothers and me. Mom quietly supported us all whenever we needed her support. Dad was a fine role model in many ways. My parents were kind, had a good relationship, and made sure that my brothers and I had everything we needed. We lived in a comfortable home and never had to worry about family debts or not having the essentials of life, as a couple of my friends did. At school, I never had any problems and when I wasn't in a classroom, I had baseball and Mr. Davidson's garage to keep me busy. It was a very happy time for me, but it didn't last forever. In fact, I remember the exact day that it ended.

Chapter 2

KELLY FIELD

On April 2, 1917, President Woodrow Wilson announced that the United States was joining the Allies in the war against Germany. After the Lusitania was torpedoed in May 1915, there was constant speculation about whether the U.S. should get into the war. For two years Wilson promised to keep us out of the war, but lots of people thought that once reelected he would forget his promise. The German High Command thought so too. Shortly after Wilson's reelection, they began an all-out offensive. It included disregarding their Sussex Pledge and resuming attacks on American ships. The Germans claimed that American ships were sneaking supplies to the British and the French. After three American ships went down in March 1917, Wilson got a declaration of war from Congress, and the United States joined the Allies. It was not a big surprise. By then we all expected it. Still, it was upsetting. Never had the United States been involved in a European war.

Before Wilson's announcement, my father vehemently opposed getting into the war.

"That war belongs to Europe and that's who should fight it. They made it. They should fight it. Everyone knows that the Kaiser has no honor, but George V and his self-centered prime minister David Lloyd George aren't much better.

Why should we send our men to die to help either side? We don't need a war! Besides, we do business with both sides. Doesn't matter who wins we lose. And if we go in and save one side or the other, every time they have a problem, they'll call us for help."

Dad was an imperialist but not an interventionalist. He believed that the United States had a responsibility to elevate the standards of civilization in lesser developed parts of the world. Europe was not one of those less civilized places.

Despite his feelings, after Wilson committed us to the war, Dad put his opposition aside and supported the American effort wholeheartedly. Once we were in the war, he wanted to win it as quickly as possible. He bought liberty bonds. He organized local food shipments to the troops. He put up patriotic banners and posters in his store windows. Mom was part of the local war effort too. She helped Dad organize local support, and two nights a week she wrapped bandages at the local Red Cross office.

To me, the war seemed like an adventure. Pictures and stories everywhere of men proudly marching off to save Western civilization. You couldn't walk down the street without seeing posters about why we should support the war. Everyone was humming new songs about going to war and not coming back "until it's over, over there." Every week nickelodeon newsreels showed men training, boarding ships, and then arriving in France. Newspaper editorials pumped up the war efforts. In school, our teachers talked about saving democracy throughout the world. When Dad went to rallies, I usually went along and heard politicians, local businessmen, even a Civil War veteran give patriotic speeches. There were celebrities—Charlie Chaplin and Douglas Fairbanks and Mary Pickford— going around the country drumming up support wherever they could. It was exciting.

Right after my junior year in high school, four of my friends signed up to join the army. A couple of others left before school started again in the fall. I was ready to go with them, but Dad said no.

"You're going to finish high school and then go to college if I have anything to do with it and I do!"

Finishing high school meant waiting a year, and I thought the war would be over by then. I wanted to be part of the action, but since I was only sixteen, I needed Dad's signature to get into the Army. There wasn't much I could do short of running away. Finally, after a bunch of "debates," Dad and I made a deal.

"I'll sign a permission slip after you finish high school.

Then when you come back you can go to college."

What Dad didn't know was that my high school started a schedule that allowed boys to graduate early. If I took three required classes during the summer, I could graduate in December. That meant I could join up before the end of the year.

On December 20, 1917, I joined the United States Army. A week later I went up to the recruiting office in Harrisburg.

At the stroke of noon, along with nineteen other recruits, I took my oath of service. My first army march was four blocks long from the recruiting office to the train station. We were arranged into four rows with five recruits each and hiked to the loud cadence of a recruiting sergeant. Right past the state capitol and down the middle of Fifth Street. As we marched, people along the way stopped and waved and cheered us. I was proud to be part of the United States Army.

At the station, we boarded a southbound train that was already carrying several dozen recruits. We were headed for boot camp at Fort Lee, just outside of Richmond, Virginia. I had never been farther from home than Philadelphia, so the ride itself was an adventure for me. Pretty quickly I found out that I wasn't alone. Few of my fellow travelers had ever been far from their homes.

The guys I was with were from the Harrisburg area.

The other guys already on the train came from Scranton, Binghamton, and as far away as Rochester, New York. As we chugged south, we stopped along the way to pick up several hundred more recruits. We made stops in York, Baltimore, Silver Spring, Alexandria, Charlottesville, and Lynchburg. By the time we arrived at Fort Lee, there were two dozen cars carrying over a thousand men. The ride had started quietly, but as we moved south it became a celebration. There were two sergeants in each car to maintain order but still lots of singing, especially popular patriotic songs. Some backslapping. Some vigorous handshakes. Lots of laughter. When we came into a new station, some of the guys stuck their heads out of the windows and shouted happy greetings to whomever they saw. Outside on the loading platforms, local crowds that had followed their sons and brothers and, in a couple of cases, their husbands to the station cheered us. In Baltimore, there was even a band playing.

We got to Fort Lee, Virginia, just before sunset. The moment we arrived the celebration ended. There were drill sergeants stationed outside each of the train's cars.

"Party's over girls. You're in the Army now!"

Anyone who still had a bit of celebration left in them as they got off the train instantly became a target for their unit's sergeant. It was an abrupt end to our ride and the beginning of our new lives.

As we climbed down from our coaches, sergeants were waiting by each door. They paired us up, then herded us into two dozen marching units, one unit per car. Each unit was then marched to a barracks that would be home throughout boot camp. My barracks became B Company.

"Men, I am Sergeant Shields. You are now in the 115th unit, 48th Brigade, 27th Division, Company B. I'll say it again. You are now in the 115th unit, 48th Brigade, 27th Division, Company B. Got that? If you can't remember it, then get someone to tattoo it onto you. That's part of your name from now on! For the next four weeks, I will be the most important person in your world. You will eat when I tell you to eat. You will sleep when I tell you to sleep. You will wash up when I tell you. You will not make a sound until I tell you it's OK. Anyone who doesn't do what I tell them to do will have a very bad time here. Now line up six across outside and no talking."

We did as we were told without a word. Sergeant Shields marched us to a tent where we were given a pile of either small, medium, or large clothing. This was our wardrobe for the next four weeks. Two pairs of khaki pants, two heavy khaki cotton shirts, a change of underwear, socks, and a pair of boots. There were four chairs at the end of the line. Each recruit, clothes in hand, was plopped down onto one of the chairs. Thirty seconds after sitting down we had no hair. It was no more than two minutes from the time we went into the tent until we exited with our uniforms in hand and our hair on the floor.

In addition to the sergeants who marched us from the train to our barracks and the supply tents, each company had a captain. Captain Brooks was our commanding officer, but Sergeant Shields was the one who was with us morning, noon, and night. He slept in a room at the front of the barracks. He marched us to our meals in the cafeteria, and he was the one barking orders at us on the drill fields. Captain Brooks usually met with us briefly after breakfast and before dinner. He had a family off the base, but during the week he lived in an officers building.

Five of the guys from the Harrisburg area were in Company B. I talked to three of them on the train, and when we saw we were assigned to the same barracks, we picked out adjacent cots. Two of them were twin brothers, Gary and Steve Wevodau.

Gary was the one who figured out that we had bumped into each other a couple of times.

"Hey, you played for Middletown—center field, right?"

"Yeah."

"We played for Harrisburg Tech. I was the catcher. Steve played shortstop. We beat you my sophomore year, but you got us back last year."

"Yeah, you guys were good. I remember a play that Steve made on a ball I hit over second. A great play. And you were a talker behind the plate. You never stopped."

"Part of my strategy. If I got hitters thinking about me, they'd think less about the pitcher. It worked pretty well."

"Especially because you guys had that great pitcher two years ago."

Gary and Steve were a year younger than me and lied about their age to the recruiting officer. There were lots of stories about other recruits doing the same thing. As long as no one objected and the recruit looked old enough, the Army was happy to have him. Uncle Sam needed as many men as he could get regardless of age. Gary and Steve had played baseball in Harrisburg and knew a couple of my baseball friends, so we had a little bit in common.

For some reason, Gary became the sergeant's favorite target. Whenever Sergeant Shields needed an example of how not to do something, he picked Gary. Some mornings the sergeant came into the barracks just before reveille and banged a thick, wooden baton against the foot of Gary's bed. "Time to get up weaver-dull." That's what he called Steve and Gary: "Weaver-dull." It didn't seem to bother Gary but it sure did get to Steve.

Boot camp was tough! Fortunately, it was only four weeks long. Under different circumstances, we would have trained a couple of weeks longer, but we were in a war and men were needed on the battlefields, so our boot camp experience was short. Still, it was four grueling weeks. For some, it was truly an ordeal. I was in pretty good shape when I got to boot camp, but there were a bunch in B Company who were not. During the first week, guys got sick on the drill fields or doing the various runs. A couple guys passed out, but we all made it through the four weeks.

Reveille came every morning just before dawn at 0600 hours. We had a few minutes to get out of our bunks, into training uniforms, and line up to march about one hundred yards to one of the two cafeteria buildings in the center of the camp. Each cafeteria fed about six hundred men three times a day. We had thirty minutes to eat, get back to our barracks, make up our bunks, and straighten up.

Training began at 0630 hours sharp. It started with calisthenics, followed by a mile run around Fort Lee with a full pack. Then off to various instruction and drills that were supposed to get us ready for battle as infantrymen. Every day, rain or shine, we shuffled through and over trenches and crawled under lines of barbed wire. We practiced handto-hand combat. We did one-hundred-yard runs with our rifles and at twenty-yard intervals bayoneted a straw dummy. Once a week we practiced using gas masks. Just about every day we practiced cleaning and rapidly reassembling our rifles, though only three times did we practice shooting and only once with live ammunition. The real bullets were being used in Europe. Training ended at 1630 hours with a mile run through an obstacle course filled with ten-foot walls, lines of barbed wire, and two high dirt mounds that had a knee-deep pool of muddy water in between them. At 1800 hours each unit lined up and marched to dinner, ate, reassembled, and marched back to our barracks. Lights out was at 2100 hours. It was a grueling four weeks.

Saturday mornings, we marched for about two hours and then got a talk from Captain Brooks. After that, we had the afternoon and Sunday to ourselves. That meant laundry, letters home, and an occasional Sunday pickup ball game. No one had a glove. We used the skinny leg of a broken table for a bat and a golf ball stuffed inside a couple pairs of old socks, tightly wrapped with electrical tape for a ball. Certainly, the equipment limited our success on the diamond, but it was fun. The Wevodau twins, especially Steve, were the stars.

The second Saturday in camp I got lucky. Captain Brooks had a Simplex Coupe like the one I had worked on at home. It didn't start when he was ready to leave camp. I was pretty sure I knew what the problem was—it sounded like a pinched radiator hose—and asked if I could help. It took me about two minutes to fix the problem. Captain Brooks was impressed.

"Malone, where'd you learn your way around automobile engines like that?"

I told him about Dad's car and working at Mr. Davidson's garage.

"I've never seen an automobile engine that I couldn't fix," I bragged.

"I'll keep that in mind. The Army is looking for men who know engines."

Toward the end of the next week, Captain Brooks pulled me out of our daily training. "There are two transport trucks that we're having engine problems with. How about looking at them? See if you can figure them out."

I had them running again within half an hour. The captain was even more impressed than the first time.

"I told you there's not an auto engine I can't fix."

After dinner a couple of days later, Company D's captain asked me to look at his car—a Model T like dozens I had worked on at home. Again, it took less than thirty minutes. I had that Model T humming long before lights out. Then the captain from Company F had a truck that needed some work. I fixed it.

Two days before basic training was over, Captain Brooks called me into the sergeant's office after dinner.

"Malone, we're really impressed with the way you can fix engines. After you fixed my car and that first truck, I wired Mr. Davidson to find out more about you. He said you are the best mechanic he's ever seen even though you're so young."

Of course, I didn't tell the captain that Mr. Davidson had only ever seen about four other mechanics.

"There's something I want you to think about. I'd like to transfer you to a tank unit or an air squadron where you could learn to fix tanks or planes. You'd have to go through another eight weeks of training, but it would be on engines. Not much running. Not much climbing. No crawling under barbed wire, and you'd have a little more free time. The Army needs mechanics more than it needs another infantryman and you seem like a natural. The other option is to stay with Company B and ship out to France on Saturday. You've got twenty-four hours to let me know what you want to do."

I didn't need twenty-four hours but waited until the next evening anyway.

"Captain sir, I still want to go to Europe and help fight the war, but I'd also like to do the mechanics' training. I'd especially like to work on airplanes."

"Malone, I think you made the right decision. You're doing your country a service. I've already done the paper work. I'll wire the Air Service before I leave tonight. And don't worry, it'll take a little longer this way, but you'll still get to the war."

Two days later my unit was sent to Newport News where it was scheduled to sail to France. Meanwhile, I was on a train headed for eight weeks of training in the Aviation Section of the Signal Corps at Fort Kelly, near San Antonio, Texas. The Aviation Section later became the Air Service and eventually the Air Force, but that was still years away.

The use of planes was still new to the U.S. military. During the problems with Mexico and Pancho Villa a couple of years earlier, planes had been used for observation, but with the start of the war, England, France, and Germany began innovating. By the time I got to Kelly, a full-fledged air war had evolved. When we entered the war, we were well behind the Europeans in the air. Part of the mission at Kelly was to catch up.

In early 1918, Fort Kelly was kind of an experimental camp. Teaching large numbers of men to fly or become mechanics was all new for the Army. Most instructors were only a step or two ahead of the men they were training. That was especially true on the flying side. The Wright brothers had made their famous flight a little more than fourteen years earlier and there still weren't many experienced fliers. We were also experimenting with how to build fighting planes as well as how to fly them. At Kelly, a French flier, Colonel Jacques Ullan, and two British pilots, Majors Bernard "Bernie" Hyde and Charles Whiteford, were ultimately in charge of the instruction, but going up in the air remained a seat-of-the-pants learning experience. Keeping the planes flyable was more predictable but not by much because of the constant technical changes to planes and engines. For me, that meant lots of opportunity to be among the first to learn about planes and flying.

Fort Kelly was divided into two facilities. I was assigned to Kelly Number One along with twenty-four other trainees. Number One was where maintenance and repairs were done. Kelly Number Two, which was about twice the size of Number One, was where pilots were trained. I was happy to be at Number One, but it didn't take long before I wanted to be at Number Two. The thought of flying, despite all the danger, was magical to me. I was young and immortal and eager for the challenge.

I discovered quickly that I was the youngest soldier at Kelly. I also learned quickly to lie about my age. The men at Number Two were all in their early to mid-twenties. Most had at least two years of college and many had their degrees. The Aviation Section wanted only well-educated men. The guys at Number One were like me but a couple of years older. They were training to be mechanics. There were also some of the new flying trainees at Number One. The military wanted all the pilots to know every detail about how their planes worked, so flying trainees were sent to mechanics' school for two weeks before learning how to fly. That meant some of the men at Number One were much older than me. So, suddenly, I became twenty years old. Of course, the camp's colonel knew I was only seventeen and probably my captain and sergeant knew, but they never shared my secret.

Training at Number One was very different than back at Fort Lee. We were expected to stay fit, but we only did calisthenics for thirty minutes once a day and we did a mile run three times a week. There was almost no marching, no hand-to-hand combat or bayonet practice. The fliers practiced shooting a couple of times a week, but those of us on the mechanics' side never touched a rifle. Discipline was also much looser at Kelly than at Lee. Some men even went off base in the evenings a couple of times. We also organized weekend ball games—mechanics versus pilots.

Another big difference at Kelly was the relationship between the trainees and the officers. Sergeant Taylor didn't pound bed frames to get us up, and he didn't bark at us the way that Sergeant Shields had. Every now and then Sergeant Taylor actually talked to us a little. He had joined the Army during the Spanish-American War but never made it to Cuba. Instead, he made the Army his life. He was also a baseball fan and coached the mechanics' team, which was good for me.

One of the first things he asked was: "Any of you guys any good on the ballfield."

"Sir, I played in high school. Played center field."

"Ya any good?"

"I started for three years. But it was a small school."

"That's OK. If you can still catch a fly ball and throw it back in, we'll have a place for you."

That first Saturday game, I was a little nervous. Everyone was older and the fliers were stronger, but I still had speed on my side. Also, most of the guys hadn't played in a couple of years and it showed, especially the fliers. I batted somewhere in the middle of the order in the first game, but Sergeant Taylor had me leading off after that.

"You're a fast little bugger aren't you? You're a junior Ty Cobb. If you can hit, you're going to score some runs for us." I could still hit well enough.

The Saturday games were supposed to be just friendly recreation, but they became rivalries quickly. I know that a few dollars changed hands once in a while. During my eight weeks at Kelly, the mechanics won six times, which made Sergeant Taylor very happy.

Captain Foultz also spent more time with us than Captain Brooks at Fort Lee. He'd talk to us after breakfast and then stop by our training sessions for about an hour every day, and was always there during our two weeks of flight instruction. He also showed up on Saturdays and rooted for us. He had flown during the Pancho Villa days but crashed and never went up again. Instead, he came to Kelly to be a trainer.

It didn't take me long to figure out how airplane engines worked. They were bigger and more powerful than the automobile engines that I was used to, but they worked pretty much the same way. There were two kinds of engines we used: a rotary and a radial. My favorites were the rotary engines. We used one called the Gnome. Rotaries were more powerful, and a pilot could start one by himself. The primary problem with the Gnome was that the spin of a rotary engine made the plane hard for pilots to control.

That meant more air training. Rotaries also drank oil and required a lot of maintenance. We didn't use many Gnomes at Kelly. Instead, most of our planes had Roberts engines. The Roberts was a pretty simple air-cooled radial engine. Planes with Roberts engines were lighter and had fewer parts but also had less power than the Gnome. To start a radial, the pilot had to engage the engine while someone, usually a mechanic, manually cranked the propeller. I saw a lot of men get plunked by propellers while starting a radial-powered plane. Also, while the Roberts was well suited for training purposes, as I later found out, it was not a fighter plane.

When I arrived at Kelly, I was told that during the final two weeks of training each mechanic could be shifted over to the Aviation Section if he was twenty-one and did well learning to be a mechanic. Not everyone in my unit wanted to fly planes, but to me the opportunity sounded great. The only problem was my age. So three weeks before my training as a mechanic ended, I gave myself a birthday. I figured that if I could get away with being twenty to train at Kelly, I could get away with being twenty-one in order to fly, and I really wanted to learn to fly. No one objected, so I became twenty-one.

The two weeks at aviation training changed my life. The first time I went up in the air I was hooked. We trained on Curtiss JN-4s, much better known as "Jennys." They had a seat in the front for the pilot and one in the back for the trainer. Jennys weren't very powerful, but they were easy to maneuver and land. During those two weeks of flight training, I learned everything I could learn about flying. The math took some studying, but I got it. The actual flying part was challenging, but maybe because of my experience driving, it came quickly. Of course, the mechanical part of flying—starting the engine, understanding and reacting to the gauges—was easy. Flying also required coordinating feet on flap pedals, eyes on gauges while scanning the sky, and using one hand to control the throttle and maintain airspeed with the other hand on the control stick. When in battle one hand also had to be on the machine gun. In case that happened, I learned to use my knees on the control stick. Planes in the air were also incredibly loud. For me, fifteen minutes in the air without earplugs resulted in a pounding earache. It was a lot to do all at once. For some, it was too much to do. Of my eighteen mechanic buddies, only two of us made it through flight training.

By the end of my second solo training flight, I knew how to take off and control the plane once in the air. Landing was a different story. My first three landings were minor adventures, but by the fourth landing I was on the mark. My problem was that the early Jennys had no brakes, so you had to judge how much runway it would take to slow the Jenny down. Fortunately, I overestimated, which meant I landed early and had to taxi back to the hangar. Planes were meant for the air. They did not hold up well bouncing over a dirt runway. I spent the second week in the air as much as I could. I figured if I got good enough, maybe I could fly in Europe.

It was at Kelly that I began to learn about war. I learned that death comes quickly and often brutally during a war. Though still thousands of miles away from the European battlefields, I saw men die or become permanently disabled every day while I was at Kelly. Learning to fly was dangerous. Future pilots got most of their instructions in a classroom or in crude flight simulators. Because not all planes had two seats and there were always dozens of men to train, instructors could go on only two or sometimes three flights with each trainee. After that, the new flier went solo. Few pilots had more than twenty hours of airtime before they were sent into battle. I later heard that more fliers died during their training than died in battle.

During my eight weeks of training, there was at least one crash every day. Most days there were several crashes. Some men survived, some didn't. Some died quickly. Some suffered before dying, and some didn't die but suffered forever. I saw men burn to death when their fully fueled planes crashed on takeoff. I saw trainees stall their planes midflight, then plunge hundreds of feet to their death. I saw landings where a trainee's plane exploded upon impacting the ground. Ironically, because so many planes went down during training, the Army built flimsy training planes that were far more prone to crashes than the planes more experienced pilots flew in Europe. Clearly, flying was not for the faint of heart.

I did well at Kelly. I knew that I was as good a mechanic as any of my fellow trainees. My trainers knew that too. Just like at Fort Lee, a couple of days before I was scheduled to leave, my captain gave me an option.

"Donnie, how would you like to stay at Kelly and become a mechanics' trainer? You're a little young, but you know engines as well as anyone we've trained this time around. We sure could use a few more trainers. Of course, there would be a promotion to lieutenant. Trainers are officers. I know you like to fly, and you'd get more airtime if you were a trainer."

This time I didn't have to think about anything.

"It'd be great to be promoted. I'd like being an officer and I'd love the airtime, but I am no teacher. Maybe in a couple of years but not right now. I want to go to France and help win the war. So thanks for the offer, but being a trainer is not for me right now."

"Yeah, I understand. I think I'd do the same thing if I were you. We old guys do better passing on what we've learned to you young guys so that you can win the war for us all. And as for flying you'll get your chance. There will always be a spot for men who know how to fly whether they've been to college or not."

Six days later I was on a train headed for Garden City, New York, and then a ship to France.

Chapter 3

OFF TO WAR

The next trip was the one I had signed up for. I was off to Europe and "the war to end all wars." Along with a dozen other mechanics and twenty pilots who I'd trained with at Kelly, I was assigned to the 94th Aero Squadron. The squadron had trained at Kelly in August 1917, then was sent to France. In March, the 94th became the first solely American squadron to fly a patrol in Europe. Soon after, a 94th's pilot shot down its first German plane. Several of the trainers at Kelly, including Colonel Ullan and Major Hyde, pridefully referred to the men of the squadron as role models for future American fliers.

All twelve of us mechanics knew each other pretty well. One, Sam Kades, was probably my best friend at Kelly. He was three years older than me and lived in Wilkes Barre, which is two hours by train north of Middletown. Sam was smart. He had two years of college at Penn State when he enlisted. He had wanted to finish college but his father, who fought in the Spanish-American War, made it clear that Sam should join up and do his part to save democracy in the world. Sam was a little taller than I am and at least twenty-five pounds heavier. He was clearly not an athlete. Watching him struggle through some of our training exercises at Kelly made that obvious. Instead, he had been the editor of his high school yearbook and school newspaper, and had written a couple of articles about his high school for a local paper. At Penn State, he had studied engineering. The thing I liked most about Sam was his sense of humor. Simply put, he could make me laugh. Just thinking about him makes me smile. As far as his abilities as a mechanic, he was good but not great. He could figure out how engines worked but often fumbled around getting all the parts to where they belonged. He volunteered to become an army mechanic because he figured working on engines behind the battle lines was better than being shot at by Germans at the front.

Sam had a pilot friend in our squadron, Ron Moore.

Lieutenant Moore knew Sam from Penn State.

"Sammy got me through calculus my junior year. I was not a math and science guy."

"Yeah, then I got to hang out with Ron and some of his fraternity friends. I was sort of an honorary member of the frat."

I asked, "How come you never joined the frat?" "Another story, another time," Ron said.

Sammy jumped in. "Nothing I could do about it, but I liked hanging out with Ron and the guys."

Ronnie had graduated in December and immediately enlisted. Like Sam, he was smart—a history major eager to go to law school after the war. Ron came from the Main Line in Philadelphia. His father was a successful attorney. Unlike Sam's father, Ron's father wanted his son to stay out of the war, but Ron felt it was his obligation to go.

"Dad had me all set for Dickinson law school. That's where he went to law school, and he knew the dean really well. He even had him to the house for dinner so he could get to know me a little bit. Dad wasn't too happy when I signed up to be a pilot."

I could identify with Ron on that one.

I remember seeing Ron in the air at Kelly and thinking that he was one of the best pilot trainees there. The three of us became good friends on our journey to Europe and decided that if we got a chance Sam and I would volunteer to be Ron's mechanic.

Our trip to France started with a twenty-four-hour train ride that took us from San Antonio to Garden City, just outside New York City. Along with nine hundred other men, we were then loaded onto the USS Saratoga. The trip to Europe was relatively uneventful. We had calm waters and good weather from start to finish. The only excitement happened two nights before we landed. One of our escort ships, the Seattle, was able to dodge two German torpedoes. Otherwise, we had smooth sailing. When I boarded the Saratoga, I was a little concerned about getting seasick but that didn't happen. After a week at sea, we docked in Liverpool and picked up several more Kelly pilots. They had gotten two weeks of additional training from the Royal Air Force before moving on to France. Unfortunately, by the time we got to England, the RAF didn't have planes or trainers it could spare. They were all needed in France. The last stop on our journey was Brest on the west coast of France. The trip from Texas to France took almost two weeks, start to finish. By the time it ended, we were all ready to get off the ship and put our feet onto the solid French soil.

During the trip across the Atlantic, Lieutenant Moore told us about the 94th Aero. He had a fraternity brother who was already in the 94th. It was one of the reasons that Moore joined the Aero forces. The squadron called itself "the Hat in the Ring Gang." Its logo was a red-white-andblue stovepipe hat inside a red circle. The hat represented the United States throwing its hat into the war. The red circle symbolized Teddy Roosevelt and his Rough Riders from the Spanish-American War. The squadron was the first American aero squad ever organized. It was led by Rauol Lufbery, a well-respected French-American pilot.

Lufbery had devised several aerial maneuvers including "the Lufbery circle" and was considered the first American flying ace. He had a reputation for being a bit quirky. For instance, before going on a mission he polished and shined the bullets he expected to use in that battle. He also had a pet lion, Whiskey, who followed him around whenever Lufbery was on the ground. Actually, he had two lions. The other one was Soda, but only Whiskey was tame enough to walk with Lufbery around the airfield. Many of his men thought he was dismissive and haughty, but everyone admired his skills and courage as a pilot. Doug Campbell was another member of the squadron. He was the first pilot flying in an American squad to shoot down a German plane. A name I did recognize was Eddie Rickenbacker. He had raced cars and set speed records before the war. They called him "Fast Eddie." He was one of the people I really wanted to meet.

Except for Fast Eddie, I had never heard of the Hat in the Ring Gang or any of the people Moore described, but I was excited to become part of the squadron.

We spent the first couple of days in Paris wandering the streets. Paris was amazing to me and Sam but not to Ron.

"Doesn't seem much better than Philadelphia. It's bigger and noisier. There are some interesting buildings. I like all the street cafes and there sure are a lot of pretty women, but otherwise, I'll take Philly."

Sam asked, "Bigger, better architecture, great cafes, pretty mademoiselles, what does Philadelphia have that Paris doesn't have?"

"They speak too much French here." We all chuckled at that.

After two days we were loaded onto a train headed for Croix de Metz Aerodrome near Toul, 160 miles to the southeast not far from the western front. Toul was little more than a farm village built by the Romans in the fifth century. It had a small hotel and a couple of shops but not much else. We arrived on May 19, 1918, the same day that the Germans shot down Lufbery. It was not a happy arrival.

The Croix de Metz Aerodrome was smaller and much less developed than Kelly. It had been built in a wheat field by the French two years earlier. In April 1918, the French transferred operation of Croix to the United States. The 94th was the first American squadron to occupy the field. The aerodrome had two dirt runways with hangars and barracks on either side. When we arrived, there were about two dozen planes scattered around the field and another two dozen being worked on inside the hangars. The mechanics and some of the pilots stayed in the barracks. A few of the pilots who could afford it stayed in a hotel in Toul a mile away. In all, there were about two hundred men stationed in the camp. Sam and I were sent to one of the barracks and told that we'd each be assigned to two or three pilots.

Maybe because the commanding officer, Lufbery, had just been killed and there was no official replacement, Sam and I were both assigned to Lieutenant Moore as we had requested. In addition to Lieutenant Moore, we were assigned to Lieutenant Moore's Penn State fraternity brother, William "Wild Bill" White. We were also put on an on-call roster, which meant that if we weren't busy on Moore's or White's planes, we were to be ready at any time to work another plane.

Wild Bill made an immediate impression. He was tall, athletic, and handsome; glib, smart, and charming. He walked with an easy swagger that translated into a core confidence in himself. He also had a reputation for being a little reckless in the air and even more reckless on the ground. The son of a prosperous Pittsburgh steel magnate, he was one of the pilots who could afford to stay in a Toul hotel. During the month since the 94th had taken over the airfield, Wild Bill had already been cited twice for disorderly conduct. His chief vices were French wine and local young women.

"The girl was just a misunderstanding. I thought she was flirting with me. Wasn't the first time a lady had winked at me since I've been here in France. So, I flirted back. She seemed to like it. How was I to know her father ran the tavern? He sure didn't like me."

It didn't take long before the war became a daily reality for Sam and me. The morning after we arrived, a squadron took off on what was called a pursuit mission. Six planes left Croix but only four returned. One was shot down and the other crashed. Periodically we also heard heavy artillery and smelled the smoke of battles coming from east of us along the front. We were only about four miles away, far enough to feel some sense of security but close enough to imagine what was happening. Occasionally we'd also see men coming from the front. Hospital vans loaded with the wounded also came by almost every day. We were learning about war quickly.

Moore and White both flew British-made Sopwith Camels. Back at Kelly, they had trained in Curtis Jennys, but the Jenny was too slow and had limited range for air combat. The Camel was among the newest, most maneuverable planes produced at the time. White had been flying the Camel for a while, but because it used a rotary engine, Moore needed a couple of practice flights. He learned quickly though. For us mechanics, the Camel was bigger and more powerful and required more maintenance, but it worked like the rotaries back at Kelly. Sam and I had no problems adjusting.

Moore, White, and two others flew off on their first missions together a week after we got to Croix. Sam and I watched as they bounced down the runway. I felt a real connection with them as they flew away. It was like the way I felt after playing a ball game back home. A real sense of team. Of course, back in Middletown if you lost you could still play the next day. This was very different. There was no tomorrow if one of our pilots lost at this game. This time all four made it back home safely. No German planes spotted.

A week later the story changed. Moore and White teamed up with Doug Campbell and his partner, Lieutenant Briggs. Briggs was at Kelly part of the time I was there and came to France with us, so I knew who he was. Ron told us what happened:

"We were flying up north for about an hour when we spotted four Fokkers. They saw us at about the same time. Two of them turned around and headed back where they came from. The two on the sides peeled off and I thought they were going home too, so I kept flying after the two center planes. Maybe a minute later I heard bullets zinging by me. The two side planes had made a wide circle around and behind us and one was on my tail. The other one was on Bill, who was beside me. Suddenly, Bill dropped down. I was afraid he had been hit and I think the Germans thought so too. We were wrong. Bill had stalled his plane. It was a great maneuver. Then he pulled up behind the two Germans and shot one of them down. The other one got away. If he hadn't done that stall, I'd probably have been a goner. It all happened so fast."

I asked about Captain Campbell and Briggs.

"They chased the two center planes. They got one but they were so far east that they were in range of German artillery.

That's what saved the other German. Campbell and Briggs had to dodge shells on their way home. Campbell's plane was hit with shrapnel, and he was hit pretty badly in his shoulder, back, and neck. They sent him back to Paris to get patched up."

I later learned that Campbell's wounds were so serious that he was sent back to the States. He ended up training pilots at Fort Kelly.

The next mission ended far worse. This time Wild Bill couldn't save his fraternity brother. Four German Fokkers dropped from a cloud bank surprising the two Americans.

"They came out of nowhere. We never saw them. Two went after me and two went after Ron. They got Ron almost immediately. I did my stall maneuver again and dropped low, maybe fifty yards off the ground. I was still over our lines so if the Germans had followed me, they could have been shot down by our infantrymen."

I had never felt as badly as I did when I heard about the crash. Ron, Lieutenant Moore, was my first friend to die. I understood that lots of people die in war. Pilots were killed every day, but I never really understood that a friend might someday be one of them until Moore was shot down. Such a good man, someone I admired, wiped out so quickly and so thoroughly. It was a pain that in time ebbed but never completely went away.

During the next few weeks, Sam and I moped around doing our job but little else. We were assigned a new pilot and kept working with Lieutenant White, but Moore's death took a lot out of us. It was as if the sounds and smells that added flavor to life had been sealed up. We took a couple of walks into Toul just to get away from the field, but the fog that encompassed us was too thick to walk away from.

A chance encounter with Captain Rickenbacker began my journey back to normalcy. He had been grounded because of an ear infection, so he spent a lot of time watching and helping the mechanics. We all knew he was an expert mechanic himself. You could tell that he really enjoyed working on engines and knew exactly what he was doing. One day after watching me work on White's plane he complimented me on how efficient and thorough I was.

"You're pretty good with those engines. Did you learn that at Kelly?"

"Yes sir, I learned about plane engines at Kelly, but I've been working on automobile engines for a long time."

I told him about working on cars back at Mr. Davidson's garage.

"I got started when I was young too…only about eleven.

Back in Columbus, Ohio. First time I saw an auto engine I wanted to figure out how it worked. Which do you like better: rotaries or radials?"

"Probably the rotaries. There's more to them. The radials are pretty simple."

"You ever flown one?"

"I got to fly a little bit at Kelly. They only had Jennys there, but it was one of the most exciting things I've ever done. I'd love to try a Camel."

"Well, there's still a lot of war left. You'll get a chance."

The next day Captain Rickenbacker came back and for about an hour watched me work on planes with rotary engines. I was doing regular maintenance, which by this time I could almost do with my eyes shut. Captain Eddie never said anything. He just watched, and every now and then nodded.

I saw him again that evening and he asked me if I wanted to walk into Toul with him. At that point, there was nothing I wanted to do more than to go to Toul with him. Since Captain Lufbery was killed and Captain Campbell had been sent back to Paris, he was the unofficial commanding officer in camp, the undisputed American ace, and the best flier at Toul. Who was I to say no?

As we walked, he asked me about my home and why I joined the aero squadron. I told him a little bit about growing up in Middletown. He seemed to understand exactly how I felt. He told me that driving race cars at 130 miles an hour was a thrill, but for him there was nothing like flying.

"Did you ever think about becoming a pilot?"

"Yeah, I thought about it since the first time I flew but there are two problems. First, I'm too young. Second, and this is the big problem, I've never been to college."

"I never made it past fourth grade. Had to quit school and help support my family. Some of the best fliers I know never went to college. As for age, I was too old when I joined the air squadron. I was twenty-seven and the army said they weren't taking anyone over twenty-five."

He added: "The thing about flying is that it's dangerous, especially in a war. You've got to be smart and brave to survive as an Army pilot"

I answered: "I've seen men die. Had a friend, Lieutenant Ron Moore, I was his mechanic. He was shot down a week after I got here. I saw a bunch of guys crash at Kelly, but I am willing to take the risk. I'm not sure how I'd do in a dogfight, but I learn quickly. Yeah, I'd love to be a pilot."

As we got back to the barracks, Captain Eddie told me he thought I was one of the best mechanics at Toul. I considered it a great compliment.

Just after noon the next day, Captain Rickenbacker came over to where I was working.

"How's it going today, Don?"

"Pretty well, sir. Just finished up on Captain White's plane and all ready for lunch."

"Ah, good timing on my part. I wanted to talk to you for a few minutes. I know you and Kades are assigned to Captain White right now, but I'd like you to transfer over to me. My mechanic is headed back to Kelly, so I need someone to work on my planes. You're the best I've seen here at Croix. I also want a mechanic who wants to fly, and I promise if you work for me, you will get airtime. It will be a lot of work, I've got two rotary planes, a Nieuport 28 and a SPAD S XIII, and once this ear problem is gone, I plan to make two flights a day, some days three. I always want a plane ready, so there'll be a lot to do. It would mean leaving Captain White. I don't know how friendly you are with him, and I don't want you to do it if you have any reservations, but I'd really like you working on my planes."

That got me out of my post-Moore blues.

I was transferred to Captain Rickenbacker the next morning. My biggest concern was how Sam would react, but he took the news well. He knew it was a great opportunity for me and he didn't want to leave Captain White. I was worried about Captain White too, but he and Sam had been together since we arrived at Croix. Sam was his mechanic.

I was just part-time with Captain White.

Three days after I was transferred to Captain Rickenbacker, the camp doctor gave him permission to fly again. Initially, he had flown a Nieuport 28 but switched to a Frenchmade SPAD S XIII, which was one of the best fighter planes built. It was faster than the German Fokker and had doublemounted, synchronized Vickers machine guns, which made the plane lethal in battle. Because the SPAD has a HispanoSuiza rotary engine, it is very maneuverable but also a bit harder to fly. For me, it meant more work. The SPAD was great in the air but not so great to maintain. Its gears were touchy, and it had a complex fuel system. The Nieuport was also a good fighting plane and had a Hispano-Suiza engine. It was fast and maneuvered well, but fragile. One of the biggest problems was that the canvas covering its body occasionally peeled off. I could see that keeping Captain Rickenbacker's planes in the air would take a lot of work. I also understood why he was so particular about who worked on his plane.

Just as he had promised, Captain Eddie took me up for a flight shortly after he was allowed back in the air. It was a beautiful June day with no clouds and a slight breeze, perfect for flying. We went up in his SPAD. That alone was a thrill to me. Just bouncing down the runway, I could feel the power. Lifting off the ground, we climbed quickly to two thousand feet. It was a whole lot different than flying Jennys at Kelly.

Captain Eddie sat in the pilot's seat behind me. Of course, the engine was so loud and we both had earplugs so we couldn't talk to each other, but when he wanted to show me something, he tapped me on the shoulder and pointed or made a hand signal.

After about ten minutes in the air, I felt him tap my shoulder. He wanted me to take over the controls. I was certainly eager but also nervous. For the next thirty minutes, I flew the plane. Captain Eddie had me banking left and right, climbing and slowly diving. Only once did he take back the controls for a few seconds. Otherwise, I flew the plane. Finally, he signaled me to circle back to the field, and much to my relief, as we dropped for a landing he took over.

"That was a good first flight. A little practice and you could be a good pilot. I think you'll get this pretty quickly. You're good with your feet and the stick. Most new pilots have a problem using them both at the same time. For you, it's probably a little carry-over from driving an auto. Next time you can take off then we'll work on landings."

I was excited. I was learning how to fly from one of the best pilots in the world. Things were getting busy at Croix, but we went up twice a week for a while. It took four more flights before Captain Eddie thought that I was ready to solo.

A second aero squadron, the 95th, began moving into the Croix de Metz Aerodrome with us at the end of April just before I got there. They called themselves the Kicking Mule squadron. The 95th was brought to the Croix a little bit at a time because there were no other American aerodromes in France. The Kicking Mule had trained at Kelly so I knew several of the mechanics and one of the pilots. By June, the entire squadron was sharing our home while another aerodrome was being built for them. As a result, there was more and more activity at the field. More flights, more maintenance work, more men bumping into each other, and more noise. In the barracks, our living space was cut in half. Dining schedules were created. The 94th ate meals thirty minutes earlier than the 95th. In general, life became more regimented and less comfortable.

One of the Kicking Mule fliers was Theodore Roosevelt's son Quentin. He had left Harvard to fly in the war and arrived in Toul in late April. He brought with him a wellearned reputation for mischief and pranks, but at Croix he was always well behaved.

My mechanic friend in the 95th told me: "He's a practical joke guy, but everyone likes him. You'd never know he was the son of a president. He gets dirty like everyone else and is staying in the barracks just like almost everyone else. The only time I've ever seen him nasty is when he competes. You don't want to be on the other side of a ballgame or wrestling match with him. Some say he's a troublemaker, but the only time I saw him around any kind of trouble, he was a peacemaker, not the peace breaker."

Captain White told me that his fellow fliers considered Quentin to be a solid officer but a reckless flier.

"He didn't fly many missions before Croix, but there are already a bunch of pilots who don't want to go up with him. He takes too many chances and doesn't always stick to the flight plan. He's not someone I want to fly with."

Sam chuckled. "Guess Roosevelt has tamed 'Wild Bill.'"

I never got to talk to Quentin, but I saw him regularly buzzing around the airfield. He was always busy doing something to his plane or exercising or preparing for a mission. In most ways, he seemed to me like a model officer.

About the time that the 95th was fully encamped in Croix, General Pershing began a major offensive. His plan was to assemble a one-million-man army in France. Once he had his men, his army would start in southern France, just south and east of Toul, and march north, fighting Germans as it went. Everyone knew it would be a tough, bloody journey and would require all the American men and equipment that Pershing brought with him. The plan upset the English and French. They wanted American forces to plug holes in the existing battle lines rather than start a new offensive. Pershing reluctantly compromised after the Russian army officially left the Allies in March 1918 to fight its own revolution. He allowed some of his units already in France to reinforce the Allied positions while at the same time continuing to work on his own plans. In June 1918, he was ready to lead his American army into battle.

The aero squadrons were a key part of Pershing's plans. He was a cavalry guy but recognized the growing importance of the air war. The plan was that Allied planes would attack German camps behind the lines, bomb German positions at the front, and observe enemy movement. The 94th's primary responsibility was pursuit, which meant shooting down German fighter planes. We were also expected to protect our troops from enemy air attacks. Because the 94th and 95th were so close to the front and to Pershing's starting point, we were among the first to join the fight.

Once the offensive began there was little time for anything but work. Three times as many flights left each day. Before the offensive, most missions included four planes and sometimes six planes. After the offensive started, a mission usually included eight planes and often as many as twelve. There were also more missions sent out each day. Instead of once or twice a day, flight squadrons usually left every two hours from dawn until about two hours before dark. Since flights were typically two hours long, it meant that planes were in the air all the time. Of course, more flights meant more maintenance work, and we mechanics were not limited by the sun. Many times, we worked long into the night getting planes ready for the next morning, and increasingly that meant stitching and gluing the canvas planes back together. Before the offensive, I often stopped by Sam's barracks and we'd talk for a while. I'd also see Lieutenant White a couple of times a week. After the offensive started, I barely had time to say hi to Sam at the cafeteria and I never saw the lieutenant. Sam said Wild Bill was in the air almost every day.

Of course, Captain Rickenbacker was very busy too. Though the official orders hadn't come through yet, he oversaw the activities at Croix. That meant, aside from flying missions, and he flew as many as he could, he had a ton of new administrative responsibilities. For instance, he made the squadron pilot assignments and scheduled flights for the 94th. He was included in Pershing's strategy decisions, then charted the flight patterns. Fortunately, he had a crew of capable subordinates, including

Lieutenant White, who helped with scheduling and personnel assignments. Still, it was a lot of responsibility. As a result, my time with Captain Eddie shrank significantly but he didn't forget me. At least once a day, as he was hustling from one place to another, he'd stop and ask how things were going for the mechanics. Also, he never took off on a flight without asking me for a detailed description of the condition of his plane.

Through the early summer, all I did was work and I was glad about that. The offensive cranked up everything about fighting a war. For the first time, the bloodshed that is part of war became unavoidable. Before the offensive, the wounded and the dead were brought to a farmhouse that served as a field hospital a mile or so south of Toul. At Croix, we almost never saw anything that went on there. That changed in June. First, there were many, many more dead and wounded. To patch up the wounded, another two farmhouses just down the road from Toul were converted into field hospitals and a barn was made into a morgue. I didn't have time to go into town, but the fliers who lived there talked about their new reality all the time. They described piles of amputated limbs waiting to be buried and men with horrendous, mutilating injuries. Men whose faces had been burned away and bodies that were irreparably broken. Some men constantly trembled and convulsed. They shook so badly they could hardly eat, drink, or walk. Most of the fliers agreed that they would rather be shot down than suffer the way they saw many of the wounded suffering. Every day, there were caravans of ambulances and trucks wheeling past Croix taking some of the wounded back to Paris and the dead to graves. At the airfield, we heard heavy artillery all the time. We had heard it before periodically, but now it was almost continuous, and when the wind blew from the east, we could smell smoke and gunpowder and death. The war became very real after

Pershing's offensive started. One day in late June I bumped into Sam at the cafeteria. I saw right away that he was not adjusting well to the new intensity of the war.

I asked, "How are things going with 'Wild Bill,' Sam?"

Staring over my shoulder and up at the cafeteria ceiling, Sam said: "It's going, that's about all I can say. He's still alive and I'm still working on his plane."

"Have they assigned you to anyone in addition to Bill?"

"No. I'm part of the pool. You know, working on other planes when Bill is in the air. I do about six a day but not all of them come back. I don't know how many planes I've lost. They keep flyin' and dyin'. Sometimes I wonder if I'm the reason they don't come back. Not a happy time."

"Sam, you're a good mechanic. If one of your planes doesn't come back, it's not your fault."

"Thanks, Don."

As we talked, he got more fidgety and started to rock slightly from side to side.

"You going to be OK, Sam?"

"I'll make it. One thing I can say for sure is that I hate war. Didn't want to come and don't want to stay, but I'll do what I have to do to keep alive."

"Look Sam, if you ever need someone to talk to, I'm here."

"Thanks, Don, I'll keep that in mind. Gotta go now. Lots of planes to fix."

The conversation worried me. Not once did Sam look me in the eye. Nor did he stop rocking. One of the things I liked best about Sam was that he laughed a lot but there wasn't a chuckle this time. He was clearly suffering. I made a mental note to see him whenever I could. Later that day when I saw Captain Rickenbacker, I mentioned Sam and he said he'd look into it.

After four weeks of fierce fighting, there were reports that Pershing's army was beginning to push the Germans north. Croix continued to send out just as many missions and there were still daily caravans back to Paris, but the sounds and smells of battle began to fade. The artillery blasts weren't as loud and there was less smoke in the air. On July 4 the rumors became reality. The 94th and 95th aero squadrons were told that because the German army was moving north, we were being relocated to Touquin, a town about fifty miles due east of Paris. We'd still be close to the front, but far enough away that we'd escape some of the visceral weight of the war.

The day before the move, Captain Rickenbacker asked me to go along on an observation flight that afternoon.

"I need someone to record the positions and movement of any remaining German units near Toul."

"Great, I can do that."

"Don't know how much of the battlefields you've seen, but you'll get to see a lot of them today."

Our weekly flights had always gone west away from the fighting, but I had seen the edges of the battlefields before. This flight was different. This time we flew directly over the battlefields from south to north and back. Seeing the full scope of the destruction from the air was shocking. It was another example of what war really is. As far as I could see in front of me the landscape was devoid of any vegetation. There were no trees, only battered stumps, no shrubs or bushes—nothing green. No livestock, no buildings. Instead, long muddy trenches snaked off in all directions. They were separated by miles and miles of barbed wire. Craters from artillery blasts pockmarked the surface everywhere. Many craters had smaller craters inside them. It looked like the surface of the moon. Aside from a few stragglers marching toward the front, the only things that reflected human activity were battered vehicles—jeeps, a few tanks, and several motorcycles. They resembled strange, charred carcasses. It wasn't hard to imagine what the landscape would have looked like with two armies fiercely going at each other as they had just a few days before. Adding tens of thousands of men in the trenches, some hiding and some shooting, and bodies on the ground and hanging from the barbed wire, and machine guns firing away with artillery shells exploding everywhere and all of it covered by a thick haze of smoke—it would have looked like one of Dante's circles of hell. I had never been happier about being a mechanic rather than an infantryman!

The move to Touquin was a definite improvement. Unlike Toul, Touquin had some shops, taverns, and several restaurants. There were also more people and most of them seemed glad to see us. The airfield was about half mile north of the town. As in Toul, the runways weren't much more than a couple of farm fields that had been cleared of crops, then pounded down and leveled. British and French air squadrons had built the field but in mid-June they transferred it to the United States. Now we were moving in. Unlike Toul, there were no hangars. Instead, we either worked on planes out in the open or in big tents. There wasn't enough room for everyone to live in the barracks so some of the mechanics were assigned to local homes. Pilots were moved into the Chateau-de-Malvisine, which was just outside the town. The chateau looked almost like a castle to me. In both cases, our accommodations were better than in Toul, especially for the pilots.

One other thing about Touquin: there were lots of women. There were American and British nurses who worked in a hospital in town, there were local women, and there were women from Paris, working women from Paris. Only the officers, which meant the pilots, were permitted to fraternize with the nurses or local young women. However, despite the orders, at least a few mechanics found female companionship, some on a long-term basis and some on an hourly basis. The nurses were at the top of the scale and they were not very interested in a greasy mechanic. Then came the local women. We were warned that local women were hunting for American husbands including mechanics. We were also warned to stay away from the women from Paris. There were stories about them robbing British fliers, and in at least one case, stabbing a British pilot. We were also warned that they probably carried an array of diseases.

It didn't take long to get back into the routine of war. The front was still close, less than five miles north of the airfield, but it was far enough away that we didn't hear or smell the fighting. We also didn't see as many of the wounded or dead. Because the hospital was at the other end of town, the ambulances and trucks carrying the wounded rarely came past the airfield. Everyone knew that there were just as many causalities as before, but in Touquin it was easier for us to put that out of our minds.

Of course, we never forgot about our pilots. The primary job of the 94th and 95th continued to be pursue and protect. We sent out as many missions as before, and every day pilots were shot down. Fewer were killed though because of a significant improvement for our fliers. When we moved to Touquin, most of our Nieuport 28s were replaced with Sopwith Camels and SPAD S XIIIs. Both were faster, more maneuverable, had better firepower, and more range than the Nieuports. They were every bit as good as the Germans' state-of-the-art plane, the Fokker. Even though a couple of pilots, including Captain Eddie, stayed with their Nieuports, most pilots were very happy to have a Camel or a SPAD. As far as the maintenance was concerned, both planes required lots of attention, so the workload for mechanics remained hectic.

Not long after we moved to Touquin, Quentin Roosevelt was one of those pilots who did not return from his mission. He was flying a morning patrol with three others not far over the German lines when they were surprised by seven Fokkers. A week earlier, something similar had happened. Roosevelt broke from formation and single-handedly chased a pair of Fokkers. He shot one of them down. This time was different. Three Fokkers briefly chased Roosevelt before shooting him down. He crashed in a wheat field two miles behind the German lines. Soon after a German photographer took a picture of the wrecked plane and Roosevelt, who had been shot twice in the head. The photo was made into a postcard and distributed all over Germany. When the High Command discovered that the dead pilot was the son of former President Theodore Roosevelt, they gave Quentin a burial with full military honors and marked his grave at the spot where he crashed. They also tried to stop the sale of the postcard but could not. Instead, the American press printed the picture in newspapers across the country to further demonstrate the ruthlessness of the kaiser and his army.

In late July, about three weeks after I got to Touquin, Captain Eddie asked me to meet him at the chateau for dinner. I had never been inside the chateau—only officers went there, so I was very curious about what he wanted.

"You still enjoy flying."

"Yes sir. I get up in the air whenever I can. It's the best part of my week."

"Yeah, I've seen you take off and land a couple of times. You look smooth out there. That's part of the reason I asked you here this evening."

I was afraid he was going to tell me that my flying days were over for a while. I was wrong.

"Don, we're getting ready for a big offensive. It's still maybe a month away but it is going to happen. Hopefully, it'll be a final offensive. We're going to need lots more pilots for this one. Would you like to be one of those pilots?" "Yes sir!"

I'm sure he knew my answer before he asked.

"It will be very dangerous. The Germans are great fliers and the flights will be low and treacherous. There are going to be lots of casualties lots of my men will be lost. Are you sure you want to do this?"

"Yes sir!"

"OK, then we should do more training. There are skills and some tricks you should know if you're going to survive as a Hat in the Ring flier. I don't want you to get shot down because I took a shortcut in your training. We need to schedule training flights. We can start tomorrow."

I hadn't flown with Captain Eddie since we arrived in Touquin, and when I did fly it was in a Jenny. I knew I had a lot to learn. The next afternoon we pulled out a Jenny and went for a flight. During the next four weeks, we'd take two flights a week.

"You're pretty good in this thing. Next time we'll step up to a rotary."

As promised, three days later he had me flying a Nieuport, which was very different than flying a Jenny. The Nieuport required a steady hand and quick responses. Takeoffs were easy but landing took more concentration. The Nieuport also had a lot more power and was more maneuverable than a Jenny. I really liked it. After two weeks in the Nieuport, I stepped up to a Camel and then a SPAD. The SPAD was just as maneuverable as either the Nieuport or the Camel, but easier to control and faster. I could see why many of the pilots preferred a SPAD.

Once I was comfortable in all three rotary planes, Captain Eddie began teaching me some of the tricks he used in midair dogfights. He showed me how to stall a plane so that an enemy in pursuit would fly over or under my plane and become my target. He taught me how to do a barrel roll and how to dive either to get away from another plane or to launch a surprise attack. He showed me how to use a cloud bank to hide. He showed me how to use the wind and the sun to outmaneuver an enemy. After he was sure I could fly the planes, he guided me to an abandoned battlefield and taught me how to use the plane's machine guns. He picked out a target, a burned-out tank or a wagon, and had me shoot at it. Flying and shooting a machine gun accurately took several practice flights to figure out.

In addition to our flights, I had dinner with Captain Eddie every Thursday or Friday night at the chateau depending upon his schedule. We talked about my flights, but he also stressed what it meant to be part of a squadron and to fly in formation.

"Don, when you're up there on a mission you're part of a team carrying out a plan. Each position in a formation is important to the safety and success of the rest of the formation. Any pilot who decides to take things into his own hands is a threat to himself, his fellow fliers, and the mission. That's what happened to Roosevelt. I was on that mission and as soon as he broke formation, I knew he was in trouble."

During our weekly dinner conversation five weeks after we started our training flights, Captain Eddie told me that both the 94th and 95th were being moved to the Rembercourt Aerodrome near the Belgian border. There had already been rumors about the move, but no one knew exactly where we were going. Now I knew.

Then he asked, "Don, do you think you're ready to fly with the squadron?"

"Sir, I feel good up there, and I'm pretty confident with the Vickers guns."

"Well, when we get to Rembercourt I want you flying with the squadron. Of course, only officers can fly, so yesterday I sent a request to General Pershing for your promotion to lieutenant. You'll be the youngest officer in the air corps. It'll probably take a couple of weeks until the promotion comes through, so I'd like you to keep this to yourself till then."

"Oh, yes sir!"

"Some of the Hat in the Ring guys may be a little wary of you at first, but they've seen us flying and you're a good pilot. As long as you remember you're part of a team, it won't take long for them to treat you as one of the squadron. At least in the air."

A week later, the relocation began. Because Pershing didn't want to alert the Germans, we made the move slowly. Among the last to go were the 94th and the 95th. It took the last half of August and early September to get everything in place. As before, the 94th's job would be not only to attack enemy aircraft but also to make low-level flights, less than five hundred feet off the ground, and attack enemy machine gun placements as well as enemy infantry. Pershing expected that these air attacks would significantly aid his infantry. On the other hand, as Captain Eddie had warned, such low-level flights added new danger for fliers who would be in range of enemy machine guns as well as enemy rifles. Likewise, at five hundred feet there wasn't any room for flying error. I could see why more pilots would be needed.

The St. Mihiel Offensive, the war's first and only exclusively American offensive, began on September 12. The attack, which lasted three days, went well. As Pershing had hoped, it caught the Germans by surprise. Their artillery was not in place and their infantry was a bit scattered. Nevertheless, the battle cost many

American lives, including fliers from both the 94th and 95th. The problem came as the Germans retreated east toward Germany. Colonel George Marshall, who commanded the offensive, had planned to chase them all the way back into their homeland but encountered problems supplying a marching army as big as his. As a result, rather than quickly capturing the Germans, Marshall prepared for a new phase in the war.

The Meuse-Argonne Offensive began in late September and lasted until the war ended six weeks later. More than one million Americans joined the French and British armies along the front. The offensive was the deadliest in American history. At least 26,000 Americans were killed and four times as many were wounded. Over 840 planes from the 94th and 95th became part of the offensive. As before, our pilots regularly battled it out with German planes, but because they were also making the low-level flights to support the infantry, our pilots didn't shoot down as many Germans as they might have under normal circumstances. At the same time, the new missions were even more dangerous than midair dogfights. We mechanics could see the new challenges. We became adept at patching up bullet holes from German machine guns. Before, if a plane came back with a bullet hole, it was unusual. During the Meuse-Argonne, if a plane didn't come back with a bullet hole, it was a good day. Of course, a bad day was when a pilot didn't come back.

Early in the offensive, there were a lot of bad days.

At Rembercourt, I was a mechanic for only a week. My promotion came through on September 19. The next day Captain Eddie called me into his office just before noon. After I got there, he presided over a brief promotion ceremony. He read a statement endorsed by President Wilson promoting me to the rank of second lieutenant and then recited an oath that I repeated. I swore to support and defend the Constitution and to faithfully discharge the duties of my office. Captain Rickenbacker then pinned a bar on my chest above my heart. It all took about five minutes, but it was among the proudest five minutes in my life. I was now officially an officer in the U.S. Army.

After the formalities, there was a small party for me. Wild Bill was there, and he brought along several of the Hat in the Ringers. I had seen Bill periodically while we were in Touquin, but not since I had gotten to Rembercourt. He knew that I was being groomed to fly and encouraged me whenever we talked. Bill was now one of the senior officers and a much-respected pilot. He had also earned the status of "ace," which meant that he had shot down at least twenty German planes.

Bill shook my hand and said: "Welcome to the Hat. It's good to have another hard-working pilot on the team. Now you'll have to get an officer's uniform." I got a pat on the back from the other fliers. One of them said that he had watched me fly and was sure I'd do well against the Germans. Another one told me that Bill had said some good things about me and that he was eager to share the sky with me. It made me feel like a part of the squadron immediately.

After the ceremony, Captain Rickenbacker took me out behind the hangar where I had been working just an hour earlier.

"This will be your plane and your hangar. It's one of the new SPADs. I'll assign a mechanic to you later today. Meanwhile, why don't you take your new machine up for a get-acquainted flight? Be at tomorrow's pilots' meeting at 0700. I'll introduce you to your new teammates and give you your first mission. Also, I want you to move your things into the chateau this afternoon. You're an officer and a pilot now."

I was up early the next morning after my first night in the officers' quarters. As I headed for breakfast, Bill stopped me and handed me a package. It was a new officer's uniform.

"Here you go, Lieutenant Malone. I hope it fits."

"Thanks, so do I."

I saw him again about an hour later at the pilots' meeting. Captain Rickenbacker opened the meeting by introducing me to the rest of the squadron. They applauded, which made me feel both good and a bit embarrassed.

Along with two other relatively new pilots, my first mission was to fly over the front lines and observe where the Germans were stationed. Bill had told me that I'd probably be used as an observer for a while, and he was right. For the next two weeks, that's what I did.

Now that my promotion was official and no longer a secret, I was eager to tell someone. Sam was at the top of my list. I hadn't talked to him since a couple of days before we left Touquin. He was still in bad shape. Bill said that Sam was staying in a house two blocks from the chateau. When I got there, I was told he was still staying there but spent most of his time at a bakery not far away. A neighbor directed me to it and that's where I found Sam. He was behind a counter putting fresh bread on shelves.

"Don! How are you? You look great. Want a croissant?"

"Thanks, I just ate but I'll take one along for later. I haven't seen you in a while and just wanted to see how you're doing.

Oh yeah, and I've got a piece of information for you."

"First, I'm fine actually, almost enjoying life here in Rembercourt. So, what's the news?"

"I got promoted to second lieutenant and…

"Now you're a flier, right? A bunch of the mechanics were betting that it wouldn't be long until you were up in the air. We all saw you flying with Captain Rickenbacker and knew that we needed pilots. Not too hard to figure that one out. I am really happy for you. Just don't get shot down!"

"Ah, you stole some of my thunder, but you're the first person I've told."

Through a door behind Sam, I noticed two women, one old and one young, kneading dough in what looked like a kitchen.

"Looks like you've got a part-time job."

Sam chuckled. "Sort of. Two days after I got to Rembercourt this girl came by where I'm staying trying to sell bread and pastries. I bought some bread and we talked for a while. She doesn't speak much English and you know I don't speak much French, so it was a longer conversation than it might have been. She told me about the shop and invited me to come by, which I did the next day. One thing led to another, and here I am."

As Sam talked, a young woman brought an armful of bread out to a couple of baskets behind the counter. She was several inches shorter than Sam, had a demure figure, shoulder-length, dark-blond hair, a fair complexion, and pale-blue eyes.

"Don, this is Brigitte. She's the one who invited me here. Brigitte, this is Don. My best friend in the army."

She did a mini curtsy, then finished putting the bread away.

"She and her mother live upstairs and run the shop. She had a younger sister who died from the flu. Her father and two brothers were killed fighting the Germans. So now it's just Brigitte and her mother. I could see that the shop wasn't doing very well, so after three or four visits, I offered to try to sell some of her stuff at the base. It was a hit and I became the outside man in the operation. Now when I'm not crawling around engines, I'm here with Brigitte and her mother."

"Sam, that's great. I'm glad you've got something that makes you happy, but let me ask. Is it being here in the bakery or is it being here with Brigitte? She looks pretty young."

"She's seventeen and it's both, but mostly it's Brigitte." He didn't have to tell me that. I could see it all over him.

We talked for a few more minutes before I had to head back to the airfield.

"Well, gotta get back."

"This has been fun. Come back and I'll give you another croissant."

"Thanks, Sam. I'll do that."

As I walked back, I thought about Sam and Brigitte. I was happy that he had at last gotten past the grief of war in general and the death of Lieutenant Moore specifically, but I was concerned about what he might be getting into with Brigitte. Several times we had been warned about becoming involved with local women. There were numerous problems that often accompanied those kinds of relationships and not many benefits in the long run. Bringing a French woman, even a new wife, back to the United States was almost impossible, and staying in France was even less likely. On the other hand, Sam was an intelligent guy and his new girlfriend had clearly lifted his spirits. I concluded that Sam deserved a little happiness, and he could deal with any problems later.

The next day I bumped into Lieutenant White and asked him about Sam. Wild Bill said that aside from on the airfield, he didn't see him much anymore, but that Sam was doing a good job on Bill's SPAD and that his outlook on life seemed much better. Bill knew about the bakery and Brigitte and was sure she was the reason that Sam was happier. Like me, he was a little concerned about the relationship but hadn't had much of an opportunity to talk to Sam about it.

Two weeks after my promotion came through, I was in the air with Captain Rickenbacker's squadron on my first pursuit mission. I was scared but ready to do battle. About half an hour into the flight, we saw two Fokkers several miles east of us, but when they saw us, they turned and ran. I did shoot my Vickers but was way out of range. The following week I was sent as part of an eight-plane squad on another pursuit mission, but the only thing we encountered was a German observation balloon. Someone shot it down. Wild Bill requested that I fly along with him on my third mission. We saw no German planes or balloons, but flying alongside Bill was special. A lot had happened during the seven months since we met. He had survived many dangerous missions. To me, he was second only to Captain Rickenbacker. I felt that by asking me to fly in his squadron, a unique, unspoken bond had developed between us.

My last pursuit was again with Captain Rickenbacker. This time there were six of us. Our mission was to take out as many machine gun placements as possible and to pursue any Fokkers that came into view. That meant flying dangerously low over German lines. Three of us were in front and three behind. I was up front on Captain Rickenbacker's left wing and Eddie Hawley was on the right wing. The plan was that if we saw any Fokkers, the front line would go after them and the back three would continue low over the Germans.

Not long after we started the attack, four Fokkers came at us. As planned, Captain Rickenbacker led our pursuit of the Fokkers. He had instructed Hawley and me that if attacked I should bank off to the left and Hawley to the right while the captain stayed in front and let the Fokkers chase him. Then at just the right moment he would dive and stall. He expected that the Fokkers would fly over him. When we saw him stall, Hawley and I were to fly back to our positions, and the three of us, now behind the Fokkers, would chase them and, with luck, shoot down a couple. We were more than lucky. The plan worked to perfection. We got three of the four, including my first (and only) kill. I didn't like shooting anyone down, even a German who was trying to shoot me down, but it was exhilarating. Before I went up again, my mechanic had painted a German kill symbol on my SPAD. Now I truly was a Hat in the Ring flier.

Back on the ground, the captain congratulated us.

"Malone and Hawley, you did a great job up there. You followed the game plan flawlessly. I'm proud of you two.

And we all got a kill to show for it. Let's go have dinner."

Captain Rickenbacker's words meant as much to me as the new symbol on the side of my plane would the next morning.

By the end of October, the German forces were crumbling. Their fate was sealed a week later when we finally broke through the Argonne Forest. The Argonne was murderous. A month of unrelenting, ferocious, deadly warfare. Initially, the American and French forces stumbled through battles, but by mid-October our armies were making noticeable progress. We had significantly more men and more equipment than the enemy. Our tanks and artillery were blasting holes in the German lines, enabling our infantry to forge steadily forward. We found out later that an outbreak of influenza behind the German lines further aided our offensive. Of course, the advance came at a huge human cost. Every foot we gained included horrendous casualties. Finally, in early November the Germans were beaten and began a last-ditch retreat into their homeland.

I saw the war end from three thousand feet. At 5:00 a.m. on November 11, 1918, an armistice was signed that called for an end to the fighting six hours later. Even though Pershing had grounded all our planes, Captain Rickenbacker had a final mission and he invited me to be part of it.

"Lieutenant Malone, how would you like to see history happen?"

"I'd like that sir."

"OK, then get suited up and meet me at my hangar in thirty minutes"

"Are we going up? I thought General Pershing grounded all planes until further notice."

"He did but he also gave me special instructions to fly over the lines just after eleven to make sure everything went according to the agreement. So if you want to go along, go get your flying gear. This will be something you'll never forget." He was right.

Half an hour later, we loaded up his Nieuport and headed toward the Argonne Forest area. It was still about an hour before the armistice, but as we approached the Meuse River, I was amazed that both sides were still battling. I had imagined that the two armies would be in their camps waiting for the official moment to stop fighting. Instead, they were attacking each other as ferociously as ever. I later learned that, ironically, the final hours of the war were among the deadliest. Even after the cease-fire moment came, it took another hour or so before the shooting stopped. And I was one of only two people to watch it all.

By the end of the war, I had seen numerous battlefields, but this last one will haunt me forever. Even in this area that had been touched only briefly by the war, the destruction was overwhelming. The land below me looked like a giant, festering wound. Trees burned to stumps, no bushes or shrubs, muddy fields pockmarked by artillery shells, burned-out tanks, but it was the dead bodies that I'll remember most. There were bodies and parts of bodies everywhere I looked. It was awful.

As we headed back to Rembercourt Aerodrome, I thought about the journey I had made during the past year. Twelve months earlier, I had been an eager kid ready to explore a new world. My reality was my family, my friends, my hometown, and graduating from high school. I had never experienced anything worse than a bad day on the ball field or a few onerous chores around the farm. That kid was gone. I had been to war. Not even eighteen and I was already a war veteran. I had seen men suffer and die. I had seen how fear and hate and despair change people. I had seen farms and towns like mine back home ripped apart and turned into desolate ruins. But I had endured it all and, in some ways, had flourished. I had worked my way up from a naïve army recruit to a fine mechanic and then to a combat pilot. I had earned the respect of people I respected. Most importantly, I had survived the war to end all wars. Now it was time to begin figuring out how my old world and my new world fit together. Time to figure out who I had really become during the past year.

Chapter 4

GOING HOME

The end of the war meant a quick return home for most of the Hat in the Ring guys. Within two weeks of the armistice, my squadron was loaded onto ships headed for home. Back in the States, Captain Eddie and company were heroes and the army planned to exploit that celebrity with a public relations campaign. Stops and rallies were planned all over the country. Captain Rickenbacker was even scheduled to meet President Wilson. Unfortunately, I did not go along. Instead, I was still in France recuperating from a force more deadly than the war itself: the Spanish influenza.

Two days before we were scheduled to leave France, I began to feel sick. A day later, I had a blazing fever, a hacking cough, and couldn't keep food down. On departure day I was in the hospital. It was the sickest I had ever been. I knew I had influenza, but no one knew exactly what kind of flu it was. There were lots of other Americans who had it too. Some thought it was a final, desperate German biological warfare attack. Others thought it was a mutant virus that evolved in mucky, rat-infested trenches. I considered it a true monster. Not the literary giant, grizzly, scaly being that slaughters people one at a time. Instead, it was an invisible, microscopic monster that killed thousands of people at the same time. We didn't know where it came from, but we know now that it killed more American troops than did the war. Worldwide, it's estimated that between twenty million and forty million eventually died.

I was lucky. The strain I had was from the first wave of the disease. It showed up in Europe late in the spring of 1918. The second, more lethal wave hit in the fall. Most who got the second strain died within three days and many within a day. Usually, it's the old and young who suffer the most from a virus. This one had no favorites. All age groups and both genders suffered equally. There were horror stories about people getting sick in the morning and dying before dinner. They'd start bleeding through the nose and ears, cough up blood, their lungs filled with fluids, and their faces turned blue. By the evening they were dead. Other victims lingered for a few days, but the end result was the same. It was an awful way to die even in a place that had seen so much gruesome battlefield death.

It took me about a week to recover. During that time, lots more men and local people were brought in with the flu. There were also men from battlefields who were too badly wounded to make the trip back home. Some of them got the flu, and in their weakened condition, they didn't last long. Even the strain that I had was far more than their broken bodies could handle.

When I was finally healthy enough to leave for home, I had a talk with the medical captain who had treated me.

"Lieutenant Malone, you'll be released tomorrow, but I want you to think about something before you go. We need someone to fly to Paris at least three times a week to pick up special medical supplies. Round trip each flight would take no more than half a day."

"I'd like that."

"Here's the rest of the proposal. We're preparing a building down the road where we can quarantine influenza patients. It should be ready in a day or two and we need people like you who have survived the influenza and have an immunity to replace some of the staff being transferred to the new building. On days you're not flying you'd be helping out with the wounded here so that some of the doctors and nurses here could work in the new building down the road. That's the proposal. I know I'm asking a lot, but please consider staying here for a while and helping."

"Sir, the flying part sounds great, but I don't know anything about medicine. What can I do?"

"We need staff people here to help amputees learn how to do simple daily tasks button a shirt, tie their shoes, or just get around without a leg or two. Basic things like that. There'd always be a doctor here to show you what to do, so you don't need to know anything medical. It may not sound too important, but for the wounded and especially amputees it will be life-changing." I told him I'd think about it.

"When do you ship out?"

"In three days."

"OK. Well, let me know before you go."

It was probably the hardest decision I made during my military experience. I really wanted to go home and see my family. I wanted to see my friends and play baseball and work on cars in Mr. Davidson's garage. Most of all, I wanted to get away from the war. On the other hand, the flying part sounded good. Once I left Rembercourt, I didn't know when I'd get a chance to fly again. Still, the thought of staying here was unpleasant.

The next day, despite it all, I decided to stay. I had watched these men put their lives on the line day after day. There were men in the hospital who had lost limbs, suffered from exposure to gas attacks, and sacrificed so much for their country. I remembered pilots saying that they'd rather crash than live with the kinds of injuries I now saw all around me. Compared to those men, I'd had a pretty easy time since joining the Army. Maybe now was my time to sacrifice a little.

The four months that followed were strange. I loved the flying part. Initially, I flew on Mondays, Wednesdays, Fridays, and a couple of times on Saturdays. They let me keep my SPAD, and on flying afternoons I did maintenance on the engine. The only thing I didn't like was that I was flying in the winter, and it was cold, but they were relatively short flights and the engine kept me warm enough.

The hospital was a different story. At first, I almost dreaded going there, but after a few weeks I began to understand how important I was to the lives of the men I worked with. I helped train them to do basic things like how to walk on one leg or how to use a wheelchair. Some men had to learn how to do things with one arm. Simple things like using a fork and spoon. There were others who were blind and had to be led from room to room. I often had to carry men from a bed to a wheelchair or a bench in the dining hall. There were men so badly shell-shocked that they constantly shook or had such bad nervous tics that they couldn't eat or drink or function without help. They kept the shell-shocked in a separate ward that was locked at night. Once a week I had night duty in the ward. There were also a few men who wore specially made masks to cover up a part of their face that had been blown away. They had to learn how to eat, drink, and speak. When they took off their mask, they looked like someone in a carnival freak show. It was terrible. I know that some of the wounded simply gave up living, but for those who persevered, I was there to help. It made me feel good about what I was doing, and I learned a lot about the human spirit.

One of the first patients I worked with was Steve Wevodau from my Fort Lee boot camp days. He was in bad shape but not as bad as some others. The 115th arrived at the front in mid-April and remained there until the war was over. During their six months in France, more than half of them were either killed or wounded. Steve made it until two weeks before the armistice. He and his twin brother, Gary, were part of a charge across a field just west of the Marne River. Steve was hit with artillery shrapnel. He lost his left arm, his left leg below the knee, and his left eye. Gary wasn't as lucky. The shell landed at his feet. It blew away the bottom half of his body, his right arm, and part of his jaw. Somehow, he survived the blast but died a short time later lying beside Steve. I couldn't imagine Steve's trauma. I remember playing baseball with Steve and Gary back at Fort Lee. They were fast, could hit, and had strong arms. They were both exceptional athletes. Now there were only pieces of one of them left. Steve died a week later.

My second day working at the hospital I bumped into Sam.

"Sam, what are you doing here? I thought you'd be on the first ship back to the States."

"Well, two months ago you'd have been right, but now there's Brigitte, her mother, and the bakery. Brigitte and her mother probably wouldn't be able to run the bakery if I left. I don't know what they'd do if that happened, so I thought about it and decided to stay for a while."

"Are you still staying at the same place?"

"No, I moved into Brigitte's brothers' room so that she would get the rent money from the Army."

I told him about my bout with the flu and that I was flying and working with the amputees. I asked what he was doing in the hospital.

"Once in a while I work in the amputee kitchen, that's where I was today, but mostly I do pickups and deliveries. I might see you out at the airfield. As for the flu, it's a killer. A bunch of Brigitte's neighbors died from it, and I think I told you that her sister died from it. You were lucky it didn't kill you too."

"It was a battle."

"Listen, Don, why don't you stop over at the bakery some night for dinner. You could get to know Brigitte a little bit and her mother is a great cook."

"Sounds good."

We set the date for two days later on Wednesday.

Wednesday evening, I arrived at the bakery right on time looking forward to my first home-cooked meal since I left Middletown. Sam was right, Brigitte's mother was a great cook. After dinner we talked for a while. I was especially curious about when Sam planned to go back to the States.

"I decided I'm not going back without Brigitte, and she won't go without her mother."

"Do you think the army will let you do that? I heard that they're not going to approve taking any nonmilitary to the States, even a wife."

"Yeah, that's the policy. I talked to Colonel Alberts at the hospital before I agreed to stay here. He said they might loosen the policy later on, so I thought I'd just wait it out." "But what if they don't?"

"I haven't really planned that far ahead but if nothing else works, I may ask to be decommissioned here in France."

"Wow! That's a big step."

"Yup, but hopefully it won't come to that."

I could see Sam was a little uncomfortable talking about the future, so I changed the subject. We talked for a while longer.

"Sam, this has been nice. The best meal I've had in about eight months."

"Well, I enjoyed hearing about your adventures and having you get to know Brigitte a little bit. Why don't we do it again next week?"

"Sounds good."

"How about next Wednesday?"

It didn't take long before I was eating dinner with Sam and Brigitte every Wednesday. I enjoyed stumbling through my limited French vocabulary with Brigitte and her mother. Brigitte's English was getting better quickly, and every week she contributed more to the conversations, which was nice. And of course, I always looked forward to her mother's cooking.

Periodically I asked Sam about his plans for returning to the States and always got the same answer. He was not going to leave France without Brigitte and her mother.

"No changes. I talked to the captain, and I talked to the colonel again but got the same answer. The Army won't transport nonmilitary. Looks like our best hope is to find some special exception. I'm also still thinking about asking to be discharged here."

It was on my visit during the first week in March that I thought Brigitte might be getting sick. She looked pale, didn't have as much energy as usual, and her clothes just didn't fit right, which made her look a little sloppy. Normally she was very particular about the way she looked. I wrote it off as just a busy time for her.

The following week Sam confirmed my observation.

Brigitte wasn't sick, she was four months pregnant. Initially, I was surprised but not shocked.

"Sam, what are you going to do?"

"We're going to get married. We've got it almost all set. Brigitte is Catholic but the local priest won't do the ceremony. I'm Jewish but there aren't any rabbis here."

"You're Jewish? I didn't know that."

"Yeah, that's the reason I wasn't invited to join the fraternity at Penn State. I haven't gone to synagogue since I was in junior high school, but just being a Jew was too much for some of those guys. So anyway, the town's Reformed pastor said that he'd marry us."

"When is all this going to happen?"

"Three weeks from Saturday. Actually, I've been trying to figure out the best way to ask you to be my best man."

"I'd be honored. Just tell me where to be and when to be there."

"It'll be a small ceremony. Just Brigitte's mother, a couple of neighbors, two nurses from the hospital, and you."

"I am looking forward to it!"

On the last day of March 1919, Sam and Brigitte were married. Sam still didn't know how or where he would be discharged, but he did know that Brigitte would not be permitted to travel to the United States with him. There were refugees being sent to the States, but neither Brigitte nor her mother qualified. Sam hoped that if he could stay in France until the baby was born that he might get a special on-site discharge from the Army. If that happened, he planned to apply for French citizenship, and then he and his family could travel to the States as French citizens. I thought that both ideas were long shots. That's where things were in late April when I left France.

After I left, Sam eventually negotiated a discharge and stayed in France. It wasn't an honorable discharge, but it was good enough for Sam. He and Brigitte had two children; a daughter, Rene Alysia, and, two years later, a son, Charles Pierre. Sam and Brigitte continued to operate the bakery, and her mother continued to live with them. Sam still planned to pursue full French citizenship. We wrote each other several times a year.

I finally left Rembercourt for good on April 29. First stop Paris, and then to Brest and onto a naval transport ship. The Atlantic crossing was much more pleasant than the trip to France. No U-boats to worry about and no sergeants to avoid. In addition to the crew, the ship carried three dozen men and more than 150 wounded. About one-third of them were bedridden. There were also several physicians and a couple of dozen nurses onboard. Aside from helping some of the men with physical therapy, I had lots of time to wander around the deck and think. It was incredibly painful and sad to watch the wounded limping and being wheeled around the deck or just trying to eat a meal. Somewhere in the mid-Atlantic, surrounded by these battered warriors, I concluded that no one wins a war. Instead, the winner is the one who loses the least.

I also concluded that a life in the Army was not for me. I had been very lucky during my time in the military. I met a bunch of great guys who I would admire for the rest of my life. I had become a much better mechanic. I learned to fly, which I loved; and I had never been on an active battlefield. Nevertheless, I wanted to go home. I wanted to restart my old life as much as possible. I knew that I was a very different person than the boy who just seventeen months ago had marched down Chestnut Street in Harrisburg and off to war in Europe, but I was eager to find out how much of that boy remained. So before we docked, I requested to be discharged as quickly as possible.

We arrived at Fort Dix in New Jersey ten days after leaving Brest. The fort was only about two hours by train from home. It had been built in 1917 to train infantry. After the war, it was used as a separation camp for soldiers, like me, who were returning to civilian life. My discharge papers were already there waiting for me when I got back in the States. Within a week I was a civilian again. It was a surreal feeling. Three weeks earlier I was in a war-shattered French village tending badly scarred survivors from the war's deadliest battlefields. Now, suddenly, I was like any other young American wandering into the future.

Throughout my time in the army, I had written my parents and brothers regularly. Writing home had not been at the top of my agenda, but I did stay in touch enough to know that life in Middletown had changed a lot for my family. In fact, part of the family was no longer in Middletown. Dad had opened a new store on Market Street in downtown Harrisburg and had bought a grand new home along the river on Front Street in Harrisburg. He rented the farm to the Schultzes. My brothers, Pat and Ray, were staying with the Schultzes until they graduated from high school. Pat would graduate in a month and Ray next year. Pat had become a star athlete, and Ray was the unofficial assistant manager at Dad's Middletown store. Meanwhile, Dad was becoming more involved in politics.

One other significant change. I had a new sister, Mary Ann. She was born in August 1917 about the time I was leaving Touquin. In April, when Mom told me she was pregnant, I was shocked but excited. I was also concerned that at thirty-nine she might have some difficulties, but she didn't. Of course, everyone wrote to me about Mary Ann and I could hardly wait to see her. Mom was very happy to have a daughter after three sons. I was sure that my brothers were already catering to their new little sister. As for Dad, I was curious about his reaction. He was never the warm, nurturing type and didn't seem to have much understanding of girls (not that I did). It also sounded as if he was busier than ever with his new store and political activities.

On May 16, decked out in my dress uniform, I arrived back in Harrisburg. There have been few times in my life when I was as happy to be anywhere as I was when I got off that train! Dad and my brothers were right there waiting for me. Dad looked like he always did—perfect posture, a brown bowler hat, a celluloid collar on a pressed white shirt with a bow tie, a flawlessly fitted three-piece suit, and well-polished shoes. Clearly, he was a haberdasher. Ray had grown a little, maybe an inch or so, and was still as thin as ever. Pat was the one who surprised me. He had grown several inches taller and had added some impressive weight. His neck was thick with new muscle. His shoulders were broader than ever, and his upper body dropped like an upside-down pyramid to his waist. I knew that he was lifting weights and had been the school's star running back. The results were obvious. Someone, probably Ray, had written that Pat was headed for Penn State to play football in the fall. He looked right for that role.

As I stepped out of the door, I heard Ray first.

"Donnie, welcome home Donnie."

Ray, Pat, and Dad were standing about three feet from the train stairs, so it wasn't too hard to hear him. Pat and Dad just smiled and waved.

Two steps from the bottom of the stairs, I heard a band begin to play and a booming voice calling to me. Dad had arranged for a small brass band to greet me as I got off the train. He also arranged for Harrisburg Mayor Keister, a fellow Republican, to greet me. It was his voice I heard above everything else. "Don, over here Don. We've got something for you. Ladies and gentlemen, let him through. Here he is, our own war hero. Let him through."

Actually, there wasn't much of a crowd, maybe a dozen people aside from my dad and brothers.

The mayor was standing on a small platform, and he pulled me up beside him, then bellowed out a short speech.

He mentioned the Hat in the Ring Gang and that I was the youngest American flier and that I had bravely shot down Germans. Meanwhile, a *Harrisburg Telegraph* photographer snapped off a few pictures. One showed up in the next day's paper above an article about "Harrisburg's Hat in the Ring Flying Hero Returns." I certainly didn't feel like a hero but was proud to be recognized as a Hat in the Ring veteran. The mayor ended by giving me a proclamation from the city thanking me for my service.

Finally, I was able to talk to Dad and my brothers. As we walked past Dad's new store, he quickly pulled me inside.

"Here he is, home from the war." Everyone cheered.

Walking to the car, my brothers wanted to talk about the war, but I wanted to talk about Mary Ann.

"I am eager to meet my new little sister. I've been imagining this since August."

Ray chimed in: "Oh, she's great. She is a cute, little pink ball with arms and legs. She laughs a lot, has started crawling all over the place, and almost never cries."

Pat added: "Yeah, but she's growing quickly. Won't be long until she'll be running all over the house."

"Your mother and I are already planning for that. If she's anything like her brothers, we'll have to hire someone just to know where she is."

"How's Mom dealing with her?"

Again, Ray spoke first: "She's been great. No question that she likes having a daughter, at least as much as we like having a sister."

"She does get a little tired," Dad said, "but nothing to worry about. And, we have an Irish girl come in three times a week to help with the cleaning."

"How do you guys like living with the Schultzes?"

Pat this time. "No problems there. Mrs. Schultz is a better cook than I thought, and she dishes out big portions.

Mr. Schultz is eager to see you. Better be ready to talk about Germany."

"I plan to stop down there once things settle down a little."

We climbed into Dad's new car, a big Buick touring car, and headed for the new house.

Mom and my new little sister were waiting for us on the front porch. Mom was standing beside Mary Ann who was babbling away in her baby carriage. Mom gave me a long hug, then reached down and handed me my little sister. I was more nervous about holding her for the first time than I had been when I flew a plane for the first time. She looked so tiny and fragile.

"Don't worry, Don, she won't break."

A few seconds later when Mary Ann grabbed my thumb, I realized that she was not fragile. As I held her, I thought about Sam and Brigitte and wondered about their approaching adventure into parenthood.

"Hold her as long as you want. She's been waiting for you to get home."

"So have I."

With her still in my arms, I sat down on a rocker, talked to Mom, and played with Mary Ann's little fingers.

"I am so glad you're home, Don. I worried every minute you were away. Then when you wrote that you were flying, I worried even more. I'm so proud of you. We all are. Your brothers talked about you all the time. Then when they found out you were part of the Hat in the Ring group, they told everyone about it. Your Dad even bragged to his political friends that the war was going to end soon because you were there. And he told everyone at the stores. He may not say it, but he's as proud of you as he can be. We're all just so glad you're back home!"

"Mom, I just did what I was asked to do. I had it easy compared to some of the guys over there."

While I played with Mary Ann, my brothers carried my duffel bag up to the room that would soon be mine, then came down to join Mom and me. After a while, Ray cut in, "Come on Mom, we want to give him a tour of the house and show him his new room." So, off we went.

I knew that there had been a lot of changes while I was away, but I didn't realize how much everything had changed. The new house on Front Street was all I'd been told that it was and more. The house was about a mile from Dad's store on Market Street. It had a sweeping view of the Susquehanna River. There was a formal entrance that led into a living room on one side and a big dining room on the other. Both looked out over the river. The kitchen was behind the dining room. It included a roomy eating nook and a pantry. Even though we didn't have a maid, there was a maid's quarters beside the pantry. Adjoining the living room, Dad had a big office with an impressive rolltop desk and lots of books. I'm sure that he had read only a few of them. There was also a bathroom between the office and the kitchen. Upstairs there were six bedrooms, four full bathrooms, and a sewing room for Mom. My bedroom was at the end of the hall. It had a great view of the river and its own bathroom. My favorite room was the first-floor enclosed patio that looked out over the backyard and the gardens that Mom put in. Mom and Dad had brought a few things from the old house, but almost all the furniture was new and there were new rugs and curtains in every room. It was quite impressive. Our house in Middletown had been modest but comfortable. This house was spacious and elegant in comparison.

Those first weeks back home were tough. It was hard to put the war behind me. I kept remembering the battlefields, especially the wounded and dead. My Kelly Field baseball buddy Gary Wevodau and his twin brother, Steve, Sam's fraternity brother Lieutenant Moore, and the many mangled survivors I got to know in the hospital. They all visited me regularly in my dreams. I'd see something or hear something, and it would trigger painful memories that went to my core. A part of me felt guilty for coming through the war unscathed and now being surrounded by such a comfortable home and loving family. I felt that I owed a major debt to those men and women who didn't come home and especially to those who survived but would carry their battle scars for the rest of their lives. I couldn't let them be forgotten.

What to do next? About a week after I got home, Dad asked me the same question.

"So, Don, what's on the agenda for the future?"

"I don't know, Dad. I'm still kind of numb."

"Why don't you look into college? That's probably where you'd be if you hadn't gone into the army. I can get in touch with some of my college contacts and see what we can do."

"No, Dad. I'm not ready to go back to school. Maybe in a year or two."

"You could go along with Pat up to Penn State."

"No, that's his adventure."

"Then how about working at one of the stores?"

"No, that's not for me."

"I could get you a job in government."

"I just had a job with the government."

"Would you want to work on the farm with Mr. Schultz?"

"No. I will probably go down to Middletown and talk to Mr. Davidson, but I'm not going to ask for a job." "He's doing well. Has several automobile dealerships. Bought the Buick from him. I'm sure he could find something for you. It would be good for his business having a war hero on his sales floor."

"I'm not a war hero and I don't want to sell cars."

After moping around for several weeks, the only thing I knew for sure was that I wanted to fly again. Floating through the sky, up there by myself, detached from the world was where I wanted to be.

I finally did go to see Mr. Davidson in Middletown. He now owned four car dealerships and employed a battalion of mechanics. Just walking through his garage, I felt better than I had since I got back home. The smells, the sounds, the sight of engines that needed attention began to reinvigorate me.

As I opened the door, Mr. Davidson came hustling across the sales floor reaching out to shake hands. "Hey Donnie, great to see ya! I hoped you'd get down here soon."

"I've been lazy since I got home."

"Your Dad said you would probably stop by soon. Said you might want a job in the showroom."

"No. Selling cars is not for me."

"Wouldn't want you sellin' cars. Waste of time. I got more important things for you if you're interested."

"Maybe."

"I always need mechanics, and I already know you're the best. Plus, with all that Army training, you're too valuable to be on a sales floor. You could be one of my lead mechanics if you're interested"

"Working on engines sounds really good right now, but I don't want to be a lead anything. I'd just be happy getting my hands greasy working on an engine. Not sure I'm ready to work full-time yet though."

"You can set your own hours if that'll get ya working on my engines. Always need people up in the Harrisburg shop. Ya want to work there, just let them know when you're available. I'll call Manny who's in charge of that garage and tell him you'll be by."

Mr. Davidson's offer felt good. A part-time job doing what I liked doing. We talked a little longer before I left. I told him about Kelly Field and about my experiences in France.

"Everyone knows about you flying with the Hat in the Ring Gang. Those guys are famous. And that you shot down some Germans."

"Just one and right at the end of the war."

"One counts."

The following Monday, I was on the schedule. I put myself down for full days on Mondays, Wednesdays, and Fridays but after the two weeks I was in the shop almost fulltime. Working on engines again was soothing and helped me begin climbing out of the dark valley through which I had been traveling since returning from the war.

The other thing that began to brighten my life was buying my first plane. While talking to Mr. Davidson, I mentioned my passion for flying.

"You know, Donnie, just about every week I get ads from the army about planes they want to sell. Sounds as if after the war they had a lot of leftovers. Now they're trying to sell them. Some are already assembled, and some are still in their packing crates."

He reached into his trash can and pulled out one of the ads.

"Here ya go. Says they are Jennys."

"Yeah, that's what they used to train fliers."

"Says you can get an unbuilt one for $100 and one that's assembled for $300 plus shipping costs."

The next day I withdrew money from my savings; I had banked more than $1,000. I wired $100 to the army sales office in Washington and ordered a Jenny. Three weeks later I owned an unbuilt Jenny.

During the next six months, my life revolved around working in Mr. Davidson's garages and building my Jenny. I spent weekdays in the garage and the weekends building my plane. I could have spent more time on the plane, but Mr. Davidson was selling more and more cars and his garages got busier and busier. Once in a while, he'd ask me to help out at one of his other lots, but most of the time I was in Harrisburg. I liked being around other mechanics even though the work wasn't particularly challenging. I also enjoyed making a little money. I had few expenses, so the money wasn't important, but it was nice to be able to get little gifts for my family occasionally.

Building my Jenny was a work of love. Each part brought back good memories of Kelly Field and airfields in France. Working on the plane was my weekend reward. Sometimes I slept over at the farm on Saturday nights so that I could work late and start early on Sunday mornings. During the war, I was always on a time schedule with my planes. Now, with no deadline, I was able to really get to know every wire, every bracket and strut, and every screw and bolt that went into the plane. Occasionally Mr. Schultz came into the barn to watch. He rarely said anything, just watched and nodded. I'm sure that he did some inspection when I wasn't there. I'm also sure he never touched anything on the plane.

It took me about four months to assemble the plane's body. Then I loaded it onto the back of a truck and hauled it down to Mr. Davidson's garage to mount the engine. It was only about two miles from the farm to the garage but there were lots of curious neighbors who watched the slow journey through town.

Many of them had only ever seen pictures of a plane. The local paper was also there. A photographer clicked off a couple of shots, and there was a short article two days later. Getting the engine built, in place, and hooked up was the hardest part of the task. Any mistake could be disastrous once up in the air. There were nights I dreamt that I was way up in the clouds and the engine fell out. Not a pretty dream!

Finally, in early April my Jenny was ready for its first flight. Mr. Schultz made a runway by extending and widening the driveway from the barn into one of the cornfields. One of the best things about a Jenny is that it doesn't need much space to get into the air. Altogether my runway was about a quarter of a mile long. Mr. Schultz had also packed crushed limestone onto the surface. It was better than the runways I had used in the villages around Paris. A corner inside the barn became my hangar. I could tell that Mr. Schultz was excited about getting me into the air. So were many of his Middletown neighbors.

"Vee vill fly soon?"

"Yep, we're going up soon, Mr. Schultz."

"Zee runway, it is OK? You need it longer? I can make it longer fast."

"It's great, Mr. Schultz. Best runway I've ever seen. I am looking forward to landing on it. You've done a good job."

"Tank you, Don. I vant a good start and end of your flyings."

I suspected Mr. Schultz would have also liked to have been an early passenger. He became my third passenger.

I made the first flight on a beautiful, warm mid-April afternoon. As expected, I had an audience, including the local paper and Mr. Davidson. Of course, Mr. Schultz was there. I got him to crank the propeller. Meanwhile, I sat in the pilot's seat, one hand fiddling with the throttle, the other on the control stick and my feet on the prop peddles. After a few cranks, I heard the engine catch. I pushed the throttle forward and gently pulled back on the stick. Seconds later I lifted off the ground. I pulled the stick farther back, cautiously getting more altitude. The Jenny didn't have a speed gauge or an altimeter, but you could tell about how high you were and how fast you were going by the position of the throttle and the control stick. In a couple of minutes, I was soaring high above the farm. It felt great. My primary concern was checking the plane's maneuverability and the gauges to make sure everything was working the way it was supposed to. Top speed for a Jenny was about seventy-five miles an hour with typical cruising speed at about sixty, and the plane could climb to about ten thousand feet. I kept the speed and the altitude well short of the limits. From start to finish, I was very happy with the way the plane responded.

Once I was sure I hadn't made any major mistakes building the plane, I took some time just to enjoy where I was. Seeing the farm and town where I had grown up was wonderful. I flew over Dad's store and Mr. Davidson's car lot. Then I went out east over the high school and the baseball field where my brothers and I had spent so much time. I also flew along the road to Harrisburg until I could see the new capitol building on the horizon. I wanted to fly over the new house but decided to wait for another day. I still had to land the plane, and I'd have hated to end my first flight on top of our new home.

Landing a Jenny is the most dangerous part of a flight. The early Jennys, like the ones at Kelly Field, sometimes lost their wheels on takeoff. The army fixed that pretty quickly, but landing was still a challenge. Landing speed was usually at around forty miles per hour and my Jenny didn't have brakes, which meant landings required as much space as takeoffs. On this first landing, I put down close to the far edge of the runway so that I had plenty of room to slow down and roll to a stop.

With the flight over, I pulled off my leather aviator's hat and goggles and I hopped out of the plane to roaring applause from my neighbors.

Dad was there with Ray. Both were smiling.

"Can't wait till you take me up," Ray said. I had already promised him one of the first flights.

"Maybe next weekend."

Dad just kept smiling. I wasn't too sure he wanted to go up, but I could tell he was satisfied.

Mr. Schultz, who almost never showed emotions, ran over as soon as the plane stopped and repeatedly patted me on the back.

"Vonderful, vonderful. I been vaiting for this. Good job, Donnie"

Mr. Davidson followed him with a smile and a big handshake.

"Great flight, Donny! You'll be the talk of the town by morning. You're going to have a lot of new friends after this."

Some of the locals joined them with more back pats and congratulations. It was a great day and the beginning of a new adventure in my life.

Chapter 5 Riding the Clouds I spent much of the summer of 1920 either up in the air or in Middletown working on my Jenny. To free up flying time, I cut my hours in Mr. Davidson's garage to three days a week. I missed the daily routine in the garage and working with the other mechanics, but having more flying time was worth it.

Almost as soon as I landed that first flight, I had a steady stream of requests for future flights. Ray was first in line. He was excited about it. I was surprised that Ray was so eager to get into the air. I made him my first passenger. Pat was still up at Penn State finishing his first year in college. As soon as he got home, I took him up with me. On both flights, we flew over the new house in Harrisburg. Mom and Mary Ann saw us and waved as we flew over. Mr. Schultz was another of those early passengers. It was the least I could do in exchange for all the work he had done making the runway and for him letting me use part of the barn as my hangar. He loved the ride.

Another early request was from Mr. Davidson. While I was building the plane, he occasionally stopped by and asked questions about flying—mostly about the logistics. What was the Jenny's range? How fast could it fly? How much weight could it carry? How much fuel did it require?

How much did weather affect a flight? He seemed to enjoy the flight. Always the entrepreneur, he suggested that I charge a fee for passengers and have a regular flight schedule. I thought it was a good idea. He said I should put an ad in the local paper, the *Middletown Monitor.*

Two weeks later I had my first paying passengers. It didn't take long before I had a waiting list. My plan was to spend two hours with passengers three days a week. I enjoyed taking people up and watching their reactions. Most were thrilled. I kept the flights to about thirty minutes. I figured that a dozen passenger flights each week would cost me almost as much as I was making at the garage, so I started charging just enough to pay the cost of the flight and have a little left over for unexpected expenses. By the end of May, I was spending three days a week in the garage and three days a week in the air or doing maintenance on the plane.

Despite the joy I had flying, there were still some dark clouds hovering over my life. The ghosts of lost comrades continued to haunt me. They visited me in my dreams. They often stopped by when I wasn't working on my plane or on Mr. Davidson's autos. Occasionally they joined me for a while on a solo flight.

One evening in late May after my last flight, a guy came out on the runway where I was working on the plane. I thought he wanted a flight.

"Looking for a flight?"

"Nah, I just wanted to look at your Jenny. You plan to put some brakes on it?"

He knew it was a Jenny and that it needed brakes, so I figured he might be a flier.

"Yeah, it came that way. I'll put some in soon. It's not a problem on this runway. Do you fly?"

"Nah. Used to work on planes during the war."

"Yeah, where were you?"

"Was at Kelly Field from June'17 until November'17. Then to a bunch of places in France for the rest of the war.

How about you?"

"I must have just missed you at Kelly. I was there from November'17 until April'18 then to Croix, Touquin and ended up at Rembercourt in August."

"Whew, Rembercourt. The Meuse Argonne. That must have been tough. I was lucky. I was in Paris during that final campaign. You a flier?"

"Not at first. Started off as a mechanic. Learned to fly at Kelly, then became a Hat in the Ring pilot in October. And Meuse-Argonne was very tough."

"Impressive. Hat in the Ring. Captain Rickenbacker. You guys were great. So, an officer. You look kind of young to have been an officer."

"Long story."

Reaching out his hand, "Phil Avillo."

"Don Malone. Nice to meet a fellow army mechanic. You're the first one I've met since my discharge."

Phil was a burly guy, two or three inches taller than me. He stood there with his hands in his pants pockets, shoulders slightly rolled forward, and arms that looked a little bit too long for his body. From his handshake, I could tell that he was strong.

As I was doing my maintenance work, Phil asked me about my Jenny, then talked about the planes he had worked on in France. It was clear that he knew about planes, so I asked if he'd like to help with the engine work that I was about to do. He almost jumped at the offer. It didn't take long to tell that he knew what he was doing. His hands moved almost without thought and went to the exact spot that needed attention. I could tell he had a mechanics soft touch when he needed it, loosening and retightening pieces carefully but with strength. One sign of a good mechanic is his hands—how he moved them and how he kept them clean enough to grip his tools and the engine parts. Phil knew what he was doing. When we were done with the maintenance, I asked him if he wanted to get something to eat. He did so we went over to Mike's Middletown Diner.

As we shared war stories at dinner, it became clear that like me, a part of Phil was stuck on those bloody French battlefields. Several times he mentioned his ghosts. I asked him how he was dealing with them. He told me about a new veterans' organization: the American Legion. I had heard about it at Fort Lee shortly before I was discharged but didn't pay too much attention. At that point, I just wanted to get home. The organization was chartered by Congress in 1919 to assist veterans. According to Phil, exactly what that support included was still evolving, but it had already become a place where veterans could get together and talk about the problems they were having adjusting to civilian life. He said that a chapter in

Harrisburg was being organized and invited me to come to one of its meetings.

"Our next meeting is Friday night. Why don't you come along? There are about twenty guys, mostly infantry but at least one was a tank mechanic. It's a good bunch of vets."

"Yeah, I think I'd like that. On Friday, I plan to finish up here about six. When does the meeting start?"

"We don't really have a formal start time. Guys start wandering in about seven. Once there are enough of us, someone starts the meeting. That's probably about eight.

Very informal."

"Where do you meet?"

"You know where the Harrisburg Diner is?"

"Yeah, on State Street just above Third."

"How about I meet you there at seven thirty?"

"Sounds good. See you then."

Aside from war stories, I found out that Phil grew up in Queens in New York City. His father worked on the new subway system. He had helped to build the system, then in 1905, a year after it opened, he became an engineer. Phil was the second of three brothers. They had all fought in the war but only Phil had survived. He enlisted along with his younger brother after his oldest brother was killed fighting for the British in Belgium. He was one of the first Americans to die in the war. His younger brother was one of the last. He was killed on the final day of fighting. I remembered flying over the battlefield where Phil's brother was probably fighting and thinking how terrible it would have been to be down there.

Phil was three years older than me. His parents had come to the United States when they were children—his father from Italy and his mother from Poland. Both grew up in tenement buildings on the Lower East Side in New York City. Both had to go to work when they were teenagers, and neither had finished high school. Phil's mother worked in a sewing factory, and his father started as a laborer on the subway and then worked his way up to foreman and engineer. Phil and his brothers had graduated from high school and all three went to Hofstra University. His dad pushed all his sons hard to get the college education he never got. Phil's older brother had graduated, and Phil spent two years there before enlisting. The war was the only excuse for not graduating that his father would accept.

After being discharged Phil tried to go back to life as it had been before the war. He moved back in with his parents in Queens and was readmitted to Hofstra, but within a month, his civilian life began to unravel. Too many ghosts, especially those of his brothers. He was unable to concentrate on school. Nor could he adjust to life in Queens. By the fall of 1919, he was wandering the streets of New York City trying to get a grip on his life. He was hired for several jobs but couldn't stick with them for more than a couple of weeks. He felt himself sliding into an ever more confusing, disjointed world. The one thing that became obvious was that he needed to get away from the city and try to find a new start somewhere else.

The following February he was hired as a mechanic by the Pennsylvania Railroad and assigned to Harrisburg. It was a good move for two reasons. He was back doing something he enjoyed: working on engines. For a while each working day he could forget about the war and concentrate on fixing engines. He also learned about the American Legion. Surrounding himself with other veterans helped him accept his war experiences. Talking to other vets eased the pain he had brought back with him to the States. He discovered that his problems were not unique. Most of his new friends carried their own invisible scars and had a hard time dealing with day-to-day life. When he and his Legion buddies got together, they began to re-create the bonds that had been frayed by the war. Phil knew he still had a way to go before his ghosts were gone but he was moving in the right direction.

As I listened to Phil talk about his problems, I could feel some of my own wounds aching. Compared to his losses, mine were small, but like his, they needed to heal.

He made the American Legion sound like a good place to start that process.

Two days later, I met Phil at the Harrisburg Diner. It had once been more of a tavern than a diner, but since January when Prohibition started, the owner wasn't allowed to serve alcohol. Despite the law, he had a back room where he served whatever his veteran customers wanted. I was never a drinker, so alcohol wasn't important to me, but most of the vets wanted beer and whiskey. Someone said that the owner had a basement full of leftover refreshments. Others claimed he was part of a local underworld.

Phil and I got to the restaurant at seven thirty as planned. About a dozen guys were already there when we arrived. During the next hour, another dozen joined in. Phil knew most of them and introduced me.

"Hey guys, this is Don Malone. Was a mechanic, then flew with the Hat in the Ring Gang. Ended up at Rembercourt just in time for Meuse-Argonne."

I was greeted with a general "Hi Don" from everyone.

A minute or two later one of the vets came over to talk.

"Hi Don, I'm Joe Munley. I'm one of the guys who organized this group and I guess I'm the unofficial leader. Glad Phil brought you along tonight. I hope to see you here again." Several others came over and introduced themselves.

One was missing his left arm. Over the course of the night, I recognized that at least four more had some physical limitation.

Just as Phil described, a semiformal program began at about eight fifteen. It only lasted for about thirty minutes. Mostly it was Joe talking about plans to get in touch with the national leadership as a step toward creating an official American Legion chapter in Harrisburg. The rest of the time was spent talking and drinking. Some talked about the war. Others talked about family or their work or sports. There wasn't much discussion about the problems adjusting to life after the war, but when someone did mention a problem they were having, there was always a handful of guys who had dealt with something similar and helped figure it out. I suspect that like others, for me it was reassuring just to know we all shared experiences and that someone was there to listen. I left about eleven feeling more secure than I had felt since I got back home.

Phil and I got together for dinner again several days later.

"How'd you like Friday night?"

"It's a good group of vets and made me feel a little better about things."

"What about Joe Munley?"

"He seems like he knows what he's doing. I like the idea of a formal chapter."

"Yeah, Joe is working hard for that. He was a sergeant during the war. Fought in some of the big battles and lost a lot of men along the way. I think he feels as if he owes it to those guys. I'm not sure how good a politician he is, but he is definitely a good organizer."

"Why would he have to be a good politician?"

"There are different ideas about what the Legion should be. Joe wants it to focus on the day-to-day problems that vets have. There are some in other places who want the Legion to be super patriotic and protect what they see as the American way, whatever that is. Those guys have this thing about organized labor. They think it is a conspiracy to overthrow our government. They want the Legion to help get rid of those un-American activities. Last year a bunch of Legion members attacked a group of International Workers up in the coal mines."

"You mean the Wobblies?"

"Yeah, the Wobblies. Some Legion guys were shot, one of the Wobblies was lynched, and the local IWW headquarters was burned down. Really ugly. Joe doesn't want anything like that to happen here."

"That doesn't sound like the American way! I just liked being with people who knew what it was really like to be in a war."

After that night, the next time I saw Phil was at the field several days later. He helped me add brakes on the Jenny. Pretty soon he was stopping by the field two or three times a week. By the end of the summer, he was helping me with the plane maintenance, serving as the cashier when I was in the air, and helping Mr. Schultz keep the runway in good shape. One thing I found out about Phil pretty quickly was that he did not want to go up in the air. He said that he had seen too many crashes and would rather keep his feet on the ground. I thought about Sam's fear of flying while we were at Kelly.

As our friendship grew that summer, Phil introduced me to chess.

"Hey Don, do you know how to play chess?"

"No. I saw guys in France playing and learned how each piece moves but that's as far as I got. Looks like a good game though."

"Want to learn how to play.?"

"Sure."

The next time he came to the field he brought a chess set for me and during the following months he taught me how to play.

"Chess is a game of strategy and geometry. The board has sixty-four squares—eight horizontal rows that are called ranks and eight vertical rows called files. People think you have to be smart to play but that's not true. Chess is all about concentration and planning. You must make a plan and figure out how your pieces can work together for your plan to succeed. I think fliers are good at the game because they know how to concentrate, they must anticipate the unexpected, and they have to think systematically."

Initially, when Phil made a move, he explained why he made the move and then described the options I had for my next move. After a while, I began to figure out some basic strategies and how the pieces could work together. By the end of the year, I could hold my own with Phil, or at least he let me think I could hold my own. The more we played, the more I came to look forward to those games.

In addition to Phil, another regular at the field was Mr. Davidson. He'd come by every week or so and talk about flying. I asked him numerous times if he wanted to go for a ride, but only twice did he go up. He spent time talking to Phil and Mr. Schultz while I was up in the air. A couple of times, he brought friends to the field for a ride or just to talk.

I kept going to the vets' meetings every Friday and occasionally on Tuesdays. I started to make friends there. Phil was always there, and Joe Munley always came over and talked to me. He was becoming more and more involved in the American Legion activities. He got us chartered as an official chapter—Post 1001—in early September. He became one of our representatives. The other one was Bobby Buffington, a former infantryman. I didn't know him very well, but he always seemed angry. He was also an advocate for the super-patriot path for the American Legion.

As the summer wound down, Phil, Mr. Schultz, Mr. Davidson, and I recognized that we'd soon be closing up the flying shop for the winter. The last week of September, Mr. Davidson suggested that we have a cookout at the field. He said he'd provide the food. We all liked the idea. Little did any of us suspect Mr. Davidson's real motive.

"Men, you've had a good summer. I'll bet you made over 120 flights. Phil, you and Donnie are the best two mechanics I've ever seen, and Donnie, what a great pilot. And let's not forget Schultzie here who kept the runway solid and the hangar perfect all summer. You guys are a great team. All you need now is a business manager and I'm just that guy."

Phil asked, "What do we need a business manager for?"

"To build a business. You know, promoting the business, following cash flow, selling our product."

I chimed in: "What product? We just take people on little flights. That's no product."

"Not yet, but I can make a product out of it."

Phil asked: "Sounds as if you have an idea. Let's hear it."

"OK, here it is. An air freight company. Documents, small packages, legal papers, sales agreements. There are plenty of things we could handle. I'll bet we could find lots of people who'd like delivery in a day. Additionally, we're right in the middle of everything. Washington, is only 120 miles away. Baltimore and Philadelphia are about ninety miles away. We might even be able to include New York City. It's only about 160 miles as the crow flies. There are a lot of potential customers in those places. You know some of those people I brought by this summer weren't here to get a flight. They were here to see the product I was selling, and several are ready to buy."

"So how are we going to do this?" I asked. "First off, we'd need money to expand everything. We'd need another plane or two, the Jennys don't have enough range, so we'd have to have bigger planes. And probably another mechanic."

Phil agreed. "I like my job at the railroad. I wouldn't have time to work both places. We'd need someone else."

"First, money is not a problem. I'll front whatever we need and if we need more, I know some people who will loan me more. So, I'll take all the financial risk." I wanted to know about planes.

"That may be the best part of this. I did some investigating this summer. Followed leads from those 'Jenny for sale' ads. I found out that there are also some Nieuports, and maybe some Camels that the Army would like to sell. I got in touch with a political friend of mine. He made some calls and I have a promise from the Army that if we want them, they will sell us as many as four rotary planes for about $750 to $1,000 each."

I was excited. "Holy cow. How'd you do all that?"

"You think those little questions I've been asking you and Phil and Schultzie for the past five months have just been conversation? My questions had a purpose."

"Mr. Davidson, you're amazing."

Phil agreed. "Yeah. Sounds like you've got it all figured out."

Mr. Davidson added: "It would be a good idea to start small. Two planes, limited flights. We'd also need to expand the hangar and the runway, but I can see real potential for growth here."

Phil, Mr. Schultz, and I agreed that it was worth a shot. The three of us had only to invest our time, and we had all winter to do that. We all agreed that mid-April would be a good time to start our new air delivery service.

During the next six months, Mr. Davidson and his lawyer worked out all the legal papers and got the financing. Mr. Davidson would own 50 percent of our new company. I would own 25 percent, Phil 15 percent, and Mr. Schultz was in for 10 percent. We decided to call our new company Eastern Air Services. We also doubled the size of the runway and transformed the barn into a full-time hangar. The big event for me came in February when a Nieuport 28 and a Camel were delivered. They were beautiful. They came by train, then we used two of Mr. Davidson's flatbed trucks to haul them to the hangar. Phil and I did a thorough check of the engines, and a week later, on one of the coldest days of the year, I took them both up for brief test flights. I was a little concerned that I'd have to relearn how to fly a rotary plane, but it all came back to me instantly. I loved flying the Jenny but flying these two planes was magical. So much more power and maneuverability. Top speed for both was around 125 and both had a range of about 180 miles. Simply put, they were almost twice the plane that the Jenny was. I was looking forward to April.

Meanwhile, life with my family rolled into a pleasant routine that rotated around Mom and Mary Ann. Dad had hired a woman to help Mom with the laundry, some of the cleaning, and other little tasks. That left Mom more time for Mary Ann, her various home projects, and once a week, her women's club. The new house was Mom's domain. It seemed as if she was constantly putting finishing touches on it. In September, she had finally gone up in the plane. She was scared at first, but once we were up in the air, she loved it. Of course, Mom's primary project was Mary Ann. My little sister had learned to walk and was beginning to explore. It seemed like every day she got a little cuter and a little more adventurous. She had us all under her spell. It became Mom's job to make sure the rest of us didn't spoil her. I may have been the worst. At least once a week I brought her a little treat—a rag doll or peppermint stick or a toy. For a hug, I gave her shoulder rides or played peeka-boo whenever she asked.

As for my brothers, Ray was about to graduate as valedictorian of his class and was headed to Dickinson College in the fall. After Pat graduated, Ray gave up playing on the school sports teams and instead worked at Dad's Middletown store after school and on Saturdays. Obviously, he was being groomed to take over the business from Dad someday. Dad bought him a little Buick roadster so that he could get to the store after school. It was a lot nicer than the Model T that I had been bouncing around in. Having his own car also meant that Ray could live at home full-time rather than spending school nights at the farm, which he had done the previous year. I liked talking to Ray though he spent most of his time studying.

Pat had a great sophomore year at Penn State. By the end of the football season, he had worked his way into the starting halfback slot and played linebacker on defense. Despite all the time on the practice field, he kept his grades well above a 3.0 average. His big news was that he had a girlfriend. Her name was Janet Simmers, she was from Jamestown in western New York, and she was very pretty. Janet wasn't the first girlfriend Pat had ever had, but she was the first one that he brought home to meet the family. They made an attractive couple. Pat, with all his football muscle, and Janet, about four inches shorter than Pat with long dark brunette hair, big brown eyes, and an alluring figure. Clearly, she was as smitten with Pat as he was with her. It was nice seeing my brother with a real girlfriend. Mom was a little concerned initially, but after Janet visited a couple of times, Mom was a fan.

Aside from his family, Dad's life swirled around politics and his business. The new store in Harrisburg was doing great. Dad liked having Ray in the Middletown store. He was happy that one of his sons was interested in the business. It also meant that Dad didn't have to spend as much time in Middletown, which gave him more time to be at home and more time to do politics. Dad and I often talked about the changes that were happening. He was happy that a Republican was elected in 1920 but was not a big fan of the new president, Warren G. Harding.

"I just don't trust him. He has too many shady friends and doesn't appear to be the brightest guy around."

"But Dad, you like that he's against the League of Nations and says he opposes regulating businesses. Wants to get back to the way things used to be."

"Yeah, he calls it a 'return to normalcy.' Sounds good, but we'll see how much normalcy he does. One thing I've learned is that you can never go back. You're a vet, what do you know about Charles Forbes?"

"Not much. I think he was a colonel during the war.

Sounds like he is going to be in charge of the new Veterans Bureau from what this guy, Joe Munley, said at a Legion meeting."

"People I know in Washington claim he spends a lot of money that he doesn't have and is a real schemer. There's also a rumor that he once deserted from the army. I'm not sure how you go from deserter to colonel to head of a veterans bureau. Another one that worries me is the new attorney general, Harry Daugherty. It's well known that he's the boss of the Ohio Gang. He was Harding's campaign manager. The story is that he controls Harding and will fix federal cases for a price. I am worried about him."

"But you like Coolidge, right?"

"Yeah, he's an honorable guy. Did a good job in Massachusetts battling those anarchist Wobblies. A real probusiness guy. Doesn't say much. Likes to stay out of the way and let people who know what they're doing do what they know. I wanted our Governor Sproul to be Harding's running mate, but Coolidge is a good alternative."

Dad also kept up with the progress of our new company, Eastern Air Services. He liked that Mr. Davidsdon was so involved.

"Dick is a good business manager—one of the best I know. If there's a buck to be made, Dick will figure a way to make it. He cuts corners occasionally but he's a good man. He'll get front money and clients. My only real concern is that you're the one who's going to do all the flying. Sounds like a lot of time in the air. Why not get a second flier?"

"We're starting small so the flying part shouldn't be too tough. When we get more customers, we'll look for a second pilot and another mechanic too."

I didn't tell Dad that I'd be splitting the maintenance work with Phil.

His regular advice was, "Just don't try to do too much."

The only real clouds on my horizon that winter were my memories of the war. They didn't come as often and weren't as depressing, but they were still there. I had made some friends at the Legion, which helped, and Phil was always there. I had become a Friday night regular at the Legion. Otherwise, things were going well. I liked living in the new house and being with Mom and Dad, Ray, and especially Mary Ann. I wish I could have seen Pat more, but I knew he was doing well at school. I continued to enjoy working at Mr. Davidson's garage several days a week, and as the winter began to melt away, I became more and more excited about the start of Eastern Air Services.

Chapter 6

EASTERN AIR SERVICES

On April 11, 1921, Eastern Air Services began operations. At 9 a.m., Mr. Davidson, Mr. Schultz, and I poured a bottle of champaign over the tail of our Nieuport. It was a workday for Phil so he couldn't be there. With the ceremonies over, I climbed into the plane and our new company was up and flying.

We knew when we first talked about our new company that we would be in competition with the United States Post Office, but we planned to go places that the Post Office didn't go. Since May 1918, the Post Office had been flying mail but had limited routes to a few major cities. For a while, the only route was New York City to Washington, but by the time Eastern Air Services was flying, the Post Office had added several other cities, including Philadelphia. The Post Office was also creating routes in the Midwest and West and a transcontinental route. Our routes would only cover towns within a 150-mile radius of Harrisburg and would serve smaller cities like Baltimore, Scranton, and Wilmington.

The Post Office airmail system had some other problems as well. The biggest was profitability. Most of what it carried was regular mail and it charged less than a dime an envelope. We planned to focus on business documents and packages, which meant we could charge more. Initially, the Post Office used only Jennys, but by 1920 it had developed its own special mail plane. It was a big plane, which meant a bigger engine, which meant more maintenance time and more mechanics. Additionally, the mail planes required longer and more substantial runways. All of that was expensive. The one thing that the Post Office planes did have was good pilots. One of them was Eddie Hawley, who I had flown with in France. We weren't good friends, but he was a Hat in the Ring guy, and I knew he was a good pilot.

The first delivery on that first day was to a banker outside Baltimore. I took various mortgage materials and architectural drawings that he needed to finance a new factory building. On my return trip, I stopped in Gettysburg to pick up some checks from a car dealer there. I felt a little strange flying over the battlefield. On one hand, it was pretty country. Everything was starting to bloom, and I recognized some of the landmark sites. On the other hand, knowing what had happened down there brought back memories of French battlefields.

Everything went as planned at both stops. Mostly, I followed the railroad tracks south, and Mr. Davidson had given me maps that took me right to the landing spots. The one in Baltimore was a paved dead-end road. It was as smooth a landing spot as I had ever been on. The one in Gettysburg was the opposite. It was just a dirt road. Not much had been done to get it ready for me. It made for a bouncy landing and takeoff. I had been on comparable runways in France, but it wasn't something I enjoyed.

Mr. Davidson was waiting for me when I got back.

"Everything go OK? People waiting for you in Baltimore and Gettysburg?"

"Yep, the stops only took about ten minutes. Went just as we planned. Only problem was the runway in Gettysburg.

It's rough."

"We'll get that fixed before the next flight there. We've got three more flights this week. Another one to Baltimore. One to Wilmington in Delaware, and one to Allentown. And next week it's Scranton, back to Baltimore, and then to Chester outside of Philadelphia."

"I am looking forward to it. Just hope the weather works for us."

"Yep. I'm trying to keep you in the air."

I had dinner that night in Harrisburg with Phil. He was excited to hear about the day's flights and the ones planned for the rest of the week.

As Mr. Davidson had outlined, I had three more flights that first week. One took me back to Baltimore, one to Allentown, and one to Wilmington. I'm not sure how Mr. Davidson found them, but he did. The two new stops that week were easy, and both were on long, paved driveways that were simple to get onto and off of.

Two of the new stops the following week went just as planned, but the last stop was a little more difficult. The Baltimore flight included a stop in York, which went well. The Chester flight also went as planned, but the Scranton flight gave me some problems. I had never been to Scranton, so I didn't know the roads and I didn't have a good map with me. I was supposed to follow a specific railroad track and land on an access road beside the tracks. The trouble was that Scranton had a whole tangled web of railroad tracks. They all seemed to run into each other. Searching for the landing spot, I had to circle over the city twice. Fortunately, on my second pass, the person I was supposed to meet saw me and waved me down. It was just a small glitch, but I made a mental note to always have a good map when I flew somewhere new. By the end of the second week, I was beginning to think Eastern Air Services might have a real future.

The rest of the summer and autumn confirmed my thoughts. We picked up enough new clients to keep me in the air most days. There were only a few times we had to reschedule flights because of bad weather, though I probably should have rescheduled several others. Adequate runways were a problem early, but by June most of the stops had found paved roads where I could land and take off. Because I was flying almost every day, I used both planes frequently, though I liked the Nieuport a little better. Phil usually came in during the evenings to help do maintenance. Best of all, after the first couple of months, Eastern Air Services was making a small profit.

The winter months were a little more difficult. From January until April, I had fewer flights, usually only one or two a week. And of course, I had to adjust to the cold weather. At the top of that list was keeping myself warm. Open-cockpit planes can be cold even in the summer. The planes' engines throw off a bit of heat, but not enough. My solution was to buy some Arctic wear. It helped. Snow was another obstacle. I didn't fly when it snowed but several times it started to snow while I was in the air. Falling snow made it hard to see and threatened to freeze up the plane's steering equipment. Twice when I ran into snow, I turned around and canceled the flight. Taking off and landing added to the snow danger. Before I started a flight, I always made sure that I'd have clean runways at the day's stops. Even worse than snow and ice were the winter winds. It was something that could not be solved before getting into the air. A couple of thousand feet up, the winds are different than on the ground. They can be fierce and gusty and unpredictable. It was often hard to maneuver through them. The wind could also slow flights down, eating up the fuel supply. The few times I knew there were particularly heavy winds I canceled the day's flight.

Despite the winter slowdown, Eastern Air Services ended our first year with a profit—$1.25. It wasn't much but it was good enough. As we got ready for our second year, we expected to add more clients but decided not to expand the area we served. In early March, Mr. Davidson and I laid out our strategy for year number two.

"Well Don, are you ready to do it again?"

"Oh yeah, Mr. Davidson, I'm ready to go.'

'We're going to make at least one change though. From now on, you call me Dick. We're partners in this thing so let's talk to each other like partners. I'm not your dad's friend in this business. I'm the guy you work with."

"OK. I'll try. Dick."

"Great, now for what we'll do next year. I've got a bunch of people who want to use our services and leads on several more. I don't want to expand the area we're serving but want to add new clients in the places where we already stop. It means you'll be flying about the same amount, but you'll be carrying more. We'll also be able to use the runways we already use rather than find new ones. How's that sound?"

"Sounds good to me. I've usually got room for more packages and if we had to, I'm sure Phil and I could carve out more space."

"If we have another year like last year then maybe we'll think about expanding our range a little in 1923. It's just a matter of time before the Post Office begins to contract out and it would be great if we could get one of those contracts. One of the keys will be to show that we know what we're doing. This past year was a good start."

"Boy, a government contract would be big."

"Yep, we'd probably need a couple of more planes, at least one more pilot, maybe more, and a full-time mechanic or two. In the meantime, slow and steady."

During that first year, I came to appreciate what a good mechanic Phil was and how smart he was. He knew the engines as well as I did, and he was quick, which meant there was always a plane ready for me to fly. He still worked full-time for the railroad but came to Middletown most weeknights. Friday nights he always went to the American Legion and I often went along. Working alongside him was something I looked forward to at the end of my flights. I liked his dry humor and his cutting assessments of current events. Phil was well-informed and opinionated about the circumstances in the nation. He was no supporter of Woodrow Wilson but was equally critical of the Harding administration. I enjoyed listening to his perspective on things, it was very different from Dad's. Phil was also a baseball fan. He liked the Yankees and their new slugging star, Babe Ruth. I liked the Athletics, even though they were one of the worst teams in the American League. We talked baseball a lot.

Getting Eastern Air started was more than a full-time job so I didn't spend as much time with my family as I would have liked. Mom and Mary Ann still ruled the house, though Mom had begun to go to local women's club meetings again. She was excited that she could now vote. Actually, Dad was happy about that too. He had been in favor of the Nineteenth Amendment. On the other hand, he had doubts about women running for political office. He claimed it was a threat to the family.

"Women need to focus on their families. Politics is tough work and women just aren't cut out for it."

Occasionally, Mom quietly got her jabs in.

"What about Jeanette Rankin? She was elected to Congress. And how about those women who got Wilson to go along with the Nineteenth Amendment?"

"Jeanette Rankin and those other women should worry more about their families."

Mom knew she was in a debate she couldn't win.

Dad didn't have to worry about Mom neglecting the family. She kept our house running smoothly all the time. Her priority, of course, was Mary Ann but after dealing with Pat, Ray, and me, Mary Ann was easy. Her one bit of mischief was that she was an explorer. Almost as soon as she could walk, she was wandering around the house and yard looking for hidden places. There were lots of little corners and nooks in the house and bushes and shrubs outside in the backyard where she could make a private, cozy nest. Mom didn't worry about her. Unlike my brothers and me, whenever Mom called her, Mary Ann reappeared instantly. It was special to me when Mary Ann shared her hideouts with me. Once in a while, we'd go to a hideout and I'd tell her a story about when I was little. She always loved my stories. My reward was usually a big hug, which I enjoyed as much as she enjoyed my story.

Pat was the source of both a high point and a low point for me during the first year of Eastern Air Services. He was a junior that year and was the starting left halfback and linebacker on the Penn State football team. Expectations were low for the team when the season started. Seven of the starters from the previous year's undefeated team had graduated. Not much was known about their 1921 replacements, including my brother. In fact, the newspapers dubbed the team "the Mystery Team."

The season started with three shellackings dished out by the team. In those three games, the Mystery Team outscored its opponents—Lebanon Valley, Gettysburg, and North Carolina

State—112-0. By the fourth game, an easy 28–7 victory over Lehigh, the Mystery Team wasn't a mystery anymore. The star was their quarterback, Glenn Killinger, who was a fantastic athlete from Harrisburg. Killinger played baseball, football, and basketball at Penn State and later played baseball and football professionally. On the gridiron, he was almost unstoppable. He was picked for the All-American team that year.

My brother and his right halfback partner, Joe Lightner, had also become campus heroes. They carried the ball about half the time, Killinger carried it the other half. Pat established himself as a rugged back who was especially effective running through the line. He was also one of Killinger's favorite receivers. During the first four wins, he and Lightner each scored four times.

Even before the season started Pat asked me to come to one of his games. I really wanted to go, but through midOctober I was very busy flying. Finally, on the last Saturday in October I got to see him play. It was an important game against Georgia Tech that was scheduled for the Polo Grounds in New York. As I was looking for one of Pat's games to go to, I mentioned the one in New York to Phil.

He jumped in, "Get me a ticket and I'll give you a place to stay."

"You'll pay for a room somewhere?"

"Yeah, at my parents' house. It's only about fifteen minutes from the Polo Grounds and the price is right."

"It's a deal."

I got in touch with Pat, and he got us two tickets on the thirty-yard line. He said that Janet would be sitting with us, which was fine with me.

The Friday night before the game, Phil and I took the train up to New York. Phil had a railroad pass, so the trip didn't cost us anything.

The next morning, we hopped on the subway and got to the Polo Grounds about thirty minutes before kickoff. The day had started cold and rainy but by kickoff it was just cold. A few minutes after we arrived, Janet sat down beside me. I introduced her to Phil, and we talked a bit.

"Pat is so happy you could come to the game. He's been talking about it all week."

"I am looking forward to seeing him play. I'm really proud of him. I know he's worked hard for this, and it's nice that it's paying off."

Watching Pat warm up, Janet added, "I just hope we do better than we did last week."

The previous week, Harvard had put a scratch on Penn State's perfect season with a 21-21 tie.

Despite the cold, damp weather, the stands were filled. It was exciting. The two school bands took turns playing fight songs, cheerleaders were busy ramping up support. The Penn State fans on our side of the field were pure energy. It was everything I had imagined a college football game would be.

The game didn't start well for us. Georgia Tech scored an early touchdown, and it looked like it might be a long day for Penn State. The following kickoff changed that. Killinger picked up the ball on the ten-yard line, then weaved his way ninety yards into the Georgia Tech end zone. Pat threw a key block on the run. After that, Georgia Tech deflated. They wouldn't score again. Penn State put up seven points in every quarter on its way to a 28–7 win.

Pat had a good game. He ran the ball for about sixty yards, caught a couple of passes, one for the third touchdown, and had an interception on defense. Killinger was clearly the star but Pat was right behind him. As I sat watching the game, I thought back to the many times Pat, Ray, and I played football back in Middletown. Back then, I would never have imagined him playing in front of thousands at the Polo Grounds for one of the best college football teams in the country.

After the game, Phil, Janet, and I went down to the field to say hi to Pat.

"I saw you guys come in. Hope you enjoyed the show and didn't get too cold or wet."

Janet chimed in: "Oh, it was great. You had a really good game, especially that touchdown catch."

I added: "Yeah, Pat, great game. I am so impressed."

"It was a pretty good win. I was afraid they had us early on, but coach figured out their offense quickly and made adjustments and, of course, we have Killer. He's one of a kind. Makes life much easier for Lightner and me."

I introduced Pat to Phil, and we talked a little longer.

"Well, gotta go. Team's got a meal to eat and a train to catch. Thanks for coming."

Janet reminded Pat: "I'll see you at the train station when you get back to State College. My train gets in about an hour before yours. You guys are on the slow train."

Phil and I left the Polo Grounds, caught a subway, and in twenty minutes we were back at his parents' house in Queens. It was a nice little duplex. Phil's parents welcomed me with open arms. His mother made something she called "bigos." It was a stew with pork and sausage and vegetables served in a big, toasted bread muffin. It was one of the best meals I had ever eaten.

At dinner, Phil's father told me about his work on the subway.

"I never like all the grease and dirt. I like clean hands and clean uniform. I like to drive the subway. Phil, he the mechanic in the family. He very good. I try to get him to come work on the subway, but he like the railroad and the airplanes, especially the airplanes. Phil say you a real good mechanic too and a real good flier."

I answered: "There are no better mechanics than Phil.

Without him, I wouldn't be as good a pilot as I am. And Phil is great to work with."

His mother asked, "Phil have any girlfriend? He needs a girlfriend."

"You'll have to ask Phil about that. I know he works a lot with me and a lot at the railroad, so I'm not sure where he'd fit a girlfriend in."

"Mom wants grandchildren, so I need a girlfriend."

The next morning Phil and I walked around New York City for a while. I had only passed through New York on my way to and from Europe and was excited to see some of the sites. I was a little surprised to see how modern New York looked compared to Paris, and even on a Sunday morning the streets were crowded with people and cars and trolleys. All the activity appealed to me.

It had been a great weekend. Two Saturdays later was not a great weekend. Penn State played Navy in Philadelphia. Midway through the third quarter, Pat took a handoff up the middle and was hit from both sides, one high and one low. His left knee buckled, and his season was over. He didn't know it at the time, but so was his football career. Penn State eked out a come-from-behind 13-7 victory, but it came at a high price for Pat.

A couple of days later Pat came home to have Dad's doctor and an osteopath check the knee. Pat was on crutches, and it was obvious that every movement hurt. I had seen serious knee injuries when I was in France, and after one look, I suspected Pat had more than just a twist. The next day the doctor confirmed my suspicions. He did an X-ray and concluded that Pat had torn his left anterior cruciate ligament, his ACL. The osteopath recommended surgery. He told Pat that recovery would take a year or longer, and even then, there was no guarantee Pat would ever regain full use of the knee.

After a long talk with Dad and his doctor, Pat agreed to surgery over the Christmas break and had already figured that his days on the gridiron were over.

That was not a happy holiday season. Pat's surgery was scheduled for three days after Christmas. Ray was home, and we all tried to cheer Pat up, but that was not going to happen. The day of Pat's surgery, Janet came to stay for a while. Mom gave her the spare bedroom with its own bathroom. Janet's invitation was open-ended, she could stay as long as she wanted. My parents both thought that having

Janet around would be good for Pat, and they were right. Janet became Pat's private nurse. Her attention reminded me of the nurses I had seen in France. Within three days of the surgery, she had Pat limping around the house on crutches, and in another week, they were taking short walks outside. By the time the spring semester started Pat was hopping around on his crutches pretty well and making plans for a schedule of physical therapy.

The night before he went back to State College, while Mom and Janet were doing the dinner dishes, I had a talk with Pat.

"How do you think things are going? You seem to be adjusting well."

"At first, it felt like my world ended. I know my football career is over, and that was one of the most important things in my life. But being here with everybody helped a lot, and, of course, Janet has been amazing. I thought about some of the stories you told me about guys in France and the things they have to deal with for the rest of their lives. I may have a bum knee, but I still have two legs and a future."

"What about school? You're going to finish, I hope. You'll be the first college graduate in the family."

"Unless Ray catches up to me. I've been thinking about school a lot. At first, I thought maybe I'd drop out and do something around here, but I like Penn State and want to stay in school."

"Good decision."

"I'm not sure what I want to do once I graduate, but I'll figure it out. I once played with the idea of teaching and coaching, but I'm not a coach, I'm a player. And I'm not sure I'm cut out for teaching. That's one of those things that if your heart isn't completely in it, you won't do a good job at it."

"Any thoughts of going into Dad's stores?"

"No. That's for Ray, not for me. Janet and I have talked about things a lot, and she convinced me that if I put as much time and discipline into my studies as I have into football that I can become a really good student. To borrow from your world, 'sky's the limit.' Right now, I'm playing with the idea of maybe going to law school. Never thought I was cut out to be a lawyer, but who knows. I never thought I could be the starting left halfback on the Penn State football team either."

"That sounds great. What about Janet? Does she fit into these plans?"

"She is special, and I can't see myself with anyone else, but right now there are a bunch of mountains to climb. We'll just have to see how things go."

I felt much better about Pat's future after talking to him.

He seemed to have a good hold on his life.

Just as Dick had planned, by the time we started the second year of Eastern Air Services, he had added eight new clients. Fortunately, we could serve all except two of them using our existing runway sites. The additions almost doubled our client base, but the workload stayed pretty much the same as it had been. For me, it meant a little more flying time. From mid-March until late October, I was in the air every day and occasionally on Saturdays. The Saturdays were usually because weather had forced us to cancel a flight or two during the week. The important thing was that the maintenance work stayed the same. Most evenings I spent working on the planes with Phil.

Increasingly, Phil's conversation drifted to American Legion activities. I still went along with him to meetings on Friday nights. He was also a Tuesday night regular. He was upset about the growing influence of members who wanted the Legion actively to promote "Americanism."

He complained: "They want the Legion to go after what they consider left-wing subversives, especially organized labor leaders, and to root out what they consider 'seditious speech.' And they want only 'good' immigrants to be allowed into the country. Italians, like my dad, and Poles, like my mom, would not have been allowed into the country had the Americanism guys been in charge."

Another time he worried about the new national commander, Alvin Owsley. "He seems power-hungry to me. He's a fan of that Mussolini guy in Italy and wants to use the Army to clamp down on those who question the government."

What Phil wanted was for the Legion to focus on the needs of veterans rather than becoming a powerful part of national politics. He was happy that the Legion had pushed for the creation of the Veterans' Bureau and a bonus retirement payment for veterans, but he saw it evolving into an authoritarian organization with the potential to trample over anything it didn't like.

"The Legion should stay out of politics and worry about helping veterans."

I could see what Phil was worried about. In our Harrisburg chapter, two sides were evolving. Phil's buddy Joe Munley, who was the unofficial local spokesman for keeping the Legion out of politics, almost every week got into a heated debate with a guy named Harper, who warned about leftist radicals and how immigrants threatened the American culture. Some of the arguments got nasty. Once in a while, he even implied that Joe was a communist. Unfortunately, though Joe had his supporters, more seemed to agree with Harper. I stayed out of the debates, but I agreed with Joe most of the time. I disagreed with Harper almost all the time.

Aside from the Legion, Phil and I often talked baseball. His Yankees team had a great season. They won the American League pennant for the second year in a row but lost to the Giants in the World Series for the second straight year.

For several years before the war, there had been a minor league team in Harrisburg. It played on a field on an island in the middle of the Susquehanna River across from the city. Now the field was used by local teams and occasionally barnstorming teams. My dad, who loved baseball, and some of his friends had talked about bringing another team to Harrisburg, but nothing had happened.

Phil and I went to a barnstorming game on the island in mid-October. One team, they called themselves Speaker's Stars, included two of Phil's Yankee favorites, Bob Meusel and Joe Dugan, as well as one of the best players in the game, Tris Speaker. They played a Negro League team, the Indianapolis ABCs. I had never seen a Negro League team before. Phil had seen the New York Cubans play the Pittsburgh Crawfords at the Polo Grounds and said I was in for a treat. He was right. I knew the major leaguers would be good but had no idea how good the ABCs were, especially their center fielder, Oscar Charleston. He made a great catch in the outfield and had three hits, including a home run. The ABCs were also fun to watch. They were fast on the bases and had a bunch of pranks that kept the fans entertained between innings. To my surprise, the ABCs beat Speaker's Stars.

"I told you those guys are good."

"Yeah Phil, I had no idea. Some of those guys could be in the major league, no question about it. That Charleston guy would be a star."

"It's going to be a while before that happens. Too many issues to deal with at this point. That new commissioner, Judge Landis, will never go along with it. The owners don't like the idea and think that fans would stay away if Negroes played on white teams. In some places, they claim there would be race riots. Nah, it's not going to happen soon if it ever happens. White America isn't ready for it yet."

"You're probably right. Even here in Harrisburg there are a lot of people who would explode if white and black players were on the same team. Still, those guys are good!"

For days after that game, I thought about the people I knew in Harrisburg and Middletown. I wondered how many of them would object to integrated baseball teams. I also came to realize that I rarely interacted with the local black population. There were white neighborhoods and there were black neighborhoods. Those who lived in one didn't go into the other one.

I wondered about my dad. He never mentioned race issues, and I couldn't think of any black business associates, political contacts, or friends he had.

I asked him about it one day.

"Well Don, there's just not much race mixing here. It's not that we avoid each other, it's just that we have separate living patterns."

"Do any black men buy clothes at your stores?"

"One or two, once in a while, but most go to the stores closer to where they live. And my stores don't sell the kinds of clothes that they want. We do fine the way it is. No need to stir things up."

A few days later I flew over Harrisburg and looked at the different parts of the city. It wasn't hard to tell the difference between the white part and the black part. Houses in the white part of the city were bigger, had nice lawns, and were closer to the river. The black houses were small, usually on tiny lots and along the railroad tracks or near the industrial areas. I concluded that maybe Dad was right, and everybody was doing fine, but certainly from the air it looked like some were doing finer than others.

Phil said that he'd only been to the black part of Harrisburg once.

"We need to change that. I know what it was like growing up in an immigrant neighborhood, and I'm sure it's tougher in a black neighborhood."

We agreed to explore that part of Harrisburg a bit.

"There are some good restaurants over there, and I've heard about a jazz club that's supposed to be really good.

We should try it out."

The next time I saw Dick I asked if he had any black mechanics or salesmen.

"There are two part-time salesmen on the Harrisburg lot but that's it. I hired them so that they would get their neighbors to buy my cars. We don't have any black mechanics. I don't think our customers would want a black person working on their car."

"Why not? There were a couple of black mechanics in the Army, and they were good."

"It's just the way it is. They live in their world, and we live in ours."

I decided that I didn't like "the way it is" and promised myself that when we hired a new mechanic, he would be black.

Chapter 7

GROWING

During the next two years, time seemed to melt away. By 1924, we had figured out how best to operate our business and had developed a degree of predictability. Daily activities had become routine and unexpected adjustments the exception. Eastern Air Services continued to grow slowly but steadily. We added a dozen new clients, I was flying five days a week even during the winter. Phil still helped with maintenance, and Mr. Schultz kept the runway well-manicured and the hangar clean and comfortable. He had even built a little addition where we could store spare parts. Meanwhile, Dick continued to find new clients and plan for the future. He was certain that the government would soon begin contracting with regional air delivery companies like ours. Perhaps most importantly, revenues grew nicely. We made almost $10,000 profit during those two years.

In mid-January 1924, Dick and I began to consider significant expansion for Eastern.

"Don, I think we're ready to take the next step. It's time to find more planes, and to start looking for another pilot, at least one more mechanic, and expand our range a little bit."

"Sounds good. Where do we start?"

"I've got a few potential clients ready to sign up. First thing, we need to add personnel, especially a pilot. Buying another plane or two shouldn't be too hard."

"What about another mechanic?"

"I'll ask Phil again if he wants to join us full-time. If not, what do you think about training one of my auto mechanics?"

"It could work. That's how I started. We'd just have to find the right one. Plane engines and auto engines aren't that much different, but a mistake on a plane engine can be a lot worse than a mistake on an auto engine."

Dick nodded his agreement. "I've got someone in mind. He's been with me for three years and has done a real good job. You probably know him. Charlie Lickty."

"Yeah, he works in the Harrisburg shop. He's black, right?"

"Yep, that's the guy. I know you want to hire a local Negro and he's a good mechanic. Think you and Phil could train him?"

"Probably. When do you want to start?"

"I thought I'd have him come and watch you guys for a while. Maybe we could start next week, and you can ease him into your maintenance work."

And that's what we did. I told Phil about the change, and he was OK with it. The following Monday, Charlie showed up late in the afternoon just before my flight of the day ended, and Phil and I began to teach him about planes. We figured it would take at least a couple of months or so before he knew enough to work on a plane by himself.

Charlie was quicker than we expected, and within six weeks he was working on the planes by himself.

A harder task was finding another pilot. There was no formal organization of pilots or list of pilots I could look at.

Instead, it was just a matter of who you knew, and I didn't know many other fliers. The first person I thought of was Eddie

Hawley, my fellow Hat-in-the-Ring friend who I knew had been flying for the Post Office. Last I heard he was living in Hackensack, New Jersey, across the river from New York City. After a couple of weeks of searching, I was sad to find out that Eddie had died in a crash. Evidently, about a year earlier he was making a night flight back from Washington, and somewhere off the coast of Delaware he went down in the ocean. Flying at night was very dangerous. I had only done it a few times and then only within about ten miles of Middletown. There were different theories about exactly what happened to Eddie. Some claimed that he got lost, went too far east out over the Atlantic and then couldn't get back. Others blamed the crash on mechanical problems. Another Post Office flier thought that Eddie might have run into a flock of sea gulls. The one thing everyone agreed about was that weather played a role in the crash. The night he crashed was especially windy and rainy. In fact, the only reason Eddie was flying at night was because weather conditions had been so bad during the day.

While I was looking for Eddie, I also looked for Captain White. He was easier to find. I knew that he was in the Pittsburgh area working for a steel company, so I started at the top, U.S. Steel, and there he was, an executive vice president in charge of production throughout the Midwest. I was impressed but not surprised. I always figured that Captain White would be successful at whatever he did. I wrote him to ask about fliers, and he wrote back that he didn't have anyone he could recommend but he was very interested in Eastern Air Services. He asked if Dick and I might be around the next time he came to Harrisburg. I wanted to see Bill anyway and was sure Dick would be OK with a meeting, so I told him to let us know when he'd be in town. We set up a meeting for June.

I also checked for possible fliers with numerous flying schools. After the war, flying schools started popping up all over the country. Most of them didn't last long but a few did. One that lasted was the Lincoln Flying School in Lincoln, Nebraska. I wrote them and Ray Page, who ran the school, sent back three names. From what he heard, one of the three had become a daredevil barnstormer who was giving shows in the East. The flier was young, smart, and a good pilot, but in Ray's opinion, he was a little bit reckless. Two months later, in May, on one of my flights to York I discovered that he was going to perform there at the end of the month.

The last day of May I flew down to York to watch the show and talk to the pilot. I got there about an hour before the show was scheduled to start. Across the runway I spotted the pilot. I was surprised at how young he was, maybe younger than me. Ray Page had told me everyone called him Slim and I could see why. He was tall and wiry thin with long arms and a shock of dirty blond hair. It didn't take long before we were talking about planes and flying. He saw my Nieuport land and wanted to know all about it.

"Hey, that's a nice plane. How do you like it?"

"Nieuports are my favorite. They handle great, have good power and range, and I think they're fun to fly."

"Is it easy to maintain?"

"It's not bad."

"How about maneuvering it?"

"I don't do tricks like you but during the war it got me out of a couple of jams."

"Never flown one but sure would like to."

"Have you ever flown a rotary plane?"

"Yeah. Flew a couple of Camels, but for barnstorming and doing the tricks I do I like a good old Jenny. You here to see the show?"

"Yeah, but I'm also here to talk to you. You're Slim Lindbergh right."

"Yep, that's me. How are you in a Jenny?"

"That's what I learned on and I still fly one now and then. I'm Don, by the way."

"Well Don, that's great'cause I need someone to fly my Jenny a little during the show. The guy who was supposed to fly it backed out this morning. I was hoping I could find someone else and here you are. All you'd have to do is take it up to two thousand feet, fly straight over the field for about two minutes, and then land. Think you could handle that?"

"That'd be easy, but I'm not sure why you want me to do that."

"I'll tell you a bit later. I'll be doin' tricks first. Then I'll land and we'll go back up together. That's it. We can talk more after the show."

I watched the show from the hangar. There was no doubt that Slim was a good pilot. He did some tricks I learned in Europe and some I would never try. The most dangerous was a death spiral. He got the plane up a couple thousand feet then stalled it, plummeting and spiraling down. He pulled the Jenny out of the plunge only a couple of hundred feet above the runway, did a low circle over the field and landed. It did create a thrill for spectators.

Then it was my turn to fly.

"OK Don, here's what I want you to do. I'm going to be in the rear seat, and you take the plane to two thousand feet, that's the important part. It's gotta be two thousand feet. Then as we fly over the runway I'll hop out and parachute down. You wait until you see me on the ground then come down and land."

"That sounds easy. That's all you want me to do?"

"Yep."

I did as I was instructed. At two thousand feet, Slim got out of his seat and stood on the struts, then, as we flew over the runway, he jumped. Parachuting was something I had never done and never wanted to do. It was dangerous under any circumstances, but what Slim did was spectacularly dangerous. From the plane, I watched him fall to about five hundred feet and pull the chute. But then, once the chute was full, he cut the chute's cords and started to fall again. I thought he was a goner but in the last few seconds, at maybe two hundred feet above the runway, he pulled a second chute that slowed him just in time to land safely. It was unbelievable to me.

"That was crazy, Slim."

"Nah, just a matter of preparation, timing, and a little courage. As long as I'm at two thousand feet, I'm OK. I do that jump at almost every show."

After the show, we talked about him flying for Eastern Air Services. He wasn't too interested, and I didn't try very hard to convince him to join the Eastern team. He was clearly a great pilot, but he was also a thrill seeker who was not ready to hang up his parachute.

"Hey Don, I really appreciate the offer, but I'm having too much fun to quit barnstorming now. I'll keep you in mind if I ever decide to get a real job."

Little did I know then that Slim and I would cross paths again a couple of years later.

Two months later, I finally found another pilot. His name was Doug Fyffe. He learned to fly in the Army Air Service at Kelly Field after the war. Doug had enlisted in 1919, about six months after the war ended, and served for three years. He expected to be part of the new Army Air Forces but was disappointed when the Army started to reduce the size of its air operations. After the Army, he became a Post Office airmail pilot for a year. He said he left the Post Office because of pay and an ornery non-flying boss who pushed his fliers to fly through conditions that Doug didn't think were safe. I immediately thought about Ed Hawley. Doug also said that he was tired of life in New York City.

I went up with Doug twice on test flights and he came along with me on three delivery flights. He flew the last of the three. I was confident that he was a good pilot and Dick, Phil, and I agreed that he would fit in with the rest of us. Phil asked him whether he was a Legion member. He said he was not, which was the answer Phil hoped for.

"Well, you'll have to come along with Don and me some Friday night to one of our Legion meetings. We've got a good group of guys down there."

I knew that Phil was recruiting new members who would agree with his attitude about the Legion.

We hired Doug in late October. He agreed to work only half-time until April when things picked up after the winter. In the meantime, Mr. Schutz said he would let Doug use the spare bedroom where Ray had stayed while he was in high school.

The final task, buying two new planes, was harder than I expected. Flying technology was changing all the time. The most exciting change was the development of an aircooled engine, which significantly expanded a plane's range, added power, and used less gas. At the cutting edge of that technology in 1924 was Bellanca WB-1 powered by a Wright J-4B Whirlwind engine. Two years after the war, the Navy had contracted with Wright Aeronautical and Aviation Corporation to build a plane that could stay in the air more than fifty hours; the Navy called it the fifty-hour test. Wright developed the J4B-Whirlwind engine and put it in a body designed by Giuseppe Bellanca, an Italian engineer who was one of the best plane designers in the world. His new plane was an immediate success. Though only a couple of samples would be available before early 1925, it was the plane that Dick thought we should buy.

After reading some information and the specs on the plane, I was eager to see one. In early October 1924, Dick and I flew up to Patterson, New Jersey, where Wright Aeronautics was located. The WB-1 was a monoplane with an enclosed cockpit, which would make it much more comfortable, especially in cold weather, and had enough room for four or five passengers. Top speed was listed at 126 miles per hour and cruising speed was 90. I asked about maintenance and was assured that it required no more maintenance than our current planes. The air-cooled engine was different but not more complex than a Camel or a Nieuport engine. I was impressed.

"Well, Don, what do you think?"

"It's a pretty plane. It has a lot more space for cargo. Need to fly one before I know how good it is. And it's expensive."

"This is the future, Don, or at least a leap into the future. You're the pilot and mechanic so if you don't like it, we'll go somewhere else, but from where I sit, this is our next step. We'll be able to expand our range, which means more clients just like we planned. I know it's expensive, but we have enough in the bank to buy one for cash and I can get us credit to buy a second. And for us to get a government contract, we need planes like this. So, you want a test flight, I'll get you a test flight."

Thirty minutes later I was on the runway with a Wright pilot and Dick ready to take a WB-1 up in the air. I had never flown a monoplane before but had no problem adjusting. The

Wright guy described the controls and gauges. They were very similar to what I was used to except they were easier to reach, read, and maneuver. It didn't take long for me to recognize how much easier it was to fly this plane. And the cockpit was warm, which I liked. The only problem I saw was that it needed a longer runway than the Nieuport or Camel.

After we landed, I told Dick that this was the best plane I'd ever flown.

"You know, Don, in five years the cargo you'll be flying will be people. Just a matter of time before people are being flown all over the country. And this plane is a link to that future."

"I've never doubted your predictions and won't start now."

"So, should we buy a couple of planes?"

"Yeah, this is the one for us."

Before we left, Dick signed a contract for two planes and agreed to send a check for the purchase within a week. Somehow Dick convinced the Wright guys to sell us one of the samples and pick it up in a few days. The second plane would be ready for us by April.

Doug and I shared flying time in the first plane initially, and as promised, the second plane was delivered in early April. By that time, Mr. Schultz had extended the runway by about one hundred yards and had paved it with cement to improve our landings. Doug had flown monoplanes for the postal service but not the WB-1. He was almost as eager as I was to get one into the air. After test flights, we agreed that it was a great plane and that Mr. Schultz's paving made landing more comfortable.

Doug and I split the delivery load during the rest of the year. Of course, Dick was adding clients all the time, which kept Doug and me in the air most days. We still used our Nieuport and Camel for shorter trips. For longer trips, we used the two new planes. Dick was expanding our reach to include stops all the way to Newark (Doug took those because he knew the area), Syracuse, and Arlington, Virginia, among other sites, so there were a growing number of longer trips.

In June, as we had planned, Dick and I got together with Captain White. After Dick told him all about Eastern Air Services, Bill laid out a proposal that would enable us to expand west into the Ohio Valley.

"Here's the idea. We build an Eastern Air Service base somewhere in the Pittsburgh area. Our goal will be to provide a delivery service in a three-hundred-mile radius of Pittsburgh. That might even include Chicago. We could link the existing operations in Harrisburg. Someone could fly to Pittsburgh and then layover and fly back the next day. And we'd have a pilot flying east with a layover here. Meanwhile,

planes would fly into the Ohio Valley from Pittsburgh. What do you think?"

Dick chimed in: "Great idea, but that would cost more than Eastern Air Services can afford right now. It would mean hiring pilots, mechanics, and several new planes, and, of course, finding clients. That's out of my network of contacts. I like the idea, but it would be very expensive." "That's where my steel company comes in. We'd finance the expansion in exchange for part ownership. Meanwhile, you would run the company with minimal involvement from my company. We'd simply want to watch cash flow and grow the business. And as for contacts, we have lots of potential customers."

"You know it would take several years before there'd be any profits."

"Yep, we figured that. We just want to get into the game. We see a huge potential for commercial flight, especially regarding passenger services. We don't have anyone who knows the air business. It is something that my company is going to do even if we do it ourselves. I thought teaming up with you guys would give us a head start."

I asked when Bill wanted to start the new service.

"Maybe early next year, sooner if we can get everything in place. For now, think about it. In a month or two we can get back together and start the actual planning and recruiting if you decide you like the idea."

Dick and I talked about the proposal several times during the following week. We both liked the idea but were uneasy because there seemed to be too many possible strings attached. Our biggest concern was that U.S. Steel would take over our company. When we described the offer to Phil, he completely opposed the proposal.

"Those guys just want to take our business. That's what they do. Find a little guy who is doing well. Dangle big bucks in front of him, then take over the little guy's business and leave him out on the street."

He agreed that with our new planes we could add flights to Pittsburgh but not with Bill's money.

Dick and I had already come to the same conclusion.

We decided that the following year, 1925, we would add a few flights west, but we weren't going to go into the Ohio Valley for a while, if ever. When we told Bill what we had decided, he was disappointed but told us to keep him in mind if we changed our minds.

At the same time that Eastern Air Services was expanding, my dad was expanding his world. It came as no surprise that he decided to run for political office. The surprise was that he was running for Congress. In June, he formally announced that he was a candidate for Pennsylvania's Nineteenth Congressional District. We expected him to run for a local office like city council or maybe even mayor, but he set his sights higher. He was running as a Coolidge Republican who wanted to cut taxes, keep the national government small, and the United States isolated. With the backing of the local Republican Party in a solidly Republican district, there was little doubt that he would win.

The announcement began a swirl of activity. Throughout the summer, Dad spent a lot of time meeting with local leaders and politicians, including the governor, putting together a campaign organization. I was impressed but not surprised by the thoroughness of his organizing. During the fall he was out shaking hands and giving speeches almost every night. I went along to speeches with him about half-a-dozen times, and as I listened, I realized how much we differed on several issues. I knew that Dad opposed membership in the League of Nations. I thought we should be part of it. My experiences during the war made it clear to me that the United States had a key role to play in Europe. The Russian Revolution, post-war conditions in Germany, social tensions in England and France, and European economic problems in general were potential threats that I thought we should help solve. Dad, like many throughout the country, saw these as exclusively European problems. Thanks to Phil, I was also a supporter of organized labor. Dad was not. He considered unionists to be un-American and a threat to our booming economy. Instead, he wanted the government to police labor but otherwise stay out of business decisions. Two of his favorite campaign slogans were "The business of Americans is business" and "The best government is the government that governs least." I didn't completely agree with either of them.

Dad's summer activity included putting my brother Ray in charge of the stores. Ray graduated from Dickinson a month before Dad announced his candidacy and, of course, he finished near the top of his class. Dad wanted him to major in finances, but Ray decided on philosophy instead. Nevertheless, there was no question that Ray would take over the business at some point. He had worked part-time in the stores throughout college, full-time during the summers, and probably knew as much about running a men's clothing store as anyone except Dad. After Ray graduated, Dad made him associate company chairman, and during the summer groomed him to take over if Dad won his election. With Ray in charge, Dad was confident that the stores would continue to prosper.

Ray jumped right into his new position. He had always been the fashion-conscious brother. In college, his classmates voted him best dressed and most likely to succeed. At Dickinson, men were expected to wear a coat and tie to class. Ray always wore a suit, often one that had been purchased within the past year. Like Dad, his shirts were starched and pressed. He had an array of ties, several of them bow ties, and a shelf full of hats. He also had a dozen pairs of dress shoes that were always shined. I especially liked his twotone wingtips. He claimed that he was a walking advertisement for Dad's stores and should make the best impression possible. He certainly succeeded at that.

Dad's campaign was exciting. He had two full-time staff people and a campaign manager who seemed to be everywhere. Mom also did a lot of work on the campaign. Now that Mary Ann was in first grade, Mom had time to do whatever errands needed to be done. Sometimes she went along with him on a campaign stop, and there were lots of stops. Almost every day Dad was out meeting with local groups and civic organizations. Weekends were picnics and rallies and local fairs and dinners. There were also lots of newspaper articles and commentary. Most supported him, though there were a few that did not. His biggest critics were a couple of labor leaders who painted him as part of the local business elite. I knew that Phil agreed with them, and he knew I didn't completely agree with Dad's stand on several issues, so we didn't talk much about the election.

One day as the campaign heated up, I asked Mom if she agreed with all of Dad's political stands.

"We agree about the things that are most important to me, like women's right to vote. When we disagree, I don't bother debating with him. There are other ways to get your father to change his mind without him realizing that's what he's doing."

One of those things was whether Mom should be able to drive. Dad had always contended that women physically were not built to drive. They weren't strong enough and their reflexes were too slow. Also, their dresses could easily get tangled in the floor pedals. During the campaign Mom showed him that he was wrong. She convinced him that if she were able to drive, she could do a lot more for his campaign. She could pick up and deliver campaign material, and she could work more hours at the campaign headquarters.

It was during the campaign that Mary Ann got her first plane ride. One Saturday in September, Dad was off to a luncheon and then a local fair in Halifax, twenty miles north of Harrisburg. He wanted Mom and Mary Ann to go along, but Mom had a morning campaign event of her own with local women. So, I offered to fly her and Mary Ann up to meet Dad in the afternoon. Mary Ann had asked to go up in the plane many times, but Mom had always said no. To my surprise, this time Mom said yes. Mary Ann had turned six a couple of weeks before and Mom felt that she was now old enough.

Mary Ann had always been an adventurer and her first plane ride was a big adventure. I flew the Camel so that she could see more of the countryside and feel the wind. She loved it. I started the trip by flying over the capitol and our house in Harrisburg then went north up the Susquehanna River. Mary

Ann provided Mom with a continuous narrative of where we were and what to look at. When she saw something that looked interesting, like a small house on an island in the Susquehanna, she tried to get me to take her closer. Her biggest thrill was when we flew into a cloud bank. Mom was not particularly comfortable in the air and especially in a cloud bank, but she went along with Mary Ann's requests. For my little sister it was an exciting day, and for me it was a lot of fun.

In November, Dad won in a landslide getting almost 80 percent of the vote. Even in an area as Republican as Harrisburg, it was an impressive win. We were all proud of him. Of course, it also meant that he would be in Washington for several months a year, but it was only four hours by train and I could fly down to drop him off or pick him up if I had to. One way or another, he would be at home on the weekends.

The victory set off an election night celebration, but the real celebration was in Washington a month later when Dad was sworn in. About one hundred people gathered in a downtown Washington ballroom to welcome the new congressman. Of course, Mom, Ray, Mary Ann, and I were there. Pat came in from Pittsburgh where he was in law school. There were lots of Dad's friends and supporters from Harrisburg, including Dick Davidson. There were also several notable congressmen including Speaker of the House Nicholas Longworth and his colorful wife, Alice Roosevelt Longworth. Mom and Alice had a long conversation; I'm sure they talked about women in politics. It was a real gala event.

Dad made a flashy entrance to Washington. I flew him, Mom, Ray, and Mary Ann to the capital in one of our new, state-of-the-art WB-1 planes. It was a well-planned trip designed more to get newspaper coverage than simply to get the family to Washington. And it worked. There were at least a dozen photographers waiting for us as we landed, and the next day there were front page pictures in Washington, Philadelphia, New York, and Harrisburg. As Dad and his strategist hoped, the arrival introduced him to Congress in very high-profile way.

Dad did have an ulterior motive for his entrance. He wanted to be on the Congressional Aeronautics Committee. That committee was responsible for devising standards for commercial air travel, which included airmail service. Of course, Dick and I were excited about that. A bill had just passed, the Air Commerce Act, that was designed to put the national government in charge of civilian aviation. The goal was to foster air commerce, which included mail services. That was pretty much what Dick and I had been hoping for since we started Eastern Air Services. If Dad were put on the committee, we would almost be guaranteed a government contract.

As Dick and I flew back to Harrisburg the next day, he was already working on a proposal.

"Don, this is it. With any luck, next year at this time we'll have a lock on air services throughout the middle Atlantic region."

"What about Bill's idea in the Midwest?"

"I'm still wary of that one. I think Phil made a good point. We should be careful dealing with U.S. Steel. Bill's a nice enough guy, but he is a company man and I am concerned his company might want to take over our company. Besides, services from New York to Washington and west to Pittsburgh, that's a pretty big territory."

"Yup. It sounds good to me."

Chapter 8

FALLING FROM THE SKY

The Air Commerce Act passed on May 20, 1926. Among its goals was to eventually create commercial air services for the entire country. We were part of the initial effort to achieve that goal. We got our contract on January 15, 1927, along with three other companies. Dad was on the Air Commerce Committee, but he claimed he had no role in us getting the contract. We joined two companies that had been flying for several months already. One flew from St. Louis to Chicago, and the other was on the West Coast from San Francisco to San Diego. One of the other new companies flew throughout New England to New York. Another flew from Richmond to New Orleans, and the third flew in the Southwest. Our contract gave us a territory from Pittsburgh to New York and south to Richmond. It was a territory with lots of potential clients. When signing the contract, Eastern Air agreed to begin providing service on July 1, 1927.

In the months between getting our contract and starting operations, we were busy. While we continued to work with our existing clients, we also hired three new pilots, bought three new planes, and had a large, full-fledged hangar and a new runway built. When the work was done, the company was using about a third of my parents' original farm. By the summer, Mr.

Schultz and his wife had built a new home on a large lot across the street from the farm. We used our old house as a place for pilots and a business office. Clearly, the farm was evolving into a full-scale airport.

Hiring the pilots wasn't too hard because the Post Office airmail was downsizing, so there were experienced pilots available. Likewise, we already knew what plane we wanted, so it was just a matter of ordering them from Wright Aeronautics. We didn't have to hire a new mechanic because Phil finally gave up his job with the railroad and became our full-time chief mechanic. He had been having problems with his station manager who never liked the union and was becoming ever harsher toward union members, including Phil. We also didn't have to find new clients, though Dick was always looking, because the Post Office provided them. One other addition was a secretary, Ellen Goodling, who managed the office and did the growing amount of paperwork. By July, we were ready to start a new chapter for Eastern Air Services.

Throughout that spring I was concerned that Eastern Air Services had bitten off a little more than we could handle. Dick kept assuring me that we had not. "Don, we can organize the stops so that you guys are in the air no more than you have been up to now. We'll have two ranges of flights. One will be short range, primarily to our old clients, and one will be long range to our new city stops. Those stops will be to the airfields where the Post Office used to fly. Pilots flying to the cities will only make one or two stops each day and deliver to only the Post Office trucks. On the other hand, they will be logging more miles. The locals will make twice as many stops but will only be flying about half as many miles."

"Sounds like a good plan, Dick, but I will be worried about it until I see it working."

"Don't worry too much, Don. I'm sure it'll work."

Dick was right. His plan worked perfectly. Two of the new pilots, George Shorb and Tom Haskins, did the longrange flights. George flew the eastern routes and Tom went south. Both had flown for the Post Office and already knew the routes and airfields where they'd be flying. The third new pilot, Mark Mathias, and Doug did the shorter routes and took turns making the three weekly flights to Pittsburgh. I flew a little of everything. Twice a week I flew the long routes and once a week a short route and once a week I flew the Pittsburgh route. That way each pilot was flying four days a week and I could stay in touch with all our clients.

On my first flight to Pittsburgh in March, I had another brush with future greatness. I was walking across the runway to the hangar when I spotted a familiar face.

"Hey Slim, what are you doing in Pittsburgh? Did you decide to give up barnstorming?"

"Don, good to see you. Yeah, I gave up barnstorming about a year after you offered me a job. Took a spot as chief pilot with a company flying mail from St. Louis to Chicago."

"You guys looking to expand to Pittsburgh?"

"Nah. Came up here to talk to someone about a little adventure I'm planning. Ever hear of the Orteig Prize."

"The one for flying across the Atlantic?"

"Yup, that's the one. I'm planning to give it a try in a couple of months."

"Wow. That is a real barnstormer's challenge. Good luck."

"Thanks, Don, I'll let you know how it goes."

Of course, everyone knew how it went two months later.

In May, Slim crawled into an updated version of the plane I now flew and became the best-known pilot in the world.

By August, Eastern Air Service was running smoothly and my concerns were gone. During the following year, we had a few minor problems that we solved quickly. As was to be expected, there were several days of bad weather, but our fleet of new planes was able to either fly through or over weather far better than the older planes. All things considered, our expanded service during its first year went very well.

With a successful flying business came more money. My money went into the bank. My only luxury was the car I drove, a Buick Sports Roadster. Phil was even more frugal. He kept what he needed to pay his bills and the rest he sent to his parents in New York. Dick was the investor. Aside from opening two new car lots, he put his money in all sorts of speculative adventures. Real estate was his favorite, but he had stock in a copper mine and a coal company, an importexport business, a couple of construction companies, and a bunch of other little businesses all over the place. It all seemed to pay off for him. On paper, he was becoming a very rich man. He kept pushing me to start investing as well.

"Don, the economy is booming. It's almost impossible not to make money nowadays. Your dad and his Republican buddies in Congress just keep helping investors get rich."

"You're the investment guy, Dick. I like putting my money where I can get at it when I need it. The bank is good enough for me."

"Now's the time to spread your money around. If you've got a few spare bucks, and I know you do, there's never been a better time to turn them into profit."

With Eastern Air doing well, I let Dick talk me into some of my own investments. His advice: "Top of the list— buy a nice house for yourself."

I had thought about buying a house. There was lots of land available, and for several years I had read about how people were buying houses cheaply and then selling them a year or two later for a big profit. I did buy two inexpensive lots outside Harrisburg but building a house was more than I wanted to do.

"Well, if you don't want to build, just buy a house."

"I've thought about it, Dick, but I like living with my family. It's a big house and now that Ray and Pat have their own places there's lots of room. I like being around Mom, Mary Ann, and Dad when he's home. And if I ever want to be alone, I can always camp out at the farm for a few days."

"Well, you should think about putting your money somewhere where it will grow. Let your money make money for you."

I did make one special investment though I didn't expect to earn much from it. Phil and I went in with a couple of guys we met in black Harrisburg and bought a baseball team in the Eastern Negro League. We had regularly gone to games in Harrisburg. Most involved Harrisburg's minor league team, the Senators. Once or twice a year we also went to barnstorming games between teams with major leaguers and black traveling teams. I was always impressed by how good the black players were and regretted that they had to work so hard to get games. The black barnstormers were clearly better than the Harrisburg minor league team and often beat the major leaguers they played. During the summer of 1927, the first of our expanded air service, a friend of Dad's who knew how much I liked baseball told me that he knew two guys who were looking for some new backers for their Eastern Colored League team, the Harrisburg Giants. I told Phil about it and we agreed to invest in the team. We each kicked in $500 and joined three other owners. Neither Phil nor I expected to make a profit. We just hoped to break even. Far more importantly, we both looked forward to being team owners and, especially, bringing the Negro League players to Harrisburg.

We were right about not making a profit. The team played only thirty-six games in Harrisburg and after expenses, home games barely paid for themselves. The team's business manager, who was also one of the owners, got a local radio station to cover games, but there weren't many businesses in the area that were willing to sponsor the team. Several of the good players also regularly rented themselves out to barnstorming teams, so they weren't always available for league games. The team disbanded the year after Phil and I became owners but, despite it all, we enjoyed the experience.

I also put a little bit of money into Dad's stores. He didn't have stockholders but allowed me to become a very minor partner in the business. My real purpose in making the investment was to show my confidence in Ray. Though technically Dad was still in charge, Ray was making all the important decisions and handling the daily operations. He had both stores doing well, especially the one in Harrisburg, but Dad had another issue with Ray.

Not long after Dad's reelection in 1926, Ray began dating his secretary. Angie had been a part-time staffer for Dad, and after the campaign Ray hired her as his secretary in the Harrisburg store. Six months later she and Ray were married. Dad was not happy. Ray and Angie had been discreet about their relationship, and in March when he announced that they were engaged, we were all surprised.

Dad was angry. While he complained that Ray should not have become involved with someone who worked for him, the real reason Dad was angry was because he didn't think Angie was right for Ray. Her parents were Italian immigrants, and for years her father had worked in the steel mill in Middletown. The family lived in a little row house near the mill. When her father was hurt at work, Angie dropped out of high school to help support her family. Her mother did domestic work sewing, cleaning, and occasionally cooking to add a bit more to the family income. Dad was even angrier when a week before the wedding Ray announced that Angie was three months pregnant.

Through it all, Mom was always kind to Angie. Mom was upset about the timing of the pregnancy but happy that she was going to be a grandmother. "Angie's a nice girl and she's smart. She has worked hard to help her family and I know what a good job she did on your dad's reelection." Of course, Dad also knew Angie from the campaign. Initially he was not as disappointed with her as he was with Ray. When Dad found out that she was pregnant, he became angry with them both. He worried that Angie had seduced Ray and was upset that Ray had allowed himself to be seduced.

I asked Mom if she knew what was going to happen once Angie wasn't living at home and helping with her family bills.

"Ray said that she wants to work as long as she can and whatever she makes will go to her parents. Her dad is working at the cigar store in Middletown and her mother does housekeeping, so they should be able to make it without help from Angie. I suspect that if they can't, Ray will help them. They may even move in with Ray and Angie. His new house has plenty of room."

Ray had bought a five-bedroom house between Harrisburg and Middletown a year before meeting Angie. He said he bought the house as an investment. I don't think raising a family was part of his plan.

The wedding was in May. Though Dad wanted a small, quiet wedding, that was not possible. The local newspapers helped to turn it into a major local social event. There was a full page of pictures and a long write-up the Sunday after the wedding. More than 150 guests attended, including several congressmen and the governor, as well as Dad's business friends. Even though Angie was Catholic, Dad, since he was paying for it, had the ceremony scheduled for our family's church, Market Street Presbyterian, which was the biggest church in Harrisburg. The reception was a gala event. It was held at the Harrisburg Country Club where Dad was a member. There was food and champagne and music and dancing until almost midnight. In the end, despite his anger, Dad gave Ray and Angie a wonderful wedding.

Of course, Angie was the star. Her mother had sewn a beautiful gown that accentuated Angie's petite figure even though she was three months pregnant. She and Ray made a very attractive bride and groom. Mary Ann was a close second to the bride. She was the flower girl. As she came down the aisle, she looked so mature and grown up. It was hard for me to believe that her tenth birthday was just around the corner.

In early September, Ray and Angie had a baby boy. They named him Timothy Anthony after my dad and Angie's dad. Mom was thrilled. During Angie's first week home, Mom was at Ray's house every day with food for the new parents, baby furniture, and supplies for Timmy. Dad also warmed up a bit. Though he didn't say it, I could tell that he was happy to be a grandparent and proud to have his first grandson named after him.

Pat's wedding two years earlier had been very different from Ray's. Pat and Janet were married in Jamestown, New York, at Janet's home. Pat was in his second year of law school at the University of Pittsburgh. He decided to go there instead of Dickinson because it was about as far away from Harrisburg as it was from Janet and her family in Jamestown. The wedding was on a cold, snowy January day, and aside from family, only about two dozen guests attended. Since then, Pat and Janet had been living in Pittsburgh. She found a spot teaching high school social studies, and after passing the bar exam the following year, Pat joined the Alleghany County District Attorney's Office.

Pat was the one who alerted me to some potential competition for our contract with the Post Office. Occasionally, when I did the Pittsburgh flight, Pat and I had lunch together. Early in January 1928, Pat told me about a case that he had recently prosecuted.

"It was a standard assault case. When I asked the victim where he worked, he said he had just been hired as a mechanic by East-West Air Company. I thought that he meant your company, but he said no. His was a new company that was planning to do air services from Chicago to New York. Afterward, I started asking around a bit and found out that U.S. Steel has created a subsidiary focused on flying and is probably going to go after Post Office contracts. Sounds as if they've got a few targeted and I wouldn't be surprised if your company is one of them."

I had already heard a few rumors about a new air company in the Midwest and Pat's news confirmed them. At that point I wasn't too concerned because our contract had just been renewed for 1928.

I called Bill White to see what he knew. "Donnie, the air project has been taken off my plate, so I don't know much. I'll see what I can find out."

A couple of weeks later he called me and said that U.S. Steel had created a subsidiary company—East-West Air.

That's all he knew.

Dick was concerned when I told him about East-West.

"We need to keep an eye on this. Stay in touch with your brother and Bill. Probably be a good idea to talk to your dad about it as well."

Phil was furious when I told him about the U.S. Steel air company.

"Those bastards will kill small businesses every chance they get. And Coolidge is with them all the way. He said he's not running for reelection, but you can bet the Republicans will come up with someone just like him. If they win again, I guarantee you that they will keep on cozying up to the big guys like U.S. Steel."

What went unsaid was that Dad was a staunch Coolidge man.

During the months that followed, Dick, Phil, and I remained wary. Eastern Air was still doing well. Our clients seemed satisfied. The only unexpected problem involved one of the new pilots, Tom Haskins. One night in early October I got a call from the Harrisburg Police Department. Tom had been arrested for public drunkenness. I went to the station and bailed him out. A week later he was fined and warned not to do it again.

The day after I bailed Tom out, I told Dick about it and told him that I'd take care of it. Tom was off that day, but when he came to work the following day, I talked to him about it.

"Hey look, it's not a problem. Just one too many one night."

I wrote it off as just what he said it was. Tom had been doing a good job, though he had also missed work several times in the previous couple of months. Of course, Prohibition was still the law of the land but there were plenty of places where people could get a drink if they wanted to.

Two weeks later, Phil told me that he had seen Tom wobbling along a street in Harrisburg and had helped him get home. Tom missed work again the next day.

"Tom, your drinking is becoming a problem. You're a good pilot, I'd hate to lose you."

"Don't worry. I said it wasn't a problem before and it's still not a problem."

"Yeah, well it looks like it's more than just 'one too many one night.' If you need help with it just let me know."

"Thanks, I'll keep that in mind, but as I said, it's not a problem."

Dick, Phil, and I kept a closer eye on Tom and were worried. I talked to him two more times, but it didn't seem to matter. Once, Dick saw him going into a speakeasy, and another time Phil saw him coming out of one. A month later and three more flying days missed, we decided to fire Tom. It hurt me to do it, but Eastern Air couldn't have a drunk pilot flying for us.

We quickly hired a replacement, Richey Barber, another former Post Office pilot. Fortunately, we never missed a flight because of Tom, and Richey worked himself in right away.

In November, Dad won another easy reelection. Just as Phil had feared, another pro-big business Republican, Herbert Hoover, a self-made millionaire and Coolidge's secretary of commerce, won the presidential election. Phil had met Al Smith, the Democratic candidate, and was a big Smith supporter. "That's the kind of guy we need in the White House. Grew up poor on the streets of New York. A real friend of the working man. Too bad he is Catholic. He'd have won otherwise."

I was surprised when Dick agreed with Phil.

"I am a little worried that the economic boom is about over and more of the Coolidge policies is going to make the end tougher."

I ask: "Why do you say that? Almost everywhere I look I see people getting rich."

"Well, you need to look other places. For instance, people aren't buying cars the way they did a couple of years ago. Some auto companies, like the Pierce-Arrow Company, are having real problems. My sales have been sliding for over a year now. If fewer cars are sold, it means less steel, and steel is the backbone of the economy. I suspect that's why U.S. Steel is looking for other ways of doing business."

Phil chimed in: "Yeah, and it means steelworkers and autoworkers will be in trouble soon. Most haven't had raises in a while and the cost of everything is going up. So, they buy on credit. If they lose their job, they are in big trouble."

"I'll give you another sign," Dick added. "The farm economy has been shrinking for several years."

"But what about the stock market and real estate?" I asked.

Dick answered: "I can't talk about the stock market' cause I don't really understand it. Seems like there's a lot of gambling going on there. I can talk about real estate, and I see some places that don't look healthy. Our local market seems OK, but there are some places that are in trouble. An example: Florida. After those hurricanes last year, that market all but died. Now there are people who own expensive land that they can't pay for. Some of these new suburban areas also seem shaky too. Ten years ago, there were more people than houses. That's changing."

Phil observed: "From what I see, lots of people bought more house than they can afford. They're betting on reselling and making a big profit. If more people are laid off, they won't be able to pay their mortgages and will be in really bad shape. I'll keep my money in a bank instead of gambling on land or stocks."

"On the positive side for us, the mail will continue to be sent and we will still have our contract," Dick added. "That's the reason we have to be careful about this East-West Air issue. U.S. Steel is going to get hungry if its steel isn't selling."

One other concern was the election. Dad traded his place on the Air Commerce Committee in Congress for a place on the Ways and Means Committee, which meant that he no longer had any voice in making airmail contracts.

Dick moaned, "There goes our ears on that committee."

Two months later, Dick's concern grew. Some of the air contracts, including ours, were delayed. The stated reason was that the new government needed a little time to get working. We were told that the current contracts would be extended until the spring or maybe even the summer.

Our contract finally came through in May, but we noticed that some of the original air companies had been replaced. The most troubling change was a new company taking over routes between Pittsburgh and Chicago. The new company was East-West Air Company, the U.S. Steel subsidiary.

"That's trouble," Dick warned.

"Yep, I bet we're on their hit list," Phil added.

"I'll see what Dad knows. Maybe it's not as bad as it looks."

It was as bad as it looked. Worse. Dad said that there were several new members of the Air Commerce Committee. At least two of them had connections to U.S. Steel, and he suspected that a couple others backed new national airlines. Also, the former committee chair had resigned and was now representing airline companies like East-West. The new guy in charge, Walter Brown, the postmaster general, planned to change the way mail carriers were paid and the way that routes were approved. Under the new system, big operators would be given larger territories at the expense of the little guys like us.

Phil was seething when he heard what Dad had told me. "This is the way it works! Small businesses like us take all the risks, spend their money, work their butts off to get things up and running, then the robber barons come in with the help of their for-hire politicians in Congress and steal it from us"

Dick was a little more positive. "If they wanted us out, they would not have issued our contract for this year. From what I've heard, the purpose of the change is to get rid of the inefficient and wasteful carriers. We certainly are not one of those. What we need to do now is continue to do what we've been doing for five years. Meanwhile, we need to pay attention to what's going on in Washington."

I was worried about the changes. As anti-government as he was, Phil's predictions about what was happening seemed pretty accurate. The Republicans, Hoover especially, talked about the virtue of small businesses but they were helping big businesses gobble them up. I knew that Dad was a loyal Republican. He was also a small businessman.

I asked him what he thought.

"The government should stay out of the way. Let business take care of itself. If that means some fall by the wayside, that's the way it goes. My stores have done well because we did things right, a good product at a competitive price. If you can't do that, then you're not going to last long. That's what American capitalism is all about. We're the richest, strongest nation in the history of the world. Part of the way we got there was because of the industry we've built. You remember what Coolidge said: 'The business of America is business.' You don't want to get in the way of that."

"But what if a business is so powerful that it can get rid of its competition?"

"As long as no laws are broken, that's one of the goals of a business. Dominate the competition."

"Sounds a lot like survival of the fittest to me."

"This isn't the animal kingdom. It's what's made us great."

Through the summer, we did just what Dick had said we should do. We worked as hard as we ever had. Dick added several new contracts as he always did. We almost never missed a flight or a delivery. We kept our clients happy and, with Dad's help, kept tabs on the Commerce Department in Washington.

Then in September one of our pilots, Mark Mathias, quit. Dick did a little checking and found out that Mark had been offered a job by East-West Air. He also found out that after we fired Tom Haskins, he started flying for EastWest as well. Both Tom and Mark were flying routes in the Midwest, but they both knew our routes.

"This is another step for East-West," Dick said when he found out about Mark and Tom. "We are in trouble. We need to get our clients to vouch for us next time we apply for a contract. You know, like a letter of recommendation.

I'm sure most of our clients would do that."

Dick began organizing right away. Meanwhile, we quickly found someone to replace Mark. This time it was a pilot, Charlie Pitts, who had recently left the army. It took Charlie two weeks to learn the routes and contacts.

September 22, 1929, I should have stayed in bed. It was a stormy day, the remnants of a hurricane brought lots of wind and torrential rain. I was scheduled to make a delivery to an important client in Pittsburgh. Because of the weather I delayed taking off until the mid-afternoon. My instinct was to postpone the flight until the next day, but I didn't. An afternoon start meant that I'd have to fly the return at night, probably in bad weather. I hated flying at night, especially over the mountains in western Pennsylvania. The light markers that guided planes through the mountains were hard to see at night under any circumstances, but during stormy weather some of the markers disappeared. It was not a flight I was looking forward to.

The flight out was tough. I tried to keep my plane above the clouds as much as I could, though there were times that just wasn't possible. A driving rain and strong swirling wind gusts made the landing in Pittsburgh a challenge. After making the delivery, I contemplated spending the night with Pat and Janet, but that would have meant late deliveries the next day and I didn't want to impose on my brother and sister-in-law, so with night falling, I rolled back down the runway headed east.

The weather on my return had improved slightly but it was still raining, cloudy, and unusually windy. About an hour out of Pittsburgh the clouds thickened, and I lost track of the direction lights. I decided to drop to a lower altitude despite the rain and wind so that I could see the lights. I kept a close eye on my altimeter and tried to stay at least five hundred feet above the ground. Then suddenly the plane hit an air pocket and rapidly fell. It was like falling off a cliff. I tried to pull up but couldn't get much height and felt the plane clip the top of a tree. Then two more treetops ripped a hole in the bottom of the plane. I was still in the air but knew I wouldn't be for long. Through the darkness I looked for somewhere to land but all I saw were trees. Losing control of the plane and only about forty feet off the ground according to the altimeter, I saw what looked like a small opening in the trees and aimed the plane for it as best I could. Several seconds later I felt the plane hit the ground and then start to flip over.

The next thing I saw was the face of a woman wearing a small cap like the nurses wore back in France. I remember a couple of bright flashes and muffled talk that I couldn't understand. Then I was back in the black again. Sometime later I saw another face, this time it was a man who was dressed in white. He kept asking if I saw him. I shook my head that I did, but he kept asking. Then he faded into darkness. Later, the woman was back. This time I tried to say something but couldn't get any words out. She heard me though and called for someone. The man in white appeared and started talking to me again. This time I understood some of what he was saying.

"You're going to be all right. You've been badly hurt but you'll be all right. You need to rest but you'll be OK."

The words were confusing but reassuring. The last thing I remembered was leaving Pittsburgh, so I figured something bad had happened to me. I didn't remember the flight or the crash. The other thing was the pain. I hurt all over but especially in my back. I tried to move my arms and legs but didn't have the strength. Instead, I just wanted to sleep.

Finally, I crawled out of my cave. I still hurt all over but was more aware of what was going on around me. My left arm was slightly suspended above me with a cast on it and my left leg also had a cast. My head seemed to be wrapped and I could see some bandages on my left cheek. It felt like there were also bandages on my chin.

"Oh Mr. Malone, looks like you've decided to rejoin us. Give me a minute and I'll get the doctor." It was a nurse and I figured I was in a hospital.

The doctor came into the room. "Mr. Malone, I'm so glad you're back with us. For a while we weren't too sure you'd make it back, but it looks like you'll survive after all." I tried to speak but still couldn't quite get my words right.

"Don't try to talk yet. I'll give you a quick rundown on where you are and then you can try some food. Your body probably wants food, though I doubt that your brain knows it at this point."

I gurgled a response.

"So, here's what happened. Your plane crashed just west of Altoona. Fortunately, it was in a field not far from a farmhouse. The good thing is that somehow you missed about a thousand trees. The bad thing is that it was not a gentle landing. We're not sure whether you were thrown from the plane as it somersaulted to a stop or whether you crawled out after the plane stopped moving. The farmer found you about forty yards away from the burning plane. He and his son loaded you up onto the back of his pickup and brought you here to the Altoona hospital. That was six days ago."

I groaned something and he continued. "It was touch and go there for the first two or three days but I'm certain you're on the mend now. You've got a broken left arm and left leg. You probably have already figured that out. You had a concussion that almost turned your lights out for good. Now that we're past the concussion, the next concerns are several vertebrae that may be fractured. I'm pretty sure of at least two. On the positive side, your spinal cord is definitely intact, and at some point, you will be able to walk again. Let's see what else, oh yeah, you've got two cracked ribs and we used forty-eight stitches to sew various parts back together. The stitches will come out in three or four days. It's a lot I know, but you're back with us and I expect you to recover. That's something I couldn't say a week ago."

The nurse came back in carrying a glass with a straw and some soup.

"I'm going to let Polly help you get some food down. She's our best nurse, so be nice to her. We'll call your family and let them know that you're finally awake. Your brother Pat was here those first couple of days and your parents are sitting by their phone. I'm sure they'll be here soon. I'll be back a little later. You and I are going to see a lot of each other for a while. In the meantime, eat, sleep, and heal."

During the next three weeks I did a lot of sleeping and ate four or five times a day. Through that first week, it seemed as if when they weren't giving me something to eat, they were giving me a pain killer that included a nap.

Dr. Barrows came by twice a day and the nurses, especially Polly, were very attentive to me. I'm sure my experience in France helped me get through those weeks. Anytime I started to feel sorry for myself or cranky about where I was, I thought about the guys in the hospital in France. My injuries were healing. Theirs never would. My life would get back to normal. They had to learn a whole new way of living. My pains were temporary, theirs were permanent.

Two days after I had rejoined the living, Pat and Janet became my first visitors and brought my first flowers.

"The doctor told me you two came by a couple of times last week. Sorry I wasn't a bit more social."

"Not a problem. Janet and I didn't expect much conversation. We're just glad you can be social now."

Janet asked, "How do you feel?"

"I ache all over but especially in my back. Can't move around much with all this plaster and these cords holding me down. Today's the first day without a headache. Aside from that, I don't feel too bad. One thing for certain, I'm not hungry. They feed me all the time."

They stayed for about an hour before Polly shooed them out. I really enjoyed talking to them, but by the time they left I was ready for a nap.

The next day Mom, Dad, and Mary Ann, carrying more flowers, visited in the afternoon and again in the evening.

Mary Ann brought one of her favorite stuffed bears.

"This is Chauncey. He came along to keep you company while you're here. He's good at taking away pains, so whenever you hurt just put Chauncey where it hurts."

Mary Ann wanted to know about everything the casts, the cords, how they put the plaster on, and how they were going to take it off. All three said they were eager to get me back to Harrisburg. Of course, they knew that it would be another couple of weeks, but it was certainly something to look forward to. Mary Ann promised to be my private nurse when I got back home.

"I'll have to get one of those white nurse's caps."

Dick and Phil came to see me the following Sunday. Like everyone else, they brought flowers. Dick told me not to worry about work.

"I hired another pilot and bought a used J4-B like our other planes so we're up and running as usual. We only missed one flight, so take your time healing. Phil and I can handle things at work."

Either Janet or Pat or both came by about every three days. Mom and Mary Ann visited two more times and Phil stopped by the following week. During the long stretches between visitors, Dr. Barrows kept inspecting my various broken bones. He replaced the cast on my arm and got rid of the cords that limited my movement. That was probably the best change that happened during those three weeks. Several days after my family's first visit and after he was sure my concussion was gone, he allowed me to read, which, again, was another big step forward. I had always been a reader but never had much time to do it. Now I had lots of time. When he told me I could begin reading, he gave me a newspaper account of my crash. "Thought you might be interested in this. It may help you remember what happened." I was, and it did. Little pieces of what happened began to appear in my memory. By the time I left the hospital I could remember most of the crash sequence.

The day after he replaced the cast on my arm, he also had my back X-rayed.

"Don, your back is not as bad as I thought it might be, but it is bad, nevertheless. You have two cracked vertebrae in your lower back. I was afraid you might have more. It is going to take a while, months, for them to heal. There's not much we can do except to be gentle with them. No casts or special harnesses. Initially, you shouldn't do anything more strenuous than reading the newspaper and eating meals. Lots of bed rest is the best remedy for the next two or three months at least. You shouldn't even go for a ride in a car. Then an easy walk around the block for a couple of months and, finally, gradual light exercise. Start to finish you're looking at six months minimally until you can begin to resume your normal activity. This is an injury that if you don't take especially good care of it, it will plague you for the rest of your life."

"I guess you wouldn't recommend that I fly a plane for a while."

"Ha, I'd say you're eight or nine months away from flying again."

Just over four weeks after I arrived at the hospital, my parents and Mary Ann came to take me home to Harrisburg. I still had casts on my arm and leg, and even though they arranged the car so that I didn't have to sit up, my back throbbed during the entire four-hour ride home. Still, I was overjoyed at getting out of the hospital.

As Dr. Barrows signed the release papers, we had one last conversation.

"I've sent your records to a colleague at the Harrisburg hospital, Dr. Levy. You also have a full record of what we did here. I expect that Dr. Levy will be in touch within a day or two. In the meantime, stay out of planes and take care of yourself."

"Thanks for all you've done, Dr. Barrows. And please thank Polly and the rest of the nurses. They made my stay more than just tolerable."

We shook hands and then Mom cautiously wheeled me out to the car where Mary Ann and Dad were waiting.

Chapter 9

THE TIMES THEY ARE A-CHANGIN'

I arrived home on Sunday, October 27, 1929—two days before the stock market crashed. At the time, I had no idea how much that event would affect my life. My immediate concern was adjusting to being home and healing.

Even though I had been using crutches during my last week in the hospital, Mom had bought a wheelchair for me.

"You should use this for a while. It'll keep pressure off your back and is easier than crutches."

I really didn't want to use the chair but figured I would for four or five days just to keep Mom happy. Turned out, I preferred the wheelchair. I moved around faster and could stop anywhere and relax. I used it for about six weeks.

My parents had moved my bed, desk, bureau, and clothes down from my bedroom into Dad's den on the first floor.

"You won't have to climb any stairs and will have a lot more things to do down here," Mom said. "You can sit in the living room and watch the river and cars on Front Street or read, and you can get snacks out in the kitchen whenever you want, or you can roll out onto the patio. I also switched all your things from your bathroom upstairs into the bathroom by Dad's den.

That's your bathroom now. If there's anything else you need, just let me know."

"Thanks, Mom. This is great. It's a lot more comfortable than the hospital."

"Oh. One more thing. I bought an Atwater Kent radio for you and put it in your new bedroom. I know how you like to listen to ballgames."

"Mom, baseball season ended three weeks ago."

"I know. I was thinking about in the spring. There are more and more good radio shows you might like. I've begun listening to this new comedy show, *Amos'n' Andy*. One of my favorite shows is *The Chase and Sanborn Hour* every Sunday night. It has lots of music and comedy skits. Last week I listened to a concert from Carnegie Hall in New York City. It was wonderful. So many new shows. I'm sure you'll find some that you'll like."

Again, I was grateful for Mom's efforts, and again she was right. One of the things that got me through those six months was the radio.

The next two months were tough. My back hurt almost all the time and my casts kept getting in the way of things I wanted to do. I was glad two weeks later when the cast on my arm came off.

I met with Dr. Levy a couple of days after I got home. He didn't want me to travel to his office downtown, so he made a house call. He checked my back, gave me some pain pills, and said he'd be back the following week.

Dad wasn't too sure about Dr. Levy initially. "Sounds Jewish to me. Gotta be careful about that."

"Dad, all I care about is that he's a good doctor and can help me heal. Dr. Barrows wouldn't have recommended him if he had any concerns about him. He will be fine, I'm sure." On my first Friday home, Phil became my first official visitor.

"On my way to the Legion and wanted to stop by and see how you are doing. I planned to come by earlier this week, but it's been hectic at work"

"Glad you've been busy. I've been reading about the stock market and was a little concerned how it was affecting our clients."

"Yeah, I'm worried too, but so far, we haven't felt much. We're still as busy as usual. The guy Dick hired to fly your routes seems to be doing a good job. Took him a week or so, but he's fit right in. Dick and I are still nervous about East-West Air. There are a bunch of rumors out there, but I'm not here to worry you with rumors. So, how are you?"

"Aside from a constant backache and these damn casts, I guess I'm OK. Mom has done a great job making things easy for me, and my private nurse, Mary Ann, has been really helpful."

"Sounds good."

"You're on your way to the Legion, how are things there?"

"Same as ever. We've still got some anti-immigrant, antieverything-but-me guys. A bunch of us try to keep them harnessed. There's some tension, but I like being with other vets. Makes me feel like I'm part of something important. There are a lot of guys who haven't recovered yet. Lots of psychological scars."

During the next hour or so, we talked about various things. Baseball was at the top of my list. For a change, my team, the Athletics, beat Phil's Yankees and then won the World Series. My only regret was that I was in the hospital the last week of the season and didn't get much information about the Series.

Phil lamented: "OK, I'll give it to you, the A's were the better team this year, but my guys will be back next year. Can't keep Ruth, Gehrig, and the rest of Murderers' Row down for long."

Then he asked, "You feel up to chess?"

"You bet! It'll give my brain something to do."

The following week I had the board all ready for him and we played several games. He also brought me three chess strategy books, which I enjoyed. During the following months, I spent many hours studying those books and moving pieces around the board.

One topic we didn't talk about was politics. Phil didn't like President Hoover before the stock market crash. I had no doubt that he liked Hoover and the Republicans much less now. Of course, Phil knew where my dad, who was home from Washington, stood, so he steered clear of a discussion that I'm sure he would have liked to have had. I did want to hear what he thought, but I agreed that at this point, politics was a topic to avoid.

"Well, I should get going and let you rest a bit. I'll stop back again soon. If not before, I'll drop by next Friday before the Legion meeting."

True to his word, he did stop back the following Friday.

In fact, during the next six months Phil became a regular Friday visitor. After a couple of weeks, he and I started to have dinner together. I always enjoyed those conversations.

As I had mentioned to Phil, Mary Ann was probably the best thing about my recuperation. She always checked in with me after school to see if there was anything I wanted. We often listened to my radio together. Sometimes she'd do her homework at my desk. Once in a while, we played board games or card games together. I taught her how to play chess and she taught me how to play bridge. "It's really easy once you get the basics." Sometimes Mom sat in as a third hand. I also enjoyed listening to Mary Ann play the piano. She had taken lessons for more than three years and was good enough to play songs that I recognized. She became my chief wheelchair pusher too.

I could have done it myself, but she liked pushing me around, so I let her. She almost always pushed me to the dinner table or into the living room to watch the river and talk, and we talked a lot. Once in a while, we'd spend a couple of afternoons doing puzzles. She made it clear that I was not to finish one until she was there. During those months she brought a little sunshine into my days. It was also during those months that we developed a special friendship.

Dick visited the week after Phil. He brought me up to date on Eastern Air Services.

"We're doing OK right now, but it is just a matter of time before this stock market crash thing bites into our clients. We've already lost three clients. I hope we don't lose any more. I'm glad we have that government contract. Without that, we'd be in trouble."

"Do you see any problems renewing the contract?"

"Not if it's based on performance, but there are strange things happening out there. More rumors about East-West Air. I wish we could do passenger flights like they do, but that's beyond us right now. We'd need a fleet of bigger planes, more pilots and mechanics, and we'd need licensing by the government. I don't see any of that happening soon."

Dick said that like the previous year, the Commerce Department was running behind and that it would be several months until contracts were renewed. "We'll just have to hold our breath and hope they do the right thing." During the next four months, the high points of my daily activities involved spending time with Mary Ann and an occasional visit. Phil and Dick continued to regularly stop in. Ray, who was busy adjusting to the falling economy, also came by weekly. He often brought Angie and Timmy along. Pat and Janet spent a weekend just after Christmas. He was very busy prosecuting in Pittsburgh. My only other regular visitor was Dr. Levy who checked in on me once a week until early February when the cast finally came off my leg. That added new activities to my days. No longer tethered to a wheelchair, I could prowl around the house, and I began taking daily walks outside. Initially, Mom was a little nervous about me wandering around on icy sidewalks, but as the weather got warmer, she stopped worrying.

I finally went back to work on a limited basis in midApril. Dr. Levy didn't want me flying, that was still several months away, but I could work on engines for a couple of hours a day as long as I wasn't lifting anything heavy. I hadn't done much mechanics work for a couple of years, and it felt good to get back to my roots. I still enjoyed grease on my hands and solving engine problems. At that point, there were few pleasures greater than standing with dirty hands beside a purring engine that I had worked on. While I was eager to get back in the air, being a mechanic again would get me through until then.

When I went back to work, we still hadn't received our Commerce Department contract. That happened on July 5. We were informed that our contract had been extended through the rest of the year but would not be renewed in 1931. The news confirmed our worst fears. During the next few days, Dick made some calls and concluded that our contract in 1931 was going to be added to the East-West Air contract just as we had suspected. Dick, Phil, and I got together a week later to map out our strategy now that we were losing our contract.

Phil was especially angry about the circumstances.

"Those Commerce Department bastards. Feed the little guy to the dragon. That's all Hoover and his buddies know how to do!"

I tried to calm him down a bit. "We worked without a contract before. It'll take some reorganizing, but we can do it again."

"I'm not sure we can," Dick chimed in. "Back then, there was no competition. Now we've got this behemoth chasing us. They're just going to add the Commerce Department contract cargo to the passenger flights they're making. Won't cost them a thing. It'll be hard to compete against that. Also, some of our other clients are having a tough time with this economy. Two more went out of business last month, and I suspect there are more on the way." "So, what do you suggest?" I asked.

"Well, we've got five months to figure it out. We're going to have to downsize, no question about that. The only questions are when and how much. It'll mean letting pilots go and getting rid of several mechanics, but as I see it, that's our only chance to stay in business. I don't think we should tell anyone about this until the end of the summer, that should give everyone enough time to find new jobs. In the meantime, we keep doing what we've been doing for the last four years."

And that's what we did.

Not long after making our downsizing decision, an EastWest vice president got in touch with Dick and asked to talk to us. Dick, Phil, and I met with him and an EastWest accountant in early August. It was clear that we were at their mercy and that they knew it.

"Look, you guys are gone after January 1. You might figure a way to hobble along for another couple of months, but you can't survive for long."

The accountant laid out what they knew about our operations and used a couple of graphs that showed we wouldn't be able to last until April.

The presentation was annoying. I felt East-West had been spying on us. It had gathered records and figures that I thought were private and used the information to show what a difficult position we would be in once our contract was gone. "We don't need to be big. We did all right before we had a contract," I said.

"The world has changed since then," the East-West vice president said. "You've got new expenses and your client base is shrinking. The reality is that Eastern Air Services' days are numbered. Look, we respect what you guys have done. You got things rolling, but the industry is moving beyond you. Eastern Air is the past, a productive past, but the past, nevertheless. We are the future. We don't want to just bury you guys. We want to thank you instead, so here's what East-West is willing to do for you. We'll buy four of your planes, which should give you enough to pay off your loans and pay your bills. We're willing to hire any of your pilots that want to come to work for us. Same with your mechanics. They'll be doing pretty much what they're doing now. We're building a new airfield and hangar not far from here and your people will be stationed there so no relocation will be needed. It should be a comfortable transition for them. I know Dick has other interests, car lots and investments, but if you and Phil want to work for us, we'd be happy to have you. And we'll throw in $2,000 for each of you."

Dick answered, "Under the circumstances, that's a very generous offer but we'll have to think about it."

"That's fine. We want you to think about it. How about we give you a week to figure things out? One way or the other, we plan to start up on January 1."

Dick agreed, "We'll get back to you in a week."

After the meeting, I asked Dick, "What other options do we have?"

"I can't see many. Basically, either we scale our operations back to the bone, though I don't know if there's enough scaling back that we can do and still be viable, or we can declare the company bankrupt sometime early next year and let the bank sell the planes. That's not something I want to do."

"Yeah, I agree."

Phil added that we need to think about the pilots and mechanics as well. What will be best for them? "You know with so many people out of work and so few jobs, I'd feel good about them having some job security."

Dick added that if everyone knows they have a job after we close, they'll be willing to work for us until then.

So, it was decided that like so many other small businesses, we would shut down operations on January 1, 1931. A week later we called the East-West vice president and gave him decision.

"Great, we'll get the paperwork started. It should be ready for you to sign by September. We'll let you know. I'm sure this is painful, but it's really not so bad. You guys will walk away with money in your pockets and no debts hanging over your heads."

The next five months were a slide toward the end of Eastern Air Services. In August, with Dr. Levy's approval, I started making short, local flights and was happy to be in the air again. Through the fall I increased my airtime always knowing that at the end of the year my flying might end for a while. East-West asked me several times if I wanted to fly for them, but I made it clear that I didn't. Phil, Dick, and I agreed to keep two planes and see how much business we could do. Phil would split his time working as a mechanic for Dick and working on our planes. Just as it was when we started, I would be our only pilot and we'd shrink our range significantly. Dick looked for clients, but he didn't have much luck. More of our old clients were going out of business, and East-West could significantly underbid us with potential future clients.

In late September, after we signed the transfer papers, we told our pilots and mechanics what would happen at the end of the year, and they all decided to go with East-West. On a Saturday in mid-November, someone from East-West came out to talk to our pilots and mechanics. He even took them to the new hangar by the river on the other side of Middletown. Everyone seemed satisfied, even eager, to make the change. Of course, for Phil, Dick, and me, it was a melancholy day. We were glad everyone still had jobs, but for us it was another big step toward an end that we knew loomed in the near future. The three of us agreed that there was no point delaying the inevitable so when everyone else left we would shut completely.

And then it was over. We had a New Year's afternoon party for the pilots and mechanics. After everyone else left, Dick, Phil, and I sat reminiscing about "the good old days." I was back home with plenty of time to ring in 1931, but rather than celebrate, I went to bed.

Two days later Phil and I began reorganizing. We moved our two remaining planes to one side of the hangar, put the tools on the mechanics' table near the planes, and swept out the hangar. I considered going for a short flight but just didn't have the energy. Neither one of us wanted to leave, so we spent the rest of the afternoon speculating about the coming year.

Phil lamented, "You know we can't survive like this for long."

"Yeah, I know. You worried?"

"No, not really. I know that Dick is having problems selling cars, so he'll probably need to lay some people off. I ought to be one of the first ones to go. You know, last in, first out."

"What'll you do then?"

"I don't know. Maybe I'll go back to New York. My dad said he could get me a job with the metro system. The subway always needs mechanics. Not what I want to do, but it would be better than waiting in a food line somewhere.

What about you?"

"Ray has said I could come to work for him, but I'd go nuts selling men's suits and socks. Dad has friends who I'm sure could find something for me to do, but I don't want him to ask for any favors because of me. I've got enough money saved to get me through for a while. I'll figure it out."

What I didn't tell Phil was that Dad and I had some growing differences about what was being labeled "the Great Depression." Dad remained a staunch, unbending supporter of Hoover and his policies. I had my doubts. Though Harrisburg hadn't been hit too hard, lots of other cities had. Officially, unemployment was up over 10% and climbing monthly. Unofficially, there were a lot more people out of work and out of their homes. Banks were failing at a record pace; businesses were closing all over the place, and food lines were getting longer and longer. Clearly, people were hurting.

Dad believed that what was happening was simply a natural correction of the stock market and real estate during the twenties. "It's the 'get rich quick' people who gambled and overspent," he said. "We're paring off the unwise fringe. In a couple more months, the economy will be stronger for it."

Dad had been saying that for a year even though things kept getting worse. I didn't buy the "paring-off" explanation. When I suggested that perhaps some direct help from the national government might help, Dad snipped at the idea.

"The government is supposed to protect us from foreign attacks. It's not supposed to manipulate business and interfere in people's lives. That's what the communists do in Russia. We have charities for anyone who can't provide for himself. That's not a government responsibility, that's for the local community to do."

Phil periodically moaned about Hoover but had always pulled his punches in deference to my dad. I'm sure he knew that I was not the rock-solid Republican my dad was. I'm also sure he didn't know how much I disagreed with Dad.

After that talk with Phil, I began thinking more seriously about my future. During the next week or so, I concluded that I needed to make some major changes in my life. I was almost thirty-one and still living with my parents. I no longer had a job, let alone a career. Phil was my only real friend. Eastern Air Services had filled my days from start to finish for five years. Then recuperating from the crash, I couldn't do much. Now, my life was missing some important parts. I thought about going to college but didn't want to go back to the life of a student. On the positive side, I still had enough money in the bank that I didn't need to make a quick decision; I was a good pilot and an even better mechanic.

One change was easy to make. I moved into the farmhouse in Middletown. We no longer needed it for the business and Phil, Dick, and I had decided that someone should live there to keep the house safe. Phil preferred staying in Harrisburg close to the American Legion building, so I moved in. Mary Ann was especially sad to see me move. For almost a year we had spent most evenings together. I regretted that I wouldn't see her as much, but felt I needed to get into a place of my own.

The next six months were gloomy. With Eastern Air Services gone, my flying time was cut to just two or three days a week and then only one stop a day. Dick hired me once in a while to make flights for him, and there were still a few former clients who hired me to make special deliveries, but it wasn't something

I could count on. The money I made from the fights usually covered my expenses but nothing more. When I wasn't in the air, I was working on the planes and occasionally did some part-time work for Dick. I also began going to the American Legion meetings with Phil again.

Initially I went up to Harrisburg several times a week, but my disagreements with Dad became ever more edgy. It seemed that the deeper the economy fell, the more staunchly he defended Hoover. So, I decided to cut the visits to once during the week and Sunday afternoons for dinner. Ray, Angie, and little Timmy were usually there on Sundays, which I enjoyed. Ray was becoming more and more concerned about the stores, especially the one in Middletown. "We're still doing OK but business is down. The Harrisburg store has the state government workers who keep it profitable, but there's not much going on in the Middletown store."

I knew that the town's steel mill had shut down and lots of people were hurting as a result. I asked about his plans for Middletown, and he had no answer. "We'll just have to wait things out."

In March, I flew out to Pittsburgh and visited Pat and Janet for several days. They were doing well. Pat had considered going into private practice but decided against it because of the tumbling economy. He had grown tired of prosecuting, especially people whose crimes were caused by the Depression. Petty thievery, small-time robbery, trespassing, or breaking into buildings.

"Pittsburgh is in bad shape. U.S. Steel has fired more than half of its workforce and there are more layoffs on the way. I know that production is way down, so they won't be hiring again soon. Without their jobs, many of those former steelworkers resort to crime to feed and house their families. I hate adding to their misery. The good thing is that I am as generous with plea deals as anyone in the prosecutor's office. Still, it is very sad."

During their visit the previous Christmas, Janet had hinted that they were considering starting a family, so I asked.

Janet answered: "Well, with the economy going the way it's going we decided to wait. I still like teaching and don't want to quit right now. We can wait another year or two."

It was during those months that I went back to the local American Legion. I hadn't gone to any meetings since long before my plane crash, and for months Phil had been pushing me to go along with him to meetings. In April, I finally did, and it was nice to be with other vets again. Phil had told me that the guys were more connected than when I was going to meetings regularly. I recognized the change almost immediately. There were no small groups scattered around the room having private conversations as before. Instead, the guys were mingling and talking to each other more. Aside from their wartime experiences and sports, the thing that seemed to bring them together was the Depression. Some had lost jobs and were struggling to make ends meet. Several of them were staying rent-free in a few rooms above the barroom. Others feared that a layoff was coming soon.

I asked Phil about it. "Many of these guys are hurting," he lamented. "Some are still wrestling with nightmares and flashbacks from the war. Then add the money issues and they've really got problems. One guy, Charlie Bancroft, shot himself two weeks ago, and I'm afraid that there are some others on the verge of doing the same. It's really getting bad."

"I thought vets were supposed to get special consideration from their employers."

"Yeah, but no one is hiring, and it seems like when there are layoffs, the vets are first to be let go."

"So, what can we do?"

"Some guys have started talking about getting our service bonuses early. They want Congress to let that money go now. I don't think that's going to happen, but it's an idea that is getting more and more popular. Aside from that, we're just trying to take care of each other. Help with food and housing and keeping our ears open for any kind of work.

The ones I really feel sorry for are those guys with a family."

As I left, I made a promise to myself that I would come back at least once a week. And I did.

At the end of the summer, Phil moved back to his parents' house in New York City. Rather than wait to be laid off by the railroad, he decided to take a job his dad found him with the subway system. I was sorry that Phil was leaving. His move created a void in my activities. We had talked to each other almost every day, and since I moved to the farm, we had dinner together several times a week. I always looked forward to hearing Phil's take on politics. I'm sure at the time he didn't realize how his opinions had influenced my thinking. I also enjoyed working on the planes together.

After his move, we stayed in touch regularly. We'd talk on the phone occasionally, and about once a month I'd go up to New York for a weekend visit. I enjoyed my visits. There was always something new to see and lots to do. We'd take the subway in the afternoon from Queens to Manhattan and spend the rest of the day watching a movie, going to a jazz club, or just walking the streets. On a visit in September, we went to a doubleheader at Yankee Stadium and watched my first-place Athletics beat his second-place Yankees twice. For the second year in a row, the Athletics were on the way to easily winning the American League.

Walking around Manhattan, there were plenty of painful signs of how bad the economy was. On almost every corner in midtown Manhattan there were people looking for work or selling apples and roasted chestnuts on the street. Numerous long lines of people waiting for food or a place to spend the night. Phil told me that the Municipal Lodging House on East 29th Street served more than ten thousand meals a day. All over the city, there were small enclaves where the homeless had built makeshift shelters. Phil called them "Hoovervilles." In Central Park where a couple of years earlier there had been a reservoir, almost two dozen shacks had been built out of salvaged wood and packing crates. A little community had grown there. They called it "Hoover Valley." There was another Hooverville in Greenwich Village, "Hard Luck Town," and "Tin City" in the Red Hook area of Brooklyn.

On a visit during late October, Phil took me to a Hooverville in the Riverside Park on the Upper West Side where a couple of dozen vets and their families lived. They called it "Fort Thomas Paine." It was a collection of flimsy shacks connected by a few dirt paths that served as streets. Several shacks were covered in tar paper, but most were just random wooden planks hammered or wired together. It was a grimy, dirty place with no electricity, and the only water came from some nearby spigots. Barrels burning wood and coal scraps were used for both heat and cooking. However, despite the living conditions, Fort Thomas Paine residents seemed more contented than I expected. They kept busy helping each other collect food and firewood, building and repairing their shanties, and keeping everything as clean as possible. They had also organized an informal camp government and chose "Commander Clark" as their unofficial mayor.

Phil knew Clark. I was never sure whether that was his first name or his last name, everyone just called him Commander. He took Phil and me to a shed that served as the headquarters. He was a short man with broad shoulders, a thick physique, and a constant smile who could have been my age or he could have been twenty years older. I liked him immediately.

"Glad to meet you, Donnie. Phil told me you are a great mechanic and were a flier during the war."

"Yep, Phil's right about the flying, but I'm no better a mechanic than he is."

"Phil's a good guy. He's helped us out with some things. What do you think of our little village?"

"It's impressive. How many people live here?"

"Oh, people come and go all the time, but I'd say we have about maybe one hundred regulars. That includes about twenty kids."

"Are they all vets and their families?"

"Yep. Each of us just sort of drifted into the park, gravitated toward one another, then decided that if we could dig trenches and live in them during the war, we can build shacks and live in them now. No machine guns or bombs here. All we have to worry about is the City and Park Commissioner Robert Moses."

"Who's Robert Moses?"

"Oh, he's the guy in charge of building stuff in the city. I think his goal right now is to build stuff that will get us out of the city. He'll probably win but it won't come easy. Part of the reason we formed our little administration here was to get the city to find a place where Moses won't bother us."

Phil asked, "Any idea where that might be?"

"Nah, not right now. There are some guys who think we should get other wandering vets from all over and move ourselves to Washington so we can put pressure on Hoover to help us out."

I added: "There're some guys in my American Legion chapter who've been talking about trying to get our war pension early. They think we should pressure our congressmen and Hoover. Maybe even have a march to the Capitol."

"I've heard that before and like the idea. Fort Thomas Paine is ready to go."

One of the things that impressed me was how satisfied everyone seemed.

Clark explained. "Don't let that fool you. Underneath, these guys are angry. They feel like they risked their lives to make the world safe and now our government has thrown them away. Wouldn't take much to set them off. There's some real anger there."

Commander walked us through camp, then Phil and I hung around for a couple of hours talking to other vets.

After that trip, I kept thinking about Fort Thomas Paine. I knew there were lots of people all over the country hurting. Dad and his Republican friends kept saying that good times were right around the corner, but the more I saw, the less I believed it. There were desperate people everywhere and the numbers kept growing. People without homes or food. There were people in Harrisburg living under a bridge or camped out along the railroad tracks. There were people wandering the streets looking for a scrap of food or, better yet, work. Like the vets at Thomas Paine, these were good people. They just wanted a chance to provide for themselves. The more I heard that a bright new day awaited just up ahead, the more I was sure that soon something needed to be done to help people. I was frustrated and getting angry.

Chapter 10

A New Beginning

On January 5, 1932, a Roman Catholic priest in Pittsburgh, Father James Cox, organized an army of twenty thousand out-of-work men from throughout western Pennsylvania. Loading up into more than one thousand cars and trucks, they began a two-day trek to Washington. During the journey, some fell by the wayside while others joined the parade. Along the way, they were fed, housed, and cheered on by eager supporters. They arrived in Harrisburg at noon on the sixth and were addressed by an encouraging Pennsylvania Governor Gifford Pinchot. Late that night, the band, which had shrunk to twelve thousand, reached Washington. After spending the night sleeping in government buildings, Cox and a few others met with President Hoover in the White House. At the meeting, Cox asked Hoover to provide public works projects to put people back to work and unemployment checks for those out of work. After the meeting, Cox reported that Hoover was cordial but refused to support either of the requests. Discouraged, some of the marchers headed back to their homes. Others, who had no home or job to return to, stayed in Washington and built a Hooverville on the swampy Anacostia Flats across the river from the Capitol.

As the caravan passed through Harrisburg, a dozen members from my American Legion chapter joined it. Three stayed and helped build the Anacostia Hooverville. During the following months, more from the chapter joined them.

In April, Phil and I went down to Anacostia for a weekend to visit some local Legion friends. Both of us were impressed and disturbed at the same time. The place was huge. There were thousands of vets, some with their families, and hundreds of shacks and lean-tos, many of them flying American flags. Some were built near signs identifying home states. That's how we found three of our Harrisburg friends, Tony Bezelko, Bob Baker, and George Mahaffie. They were camped out in a shanty right behind the Pennsylvania sign.

Tony shouted: "Hey Don, you brought our old buddy turned New Yorker. How's it going, Phil?"

"I'm doing OK. Looks like you guys have stepped up in the world."

George responded: "Not sure it's a step up, but it feels better than being in Harrisburg. The guys here are just like us. Fed up with being stepped on and ready for some changes. All we want is the bonus that we're supposed to get."

Tony laughed and added, "Yeah, homeless, unemployed veterans with nothing better to do than ask for something we've already been promised."

Bob and George took us on a tour of the camp. In most ways, it looked like Fort Thomas Paine, except much bigger and more families. George said unofficial neighborhoods had been built around the state signs and each neighborhood had a leader. The ultimate leader was a guy named Waters from Oregon. Just like Thomas Paine, there was lots of activity building and mending shelters, and keeping things as clean as possible.

Phil observed to George, "Looks like you all stay busy."

"Lots to do. Seems like new people coming in every day now that the weather is getting nicer. And we play a lot of cards too."

Bob said, "And there's another camp on Pennsylvania Avenue right across from the White House. A bunch of buildings that are scheduled to be torn down. Right there where Hoover can see us every morning when he wakes up."

I asked, "Where do you get the food for everybody?"

"Sometimes it's a challenge but we find it. Each neighborhood figures it out for itself and if there's anything left over, we share. There are people who donate stuff and some local Legions chip in. It'd be great if when you get back to Harrisburg you could get our chapter to help out a little. Plus, there are a couple of local grocers and restaurants that give us what they haven't sold. The superintendent of the Washington police has also sent us food and blankets. He doesn't want everybody to know about that, but he's helped."

Bob added, "He fought in the war and seems to agree with what we're doing as long as it stays peaceful."

It was a confusing weekend. On one hand, I felt bad for the guys at Anacostia. They had not fought in the war to live like they were. Their clothes were tattered and dirty. They had to scrounge for food and had almost nothing of their own. On the other hand, the bond that they had shared during the war brought them back into a brotherhood many thought they had been left behind in Europe. After my visit, I felt a little bit of that renewed bond too.

The next time we had a Legion meeting, I organized a committee that weekly figured a way to get food and supplies to Washington. Usually, one of our guys drove down to Anacostia every Wednesday and then reported back at our Friday meetings.

After that first trip, Phil and I agreed to visit Anacostia on the last weekend of every month. Each time we did, the camp got bigger. On our trip in June, we bumped into Commander Clark.

"Hey Commander, I see you've relocated."

"Hi Phil. Robert Moses was ready to invade Fort Thomas Paine, so we decided to come down here. We moved about three weeks ago. This is really a big show. Someone said there are fifteen thousand of us. It just goes on and on."

"Looks like you guys have settled in pretty well."

"I still like our New York home better, but it feels really good to be with so many of our people."

On July 28, two days before Phil and I planned to make our July visit, everything changed in Washington. Hoover decided that the vets were a threat, and it was time to get rid of the encampments. He ordered the city police to drive the vets out of Washington and destroy the encampments; there were now four of them. Initially, everything was peaceful. First to go was the Pennsylvania Avenue group. They slowly began to march back toward the river and Anacostia, but along the way some guys started throwing rocks at the police. In the melee that followed, several on both sides were hurt and at least one person was killed. The president immediately called in Douglas MacArthur and his army. Hoover claimed that the riot was part of a communist insurrection. During the afternoon, MacArthur and his men with bayonets in place, gas masks on, and followed by tanks, pushed the veterans back to Anacostia. That night the army attacked all four encampments, driving everyone out and then setting fire to the camps. By the next morning when Phil and I arrived, all that was left was smoke and ashes.

Phil and I were nervous about the trip, but we wanted to see for ourselves what had happened. We decided to take an early train rather than drive. As soon as we arrived, we saw men on their way north. A couple of guys outside the station told us about the confrontations.

"It was terrible. Our own army attacked us like we were a German infantry squadron. We were at Pennsylvania Avenue at first, then went over to Anacostia. Didn't matter where we were, they were going to get us and they did. I had a buddy who was bayoneted in the leg and another one who was knocked unconscious by a guy on horseback. We were all gassed. I don't know how many were killed. It was brutal what they did to us."

Phil asked: "So, who's left? What are you going to do?"

"Don't know how many are still here—I didn't think a lot about it. Colonel Waters says the plan is to go back to Johnstown and figure out what to do next."

His friend chimed in: "I'm not going to Johnstown. I'm going back to my Hooverville outside Cincinnati. Just gotta figure out how to get there."

"Yeah, I'm going home too. I don't think many guys are going to Johnstown."

Phil and I spent the rest of the day roaming around the city. There were troops all over the place, so we were very careful. We saw stragglers everywhere being pushed along by either the police or the army. We walked past the Pennsylvania Avenue camp and over to Anacostia. Both were still smoldering. It was hard to believe that a day earlier, thousands of vets, and in many cases their families, had lived there.

Wisely, we decide to take an evening train back to Harrisburg.

Throughout the spring, my visits to Washington broadened the breach between my father and me. He steadfastly continued to support Hoover. He claimed the protesters at Anacostia were nothing more than troublemakers and dupes or a communist insurrection. I disagreed.

"Dad, have you talked to any of the men or gone over to Anacostia?"

"No, I can see from the newspapers what their squatters' camp looks like, and I know what they want—a handout."

"What they want is something that they've already been promised."

"And they'll get it when they were promised to get it, not a decade ahead of time. Look, the government can't afford that kind of payout right now. It would create a big deficit. If we just follow President Hoover's plans and be cautious with the money the government spends, we'll soon have more than enough to pay those guys when we promised to pay them."

"But Dad, those vets put their lives on the line for us. Now they need help. What about government work projects like some people are talking about? You know, road building, new schools, repairing public buildings. There are lots of worthwhile projects that would help get people back to work. And that means paychecks, which means, among other things, more taxes being collected to pay for the work projects."

Dad snapped back: "That's not the way our government works. If the government creates those kinds of projects, soon people will get dependent on the government. That would be the end of our capitalistic nation and lead us right into communism. Is that what those protesters want?"

"Of course not. What they want is a chance to get back on their feet."

"Well, that's what Hoover is trying to do."

"Hoover is just trying to bail out big business."

"Big business is part of the solution. New production means jobs."

It was a debate I couldn't win. Even as the economy continued to plummet and the homeless population continued to grow, Dad stuck to his "Believe in Hoover" mantra. I finally decided to avoid talking to him about Anacostia, Hoover, and the Depression. We could talk about family or baseball or the stores but not politics.

My brother Pat agreed with me. On a Father's Day visit, he and Janet and I teamed up against Dad. It made no difference. Dad remained fixed on Hoover. Instead of Anacostia, Pat and Janet talked about the Hoovervilles in Pittsburgh. Pat agreed that something soon had to be done. He also agreed that work projects would help.

Pat suggested: "We should do what the governor of New York is doing. He's created some public projects there that seem to be working."

Dad quickly rejected the idea. "Everybody knows that Roosevelt's just maneuvering to run against Hoover. I haven't seen any big successes in New York. He just wants to make everybody dependent on him and his big government. What he's talking about would kill any economic recovery."

We went back and forth for a while, but in the end, Dad hadn't moved an inch and neither had we.

Pat later confided to me that he was thinking about leaving his job and joining the public defender's office. "I just can't prosecute homeless, desperate people anymore.

It would mean a smaller paycheck, but I'd feel a lot better about keeping people out of jail than putting them in."

Janet added: "If Pat changes jobs, I'll keep mine even though my salary has been cut two years in a row. We'd have to economize a bit, but we could do it. And we can wait a while longer to start a family."

I wasn't sure what Ray thought about Dad's solution to the Depression. When I asked him after dinner one Sunday, he really didn't agree with one side or the other.

"I don't know, Don. Things in Middletown are bad. Lots of unemployed steelworkers wandering around. You know that Dick Davidson closed his lot in town. On the other hand, here in Harrisburg there's not too much to be upset about. The only obvious sign of problems is a small Hooverville down in the Shipoke area along the river. Otherwise, people here seem content."

"How about the stores? Are they doing OK?"

"We may have to close the one in Middletown. It's been losing money for two years. Dad wants to keep it open because it was his first store and he's sure the economy will turn around by the fall or early next year at the latest. The store in Harrisburg is doing fine. Not as much profit as a couple of years ago, but it's doing OK."

"What about Angie's parents?"

"You know they are living with us now. Angie brings her mother things to sew from the store. She's become our unofficial and unpaid seamstress. Aside from that, they watch Timmy during the day so that Angie can help me at the store. She always said that she wanted to go back to work and she's a great accountant. She handles the day-to- day money stuff better than I could."

"So, you agree with Dad about Hoover?"

"Not completely, but I don't disagree with him too much either. He is still my boss even if he's not around much. I just try to stay away from debating with him. And Harrisburg is not a great place to be criticizing Republicans, especially when you're trying to sell them suits."

I told Phil about my growing differences with Dad, and he said I had a decision to make.

"Either you keep your mouth shut around your dad and his buddies or you speak your mind and let the chips fall where they may."

A few weeks after the trip to Washington it became almost impossible to keep my mouth shut. Dad was beginning to gear up his reelection campaign and expected me to help. It was something I just couldn't do. I wanted him to win because he was my father, but I disagreed with almost everything he supported. Meanwhile, I was quietly working with the Legion to support the candidate running against Dad. As Dad started to organize his campaign, he scheduled me for various activities. He liked to take his "war hero" son along with him to speeches. I never enjoyed that role before, but this time there was no way I could go along with those plans. It put me in a tough spot.

In addition to my problems with Dad, I had work problems. Since midspring, I was making only one flight a week and had to dip into my savings to pay my bills. Fortunately, I had few expenses and several thousand dollars in the bank. Dick gave me some part-time work, but his car lots were not doing well. Since the beginning of the year, he had closed one lot and had cut down his staff at two others. He offered to hire me full-time, but that would mean getting rid of someone, and I couldn't justify replacing his full-time people, so I just filled in when he needed me.

It was Phil who came to my rescue. On a visit in midAugust, he told me about rumors that an airfield in Queens near his house was about to expand and might need pilots and mechanics.

"It's the only airfield for the city. The other one in the area is at Newark and that's too far for New Yorkers. The new place used to be an amusement park, Gola Amusement Park. I went there a lot when I was little. A couple of years ago, someone bought it and converted it into an airfield. Glenn

Curtis Airfield. Not much of a field, only two runways and a hangar, but a great location for flying. With more and more commercial flying, some people think it might make a great place for a full-service airport."

"That sounds great. Any idea when it might be up and running?"

"Sounds like in the next year or so, but I'm pretty sure that there are already people flying there. Next time you come to the city we can check it out. It's only a mile or so from the house."

I liked the idea, and the following weekend took a train up to New York.

Glenn Curtis airfield wasn't much more than my airfield in Middletown, but it was perfectly situated. It looked out over Jamaica Bay and Long Island. I could see potential access to the entire Atlantic coast, a perfect spot for air routes. And of course, New York City was golden in terms of cargo flights and, with passenger service growing as everyone knew it would, Glenn Curtis could become one of the primary airports in the East and maybe in the nation.

I was excited about the possibilities.

The person in charge of the field was Joey Olivetti. Turns out he was born in Italy and flew for the British Royal Air Force during the war. He hadn't flown much since then. Instead, he helped build and manage airfields. Glenn Curtis was his fourth. He also operated several flying schools. He said he and his partners planned to triple the size of the field during the next couple of years.

"Right now, things here are in a holding pattern. We had some trouble convincing the guys who owned the land to sell to us, and the city has thrown up some roadblocks, but we're on track to start the expansion by the first of the year. Our goal is to find some tenants who could use this as their base of operation."

"Are you looking for big tenants or would you work with individuals?"

"At this point, we'll take anything we can get. Long term, the plan is to get a couple of air companies to use this as their home base. Passenger carriers are the future of commercial flying."

"I've got a plane. How much would it cost to keep it here?"

"Not much—how's ten dollars a month sound? You'd have to buy insurance on the plane, do your own servicing, and you could buy fuel from us."

"That sounds like a good deal. I live in Pennsylvania right now but plan to move up here sometime during the next few weeks."

"Just pay me when you get here. We can go from there."

I asked: "Do you know of any flying jobs? I had an air delivery company for a while and would like to get back in the air. I'm also a pretty good mechanic." Phil chimed in, "No, he is a great mechanic."

"We could use a part-time mechanic. Not many planes here now so there's not much engine work, but I could give you some hours every week. Enough that you could pay the monthly rental and insurance on your plane. We can talk specifics after you move up."

My conversation with Joey sealed the decision to move to New York. When I told Phil, he said I could room at his house for as long as I wanted.

"My parents consider you to be almost part of the family now, and I know they'd like to have someone in one of those empty rooms. They don't say it, but they still really miss my brothers. I'm sure they'd like you filling one of those rooms."

"Sounds good. I'd want to pay room and board."

"Probably wouldn't be necessary. We can talk to them about it." We settled on twenty dollars a month.

I was nervous about telling my family about the move, especially Dad, but they took it better than I expected. When I told Mom, she said she'd miss me, especially at dinner on Sundays, but was happy I had found something I wanted to do. Mary Ann immediately began planning visits. "When can I come up and see you? We can go to some Broadway shows and I've never been to the Statue of Liberty. And we can shop on Fifth Avenue. I'll miss you, but I'm looking forward to visits." Even Dad took the news well.

"Too bad you won't be here to help with the campaign, but we'll muddle through, I'm sure. It's probably a good move for you. There're more opportunities up there."

He was right about the election. Despite the Roosevelt landslide, Dad got almost twice as many votes as his opponent. Of course, by that time I was in New York and able to enjoy Roosevelt's victory. It was the first time I voted Democratic and I felt good about it. It was also nice being surrounded by Phil and his family, all of whom were strong Roosevelt supporters.

Two weeks after telling my family about the move, I was in New York and my plane was at Glenn Curtis. At the top of my agenda in my new hometown was finding a job. Phil said the Transit Authority wasn't hiring but he'd keep his ears open. Joey at the airfield suggested I consider driving a cab. "Ask for Vinnie and tell him I sent you." I liked the idea, and on my first Monday morning in New York City I went to the Checker Cab office in Brooklyn. I talked to Vinnie, a big guy with a few extra pounds but more than enough muscle to make up for it, and he hired me instantly.

"Joey says yous OK, then yous OK. Here's a book of the streets. I'll give yous a week to learn it, then come back next Monday at ten and I'll give yous a schedule. Probably Wednesday through Sunday, two to eleven in Manhattan, so learn them streets first. We'll get yous set up for the union too. Can't drive without bein' in the union."

It didn't take me long to figure out that you didn't want to get Vinnie angry. Some of the other drivers described times when he had "disciplined" cabbies. They said he knew how to hurt someone without leaving marks. There was also a rumor that Vinnie, and Joey too, had some nasty friends who could make people disappear. Adding credence to the rumors, two of his friends, wearing expensive suits, stopped by every afternoon and picked up a fat envelope from him.

Fortunately, Vinnie never got angry at me.

I learned the streets in Manhattan quickly. Numbered streets go east and west, the avenues north and south. The rest of the city was a bit more difficult, but I learned it quickly. I also always had my book of streets with me just in case a fare wanted to go somewhere I didn't know. While I tried to stay in the midtown area, within a couple of weeks I felt confident enough to taxi people anywhere in the city. I also figured out where the best tippers were and when they most needed a ride.

One of the things I liked about driving a cab was the array of people I met. Most were friendly and seemed to enjoy talking. The ones who were visiting were usually fun to talk to. They were excited about being in the city and eager to find out about restaurants and sites to see. After the first week, I made sure I knew a dozen or so good restaurants and all the shows on Broadway. Businessmen were the toughest to please, but most were at least pleasant. Some made recommendations to me about future jobs or investments or personal matters. Once in a while, we talked a little bit about my war experience and my flying. Every now and then I also had a "working woman" in my cab on her way to or from a customer. They were quiet fares.

The most exciting rider was a guy I picked up early in July 1933. The Yankees were in town and there were always fares out by Yankee Stadium after a game. This day I got to the stadium a little late. A guy right outside the main gate ran over and climbed into my cab. On the ride we talked about the game. He was going to the Ansonia Hotel on Broadway on the Upper West Side. When we got there, he held out a fifty-dollar bill.

"There's a Bubba Tyler's tavern two blocks up on SeventyFourth. Get two cases of Heineken and two fifths of Johnny Walker Red, then bring them to me in the penthouse, top floor, of the Ansonia. Tell Bubba's it's for Joe and George and to put it on our tab. I'll give you the fifty when you deliver."

Fifty dollars was more than I made in two weeks, so I was happy to take some time away from the cab even though Vinnie might not like it.

I did as I was told and when I got off the elevator at the penthouse floor, I heard a booming laugh, some music, and lots of chatter. It was clear that there was a party going on. My rider opened the door, slipped the fifty dollars into my shirt pocket, and told me to put the alcohol in the kitchen. As I walked to the kitchen, I looked into the front room and standing there was Babe Ruth himself. I was making a delivery to Babe Ruth, and his teammates—third baseman "Jumpin" Joe Dugan, pitcher Waite Hoyt—and several very attractive women. The Babe was wearing a jacket and open shirt and had his arm around one of the women.

"Hey kid, thanks for the booze."

"No problem, no problem at all, Mr. Ruth."

"You a Yankee fan?"

"No, I'm an A's guy but I love baseball. My housemate is about the biggest Yankee fan around and you're his favorite."

"I guess that makes it all right. Tell your buddy he's a smart guy."

I couldn't wait to get home that night to tell Phil about my delivery.

"Hey Phil, dropped a guy off at the Ansonia between Seventy-Third and Seventy-Fourth today."

Phil beat me to the punch a bit. "Did you know that's where the Babe and a couple of other Yankees hang out?"

"I do now. I delivered beer and whiskey to the Babe, 'Jumpin' Joe, and Hoyt."

"You got to meet him?"

"Just briefly, but yeah. I met all three and got a pat on my shoulder from Ruth. When I told him that you are a fan, he told me to tell you that you're a smart guy."

The following evening, I went back to where I had picked up Dugan but no luck. The Yankees were out of town for a week. When they returned, I was back at my spot. It took two more days until I again saw Dugan waiting for a ride.

"Hey, I remember you. You're the beer guy."

"Yep, I sure am Mr. Dugan."

"Don't need any beer tonight, we're pretty well stocked, and call me Joe."

"That's OK. I'm just happy to have you in my cab."

This time on the ride in we talked about the game and baseball in general. The Yankees had won, and he had a couple of hits, so he was especially talkative.

During the next ten days, I taxied Dugan home four times and made one more beer run for him. The last time I picked him up I did something that Vinnie would definitely not have liked. I took Phil along with me. I picked him up just before I drove out to Yankee Stadium. I had made arrangements with Joe to pick him up. He said it was fine if I brought my Yankee fan housemate with me. Phil was thrilled when Dugan hopped in. He was even more thrilled when we were invited up to the penthouse. I hadn't expected that.

As soon as we stepped into the room, Ruth boomed out a greeting to Phil.

"Hey kiddo. You must be the smart one of the pair. You know we're going to beat the pants off old Connie Mack this year. You can bet on it."

"No doubt about it, Mr. Ruth, especially with the year you're having."

"You two stick around a bit. Get yourselves something to drink. I'm gonna need a cab in a little while."

Phil and I did as we were ordered. Phil had a beer and since I was driving, I had a ginger ale. I was a little nervous about being out of the cab for so long, but this was worth a few whacks from Vinnie if he found out. Ruth kept talking to us as if we belonged there. We told him about owning a Negro team in Harrisburg.

"Hey, I played there once. Hit one into the river. They should let Negroes play in big leagues. Some great players out there, but it ain't going to happen as long as the Judge runs things." It was obvious that Ruth was no fan of baseball Commissioner Judge Landis. At one point while we were talking, the Babe came over and put his arm around Phil's shoulder. It was an evening neither of us ever forgot.

About an hour later, Ruth bellowed: "Goin' to Chicago tomorrow and gotta spend a little time with my wife. How about you two drive me up to my apartment on Riverside Drive?" He gave me a twenty-dollar tip.

The next day, the Yankees started a two-week road trip. After they got back, I only saw Joe three more times and never got back to the penthouse.

Chapter 11

WORKING WITH CAPTAIN EDDIE AGAIN

Construction on the airfield began in early May 1934. By that time, I had been working at the field two mornings and all day on Mondays each week for almost eighteen months. It took a couple of weeks to clear and level the land for the new runways and another two weeks to pave the surfaces. While that was going on, two new hangars were being built behind each runway. Joey said he had six new renters and was working to get a couple of air companies signed up. He had also renamed the airfield. It was now North Beach Airport.

One morning about a month after construction had started, I was working on a plane and saw Joey with someone inspecting the runway surface. They walked out to the end of the runway. One of the men looked vaguely familiar but he was too far away to see clearly, so I went back to work.

Half an hour later, as Joey was walking the visitor to the parking area, I recognized the visitor. It was Captain Eddie. Instantly, I bounced out of the hangar and ran over to the two men.

"Captain Eddie! I saw you and wanted to say hi."

"Don, it's great to see you. You've hardly changed. What are you doing here?"

"I'm Joey's part-time mechanic."

Joey jumped in, "You two know each other?"

Eddie answered, "Don was one of my wing guys during the war. He was the youngest Hat in the Ring flier. What were you, about twelve back then?"

"Actually, I was seventeen."

"One of the best mechanics we ever had and a fine pilot."

"You taught me everything I know."

"Last time I saw you we were flying over battlefields watching the war end November 11, 1918."

"I'll never forget it."

"It sure is good to see you. I've got some things to talk over with Joey, but I'll come back, and we can catch up a little bit."

When he came back, we talked for an hour before Eddie had to go. I told him about my flying adventures including my crash and about Eastern Air Services.

"You still flying?"

"Whenever I can. My plane is in the hangar."

I knew a little about his post-war story, but he filled in some details. I knew he had started an automobile company, Rickenbacker Motor Company, which had gone out of business in the late 1920s. About the same time that Rickenbacker Motors shut down he bought the Indianapolis Speedway. He told me that after the speedway, he became the assistant general manager of General Motors with plans to head up an air company subdivision. That's the reason he was meeting with Joey. He was considering making Joey's airfield his central headquarters when it was expanded.

"It's been great talking, but I've got another appointment in midtown in an hour and I've got to leave. Give me your phone number and we can find another time to get together."

After Captain Eddie left, Joey came over from his office.

"I didn't know I had a famous flier working for me. I'm impressed. My RAF buddies talked a lot about the Hat in the Ringers. How many missions did you fly? Any kills?"

I told Joey my war story and how I became Captain Eddie's mechanic and eventually his wingman for a couple of missions. I kept the story humble, but I could tell Joey was fascinated.

"This is great. I gotta figure a way to let people around here, especially potential customers, know about you."

He didn't waste any time. The next day Vinnie started calling me "Ace" and asked how many Germans I had shot down. I told him and then asked that he not spread that around. "Hey, no problem. I know how to keep secrets." I had no doubt that a secret was safe with Vin.

Ten days later, Captain Eddie called and suggested we have dinner at an upscale midtown restaurant, Barbetto's Italian Restaurant. While we ate, he told me about his plans for his new air company.

"I convinced General Motors to get into the air transportation business and create a major air company. After the airmail scandal during the Hoover years, the new administration decided to reorganize the mail service altogether. Clean it up from top to bottom. That's created lots of new opportunities, especially in terms of passenger services, and GM is ready to explore them."

I told him about what happened to Eastern Air Services and how a U.S. Steel-backed company stole our routes.

"Sounds like you guys were victims of the scandal. There were a couple of dozen companies like yours that were put out of business. There were also cities that lost airmail service. Now U.S. Steel has teamed up with the Boeing Company and they've created United Air Company. They have a headquarters in Seattle and one in Chicago and will soon dominate air services in the Northwest and the upper Midwest. There are two other new companies, American in Texas out to the West Coast and Pan American in the Southwest and Mexico. What GM and I plan to do is merge together the remnants of those small Eastern companies like yours and create a major air company that can dominate the East Coast from Miami and Cuba to Canada."

He went on to tell me that he wanted to make New York

City his headquarters with, eventually, another center in Miami. The problem was that New York didn't have an airport big enough. With a couple new runways, Joey's North Beach airfield would be big enough.

"We're getting help from the new mayor, La Guardia, who wants to bring better transportation to the city—new roads and bridges and an airport. Even though he's a Republican, La Guardia is a big FDR supporter and is getting major New Deal money. That's what is paying for the construction that you've been watching out there. Once the North Beach is ready, we'll start moving our planes in and begin flying. We're shooting for a 1934 start."

"Sounds exciting."

"It is."

"Don, you know I'm a direct person. I don't beat around many bushes so here's part of the reason I asked you to dinner tonight. After we talked last week, I did some research. Talked to several people including Bill White, you remember "Wild" Bill out in Pittsburgh.

"Sure, I do. Haven't talked to him recently though. He was good about keeping us informed about the U.S. Steel plans."

"He was sorry to see you go out of business. I also talked to Dick Davidson in Middletown. He told me all about Eastern Air Services and said you really worked hard to keep it going. And I talked to several satisfied customers. Everyone had nice things to say about you and your company. So, here's the question, do you think you'd like to be part of our new company?"

"I'd like working with you again but what would you want me to do? Any flying involved?"

"I can see several jobs for you. Of course, we'll be looking for pilots. I thought you might want to be in the air. We'll also need mechanics, but with your experience running a flying company, I'm thinking about something that includes some management and some flying. Of course, I'm talking about a full-time position."

"Yes sir, Captain Rickenbacker, I am ready to go!"

"Then consider it done. One thing. Don't mention this to anyone. I have some negotiating to do, and I'd prefer to keep the media out of this for a while. As for Joey, you've probably already figured this out. Joey has some tough friends. In fact, Joey is a very tough guy himself. I only want him to know what he needs to know."

"Yeah, one of Joey's friends, Vinnie, runs the cab company where I work. I've seen some of his other friends. They all look like people you want on your side."

Captain Eddie went on: "From what I've heard, Vinnie arranged the muscle that convinced the previous owners to sell their land to Joey. It was not a particularly happy transaction."

"One other thing, Don. How would you feel if we used your company's name? I'm thinking that Eastern Airline Company would be a perfect name for us."

"I'll ask my partners, but I don't see any problems." There weren't. After a little legal work, Eddie's new company became "Eastern Airline."

We talked a little longer, finished dinner, and shook hands.

"I'll be in touch with you again soon. I have some people I need to talk to, and it would probably be a good idea if you were there for at least one of those conversations."

"Just let me know. I'll be there."

Knowing how Captain Eddie operated, I figured it wouldn't be long before we talked again. I was right. Two weeks later, he called to set up a meeting at the airfield. He said a friend of his wanted to look over the North Beach and had some ideas about planes.

I was surprised to see who it was, and with a big smile on my face, trotted over to meet them.

"Hi Slim. Nice to see you again."

"Nice to see you too. I didn't know Ed was talking about you when he said there was someone at the field who he wanted to join us. A good choice, I'm sure." We shook hands.

"You two know each other? How'd that happen?"

"Don was my pilot for a show I did back in my barnstorming days. Only one show but he did a great job. One of my best jumps. Then we bumped into each other out in Pittsburgh just before I made the flight."

I added: "I even offered him a job at one point. He wanted to go to Paris instead. It was a good choice on his part."

"Don, I didn't know you had friends in such high places."

I replied, "Just two and they're both standing in front of me right now."

"Charles is going to help me decide on the planes to buy, and I thought it would be good for you to be in on the conversation too."

For the next hour, the three of us walked over the new runways. Captain Eddie and Lindbergh talked a lot about the surface quality and length, the kind of planes the new company should consider buying, and where a passenger terminal and cargo buildings should go. Aside from a few comments about the planes, I did a lot of listening. Pretty quickly it became clear to me that Eastern Airlines Company was going to focus on passenger flights. Cargo and the mail would be a distant second.

After Lindbergh left, Captain Eddie and I talked a bit more.

"Charles has great contacts with manufacturers. They all want him to test their planes, so he knows what's going on in the industry. We talked last week. He told me about a new plane that Douglas Aircraft is building. It's the DC-2, which is actually a new version of their DC-1. It'll be big enough to carry the mail, some cargo, and up to fourteen passengers. It'll also travel at just over two hundred miles an hour and has a thousand-mile range, which will be good for us. The only problem is that it's not scheduled to be ready until next spring. So, what I plan to do is to have a look and maybe order a small fleet."

"I've read a little about the DC-1. Sounds like a big plane. Haven't seen one yet."

"Well, here's your chance. I'd like you to go along with me when I look them over."

"Count me in. Just tell me when and where."

"The when is early next month. I made an appointment with Douglas for August 5. The where is Santa Monica, California, at the Douglas plant."

"That's three weeks from now and it'll take several days to get there. I'll have to clear that with Joey and Vinnie."

"I'll give you another option. Quit those two jobs and start working for Eastern Airline Company on August 1. You'll be our operations manager in charge of pilots, flight scheduling, and overseeing plane maintenance. To start, we'll pay you double what you're making here and with Vinnie. How's that sound?"

"That sounds great. I'll give notice to Vin and Joey tomorrow and pack my bags for California."

And that's when I started working for Eastern Airlines.

I went home that night and told Phil and his parents that I was going to start a new job in August and would be away for about ten days. Phil was curious about what I'd be doing. When I told him, he was happy I'd have a chance to fly again. He also promised to keep quiet about the job. I wasn't too concerned about Phil telling anyone. The only people he saw were the guys at the machine shop where he worked and a few vets at the local Legion. Since returning from Washington, he had lost some of his enthusiasm for the Legion. Fort Thomas Paine was gone and by then most of the vets there had moved out of the city. We heard that several had found jobs on New Deal projects. A handful of others, including Phil, got together every couple of weeks, but there were no formal meetings like before.

Two weeks later, I was on my way to California. Captain Eddie, who was already there, sent me a plane ticket on the Tin Goose, Pan American's transcontinental flight. The trip took four days and included overnight layovers in cities along the way. Once in Los Angeles, I went downtown to the Roosevelt Hotel where I'd be staying.

"I'm glad you made it in one piece, Don. That's a long trip."

"I think I'd rather fly myself than sit on those planes for four days. I'm here now though and ready to work."

Eddie smiled and said: "I've made an appointment for tomorrow at Douglas Aircraft Company. We'll probably need at least three days out there. One day to look, one day to test, and maybe a third day to purchase and schedule deliveries if we see something we like."

The next day at ten, we were at the Douglas Field in Santa Monica. Don Douglas, the founder of the company, and Eddie were longtime friends. Eddie had tested a couple of Douglas's early military planes.

"Don, meet Don Malone. He's the Eastern Air operations manager, which includes overseeing the planes we fly. He also flew with me during the war."

"That's a name I won't forget." We shook hands and he walked us over to one of the production hangars where two new Douglas commercial planes, the DC-2 and the DC-3, were being worked on.

"Ed and Don, this is John Northrop. He's the lead engineer on these two projects. He can give you specs on both planes."

We spent the next three hours talking to Northrop about the two planes. He gave us a production schedule and specific details about both planes. It sounded as if there were only a few differences between them. The DC-3 was a little bigger, could climb a bit higher, could fly a little faster, and was designed to carry fourteen passengers instead of twelve.

The two big differences were that the DC-3 had more than twice the thousand-mile range of the DC-2, and the DC-3 would not be ready for another twelve months. The DC-2 would be ready by March.

The following day, Captain Eddie and I tested both planes. One of the Douglas test pilots took us up. At first, I was a little overwhelmed by the plane. It required a pilot and a co-pilot to fly it and had an engine on each wing instead of a propeller in front of the pilot, which was something new for me. Each engine had to be started independently. There were also gauges for each engine, which meant there were a lot more instruments to watch. The planes were roomier than any plane I had ever flown. The cockpit, which was right at the front of the plane, sat much higher than in any of the planes I had flown. I had to climb up onto the wing to get into the cockpit. Also, while it was parked, the plane's nose looked well above the runway. Clearly, flying these planes would be a new experience for me.

We climbed into the DC-2 first. Before we took off, the test pilot explained the gauges and the basics of maneuvering the plane. Eddie, who sat in the co-pilot's seat, took the controls almost as soon as we were in the air and flew the plane for the next two hours. Reluctantly, he let the test pilot land it. I sat behind them and watched. Though there were more gauges, including some that were above the pilot rather than in front of him, by the time we landed I felt comfortable with the control panel.

After lunch, we took the DC-3 up. This time Eddie sat in the pilot's seat and I got to be the co-pilot. The test pilot sat in the middle. We cranked up the engines, raced down the runway and into the air. Eddie flew for about an hour, then asked me if I was ready to fly. "This is easier than it looks, Don. Just enjoy yourself." I was nervous initially but with a little instruction from the test pilot, I began to feel sure of myself. I liked not having a propeller in front of me. The view was much broader than in my plane. I also adjusted quickly to the flaps and to the pedals that moved the rudder. Both were a little harder to operate because it was a much bigger plane than mine, but the DC-3 handled better than I had expected. After an hour, I handed the controls back to Captain Eddie. I had really enjoyed my flying time. I was surprised how easy it was to maneuver such a big, powerful aircraft. Eddie flew a little longer, then landed the plane as if he had been doing it for years. This time, we had been in the air for almost three hours.

Back at the hotel, Eddie asked me, "Well, what did you think of those two planes?"

"I loved flying the DC-3 and if the 2 is similar, I'd be happy with either."

"The 2 is as easy to handle as the 3, but not quite as powerful. While I think either plane would suit our purposes initially, in terms of long-term plans, we need to have a few of the 3s." I asked about the cost.

"Don't worry about the money. Our well has a bottom but it is very deep. Between General Motors, New Deal money, and La Guardia's money, buying these planes will be no problem. I'm thinking that we buy eight 2s. We can get things started with them and we'll order eight 3s for the earliest delivery possible. I'll push Don to have them to us as soon as they come off the production line."

The next day, we were back at Douglas ready to buy some planes. Just as we had talked about, Eddie bought eight DC-2s and contracted for eight DC-3s with a February 1, 1935, delivery date. Douglas also agreed to send two test pilots to train our pilots.

After buying the planes, Eddie and Don went out to talk to Northrup while I got a lesson in flying our new planes. With me as the pilot, one of the test pilots walked me through taking off and landing. Again, I was surprised how easy it was even though the plane was much bigger than anything I had flown before. After several takeoffs and landings, I was ready to go.

The months after I got back from California were busy. My top priority was hiring ten pilots, ten co-pilots, and six mechanics. Half of the new hires were going to be stationed in New York and the other half would be in Charleston, South Carolina, which we decided would be our Southern headquarters. I asked Phil if he was interested but he didn't want to leave the Transit

Authority. He did recommend two guys. I hired them both as well as a mechanic I knew at Vinnie's garage. The other two answered an ad we placed in Charleston. Finding pilots and co-pilots was harder. I checked with local flying schools looking for interested instructors rather than new pilots. The planes we'd be flying were well beyond a new flier. I got four local instructors to sign on. I also hired six former Post Office pilots. The other ten were products of various contacts Eddie had. Lindbergh was one of those contacts. He recommended four fliers in Charleston who we hired. By December, we had our corps of pilots and co-pilots. The Douglas instructors were scheduled to work with them during the two weeks before Christmas. One week in New York and one week in Charleston.

In addition to hiring mechanics and pilots, I went along with Eddie to look over the airfields that we planned to use. During the week before Thanksgiving, we inspected fields in Boston, Philadelphia, Washington, Richmond, Savannah, Charleston, and Miami. Our business manager, Gary McClellan, also went along on the trip. Gary and Eddie had worked together for several years. When the air company was organized, GM moved him over to Eastern at Eddie's request. Gary was the guy who paid the bills. I had never met him before but liked him immediately. I knew that if Eddie requested him, he was good at what he did. He also had a great sense of humor. He kept us laughing throughout the trip. On the trip, we flew the first DC-2 delivered to us. I shared flying time with Eddie, which I enjoyed.

Gary and I became good friends pretty quickly. He lived in Queens, not far from the airport, was married, and had two sons. They were all baseball fans. That summer, Eastern's first, Gary and I went to six Dodgers' games at Ebbets Field, three of them with his ten- and eight-year-old sons.

They were Cincinnati fans, and whenever the Reds played Brooklyn, Gary tried to get to a game. He had grown up in Cincinnati and went to Xavier University where he was on the baseball team. He had also played on the basketball team, but baseball was his favorite. After the games and a few other times, he had me over for dinner. I enjoyed my meals at his house. It reminded me of when my brothers and I were growing up. Also, his wife, Helen, was a great cook. I always looked forward to meals she cooked.

A year after Eastern started flying, Gary helped me find my first house. I had been feeling guilty about my irregular schedule and the way the Avillos catered to it. There were many nights I got in very late, but Mrs. Avillo always cooked me a meal. There were other times when I expected to be home but wouldn't show up for a day or two. I mentioned how I felt to Gary one day.

"Why don't you buy a house of your own? There are plenty out here in Queens, and Long Island is booming with affordable homes. We almost bought out there."

"I don't know anything about buying a house. Besides, I'd only be there a couple of days a week with my schedule the way it is. I should just rent something."

"You rent; you have no equity. No equity makes it harder for you to get credit. No credit means it's harder to buy big things like a car. No, you need to buy a house."

"I have some money saved, but I don't think I could afford a down payment."

"I'll talk it over with Eddie. Eastern may be able to float you a small down payment loan. You could pay it back monthly based on what you can afford."

"That would be nice. Better than borrowing from Joey and his buddies."

"No, you definitely don't want to borrow money from Joey. Don't ever borrow from Joey."

Two weeks later, Gary introduced me to his real estate agent, Dylan something or other. He showed me about eight houses in Queens not far from the airport. I liked a threebedroom house on Murdock Road just off Rockaway. It was bigger than I needed, but Dylan convinced me to buy it.

"With this one, you will have lots of room for family visits."

I hadn't seen my family much since I moved to New York. I especially missed Mary Ann. She was in high school now and always excited about coming to visit. Her only trip so far had come about two months after I had moved to the city. We went to the Metropolitan Museum and window shopping on Fifth Avenue. I also took her for a ride in my plane. The thought of having her and the rest of my family visit made me feel good.

Eastern Airlines opened for business on January 1, 1934. We didn't have many passengers during those early days.

Initially, we flew mostly airmail and cargo. In the spring, we slowly began to pick up passengers. Gary had figured that it would take a couple of years before we'd see any real profits and he was right. Our first two years ended in the red. But we had lots of money behind us so early profits weren't necessary. As long as we didn't lose too much money, we were OK.

I was on the go constantly during that first year. My primary task was to create and then manage a schedule for the pilots, co-pilots, and the mechanics. Gary worked out the daily stops and I assigned pilots and co-pilots to routes. Each day, two planes, one in the morning and one in the early afternoon, started in New York and flew to Boston, then south to Washington and back. Two others started in Charleston and flew to Miami, then north to Richmond and back to Charleston. Pilots and co-pilots usually flew their routes every other day and were in the air about eight hours. I also worked out schedules for mechanics. Three of the mechanics we hired were at our Charleston hangar and the other three were at North Beach. Just before we opened for business, I made arrangements at airfields where we didn't have a mechanic to use local guys when we needed them.

I got a lot of flying time myself that first year. I always had a suitcase packed and ready to go. Typically, I made a stop at all our airfields every week, which meant I spent at least three days each week away from home. I tried to meet with all our pilots and co-pilots at least once every two weeks. There were also several times that I substituted for either a pilot or co-pilot when someone wasn't able to fly. I wanted to keep tabs on our mechanics too, especially at the fields where we had to hire part-time people. I still enjoyed getting into an engine, and I think I surprised some of the mechanics by working on planes with them occasionally.

Another thing about the job that I enjoyed was training pilots. I had never considered myself a teacher and was surprised how much I liked instructing new pilots and sharing information with our experienced pilots. The co-pilots were my favorite students. None of them had flown planes like ours before, so they all needed instruction before they could fly. For some of the new pilots, our planes were also a step up. In both cases, I arranged meetings, sometimes one-on-one, and sometimes in small groups, to give them the basics. When possible, that included a short flight. I always had the co-pilots go on their first trip as an observer, and I went with them as the flight's co-pilot. Usually, I found that the co-pilots were especially eager to learn. It always reminded me of the excitement I felt flying that DC-2 for the first time. Of course, teaching also meant that I had to stay up to date with new flying techniques and any changes from Douglas. To do that, I read Douglas manuals, talked to test pilots whenever they came east, and I began reading books about planes and flight in general. I learned a lot trying to stay ahead of my students.

During that first year, the one thing that became irritating to me involved the traveling conditions I had to put up with. On overnight trips, the places where I stayed were not especially comfortable. In many of our hangars, we had a room where I could spend the night. The rooms had little more than a cot, a sink, and a radio that I could use to listen to ballgames or music. At other stops, there were shoddy, "pay-by-the-hour" inns close to the airport. Eating on the road was also a negative. While I usually carried several sandwiches with me, they were no substitute for Mrs. Avillo's home cooking. And then there were the many nights alone. I had always been a solitary person, but after a year on the road, it became lonely.

Everything considered, our first two years were good ones. Once in a while, I'd have a problem with a pilot or co-pilot. On two occasions, that meant firing someone and hiring a replacement. Keeping our mechanics was a bit more difficult. The New Deal generated new jobs and mechanics were in ever greater demand. The parttimers I worked with were especially hard to keep. It meant that at some hangars we occasionally didn't have a mechanic immediately available, but I worked out a substitute system pretty quickly. We also had days when flights were canceled because of weather conditions. It wasn't hard adding cargo or mail to a later flight, but passengers were not as easy to satisfy.

Mayor LaGuardia was right when he predicted that our North Beach Airport would become New York's primary airport. During Eastern Air's second year, two new runways and two new hangars were added to the field. A grand, new terminal building connecting all six runways was also built. Now passengers had a comfortable central place where they could wait for flights. The terminal even had a restaurant. Unofficially, the newspapers began calling the airport LaGuardia's airport because of all the money the city had been spending to expand it. Fortunately for Eastern, no other major company set up shop at the field, but I knew it was just a matter of time until they did. I bumped into Joey one day and he confirmed what I suspected.

"We're trying to get some competition in here for you soon, Don. When we get done with these two runways, we're planning two more. That'll make ten altogether. Any major flying company should be eager to join us here. As long as the mayor and his buddy in the White House are willing to send us money, we're willing to build runways. In a few years, this will be the biggest airport in the East and one of the biggest in the country." I knew he was right.

Chapter 12

CAT

Just as Gary had predicted, Eastern's first profit came in our third year. It wasn't a big profit, but we were in the black. Early that year, we had added new stops in Pittsburgh, Baltimore, Charlotte, and Atlanta, and doubled the number of our pilots. We also bought eight more DC-3s, which enabled us to keep each pilot's workload at what it had been during the first two years. The new stops almost doubled the number of passengers we carried, bringing the total up to just over five hundred a day and, in turn, was the source of our first annual profit. The expansion had been a gamble. Eddie and Gary argued in favor of it. GM strongly disagreed but ultimately admitted Gary and Eddie had been right.

Of course, I was happy about the profit, but I was especially happy about the expansion because it reduced my nights away from home. As part of the expansion, we hired someone, Kenny O'Leary, to help me manage our routes from Washington south. Kenny met with me in Washington most Wednesdays to go over his territory, but otherwise I visited our southern routes only about once every three months. That meant I could be home at night for a change—something I liked a lot. I still trained all our new pilots and co-pilots, but they now came to

New York for their training. That also enabled me to end my days at home instead of on the road somewhere.

The new leisure time gave me an opportunity to begin fixing up my house. During the year after I bought it, I did little to furnish it. I had a bed and beaten-up bureau, a small dining room table, and a couch. My walls were almost bare, and the only curtains were in the bedroom and living room. Two rooms were completely unfurnished. It was a spartan existence. Filling those blank spaces became a priority.

Rather than pay for a house of new furniture, Gary suggested that I go to some estate sales.

"Half our stuff came from estate sales. You can find some real bargains."

"I've never been to an estate sale. What do I need to know?"

"It's easy. Two pieces of advice. Take a list of things that you're looking for, and don't buy something just because it's pretty and inexpensive. Helen did that regularly. Other than that, have fun."

Phil went with me to my first adventure into the world of estate sales. We hadn't seen each other for several months, and it was good to reconnect a bit. We talked a little baseball, a little politics—he was a real FDR supporter—and about his job. He was now a foreman at the transit company and still enjoyed it. I told him if he ever wanted something else, Eastern would hire him in a second, but I was sure that he had become a transit lifer like his dad.

Even though I didn't buy anything that first time, I enjoyed it. I saw some nice pieces and talked to several estate sale regulars who gave me tips. I came home looking forward to my next sale and even more eager to fill my empty spaces.

Two weeks later I was at a sale in Brooklyn. There wasn't anything that interested me, but as I was prowled around, I chatted with an attractive woman I had seen at the previous sale. She clearly knew what she was looking at. She rattled off styles and dates of almost everything she touched. She also knew what was authentic and what had been copied or repaired.

"So where did you learn all this?"

"My parents had a second-hand store in the Ukrainian Village part of the Lower East Side. I helped out from as early as I can remember, which means for about thirty years. If you see something enough, you get to know what it is, and that's how I know what I'm looking at."

"All on-the-job training."

"Sort of. I do have a degree from NYU in history and I read a lot, but my foundation came from my parents."

"Do you still work for them?"

"A little bit. If I see something that I'm sure they can sell, I'll get it, but my real job is finding things and decorating for clients. People who want to furnish or refurnish an apartment or a house hire me to do it for them. We talk about what pieces they need and what styles they'd like and, of course, how much they are willing to spend, and then I go out and find what they want. I often buy new, but the things you can find at a good estate sale are often better made and fit my clients' requests better. I also really enjoy wandering through these sales."

As we were talking, I followed her into the bidding room.

"Here's my tip of the day. Always sit toward the back of the room. That way you can see who you're bidding against."

"Thanks, I'll keep that in mind, but I don't think I'm going to bid on anything."

"Too bad. There's a big sale next week out on Long Island. There should be a lot of good items. You might find something there."

The next week when I got to the sale, I immediately spotted the woman I had met. She was wearing a fashionable tweed jacket, dark tan pants, and what looked like riding boots. She was easy to pick out because she was the only woman not wearing a dress or a skirt. The outfit reminded me of a Katherine Hepburn movie. The ultimate defining characteristics were the pencil behind her ear and the legal pad she carried.

As I walked over to her, she waved. "You know, last week I didn't even give you my name. I'm Don Malone."

"Yeah, I thought about that later. Sometimes I get so caught up in these sales that I forget basic etiquette."

She stuck her hand out for me to shake. "I'm Catherine Kelly, but everyone just calls me Cat."

For the next two hours, Cat and I wandered around looking at all sorts of things for sale. I told her what I was looking for and she gave me recommendations when she saw something that she thought I might like. Listening to her describe what we were looking at was an education itself. This time when the bidding started, we sat together at the back of the room. She bought several items, including a large bureau, matching bed frame, and nightstands. With her encouragement, I bought a big fat living-room chair, a small table for beside it, and a floor lamp.

"If you don't have a way to get your stuff home, I have a guy who's going to pick my stuff up on Monday and I can have him drop your chair and lamp off if you'd like."

"I'm going to take the lamp, but a chair and table dropoff would be great."

What had become my weekend quest continued the next Saturday. This time, Cat and I had agreed to meet two hours before the bidding outside the bidding-room door. It was a sunny, warm late-April morning, the first real spring day, a great day to be outside.

"OK, Don, today let's see what we can find for you. How about a sofa, some rugs, and maybe another lamp or two?

Maybe even a dining room set."

"Sounds good to me, but I don't want to interfere with your business."

"Don't worry. I'm between clients. I finished one job yesterday and have to meet with some people next week about three other jobs. I'm just looking for odds and ends today, so let's see what we can find for you."

We spent the morning meandering through things that were going to be auctioned off. As she always did, Cat took notes and carefully inspected. She found a couple of rugs and a sofa she thought might be right for me. I saw several things I liked, including two end tables, but she warned me about them. "They look good, but the legs have been replaced on one and they look wobbly on the other." I also saw two lamps I liked. We bid on all the items, and I ended up with a rug, both lamps, and a sofa. I was excited.

"I'll have my guy drop them off at your house on Monday."

"Thanks. This has been great. I never would have found those things without your help. How about I compensate you for your time with a late lunch this afternoon?"

She agreed and we went to a little restaurant close to the airport.

"So, Don, you know what I do, but you haven't told me about what you do."

"I fly planes. Actually, I'm the operations manager for Eastern Airlines, which means I fly around and make sure our pilots have everything they need and that all our planes take off and land when and where they are supposed to."

"Oh, that sounds exciting. How did you end up at Eastern?"

I gave her the five-minute version of my war experience and the Hat in the Ring Gang, a little bit about my company, and then about Eddie and Eastern.

"Wow, a Hat in the Ring pilot. I've read about you guys. And now an airline executive. That's exciting."

"The title sounds more important than it is, but I really like the job."

"So, what do you do when you're not flying around or going to estate sales?"

"Actually, not a lot. I'm a big baseball fan and go to games with a good friend. He's a Yankees guy and I'm an Athletics guy, and whenever the A's are in town we go to some of the games. Once a week, we also try to get together to play chess."

"Chess. You play chess. I love chess! My father used to play in tournaments and is still really good. He taught me how to play when I was four or five. It's a great game! Maybe we can play sometime."

"Sounds good, but before we play chess, you've gotten my story, now it's your turn. Tell me more about yourself."

"You got most of the important information last week. The rest is that I was born in Ukraine in 1906. No brothers or sisters. When I was two, my parents immigrated to the United States. My real name was Katrina Kalecki. The immigration people at Ellis Island changed it to Catherine Kelly and that's who I've been ever since. My parents still call me Katrina, but I'm Cat to everyone else. We ended up in the Ukrainian Village part of the Lower East Side where my parents opened up their shop."

We talked for almost two hours. She told me more about her parents and growing up. I told her about my parents and siblings, life in Middletown, and I mentioned that Dad was a staunchly Republican congressman, but that I was an FDR supporter. She was especially intrigued about my flying.

"It must be great flying all over places. I've never even been in a plane."

"Well, we can fix that. Let me know when you have a couple of hours and I'll take you up."

"Oh, that would be great! I'd love it. How about next Sunday?"

"Perfect. Sundays are never busy at the airport. I will warn you though. Once you go up, you may not want to come down. As much as I fly, I always look forward to the next time."

"I'm so excited! I'll count the days! It will be so much fun. I just hope it doesn't rain."

Her enthusiasm made me happy also. I expected that I'd be counting the days too. As we left, I asked her about a sale the next week.

"Oh yeah, yeah. I'm so excited about flying that I forgot."

She told me where it was, and we made plans to meet at the bidding-room door again.

That week, I thought a lot about Cat. She was unlike any woman I'd ever been involved with. I had had numerous girlfriends along the way. Some had been especially important to me at the time. There was a girl in high school who I liked a lot and dated exclusively. We might have stayed together if I hadn't joined the Army. In France, while I was working at the hospital, there was a nurse that I dated, but we both knew we were in a wartime relationship. Shortly after I recovered from my crash, I went out for a while with a teacher who Phil had introduced me to, and during my

first year in New York there was also a woman I liked and saw regularly for several months. With each one, there was a specific quality or two that was appealing to me. With Cat, it was the total package.

The obvious was that she was what I considered "quietly" attractive. Nothing flashy or showy but elegant and fashionable. She was about five inches shorter than me. Light brown hair that was always stylish and worn down on her shoulders. A trim figure, engaging smile, and a pretty face.

Aside from the physical attributes, she was clearly an intelligent, well-read woman, but sort of humble about it. She was also self-assured, poised, and professional about what she did, which I liked. She seemed to be a thoughtful and kind person who genuinely cared about people. Maybe it was a product of her immigrant background. She was friendly with people unless she felt snubbed and then she was feisty. I liked that. There were several people at the auctions, one woman in particular, who disrespected her, and a couple of men who tried to bully her. She immediately let them know not to do it again. One other quality that I liked was her enthusiasm. When she was excited about something, a special sale item she had found or the promise of a plane ride, her face lit up and the excitement just bubbled all over her. Of course, there was still a lot about her that I didn't know, but what I did know was that I wanted to get to know more about her.

By the time that Saturday arrived, I was eager simply to see her again. We had another fun afternoon talking, looking at furniture, and bidding on items. This time, she bought a dozen items and helped me decide on a desk and two bookshelves. Afterward, we went for a casual lunch again at a Brooklyn diner near the sale and made plans for her first plane ride the next day. We agreed to meet at the Eastern lobby at two o'clock.

Sunday was a beautiful day with almost unlimited visibility. A perfect day for flying.

"I have really been looking forward to this. I've been dreaming about it all week."

"I think you're going to enjoy it. We'll take my plane, which is smaller than the company planes, but it'll only be the two of us, so we won't need much space. Is there anywhere you'd like to go?"

"No. Just up in the air."

We got loaded up into the plane. I gave her a spare flight jacket that I kept at the hangar, then we buckled in and up we went. I started the flight by heading west over Manhattan to the Statue of Liberty, then up the Hudson to the northern tip of the island, and back down over Harlem and the Bronx to Broadway and south to Battery Park. Along the way, we flew over Yankee Stadium, Central Park, and the Lower East Side where she grew up. I ended the trip flying east to the ocean, then up over the southern part of Long Island, and back to the airport. We didn't talk much along the way because of the engine noise, but from the smile on her face I could see she was enjoying herself.

"That was fantastic! You were right, I didn't want to come down. What spectacular views! That was definitely one of the most exciting things I've ever done maybe the most exciting. And you get to do that every day."

"Well, some days are better than other days. This was a near-perfect day for flying. I'm just glad you enjoyed it." "Oh, I did. Now how about I take us to dinner. One of the many things I like about New York is how many restaurants are open on Sunday nights. I know a nice little Italian place not far from here."

"That's fine with me."

"I have just one favor to ask. You said you live near the airport. If it's not too far out of the way and if you're comfortable with it, I'd really like to see your house and the spaces we're trying to fill."

I always kept the house clean, so a quick visit was fine with me. It took about half an hour to get there and for her to look around. True to her habits, she brought a pencil and pad to take notes. When she was done, we left and went to dinner.

Throughout dinner Cat talked about the flight and furnishing my house and what we each had scheduled for the coming week. As we left, she thanked me again.

"What a wonderful day. I absolutely loved the flight."

"We can do it again sometime if you'd like. Pick a city Eastern flies to that you'd like to see, and we'll fly there some Sunday and make a day of it."

"Oh, what an offer. I'd love to do that. You just name the day."

"Next Sunday I promised my friend Phil I'd go to a Yankees game with him, but the following Sunday is OK."

"Oh boy. I'll mark it on my calendar with stars!"

"Where to?"

"How about Washington? I've never been there and have always wanted to see the Capitol building and the Washington Monument and the Lincoln Memorial or the Smithsonian. I've read lots about the museum and the art there."

"Make a list and we'll do as much as we can."

When we got to our cars, she came up to me and gave me a short but affectionate hug.

"Thanks for a great day. I look forward to seeing you next Saturday."

I was a little surprised but returned her hug with one of my own.

"You're welcome. I look forward to seeing you too."

When we met the following week, Cat said that after her walk through my house she had a better idea of what might look good and, at the same time, what I might like. She was right. We found a perfect bedroom set—a queen-sized bed, nightstands and lamps, and a bureau with a mirror. She called the set Arts and Craft style. When the furniture was delivered, there was also a classic Staunton chess set that came along.

First thing when I saw her that week, I thanked her.

"Thanks for the chess set. It's beautiful."

"I hoped you'd like it. It's just a little thank you for the flight last week. And besides, I like to play on good boards when I play chess."

The next week she found a big Persian rug for the living room and a woven one for the bedroom. "You have to be careful buying rugs. If it's not good quality, it will fade, or the edges will unravel, or paths will get crushed into it." During our regular post-sale dinner, our approaching trip to Washington was a primary topic of discussion. It was obvious how excited she was about the trip. She had a couple of travel books and had tentatively mapped out a route that would enable us to see most of what she wanted to see. I doubt she suspected that I was almost as excited as she was. When we parted, we shared another soft little hug.

Trip day was a warm, late-May day. Cat agreed to meet me at my house so we could drive to the airport together. I figured that if we were in the air by nine, we could be in D.C.

by eleven. That would give us six or seven hours to sightsee.

The flight was a bit bumpier than the one two weeks earlier, but it didn't seem to faze Cat. She really enjoyed seeing the Capitol from the air. "It looks so intricate from up here." We landed, took a cab to the Washington Monument, and, just as I had planned, were ready to start seeing the sights by eleven.

I told Cat, "You've got the map and the agenda, I'll be the guide."

"I just want to stand here for a few minutes. It is just so inspiring to look one way and see the Lincoln Memorial and the other way down the mall and see the Capitol building."

"Yeah, I never get tired of this view."

We walked around the monument a couple of times, then climbed up the steps to the top.

"Oh, what a wonderful view," Cat said. "This is even better than down on the ground. The Capitol is just majestic, and the river looks so sparkly and pretty."

I knew Cat was a Jefferson fan, so I pointed out the site where they planned to build the Jefferson Memorial. "It's supposed to take a couple of years. I read somewhere that it will be as impressive as any of the memorials here in Washington. A circle of tall columns with a giant statue of Jefferson in the middle."

From the monument, we walked down along the reflecting pools under the cherry trees to the Lincoln Memorial.

"You should see these trees when the blossoms are out. We missed it by about a month or so. I've only seen them in bloom once, but it was unforgettable. The blossoms and sky reflect off the pools. It's like an impressionist painting.

Just beautiful."

When we got to the memorial, Cat inspected every element from the sculpture to the columns and the quotes on the walls and the masonry throughout. She even went behind the building so she could look across the Potomac. Then it was back up the other side of the reflecting pools and onto the mall. We bought sandwiches and sodas from a vendor in front of the Smithsonian and ate on a bench under the trees.

"This is such a wonderful place. These are incredible buildings. So much to see and everything is so pretty. I'm so glad you brought me here. This is such a wonderful day.

I really appreciate it all."

"I'm having fun just watching you enjoy things."

As we walked up toward the Capitol building, our next stop on Cat's agenda, she softly bent her shoulder into mine and slipped her arm through mine.

We spent about an hour wandering around the Capitol building. She was again especially interested in the architectural details and the statues.

"Have you ever been inside?"

"No, but I'd like to see it someday. They have tours during the week. Hard to believe that my dad actually worked in there."

Next was the Supreme Court building and then to the White House.

I asked Cat, "How'd you like to be the decorator for that house? I'll bet it'd take a lot of estate sales to fill it."

"I'd like to give it a try."

We decided we didn't have enough time to see much of the Smithsonian, so we walked around a little bit more and then hiked back to the Washington Monument and looked for a cab to take us back to the airport.

When we plopped down in the cab, Cat slid close beside me and put her head on my shoulder.

"We must have walked fifty miles today, but I think I could go for fifty more. It was so much fun."

I put my arm around her shoulder. "Me too."

At the airport, we bought a couple of sandwiches and sodas that we ate on the way home. The flight back to New York went smoothly. We landed at about eight, just before a beautiful sunset that capped off a great day. I cleaned up the plane, filled the tank, and checked the vitals before we left the hangar. We were back at my house at nine.

"I don't have much to eat, but there is cheese and crackers, and you're welcome to have a glass of wine. I'm flying tomorrow, so I have to stay with lemonade."

"Lemonade is fine with me."

We chatted and ate cheese and crackers for a little while before I walked her to her car. As we walked, she snuggled up against me and put her arm through mine. When we got to the car she reached up and put her arms around my neck. "I want to see more of you, Don. I like being with you." I put my arms around her waist.

"I like you too and would like to see you more."

"How about dinner at my place sometime this week?"

"Sounds great. Any night except Tuesday. I have to go to Pittsburgh on Tuesday."

"OK then, Wednesday at six."

"I'll be there."

She got up on her tiptoes and gave me a little kiss and another hug, then got in her car and drove home.

The next day she called to give me her address.

"It's a studio in Greenwich Village above a little storage space that I use."

Her apartment was on MacDougal just above Prince Street, an easy subway ride from my house. I'm sure I passed by it when I was driving a cab. I got there, opened the door, and climbed a flight of stairs. She was waiting for me at the top of the stairs.

"The door downstairs has a squeak that I can hear when someone comes in."

It wasn't a big apartment, but there was more than enough room to be comfortable. To the right of the door was a large front room with three windows that looked out onto the street.

Cat had a large sofa looking out toward the windows with a coffee table in front of it and end tables on either side. Two chairs with floor lamps were near each front corner by the windows. There was also a tall bookshelf packed with books on the wall to the right of the door. In front of me, the dining table that was set for our dinner, an attractive tablecloth, and candles ready to be lit. Against the wall behind the table was a big rolltop desk full of slots filled with neatly arranged papers. The high ceiling gave the room a spacious appearance. To the left was the kitchen with a loft bedroom above it. All the walls were filled with knickknacks and paintings. While it could easily have appeared to be an eclectic collection of odds and ends, everything fit together perfectly.

"Well, welcome to my world. What do you think?"

"This looks so cozy. I like it, especially all the interesting things on the walls."

"That's the Victorian decorator in me. Dinner will be ready in just a few minutes, gotta get the beans steamed.

We're having Ukrainian chicken, roasted potatoes, and green beans. A standard Ukrainian dinner. I have a bottle of wine if you want any. Otherwise, there is tea, ice water, or lemonade."

"I'm not flying tomorrow. I am going to observe our Philadelphia crew instead, so I can have a glass or two tonight."

I helped her bring the plates to the table and lit the candles while she poured us each a glass of wine. The meal was great. As we ate, we chitchatted about the events of our day and plans for the rest of the week. After dinner, we walked down to a corner shop and got ice cream cones.

"I was going to make some Ukrainian honey cakes but I'm not much of a baker."

We walked down the block to Hudson Park, sat on a bench, and finished our ice cream. When we got back to her apartment, I helped her with the dishes—she washed, I dried—she poured us a glass of wine and we sat down on the sofa. As soon as we sat, she reached over, took my hand and put it over her shoulder, and snuggled close to me. I pulled her closer and whispered: "This is really nice. I like being here with you."

"And I like having you here. I am usually a pretty private person, but I felt comfortable with you ever since that first day we talked, even before I knew your name." I pulled her closer and kissed her.

For the next hour or so, we snuggled and hugged and talked and kissed on her sofa. At about ten, I reluctantly said I had to go, but we made plans for the weekend.

"No estate sales this week. How about if you come over here Saturday around eleven and we can look for a painting or two for your walls? There are a bunch of small galleries in the Village where you can get original art at a very reasonable price. There are also lots of fun shops."

"Sounds good to me."

That Saturday began a new routine for both of us. One day each weekend we spent at her apartment and one day we were at my house. Sometimes we did special things like going to a movie or listening to a neighborhood music performance. A couple of times, I took her to ballgames at Ebbets Field. She wasn't a baseball fan but enjoyed going to games. What she really enjoyed was watching the quirky array of Dodger supporters. One time during the summer we flew to Philadelphia and spent the day there. Another time we flew to Boston. We also saw each other once during the week, usually Wednesday or Thursday, for dinner and a walk. Once, Cat got complimentary tickets to a great new musical, *Babes in Arms,* for which she had helped furnish the set.

Until the first Saturday in July, the only difficult thing about our time together was leaving. That night, we went to a Fourth of July concert in Central Park. It was late when we got back to Cat's apartment and we cuddled our way up to her bed where we stayed for the rest of the night. Drifting off to sleep with her curled up in my arms, then waking up beside her was wonderful.

Sunday morning felt like the beginning of a new life, and in many ways it was. Throughout the rest of the summer, we were together much more than we were apart. We added Friday nights to our routine, at least one weeknight, often two, and spent the weekends together. Just being together made everything right. Some days we went to the beach, other days we wandered through a park, and some days we just rested at home. We had picnics and cooked out. She got me to read more, and we played chess every Sunday. By September, Cat had clothes in a closet and bureau drawer at my house and I had clothes in an armoire in her apartment.

In mid-September, we took the next step in our relationship. I met her parents. She visited them almost every week on a day when we couldn't be together. They were old country people and had certain ideas about who she should see and who she should not see. Initially, I didn't qualify for the "should see" list. I was an American, not a Ukrainian. I didn't belong to the Eastern Orthodox church, nor did I have a college degree. However, over the summer, Cat tore those walls down brick by brick and by September was ready for them to meet me. One Sunday afternoon, I went along with her to dinner at her parents'. They lived in the heart of the Ukrainian Village part of the Lower East Side, only six blocks from her apartment, but it felt like six thousand miles. After a somewhat icy reception, they began to warm up, and by the end of the afternoon, all was well. They clearly adored their daughter and were happy if she was happy. They welcomed me into their world, and they became a regular Sunday part of Cat's and my routine.

One day in the early autumn, Cat and I had a long talk about our future. We agreed that as far as we could see into the future, we saw ourselves together. However, neither one of us was eager to get married. Cat was happy with our life together and her life in Greenwich Village. She was concerned that marriage might create new expectations and pressures. I agreed. Having children was also not a priority. We both enjoyed our careers and the independence we had. We liked being spontaneous sometimes and being able to relax with no responsibilities. Having children would change that. We'd both have to make major career adjustments and the opportunity to enjoy the things we did now would be limited. Our conclusion was that we didn't want to change our relationship. Someday we would probably get married and maybe even have children, but neither of us saw that in the immediate future.

Instead, we agreed to continue enjoying our lives as they were together.

Chapter 13

AN OLD FRIEND RETURNS

During the summer that Cat and I began our relationship, tensions were growing at Eastern between Eddie and the General Motors board. Emboldened by our first profits, Eddie wanted to expand the company's reach to Havana, New Orleans, and possibly to Louisville and Cincinnati as well. Gary figured out the financing and showed that the new cities could add to the profits within two years, three at the longest. The board objected. It was willing to add Havana but nothing more. By the summer, the wrangling had grown intense. Late in 1937, I asked Gary about Eddie's maneuvering.

"I can't tell you too much, but he's been talking to some outside money people. Next time you see Eddie, you might ask him."

That's what I did. Early almost every Monday morning, Gary, two others, and I had a planning meeting to go over the coming week's activities. Eddie usually ran the meeting. The Monday after I talked to Gary I waited until our meeting was over and talked to Eddie privately.

"I've heard some rumors and I'm curious about what's going on with GM."

"Don, it's not anything you need to worry about. You'll be here as long as you want to be here. I promise that you will be one of the first at Eastern to know about any changes." Just after New Year's, Eddie stopped by my office.

"Don, it's time to answer your question. Sometime this spring, Eastern is going to fly solo. No more GM. I've got five investors who are backing me and GM has agreed to sell us Eastern Air. I'll be the majority stockholder and the others will share 49 percent. We've got the lawyers working out all the specifics right now, but the deal is done. We'll be independent by April."

"Wow, what does that mean in terms of operations?"

"It means we add all the stops I've been talking about, plus Tampa. One of the investors wants to add Tampa, which Gary says will be a good addition. He thinks that with those new cities on our list, we'll be able to dominate everything east of the Mississippi."

"That sounds great. I guess I'll be training some new pilots and co-pilots soon, and we'll be buying a bunch of new planes. I'll like that."

"Yeah, you know the procedure. We'll get going at the end of the month or early in February. Probably buy some more DC-3s and hire a dozen or so pilots and some co-pilots. One thing, I told you that you'd be first to know and you are. Only the investors and Gary know from our side, and a few on the GM board know on their side. It'll be a while before this goes public, so please don't tell anyone."

With one exception, I lived up to my promise. I had to tell Cat, but I knew she would keep the secret.

A few days later I saw Gary in the terminal. He asked if Eddie had talked to me, and I said he did.

"Within the next few days, we should begin the planning process."

I told him I had a couple of flights scheduled for the middle of the week but could change them if I needed to. We talked a little longer and decided on Wednesday morning.

"Did Eddie tell you who the investors are?"

"No, he just said that there were five of them."

"I probably shouldn't tell you this, so don't let anyone know. You'll officially find out soon enough. One of the investors is Joey Olivetti."

"Our Joey? The guy who manages the airport and has some nasty friends. That doesn't sound good, but he's only one of five investors."

Gary looked concerned. "Those guys have ways of taking over businesses. They have lawyers who know all the loopholes and how to maneuver through them and, of course, Joey has muscle. Additionally, his people will probably be involved in running the Miami operation. He is the one who wanted to add Tampa to our list of cities. The prize for him and his guys is Havana. I've never been there, but from what I've heard, anything goes in Havana—gambling, prostitution, drugs, anything. In Tampa, one of the bosses is Santo Trafficante. He's fighting it out with two other gangs and direct, regular access to Havana will enable Trafficante to dominate his rivals. Joey and his guys up here want to get a piece, probably a big piece, of Trafficante's operation."

"Wow, I knew Joey had some dangerous friends, but I didn't think he was that important."

"Joey's not the top guy, but he's close. He's probably the one who will be running the Miami airport by the time we start our Havana flights."

"I hope Eddie knows what he is getting into."

"Eddie's a big boy. He can play as tough as anyone, but Joey and his guys have no rules and that's what worries me.

One of the things Eddie has going for him is his reputation. He's well respected. Even President Roosevelt is his friend. That's perfect for Joey's guys. Who would suspect that anyone like Eddie would have mob business partners? On the positive side, I doubt that Eastern will have many labor problems. Joey's guys will make sure of that. You know how Eddie hates organized labor. Well, now he will have some help with unions."

I asked, "Will we include Joey when we start planning the Havana-Miami-Tampa runs?"

"Probably and I wouldn't be surprised if he wants to be involved in the New Orleans planning as well."

I was troubled by what Gary told me, so I started reading the Tampa newspaper for information, and it didn't take much searching. Evidently, there had been a gang war going on for several years between Charlie Wall's gang and Ignacio Antinoni and his gang. Both operated out of the Ybor City section of Tampa. Trafficante got into the competition late but was equally brutal. I worried about Eastern becoming a part of a gang war.

We started planning the following week. Gary was right. Joey was there, but he only cared about the flight schedules to and from Miami. He wanted two daily round-trip flights from Miami to Havana and from Miami to Tampa. He also proposed: "I know some people in Havana who, I'm sure, can get us prime space at the airport. They'll also be able to get us some mechanics and staff. Otherwise, you guys know what you're doing, just keep me up to date about Florida." Otherwise, he let Gary and I do all the planning.

Eastern Air officially separated from General Motors in April. As always, it was a busy time, though, for me, not as busy as previous openings. I already had an assistant working our southern fights. Now I'd have another assistant overseeing the western flights. Officially, I had a fourth operations assistant who dealt with the Florida flights, but I would have little contact with him. I was happy about that.

As Gary had predicted, just two weeks before our opening, Joey became the airport manager in Miami. The day before he left, I went over to the main terminal building and wished him well.

"Donnie, I appreciate that. Probably won't be seeing you much anymore, but anything you need, just let me know. You're a straight-up guy. I like that. You have any problems with anyone, I'm the guy to see."

"Thanks, Joey. I'll keep that in mind."

"Look, Donnie, I know you know who my friends are. You don't have to worry about them at all. And if you need something, just ask. No strings attached, it's yours. Got that no strings attached."

"Got it. Thanks again, Joey, and good luck in Miami. I'll miss you up here."

I never planned to take Joey up on his offer, but six months after he made it, I asked him for help.

In late July, I got a letter from my old mechanic buddy Sam Kades. It had been a couple of years since either of us had written, so I was surprised to hear from him. In fact, his letter came to Phil's parents' house. I knew that he and Brigitte had moved to Metz close to the German border about ten years earlier after Brigitte's mother died. They operated a successful bakery and an even more successful restaurant there, and from his previous letters, they were doing well. That had changed.

Sam wrote to ask if I could help him and his family emigrate to the U.S. He had grown increasingly concerned about the rise of Adolf Hitler and his Nazi supporters.

There seemed to be few restraints on Hitler's ambition and Jews were among his primary targets. Because Sam was Jewish, the rest of his family was also considered Jewish by the Nazis. He described a growing animosity that was spilling over the German border. There had already been several incidents in Metz that reflected the tensions. Sam was certain that conditions would get much worse before they got better. He also feared that it was only a matter of time before he and his family were targeted. His main concern was for seventeen-year-old Charles. If there were new hostilities between Germany and France, which Sam thought was almost unavoidable, Charles would either be inducted into the French army or taken by the Germans. He also worried that if Germany invaded, it was possible that his family would be seized and interned somewhere.

Since Sam was still a U.S. citizen there was nothing prohibiting him from bringing his family to the States. The problem was finding a ship to get them here. People in Germany and France were fleeing in constantly growing numbers. The result was that ships were booked more than six months ahead of departure. Additionally, authorities in Europe and in the United States had begun to require immigrants to meet ever more stringent qualifications in an effort to keep the immigration numbers down. Sam figured it would take at least a year to leave unless he had a sponsor in the United States. Depending upon the availability of ships, he and his family would go to the front of the line and could be out of France within a couple of months if he had a sponsor. He was writing me to ask if I could be his sponsor.

I had no problem meeting all but one of the requirements of sponsoring Sam and his family. I could provide them with a residence. I could find him a job, and I could provide details of our long-term relationship. The requirement I'd have a hard time with was identifying the ship that Sam would sail on. Sam had already said that without a sponsorship, it would take a year to book passage and I couldn't sponsor him until I knew the ship he was sailing on. The solution was for me to book Sam's passage and that proved difficult.

Sam was right. Available passage from France was almost nonexistent. The earliest openings I could find were more than ten months away, in June of 1939. That was too long to wait, so I looked for another solution. The following Monday after our next weekly meeting, I talked to Eddie about Sam. I told him the circumstance and emphasized that Sam had been a Hat in the Ring mechanic.

"Yeah, I vaguely remember Sam. Kind of heavy set with black, curly hair."

"That was Sam. He and I were partners before I became your mechanic."

"Well Don, I'll see what I can do. I know some people who may be able to help, but I can't guarantee anything." The next day I got a call from Joey in Miami.

"Hey Donnie. Heard you were looking for help getting a friend and his family out of France quickly."

Of course, I didn't have to ask where Joey got his information. I was just surprised that Eddie would work so closely with Joey.

I explained the situation.

"Let me see what I can do. Why don't you come down to Miami and we can figure things out? When's the next time you plan to be down here?"

"I could rework my schedule and come down in two days from now, on Thursday, if that gives you enough time." "Sure, no problem. When you get here, come on over to my office in the main terminal building."

Two days later just before noon, I was sitting in Joey's office.

"I did some asking around and I think I got something that you'll like. There's a ship leaving from Genoa, Italy, the *Cristoforo Colon*, on December 15, that's six weeks from now. It's a two-week trip and ends up here in Miami on December 30. I booked adjoining cabins for your friend and his family. They'll have to take a train from wherever they are in France, but that shouldn't be a problem. I could get something in late January if December is too early, but from what you said, the sooner the better."

"Joey. This is great. I'll wire Sam this afternoon and give him the good news."

"Here's where you can pick the tickets up. I've got a driver who can take you there. Just tell the travel people I sent you and everything should be ready. There's a Western Union office on the way where you can send your telegram. When your friend and his family arrive in Miami, someone will be at the dock to pick them up and then we'll get them up to New York right away. If they need anything else, just let me know."

"You think of everything Joey. I am going to try to be here to meet him but if I can't I'll let you know. Thanks Joey! This is great."

"Hey, no problem. Just wanted you to see that my business associates and I do good things for people no strings attached."

"Got it."

I wired Sam that afternoon on the way back from picking up the tickets. The next morning, I got a return wire saying the arrangements were good. I sent him a certified package with the four tickets and connections.

At the time we made the arrangements, no one could have known how lucky Sam and his family were. Two days after they left Metz, the night of November 10, the vicious assaults that Sam had feared occurred. It was known as Kristallnacht, or "The Night of Broken Glass." Nazi supporters throughout Germany vandalized Jewish homes and businesses and attacked Jews. More than twenty-five thousand men were arrested and sent to concentration camps. It was the first large-scale, overtly violent attack on Jews and set the tone for years to come. Had Sam chosen to take the later ship, he and his family may not have made it out of France. Fortunately, they had left for Genoa just two days earlier and were safe in their hotel, tickets in hand, waiting for passage to the United States at the time of the attacks.

That year, Thanksgiving had special meaning knowing Sam and his family were safe.

Cat and I spent Thanksgiving with Ray's and Pat's families, Angie's parents, and Mary Ann at my parents' house. Cat had already met my parents and Mary Ann, and Ray's family, but this was the first time since she and I had been together that we were with my entire family.

I enjoyed getting updates from my brothers. Both were doing well. Pat, along with two partners, had opened their own law practice in Pittsburgh, and both he and Janet seemed happy. I asked him about his new firm, "The first two or three years are always a challenge when you go out on your own, but Malone, Metzger, and Rowe is holding its own. It's nice being able to pick my own cases rather than have someone plop a file on my desk and tell me it's mine."

He said Janet loved the school where she was teaching.

"Janet says that the school really accommodates their teachers. Her kids, many of them are first or second generation, are very motivated. The parents keep them on task."

I asked about plans for children and he said none were planned in the foreseeable future.

"Her income is still what keeps us out of debt. I pay the mortgage; she puts food on the table."

I knew that Ray was doing well running the stores. Mom updated me regularly. He had saved the Middletown store when it appeared there was no way around closing it, and the Harrisburg store was more profitable than ever.

Mary Ann was now a junior at Cornell. She visited me several times each semester, so I knew what she was up to. She loved New York and was considering graduate school at Columbia. She and Cat got along very well. Often when Mary Ann came to visit, Cat took her "antiquing" or clothes shopping. The three of us occasionally went to Broadway musicals, which was a real treat for her. I teasingly referred to them as "my favorite two girls," to which Mary Ann always shot back "women, your favorite two women."

The one cloud over the gathering was Dad. I hadn't seen him since March, and he had aged noticeably since then. He was as impeccably dressed as ever, but his solid, upright posture had been replaced by a slight stoop. He also clearly didn't have the energy and gusto he once had. I asked Mom about him.

"Part of it is just the aging process, but I think he has never gotten over losing his reelection two years ago."

In 1936, the year FDR won an easy reelection, my father was thumped the way he had always thumped his opponents. It was the first time since the Civil War that Harrisburg would be represented in Congress by a Democrat.

My father took it personally.

"He had considered running again this year, but local Republican leaders convinced him to sit it out. That was another blow to his ego. At the stores, even though he still goes into the Harrisburg store several times a week, Ray runs the show. Your dad still goes down to the Tuesday Club once a week and sees his old friends, but aside from his family, the two most important things in his life have been whittled down and he's having a hard time adjusting."

I felt bad for Dad, but I also felt bad for Mom. She had always known how to sustain his spirit. She was invigorated by his success, and most of her volunteer activities in one way or another supported him. Now she was also drifting through life a bit. I made a mental note to visit more often.

As scheduled, Sam and his family arrived in Miami on December 30. I wasn't able to fly down, but just as promised, Joey had someone meet them. He booked a hotel suite for the four of them and got them on a train bound for New York the next morning. The following evening, January 1, Cat and I picked them up at Grand Central.

Even though Sam had changed during the past twenty years—less hair and more stomach—I spotted him right away.

"Welcome to New York! It's great to see you and Brigitte again. Safe and sound." I hugged them both.

I introduced them to Cat, and they introduced us to their children. Charles was taller than Sam, maybe six feet, with a slender, wiry frame. Rene was the mirror image of Brigitte twenty years ago.

"Don, I can't tell you how glad we are to see you and how much we appreciate all you've done for us. We can never thank you enough!"

"The real hero here is Joey. All I did was ask him what he could do, and he did the rest."

"He seems like a nice guy."

We picked up their luggage, twelve pieces in all, and took two taxis back to my house. Cat and I showed them the house, then we made dinner for them.

"I plan to stay at Cat's until we can find you a place of your own. A friend of mine, Gary, who is the business manager at Eastern, owns a house in Brooklyn that is vacant and there are plenty of houses for sale or rent available. You shouldn't have a problem finding something."

The next few days were especially busy. I tried to keep my work schedule limited so that I could help Sam find a place to live. Cat also pitched in with the search. By the end of the week, Sam and Brigitte had found a house in Garden City on Long Island. Garden City was one of the fastergrowing towns on Long Island. Lots of newly constructed, affordable housing, a growing population of middle- and upper-middle-class families, and a vibrant commercial center. I felt a certain attachment to Garden City because it was near Roosevelt Field where Lindbergh took off on his famous flight. Cat took Sam and Brigitte to an estate sale that Saturday and they found several rooms of furniture.

By Tuesday they were moved in.

Next on Sam's agenda was opening a restaurant.

"Don, I want to get your opinion about something. When we were in Miami, Joey and I talked about what I planned to do here in New York. I told him eventually I wanted to open a restaurant like the one we had in France. He asked me about it and said he might be interested in helping with the financing. He said I should talk it over with you before making any commitments. So, what do you think?"

"Joey has always been good to me. He helped me get a job when I moved here. Since then, he's done little things to make my life easier, and, of course, he's the reason you're here. On the other hand, Joey is a tough guy with some very tough friends. People involved with them don't want to say no to them. They play by their own rules, which sometimes includes really bad things for anyone who they think crosses them, and crossing them doesn't take a lot."

"Yeah, I figured that. We had gangsters in France too, but I always steered clear of them and never had any problems." "Let me talk to Joey before you commit to anything." I called Joey the next day.

"Look, Donnie. Me and my guys invest in lots of legit businesses. Sam seems like a great investment opportunity. He's got years of experience operating a restaurant. We don't want to interfere with anyone who's running a successful business. All I ask is that Sam treats us fair like he would anyone else. I'm sure some of my guys will try Sam's restaurant, and some may even become regulars, but we won't do business there. The most we might do is ask for a special table once in a while. It will be Sam's restaurant. You know, no strings attached."

The next day I told Sam that if there was any way to open his restaurant without Joey's help, he should do it.

"Don, I have two options at this point. I could work in someone else's restaurant for several years or I could open one of my own. Doing option number two will take more money than I have, but I think it is the better choice even with Joey's guys on board."

"I just want you to know what you're getting into."

In the end, Joey became a 25 percent owner. I just hoped that Sam wouldn't regret it.

Le Petit Chateau opened four months later a mile away from Sam's house in Garden City. Sam had found a fourbedroom Cape Cod house that he redesigned into two cozy rooms that could seat two dozen diners and expanded the kitchen to create what he called a "chef's kitchen." Sam and Brigitte did the cooking. Brigitte baked bread and pastries, and Charles and Alysia shared duties as host/hostess and waiter/waitress.

Cat and I were among the first diners in the restaurant.

"Sam, this is great. It looks so warm and comfortable."

Cat added, "I like the French décor."

I had bouillabaisse and Cat had coq au vin.

"Sam, this food is wonderful. Keep it up and you'll have people lined up around the block."

They did, and within a year Le Petit Chateau had become a favorite of Long Islanders as well as New Yorkers in general. I was happy for Sam and his family, but still a bit worried about Joey's connection.

Chapter 14 The Winds of War The world changed in September 1939. Hitler invaded Poland. In response, England and France declared war against Germany. It was the beginning of another world war though most Americans, including myself, didn't know it at the time.

Until Sam and his family moved to the United States, I hadn't paid much attention to what was happening in Europe. I knew that Adolf Hitler had wrestled his way to power in Germany and that he was rebuilding the German military, especially his air force. He called his new air force the Luftwaffe. I had read about the new German planes, particularly the Messerschmitt fighter plane that had first been used two years earlier during the Spanish Civil War. It could travel at over 400 mph, the fastest plane ever built, and had a new wing technology that made it very maneuverable and, apparently, very effective. I wanted to fly one someday.

I was also aware that a nasty autocrat, Benito Mussolini, ran Italy, and after the Spanish Civil War a fascist, Francisco Franco, was in charge in Spain.

Most of what I knew came from newspapers and quotes from Captain Eddie. Along with Lindbergh and a number of congressmen, he was labeled an isolationist. I had heard him complain about FDR's growing interest in both Japan and Europe. He thought the United States should stay out of any foreign adventures. He argued that it was part of a scheme by big business and banks to profit at the expense of American soldiers and workers in general. After Kristallnacht, Eddie's opposition began to ease, but in September 1939, he was still strongly opposed to getting involved in the European war.

My friends were split on what we should do about the German attack. Of course, Sam was vehemently in favor of helping the French and British get rid of Hitler. He worried about the fate of Jews and was sure that Hitler's quest for power would not stop at the Atlantic. Phil agreed with Eddie that we should stay out of the problems. In his opinion, getting involved was part of big business's plan to kill unions. Gary felt that England and France were our closest allies, and we should help them, just not by sending troops. Cat generally agreed with Gary but, because her mother was from Poland and still had relatives there, Cat was upset about the German invasion.

During the next fifteen months, the war in Europe was like a bad tooth that kept getting worse. At first, it was a dull pain, but the longer it went untreated the worse the pain became. We all expected the British and French to yank the abscess quickly, but instead it appeared to be growing ever more ominous. In the year that followed the attack on Poland, France fell to Hitler and the British suffered under a withering bombing campaign from the Luftwaffe. The success of Hitler and Mussolini, after Italy joined the war in June 1940, alarmed a growing number of Americans, including Captain Eddie. That year, Roosevelt ran for an unprecedented third term, and he resisted overt support of the Allies probably in exchange for votes.

Of my friends, only Phil agreed with FDR and remained staunchly opposed to the U.S. becoming involved. Cat and I concluded that the U.S. should assist the Allies in every way short of sending troops.

I was a bit surprised that as conditions in Europe deteriorated, Eastern Air's business continued steadily to grow. Even more quickly than Gary had predicted, the revenues from our new stops brought profits in only a year. The Florida routes were the source of the success. While it went unstated, Joey and his associates were transforming Cuba into their own bonanza. Everyone knew that gambling, prostitution, and drugs attracted certain visitors, but Joey's friends were also building luxurious hotels geared toward traditional visitors. Of course, they were also expanding their illicit activities as well. There were also rumors that Joey's associates were paying off the Cuban government. Some said that the powerful Cuban leader, Fulgencio Batista, was on Joey's boss's payroll. I was happy about the profits, but I didn't like that Eastern had any part in what was happening in Cuba.

While in some ways the months after the German invasion were great for Eastern, they became difficult for my family. Two weeks after the attack, I got a call from Mom. Just the tone of her voice told me that something bad had happened.

"It's your father. This morning he had a stroke. He had just come downstairs and stumbled across the living-room floor, then fell. He was saying something I couldn't understand and trying to get up. I helped him to his chair, then called the doctor. They took him to Harrisburg Hospital. He's in intensive care now. His doctor said it would be a day or two before we know how bad it is, but he's sure some significant damage has been done. I've already talked to Ray and will call Pat as soon as I hang up with you."

"Mom, is there anything I can do? Do you want me to be there? I can be there in three hours."

"No, not now. I'll call you when we know more, probably tomorrow or the next day, and we can make plans then."

When she called two days later, the news wasn't good. Dad had had a massive stroke followed by a smaller one. Mom called it a thrombotic stroke. It was caused by a blockage of a major artery on the left side of his brain, so it affected his entire right side. Mom said that at this point his speech was slurred, the right side of his face had lost most of its movement, and he had limited use of his right hand, arm, and leg. It would take a few more days, maybe a week, to determine the full extent of the stroke, but there was clearly significant, long-term damage done. Mom said that Dad would be in the hospital for at least a week and then would need lots of physical therapy at home.

During the next few days, Ray, Pat, and I phoned each other several times to set up a plan to help Mom take care of Dad. She had already decided to hire a nurse to help during the weekdays, so my brothers and I agreed that we would take turns staying with Mom on the weekends. We also agreed that Mary Ann should finish college before we asked her to do anything. She was set to graduate from Cornell in early June. Of course, Mary Ann rejected our plan. She wanted to be there every weekend, but after some negotiating, my brothers and I got her to agree that she would take a turn every fourth weekend.

"And when I graduate, I'll look for a teaching job here in Harrisburg. That way I can be here as long as Mom needs me."

Which is what she did. She was hired to teach English at the local high school. As much as my brothers and I would have liked her to go right off to graduate school, it eased our minds knowing that after June, Mary Ann would always be there during the hours when the nurse was not.

Dad came home a week later. It was a Wednesday. Cat and I flew over on Saturday for our first weekend visit.

When we got to the house, we talked to Mom for a few minutes, then she took us to see Dad. Mom had fixed up the downstairs bedroom where I had been during my recovery ten years earlier. "He's in pretty bad shape so don't be too alarmed when you see him."

Dad was slumped into the big, cushiony chair in the corner of the bedroom so that he could either look out the window or across the room. He raised his head slightly when we entered. His right eye was frozen half shut, and he couldn't move the right side of his face. His mouth was set in a motionless half-smile. His right arm was tucked close to his body, and his fingers were rigidly curled at the knuckle. We already knew that he couldn't move his right leg.

I walked over and patted him on the shoulder, and he tilted his head up just a bit. Cat and I chattered about our flight and politics and events in our lives, but he never made eye contact and didn't seem to be listening. Instead, he sat with a vacant, blank look staring at the wall behind us. A couple of times he grunted something indiscernible, but when we asked him to repeat it, he didn't. Aside from slightly moving his left arm at one point, he sat motionless. It was sad seeing him in such a weak, helpless condition.

After about half an hour, Mom came back into the room.

She brought a tray with a couple of sandwiches and tea for Cat and me and a bowl of soup, a cup of fruit, several pills, and a glass of juice with a straw for Dad.

"It's Dad's lunchtime. He's still on a very restricted diet."

She pulled a chair over beside him and started feeding him while Cat and I continued to talk. It was clearly a struggle for him to swallow his food. Despite Mom feeding him tiny spoonfuls of soup and fruit, he seemed to gag slightly several times. After he had eaten all that he was going to eat, Mom gave him his medication and asked me to lift him into bed for his nap. Until I picked him up, I didn't realize how much weight he had lost and how frail he had become. It was almost like lifting a child.

Back in the living room, Mom gave us an update on the prospects of his recovery.

"He's scheduled to start physical therapy next week. Someone will come here every day for a while. The doctor said that at best he will always have trouble walking, his arm and hand will have limited usage, and his speech will probably always be a bit impaired, but the therapy will help him minimize his problems. It'll take at least several months before he can take care of himself."

Cat asked, "Will he be able to read or take a walk or even brush his teeth by himself?"

"We're not sure how much he'll get back. At best, he'll need a cane and will have a limited range, maybe around the block. His days at the store or at his clubs are probably over."

I followed up, "What about his ability to think and reason?"

"The doctor hopes that he gets back to 75 or 80 percent. It will be a while before we know what that means exactly. I just hope he'll be able to enjoy being with people and talking to them again, even if it's not at the same level as before. He's always enjoyed socializing. I'd hate for that to be taken away from him."

Cat and I spent the rest of the weekend with Mom. I could see the toll Dad's stroke was already having on her. She had moved a rollaway bed into Dad's room in case he needed her during the night. Unfortunately, she didn't get much sleep as a result. She was also with him during the day whenever he was awake. She washed him, fed him, and helped him change positions to make him comfortable. She read him the newspaper, played records, and tuned the radio to shows that he liked. Several times a day while we were there, Cat and I took her place in Dad's bedroom so that Mom could get a little rest. Otherwise, Dad's needs consumed her almost completely. During the week, the nurse would be helping, but even then, there would be a lot for Mom to do, especially during the evenings after the nurse left.

I told Pat and Ray about the weekend. Ray had already visited our parents, and he simply confirmed what Cat and I had seen. The following week, Pat had a similar experience.

"I'm also worried about Mom. She looks tired and I think she's lost weight. We don't want two parents with strokes." I agreed but none of us had a solution.

"Maybe when Dad starts improving, Mom will be able to rest a little more."

That didn't happen. Dad's recovery went very slowly with minimal improvement. During the first six months, with the physical therapist's help, there was small but noticeable progress. Dad was able to move his right arm, hold a fork, spoon, and toothbrush, and his curled lip flattened a bit. Though he was still unable to speak, he developed his own method of communication using his arm to point and various grunts. He was also able to stand with the help of something to hold onto and he could plop himself into his wheelchair though he couldn't wheel himself. He spent many of his waking hours in the wheelchair looking out over the river or on his favorite living-room chair listening to music. We could tell that he enjoyed having family around him but knew how frustrating being unable to talk with us must have been for him.

Mom continued to show the effects of her new duties helping Dad. She developed a daily routine that included an afternoon nap while Dad was napping, and she adjusted to getting up with him in the middle of every night. Still, she always looked tired and had lost enough weight that her clothes hung more loosely. She also looked as if she had aged about ten years. Had it not been for the nurse and our weekend visits, I'm not sure how Mom would have managed.

Eighteen months after his stroke, Dad died. It was not completely unexpected but was a shock, nevertheless. Mom thought he just decided to give up. During his last months, he seemed simply to withdraw from life. His days were reduced to long naps separated by a couple of hours in his wheelchair watching out the window. He rarely paid attention to anything or anyone around him except Mom. He no longer listened to music on the radio and had no interest in hearing about politics or the stores. He even ignored Mary Ann when she played the piano. He had always loved listening to her play. During those last months, he became a slowly shrinking shell of himself. It was sad to watch a man who had once commanded attention whenever he walked into a room fade away as he did.

One morning in early May, Mom woke up and saw that Dad was having a seizure. She called his doctor immediately but by the time he arrived, Dad was dead. The doctor said that Dad had just not been strong enough to withstand another stroke, even a mild one.

Of course, our concern was now Mom. A few days after the funeral, my brothers, Mary Ann, and I talked to her about the future. She decided, at least for a while, to stay in the Harrisburg house.

"It's been my home for more than twenty years. I'm comfortable here. I know it's much bigger than what I need, but for now, it's where I want to be."

Mary Ann decided that she'd stay too.

"I enjoyed my year teaching. I learned a lot. I still want to go to graduate school, but another year teaching will be good.

Even if Mom moves, I plan to stay with her and spend another year teaching English."

As far as money was concerned, Dad had left Mom enough that she would be comfortable for the rest of her life.

Ray added: "Mom also now has part ownership in the stores. As long as I keep them profitable, she'll have a nice income each year."

It took Mom several months to get past Dad's death, but with Mary Ann's daily attention, weekly visits from Ray, and monthly visits from Pat and me, she regained her smile and her energy. She spent the next two years in the house, then sold it and moved to an exclusive apartment building about a mile closer to the center of Harrisburg. She had three bedrooms on half of the third floor, which was the top floor. Her apartment looked out over the Susquehanna River and, because of the height, it had an even better view than the house.

When Mom moved, Mary Ann, after three years teaching English, decided the time had come for graduate school.

She enrolled at Columbia. Cat and I were happy to have her so close. For a while, she visited at least once a week, but by her first spring in New York, she had a part-time job in a bookstore as well as a couple of challenging courses, so we saw less of her. We also knew that her social life was growing as well.

After Dad's stroke, another concern began to share space in my mind with my concern for my parents. Conditions in Europe were steadily deteriorating. During the summer of 1940, the constant bombing of England and the capitulation of France demonstrated that Hitler was not going to halt his quest for power soon. The addition of Mussolini to his forces after France fell was further alarming. The German invasion of Russia a year later made it clear that Hitler's goal was total domination of Europe. Meanwhile, there were growing rumors about Hitler's work camps for Jews. Of course, Sam was my chief source of rumor information. Almost every time I saw him after France fell, he had new stories about the grim fate of Jewish friends in France and Germany.

Eddie added intensity to my growing fear. After the German assault on Russia, he began unofficially consulting with the army air force a couple of times a month. By mid-1941, he was actively advocating that the United States officially join the Allies. Like many others, he argued that England, France, and Russia would not be able to stop Hitler without our involvement. We were already providing equipment and supplies, but Eddie now wanted our military to once again join the European armies in fighting Germany.

Eddie was also one of the few who warned that Japan was an ever-growing threat in Asia. In 1937, after a decade of tensions, Japan began an aggressive campaign into China. Many leaders in the United States saw no vital interests at stake, so we remained uninvolved for the most part. Bogged down in its war, Japan in early 1940 defied a commercial agreement with the United States. Eight months later, it signed a defensive pact with Germany and Italy. The following summer, Japan began a steady march into southeastern Asia. Most still marginalized the Japanese expansion. Eddie did not.

Through the autumn as hostilities grew in both Europe and Asia, many Americans continued to resolutely oppose military involvement outside our borders. Then the world stopped. On December 7, 1941, Japan launched an attack on American forces at Pearl Harbor. The attack devastated our Pacific fleet and stunned all Americans. The next day, Roosevelt declared war on Japan, three days later Italy joined the war against the United States, and the next day Hitler also declared war against the United States. In response, the United States joined the

Allies, and the world was again at war. For the United States, that meant a war on two fronts.

A few days after the attack on Pearl Harbor, Eddie formally agreed to help the Allied air forces. He announced that he was taking a leave of absence from Eastern Air to assist in the war effort, and he put Gary in charge of Eastern Air. Eddie spent the next month inspecting and assessing both American and British air capabilities. The Monday after he got back from England, he asked me to meet with him in Washington.

"Don, I'll cut right to the core. You know our air forces are in terrible shape. We don't have enough planes and we don't have enough combat pilots. We need to correct those deficiencies immediately if we're going to win in Asia and in Europe. I'd like to know if you'd be willing to help with the rebuilding."

"How can I help?"

"You'd be involved with the training. We need to build new training fields fast and find people who can train pilots. We're going to hire flying school trainers to do the basic training, which is the first phase of training. We've got a handful of military pilots to do the combat training, which is the final phase of training. What we don't have are people to do the advanced training. People who can teach men who know the basics of flying how to become experienced enough to move on to combat training. In a lot of ways, it's what you've been doing with our new Eastern pilots. Each phase of training will take three months. Your job would be both to train as well as oversee the intermediate training."

"Sounds good so far. Would I have to rejoin the Army or could I stay a civilian?"

"Whichever you'd want. If you rejoin, you'll be promoted to captain. If not, you'll be an individual contractor."

"What about pay?"

"If you rejoin, you'll be at the captain's pay grade but also have all the military benefits, including housing. If you stay a civilian, you'll be paid something comparable to what you make now, maybe a little more, but you'll only have a few of the benefits."

"And where would this happen?"

"We're building bases in two places. One is Texas. We already have several training fields there. Kelly is one of them, but there will be more. The other sites will be in California. There aren't many fields there now but they're going up quickly. You could go to either."

"Boy, if they were on the East Coast, I'd say yes right away, but I'll have to talk to Cat about Texas and California.

When would we have to leave?"

"As soon as possible. Talk to Cat. I'll be back in New York early next week. You can give me your decision then. We need to do this fast. And here's a little added incentive. You'll be flying the best combat planes in the world. The best ever built. I've flown a couple of them. They are special. Fast. Extremely maneuverable and unlike anything you've ever flown."

That night, Cat and I talked into the early morning about Captain Eddie's proposal. She agreed that if I went, she'd go with me and I agreed that if she didn't want to go, I'd stay in New York with her. We both liked the idea of California better than Texas. Cat was concerned about leaving the business she had built but was ready to start over in California. We talked about what we'd do with our houses. She didn't want to sell her studio, so we decided if we went, we'd rent it while we were gone. I'd sell my house. Her biggest concern was for her parents and that question didn't have an immediate answer.

"I would be so worried about them. They're getting old and both are slowing down. I don't know what I'd do if something happened to them and I wasn't here."

"Maybe we could take them with us."

Cat wasn't sure they'd want to leave New York but thought it might be a solution.

"We need to talk with them and see what they'd want to do."

I brought up one final issue. "You know, if we go, we should probably get married."

"Is that a proposal? I thought about that too and agree. There are a lot of reasons life would be easier in California if we were married."

The next evening, we talked to her parents and laid out the possibility of them coming with us.

Her father was adamant: "You go. This sounds important. This country has given us so much. We can give a little back. You go. We like having you here, but we don't need you here."

Her mother added: "We'll be fine. We've got lots of friends. We can visit. We won't be lonely. You go help us win the war."

The following morning, I told Eddie that we had decided to go and would like to be in California and that I wanted to stay a civilian.

"That's great, Don. I'll get things moving this afternoon. I'm really happy you're going to be out there. It'll probably take three or four weeks to get all the paperwork done and have everything ready for you. If you'd like, I'll have the Army find you a furnished rental house."

I saw Gary later that day. He already knew that I would be gone for a while.

"I talked to Eddie about it over the weekend. He hoped you'd agree to his offer. I'm glad you did. I've got some ideas about how to replace you here until you get back. We're going to have to scale down operations during the war anyway. I don't know how much but I expect pretty significantly. A handful of our pilots have also signed up to fly for the military. They are just waiting for their assignments. So, don't worry about us, we'll survive, and your job will be waiting for you when the war is over."

Gary was right about cutting back. Gas rationing, rubber rationing, and the use of our planes to transport military personnel and supplies all had a major effect on us. Most air companies lost money during the war, and some went out of business, but despite it all, Gary kept Eastern profitable, even though, except for the Florida routes, we flew less than half as much as we had flown before the war. Only the Florida routes to Cuba continued pretty much as they always had been. I'm sure Joey's contacts had a lot to do with that. It was probably those routes that kept Eastern profitable through the war.

That night, Cat and I had dinner at Sam's restaurant to celebrate our decisions to go to California and to get married. We told Sam and Brigitte about everything. On my way home from the airport, I stopped at a jeweler's and bought an engagement ring for Cat. I asked Sam to serve it to her for dessert. He did something even better. After dinner, he and Brigitte brought Cat and me a bottle of champagne and four glasses with the ring looped by a ribbon around the neck of the bottle.

"Oh, Don, the ring is beautiful, and it fits perfectly. I love it!"

The next two weeks were very busy. I put my house on the market immediately and the real estate agent had prospective buyers scheduled even before we left for California. Cat knew a couple of people who were eager to rent her place, so that was not a problem. We decided to store most of her furniture, and one of the auctioneers she dealt with regularly agreed to sell mine. We both had various accounts to close and packing to do, and, of course, we had a wedding to plan.

Cat's parents were very happy about the wedding. They had been hoping for a long time that we would finally get married. They wanted to have the wedding in their church, and, despite the last-minute arrangements, were able to get it scheduled for the Saturday afternoon before we planned to leave for California, which was perfect. I called everyone in my family to tell them the news. They were all excited, Mom especially. Only Pat and Janet were unable to come.

Aside from Cat's parents and my family, there were only a dozen guests, but because it was a small church, it looked like more. The ceremony was simple and brief. I had no best man and Cat had no maid of honor. Ray was the usher even though there weren't many guests to usher in. Gary and his wife were there, as was Phil. I hadn't seen Phil for about two months, and when I told him about the wedding and our plans, he was surprised. After Pearl Harbor, like many others, he had come around to support the war. He even planned to volunteer to help out on the home front. I had hoped Eddie would be there, but he had flown to England two days earlier. Eddie was a grand advocate of marriage. I knew he was happy that Cat and I were finally getting married. He arranged for a dark-red 1942 Buick Special convertible to be waiting for us when we arrived in Los Angeles. It was our wedding present from him. That evening after the ceremony, Sam closed the restaurant and catered a reception. It was a wonderful day.

On our way to her studio, I said to Cat, "If I'd have known getting married was so much fun, I might have pushed for it a long time ago."

"It was a beautiful day, and I am very happy we finally did it. I like being married to you. It just feels right. I didn't realize how right it would feel, but I do like us officially being two halves of a whole. However, it'll take a while to get used to being a 'Malone,' but I'll adjust."

"Katrina Malone I like it."

On Monday morning, Cat and I climbed onto a train and headed west. We decided to take a little time getting to our new home and relax a bit. Neither one of us had taken a vacation in a couple of years and a little decompression time sounded very good to both of us. It was, after all, our honeymoon.

Cat had never been west of Pittsburgh, so she was especially excited watching the country roll past. We had a sleeper car, but she didn't want to sleep because she was afraid that she might miss something important. We did make two stops along the way. We spent a day sightseeing in Chicago and a day in Denver.

One week after our wedding, we arrived in Los Angeles to our new world and our new life.

Chapter 15

VICTORVILLE

Victorville is a small town about seventy-five miles northeast of Los Angeles. It is at the southern edge of the Mojave Valley and is cut off from Los Angeles by the San Gabriel Mountains immediately to the west. The town was built close to a California Southern Railroad station. It was initially a farm community, but shortly after the turn of the century a major cement factory opened and became the town's primary industry. In 1941, the United States Army established an air training base there and four auxiliary fields in the area surrounding the town. Cat and I lived in Victorville for three years.

We arrived in our new hometown three days after getting to Los Angeles. One of the first things we both noticed was the heat. It was late February, there wasn't a cloud in the sky and the temperature was in the mid-eighties. When we left New York, it was fifty degrees colder with snow on the way.

Cat was the first to comment: "Not bad for the middle of the winter. I think I could get used to this."

It wasn't hard finding our house because there just weren't many streets in Victorville. The house was a recently built ranch-style house with two bedrooms, a living room and dining room, a small kitchen, and a yard full of scrubby grass. The furnishings could best be described as basic. A sofa, two chairs, a dining room table with four chairs, and two bedrooms with double beds and a dresser. Cat was ready to redecorate almost as soon as we stepped inside the house.

"I've got to get something on those walls soon or I'll explode."

It was more than just the walls that exasperated Cat. Though she liked the weather when we arrived, life in Victorville was not easy for her. She had never lived outside New York City and was used to a much faster pace of life. Some people have a hard time dealing with the traffic and noise and the grit of a city. Cat expected it. She expected taxis to be waiting when she needed one. She took for granted the array of New York's shopping experiences we left behind. Department stores, various specialty stores, little corner groceries, and bakeries on almost every block were all part of her normal habitat. Likewise, she missed the various restaurants, movie theaters, art galleries, and musical performances we patronized back East. Victorville had three restaurants, a movie theater, and a tiny, part-time art gallery. She longed for the ethnic diversity of the city. Walking down a street and hearing various languages or smelling ethnic foods cooking and enjoying the many cultural celebrations energized her. In our new home, the diversity was exclusively Mexican, which Cat liked, especially the food, but it could not replace what we had left behind. Even the weather, which was initially inviting, became blistering hot during the summer. From June through September, the temperature always topped ninety degrees and often hit triple digits. Neither one of us was prepared for that. Nevertheless, despite it all, Cat kept a good attitude about everything and made the best of what we had.

"It's my tour of duty. If men and women can go off to fight, I can deal with life in Victorville."

I had instructions to get in touch with the base when I got into town and someone would be out to get me. We got to Victorville on a Friday. I was surprised to discover that our phone was already connected, so I called as soon as we had carried our bags inside. My contact was Major Robert Duffy.

"Hi Don, good to hear from you. I'm eager to get started working together. I've heard a lot of good things about you from 'Hap.'"

"Hap" was General Henry Arnold, the commanding officer of the U.S. Army Air Corps. Arnold had been largely responsible for reorganizing the Army Air Forces to provide it with new autonomy by bringing it under a single command. The change was part of the creation of the Army Air Corps in June 1941. Arnold's grand plan called for an extensive expansion of the air corps' activities. That included a new method of training along with hundreds of new planes and, of course, significantly more men. That's what brought me to Victorville.

"It's Friday afternoon and most things here are winding down for the weekend. I'm sure you and your wife have plenty of unpacking to do, so why don't I pick you up on Monday morning at about 0800."

"Sounds good to me. Do you know where I live?"

"Oh yeah. We have a couple of other civilians who live close to you. On Monday, be ready to fly. I want to take you to our auxiliary bases and show you around."

"I'm looking forward to it. See you Monday."

That weekend, Cat and I went out to explore our new hometown. Almost everything we needed was on a threeblock section of 7th Street. A grocery, a drugstore, a restaurant, even a gas station. It was certainly different from New York, but it would provide the basics. We also prowled around the rugged desert countryside just outside the town.

Its natural beauty was striking but stark.

Major Duffy showed up right on time on Monday morning. The first thing he did was issue me three sets of pants and shirts that I was expected to wear when I was on the base. I changed clothes quickly. Duffy appeared to be close to my age. He told me later that he learned to fly at Kelly Field but joined the Air Service just two weeks before the war ended. He had been flying ever since.

"I hope you're ready for a full day."

"Yes, sir, I am."

The drive to the air base took about twenty minutes, which was enough time for Major Duffy to tell me the basics about how things operated. He was fourth in command. Technically General Arnold was the commanding officer though he was only at the base irregularly.

"You'll like General Arnold. As long as you do your job, he's easy to work with. He's an army lifer. Taught to fly by Orville Wright back in about 1910. Spent most of World War I in Washington doing administrative duties. Worked his way up the chain of command through the Army Air Service and knows as much about air technology as anyone. He's also a great planner. You'll probably get to meet him sometime next week. Colonel Wolfe is second in command though because Hap is gone most of the time. Colonel Wolfe is usually the ranking officer at the base. Then there's Major Cartwright who has a few years seniority over me. He and I share most of the training responsibilities, but he works with bomber pilots a lot and I work with fighter pilots."

I was impressed by the size of the base. It had seven hangars and four runways—three that formed a triangle and one that split the triangle in half. The auxiliary fields at Hawes and Helendale also had four runways. The other two auxiliary fields, Mirage and Grey Butte, had three runways that formed a triangle. Duffy said that the Victorville base covered almost 2,200 acres. The auxiliary fields were a bit smaller and had no hangars.

We spent the morning touring each of the base's hangars.

I paid particular attention to the mechanics.

"How much about the planes' engines do the pilots learn?"

"Just the basics. Not like in the old days when we learned to fly. Had to be a mechanic first. We need to get these guys in the air as quickly as possible. They do the flying and we let the maintenance up to the mechanics. Also, the engines are getting more and more complex." I looked forward to spending some time with the mechanics and getting to know more about the planes.

After lunch, we went flying.

"This is a T-6 Texan. We call it 'the Six.' The other one I like is the Vultee BT-13 Valiant. We call it 'the Valiant.' We have a couple of other trainers, twin-engine Beechcraft and some Piper Cubs, but the Six and the Valiant are the two you'll be flying most of the time."

Both were two-seaters. The Valiant had a slightly faster top speed. The Six had a bit more range. I was eager to fly both, but Major Duffy hopped into the pilot's seat. Even as we lifted into the air and banked tightly west, I could feel the response and maneuverability of our plane.

Our first stop was at Grey Butte, west of Victorville, then we flew in a quarter arc, from nine o'clock to twelve o'clock, northwest to the other three auxiliary bases. The bases were about thirty-five miles apart. All four were used for takeoff and landing training by planes from Victorville. Though none had support buildings during the day, there was usually a small staff on-site to maintain the runways—look for cracks and keep the sagebrush and coyotes off the runways. During the next three years, I would spend many hours with trainees landing and taking off from these runways.

After the last stop, Major Duffy asked if I'd like to fly the Six a bit.

"I'd love to, Major."

"All right but there's one stipulation. You're a civilian so you can call me Rob from now on."

"It's a deal, Rob."

We traded seats and I took the controls. Rob told me to fly east over the Mojave Desert. For the next hour, that's what we did. From twenty thousand feet, the Mojave looked beautiful but desolate and imposing. We flew east to Clark Mountain near the Nevada border, then circled west back home. I would have stayed up longer, but we were running short on fuel.

"Did you enjoy that?"

"Absolutely. A great plane too. It's been a while since I've flown a two-seater. I've gotten used to the DC-3 which doesn't maneuver like this one. This Six is lots of fun."

"Well then, you're going to enjoy the rest of the week. The plan is that you'll work with me doing some combat training. Just four days, but you'll get to see what the bomber and combat trainees need to know by the time they're done with you. Tomorrow you'll be in a Douglas Havoc bomber. It flies like the DC-3, but is a little bigger and has a few attack gadgets. You shouldn't have any problems with the Havoc.

Then the rest of the week, you'll get to fly both the Spitfire and the Mustang fighter planes. I think they are the best combat planes in the world. It was the Spitfire that saved Britain last summer and the Mustang is even a bit better. It has a bigger range and more firepower. Flying those two planes will be something new for you, I'm sure."

"That sounds great. I'm excited! Don't know whether I'll be able to sleep tonight!"

Rob was right. The two planes were unlike anything I had ever flown. Both cruised at about 360 mph and several times I took them over 400. It was exhilarating. They were also unbelievably maneuverable. Banking was tight and quick. Both could climb rapidly. I took the Mustang up to thirty-eight thousand feet, higher than I had ever been. It felt as if the planes knew what I was thinking and responded instantly. I had to practice landing several times before I felt comfortable. Basically, the landing principles were like in other planes, but it all happened much faster. Takeoffs were wonderful. I could get into the sky almost instantly. The only other adjustment was the control panel. A couple of new switches to learn, including a bomb-release on the Mustang, but I had no problem with them.

"Will I be able to fly these guys while I'm training pilots?"

"Oh sure, we want you to take them up for a short flight at least once a week to stay fresh. You can plan a few late afternoon trips for yourself." Flying those two planes was something I looked forward to every week.

In addition to flying, throughout the week Rob and I also went over the specific skills that I would be expected to help advanced trainees learn. Primary training was done by civilian flying schools throughout the region. As a result, trainee cadets came to me with different sets of skills.

My job was to make sure that the advanced trainees met the Army Air Corps flying standards and then help them develop basic combat skills like flying in formation. I would get a new group of between six and ten trainees every three weeks, which meant I had three groups at different stages of training all the time. At the end of their time with me, they would move on to combat training. Some would learn to fly bombers, and some would fly fighter planes. The flight training process was much more involved and thorough than when I learned during World War I. It was still dangerous, but there were far fewer crashes and deaths. From start to finish, trainees spent more than two hundred hours in the air compared to about twenty hours when I learned.

While I was flying around the desert that first week, Cat was trying to figure out how to put herself back in business. It didn't take long for her to conclude that her days of buying and selling furniture were probably over for a while. There were no Long Island estate sales or Upper East Side apartments to redecorate. Instead, there were basic ranch homes furnished like ours by families who neither wanted nor could afford much more.

After our first month in Victorville, Cat began to volunteer at the local history and art museum to fill her time. Within two months, she had worked herself into a part-time position. Four months later, the museum director retired, and Cat was invited to take the position. The job didn't pay much, but Cat enjoyed the work, especially scheduling and preparing the art exhibits. She was able to get several impressive visiting exhibits, including one that featured two Edward Hopper paintings and a George Bellows painting.

She also brought more media attention to the museum, which helped bring new visitors and members. During her two years as director, the museum remained small, but Cat brought it to a new level of importance in the community.

The air corps became one of her regular targets for donations to pay for exhibits. That included one exhibit that became particularly upsetting to her. About a year after she became the director, Colonel Wolfe called Cat and asked if she'd be interested in an exhibit of local Japanese folk art. Because of the war, she was a little nervous about the idea but agreed to look at what it might include. I was surprised when she told me about it.

"It's from a place called Manzanar, about 90 miles from here."

"Manzanar! That's a Japanese detention camp. Are you sure you want to get involved with that?"

The following Saturday we drove up to the camp.

Cat and I were both immediately alarmed by what we saw. The camp was surrounded by a high barbed wire fence with eight guard towers that were manned by armed military police. As we drove in, we counted twenty-four housing barracks. We later were told that there were thirty-six blocks of barracks with fourteen barracks in each block, and each barracks housed about two dozen internees. Built quickly on a dry, barren plateau, there were no paved streets, no trees, or shrubbery, and dust blew everywhere. It looked grim. Aside from the barbed wire and guards, Manzanar reminded me of a bigger version of Fort Kelly when I was there.

Colonel Wolfe had given Cat a contact person who was waiting for us at the entrance gate.

"Hi. I'm Lieutenant Janice Burris. I'm the activities director here. We can walk over to the community building and look at the art our people have made since coming here. If there is anything you'd like for an exhibit, let me know. We have an internee advisory council that will have to approve lending material, but I'm sure they'll be happy to cooperate. In the meantime, I know it was a long drive and if you're hungry, we can also have lunch at the community building."

"That sounds good. Don and I are both very hungry."

"I hope you like Japanese food. We have some great cooks here."

The meal was almost worth the trip by itself. Miso soup, fried rice, and chicken curry. We had both eaten Japanese food in New York, but it wasn't as good as what we got at Manzanar.

After lunch, we spent a couple of hours looking at a collection of art done in the camp. There were several vivid silk paintings of Japanese landscapes, numerous long hanging scrolls, and Japanese calligraphy done with various brushes and inks. Janice called the calligraphy shodo. Cat especially liked the daruma dolls, which were round, hand-painted representations of Japanese faces. There were also numerous woodblock prints called ukiyo-e.

Cat was impressed. "There are some things that are amazing. You have some real artists living here."

"We don't have any trained artists, but I agree the work is incredible. I'm no expert, but some of these pieces are just beautiful. They were all made by internees who were just interested in doing art and they didn't have much to work with. They had to find all their materials here in the camp. Even the silk is from remnants."

The more we inspected the collection, the more excited Cat got about an exhibit.

"I'd love to show many of these things in our Victorville museum. I'm a little worried about how my board will react to showing Japanese art, but I think I can convince them about how exceptional these things are. How does a fourmonth exhibit sound?"

Janice smiled. "Sounds good, but as I said, I'll have to get approval from the advisory council. Let me know specifically which pieces you want, and I'll ask for permission to lend them to you. I really want the world to see how special these things are and how talented some of our people are."

Cat picked out two dozen various pieces.

"I'm really excited about this exhibit," she said. "I'd like to do this as quickly as we can. If everything goes right, how about if we plan to come back up here in four weeks to pick up the pieces?"

That was fine with Janice.

Four weeks later, Cat and I were back on the road to Manzanar. Since our first visit, we had talked a lot about the exhibit but more about Manzanar. Cat read about it in some old newspapers at the museum and was curious to see more of the camp. The newspapers made it sound as if it was a relatively accommodating place for local Japanese to sit out the war. What we had seen was definitely not comfortable. It was opened in March 1942 and was the first of ten similar camps throughout the West. Most Japanese living along the West Coast were relocated to the camps to make sure they wouldn't help Japan.

When we got there, Janice took us to lunch again at the community building. While we were eating, Cat delicately asked if we could get a short tour of the camp after lunch. Janice agreed. "We aren't supposed to show people around so if anyone asks, we'll say you need to get some information from the artists."

After lunch, we walked down along a row of barracks toward the middle of the camp. At one of the buildings, Janice knocked on the door, and a middle-aged Japanese woman opened the door and invited us in.

"This is Mrs. Ichiro. She did a couple of the daruma dolls that you're taking."

We spoke for several minutes. I expected an accent, but she had none. Mrs. Ichiro, her husband, and their three teenage children lived there. They were from Rancho Palos Verde, an upscale, Los Angeles suburb. Mr. Ichiro was a lawyer. They had lived in a comfortable, well-furnished, five-bedroom house.

"The Ichiros were lucky. His law firm put the family's possessions into storage for them. Many of the people here lost almost everything they had when they were brought here. They only had forty-eight hours to do something with their things, and if they couldn't figure anything out, they lost everything."

Like everyone else, the Ichiros now lived in one room and shared their barracks with three other families. Their room had a stove, five cots with straw-filled mattresses, and a light bulb hanging from the ceiling. Several hanging scrolls, a dozen daruma dolls, and two silk paintings were the only things that gave the room any appeal. After we were back outside, Cat asked Janice about the fact that Mrs. Ichiro had no accent.

"Most of the people here were born in the United States and have never been to Japan. Some can't even speak Japanese."

"So, they are native-born American citizens. Actually, they are more American than I am. I was born in Ukraine and didn't get here until I was two."

"Mr. Ichiro is on the advisory council. He also writes for the camp newspaper, *The Manzanar Free Press*."

I asked, "There's a camp newspaper?"

"Yeah, the residents have created a full-service little village here. I mentioned the advisory board, which functions as a village government. The internees have organized a cooperative store that sells the fruits and vegetables grown here. There is a cooperative bank. We have a school and several churches. There are also sports fields, musical performances, numerous recreational programs, and, of course, lots of art. More than half the camp population are children, so their parents have arranged various recreational activities for them."

I asked, "All of this was done by the internees?"

"That's right. They've done it all."

"Wow! On one hand, the living conditions look so grim. Enclosed by barbed wire fences and armed guards. Five people living in one room and four families sharing a building. No privacy. Communal showers and toilets and dust flying around everywhere. On the other hand, it seems like a pleasant little community."

"That's the contradiction of this place. When newspapers report about life in Manzanar, they print nice little stories about the good stuff. The reality is much worse. This is a throwback to early Indian reservations or the concentration camps the Spanish built in Cuba fifty years ago. Part of the reason I wanted to do an art exhibit was to show people how exceptional the internees are, and, possibly, give a few of them a chance to get outside the camp for a while."

Cat agreed. "We can help you with that. I'll put together an opening event that will include the artists. It'll be a couple of days outside Manzanar."

On the way home and for the next week, Cat and I talked about life in Manzanar a lot. We concluded that it was almost inhumane what was being done to the people there. They were prisoners. The only reason life was tolerable was because the prisoners had not rebelled but instead organized and created a community themselves. We both vowed to help the prisoners as much as we could though there wasn't a lot we could do. Fortunately, by the time of the exhibit in late 1944, camp life had begun to improve. Limited time outside the camp was allowed, and the restrictions within the camp had eased.

The Manzanar exhibit went well. The art was impressive, and Cat did a good job displaying it. She also had Janice take pictures of the artists amid their living quarters. It was a subtle way to show the dreadful conditions at Manzanar. As she had promised, Cat also had the local media there as well as reporters from Los Angeles, San Jose, and San Francisco. The reviews were great but the stories about the artists were even better. They were described as talented, kind, and loyal Americans. A couple of the stories even described some of the actual living conditions at Manzanar.

For two years after the exhibit, Cat stayed in touch with Janice. Both were happy in late 1945 when the camp was closed. I was not surprised to find out that General Arnold was also glad when the camp was closed. He had implied to Cat several times that he hadn't supported the creation of Manzanar, but neither Cat nor I realized how much he opposed the internment camp idea altogether.

I met General Hap Arnold two weeks after Cat and I arrived in Victorville. Rob was right when he said that I would enjoy working with Hap. We met every two or three weeks to talk about the cadets I was training. I was impressed by how knowledgeable he was about every aspect of the training process and how concerned he was about the cadets' well-being. It was obvious that he had a clear vision for the air corps. In many ways, he reminded me of Captain Eddie. I wasn't surprised to learn that the two of them were close friends and that Hap consulted with Eddie regularly.

The first time I saw Captain Eddie after Cat and I moved to Victorville was in the middle of October 1942. During the early months of the war, he had been busy traveling to Europe and throughout the United State assessing the air corps on behalf of General Arnold. His visit to Victorville was to meet with Hap for two days about a new mission to the Pacific islands that Eddie had agreed to tackle. The night before he left, he invited Cat and me to have dinner with him, his aide, Hans Adamson, and Hap in the officers dining hall. Of course, we agreed. We hadn't seen Eddie since we were married and were eager to catch up with him a bit as well as thank him again for the car that he had given us for our wedding present.

True to his habits, Eddie bounced into the dining room precisely at seven as was planned. A few minutes later Hap joined us.

"It's nice to see you two again. It's been a while. I've heard some good things about the work you're doing with the cadets, Donnie."

"I'm enjoying it and enjoying working with General Arnold."

"Yeah, Hap is a good boss, he's smart, and he knows his business."

During dinner, Eddie, Hap, and Eddie's aide talked a bit about the mission that Eddie and Hans were about to begin.

Eddie had agreed to tour the air corps bases in Hawaii and the Pacific and report suggestions to Hap about how the bases could be improved. We had just begun to recover from the Pearl Harbor attack, and Hap wanted Eddie to assess what needed to be done. It seemed like a straightforward job, but from the way he and Hap were talking I suspected that there was something more on Eddie's agenda. Eddie and Hans flew off to Hawaii the next morning. A week later, the world found out more about Eddie's mission. He had agreed to orally deliver a top-secret message to Douglas MacArthur, who seven months earlier had escaped the Japanese invasion of the Philippines and was in Australia already plotting his return. The plan was for a Flying Fortress bomber carrying Rickenbacker and his team to refuel on Canton Island, which is about midway between Hawaii and Australia. That was the plan, but unfortunately, because of faulty navigational equipment, the plane flew off course, ran out of fuel, and crashed into the Pacific.

News of Rickenbacker's disappearance was flashed around the world. Like many, I was shocked when I heard that Captain

Eddie had vanished somewhere in the middle of the Pacific, but I was confident that he would survive. Just six months earlier, he had survived a terrible crash outside Atlanta, and I was certain that he would prevail once again. However, during the following weeks, my confidence ebbed almost daily. I was just about ready to give up hope when, after three weeks of searching, the military called off the official hunt. Then amazingly, twenty-four days after the crash, he and eight of the nine on board the plane were found drifting about five hundred miles west of Canton Island. All were badly dehydrated, malnourished, suffering from exposure, and were at the brink of death, but they had somehow survived the ordeal. Later, they all attributed their survival to Captain Eddie, who himself was too weak to walk and had lost more than 60 pounds by the time of his rescue.

Several weeks later, Eddie delivered his message to MacArthur, completing his mission.

I saw Captain Eddie again briefly about a year after his brush with death. He had come to Victorville for the day to meet with Hap. We only had a few minutes together, but even in that time it seemed to me that Eddie had changed. He was a bit distant and not as focused or decisive as he had always been. Rather than talking about the course of the war or the air corps, he talked about his post-war plans at Eastern Air and the possibility of selling his shares in the company and starting something new. He wasn't sure what that might be, but he seemed to be looking for a new challenge. I mentioned entering politics, which he rejected immediately.

"People like me OK now, but if I were elected to something, they'd change that tune quickly."

As bad as it was, Eddie's crash wasn't the worst moment during my time in Victorville. Even though I enjoyed training cadets more than I thought I would, there was a trap. It was very easy to become attached to them. After the first year and several fatal training crashes, I learned not to get too close to trainees. It was harder separating myself from the two dozen or so pilots I had trained who died in combat. Each one left a scar. I often thought back to my experiences during World War I and the deaths I had seen there. This was a different kind of sorrow. In Europe, I was surrounded by the war. In Victorville, the war, in many ways, was a concept rather than a reality. I was detached from the fighting. During my war, there was so much carnage that I became somewhat numb to it. Even when it included men I knew well. In this war, it was as if each lost pilot I trained had flown off into a void and vanished, never to be seen again. There was no carnage, just a permanent absence. As I did after my war, I wondered about those exceptional men and the many unfulfilled gifts and talents my pilots took with them. I accepted that this was a war that had to be fought, and in war there are casualties, but that didn't soothe the sting I felt when brave comrades were lost.

Cat and I left Victorville in mid-October 1945, two months after V-J Day. We had made some good friends in the town and at the base, and we were encouraged to stay. Hap even offered me a position, but Cat and I never considered making California our permanent home. We were Easterners. We had enjoyed the West and getting to know Los Angeles. We especially liked our two trips to San Francisco. It was a city with many of the things we had left behind in New York, but it didn't have Broadway, the Metropolitan Museum, Central Park, or major league baseball. I missed going to Athletics and Dodgers games. I even missed the Yankees.

Of course, most of all, we missed our families. We hadn't seen our families since we left New York. Cat talked to her parents almost every week, but after three years that wasn't enough. She wanted to see them again. I was also eager to see my family, especially Mom and Mary Ann. As with Cat's parents, Mom was getting old, and there was always a dull fear that I might never see her again. Mary Ann had earned a master's degree at Columbia and was working for a publishing house in New York City. She was also seriously involved with a physician in the city. The rest of my family was convinced that marriage was in her near future. I wanted to meet him before he became my brother-in-law.

So, two months after the war ended, Cat and I packed up the car and headed east.

Chapter 16

RETURN TO NEW YORK

After the war, I was happy to return to my old job at Eastern Airlines. Gary had done a great job guiding the company during the war. While government subsidies enabled competitors to survive by a thread, Eastern Air took no subsidies but instead continued to earn profits on its own. Throughout the war, the company also maintained most of its routes. The Cuban routes remained as popular and as profitable as ever, while the other routes held their own. The company also contracted with the military to carry men and materiel. By any standard, Eastern Airlines remained a solid enterprise.

During the last months of the war, I had been in touch with Gary about once a week. He had plans to further expand the company beyond Cuba in the Caribbean, as well as to Mexico and Canada. Gary claimed that the changes would make Eastern Airlines the largest air company in the country. The expansion would also include reordering the company's administration a bit, and he assured me that my return would fit nicely into those plans.

Cat and I got back from California in early December.

We had planned to move back into Cat's loft in Greenwich Village, but instead Gary offered to temporarily rent us one of his houses in Brooklyn so we could look for a new house.

He also gave us some time to look for something.

"This Christmas season has been pretty busy for us and I'm sure you two could use a little time to get your feet back on the ground. Let's wait until after the new year for you to start back at Eastern."

Cat and I were glad to have the extra time. We went house hunting immediately. She wanted to be in Manhattan, which was fine with me. We both liked being close to the restaurants and entertainment in the midtown area even though it meant a little longer commute for me. Within a week, we found a cute little two-story, three-bedroom townhouse on Nineteenth Street near Gramercy Park. It had a living room, dining room, and a large kitchen on the first floor. The three bedrooms were on the second floor. We spent the next two weeks moving things that Cat had in storage into our new house and visiting Cat's old haunts to find additional furnishings. My prize was a big rolltop desk that had dozens of little drawers and shelves. Cat found several lamps, some things for the walls, and a settee for our bedroom. By the time I started back at Eastern, we were comfortably settled in.

Cat and I also used our time to catch up with our families. Cat's parents were at the top of the list. The day after we got back, we spent the afternoon and evening with them. Both were healthy and neither had lost a step since we left. They had lots of questions about our plans and were happy when we told them we had no plans to leave the city. Three weeks later, they became the first visitors to our townhouse.

We spent Christmas with my entire family at my mother's apartment in Harrisburg. I was especially curious about Mary Ann's boyfriend. A couple of days before we met him, Mary Ann called and made it clear that I was to skip the "big brother" interrogation, Pat and Ray had already done that. I promised to be on my best behavior.

"And remember, he's David, not Dave."

With a little help from Cat, I was able to live up to my promise. "Don and Cat, this is David Whiteford. Dr. David Whitefield, so if you ever need a doctor in the city, he's the guy to call."

David was a little taller than me, had broad shoulders, and looked fit. He was two years older than Mary Ann and said he had played baseball and basketball at Columbia. Now he regularly played squash at a club in New York.

"I've never played squash but hear it's a good game."

"If you're ever interested, let me know and I can take you to the club. Mary Ann said you played baseball at one time so you should pick squash up quickly. I think it's a great game. Mary Ann also told me to warn you that I'm a big Yankees fan."

"I'll keep that in mind. For over twenty years, I have had a very good friend who is as big a Yankees fan as there is. I think I can tolerate another one."

We talked about California and training fighter pilots.

He said he had some experience with injured pilots in Europe.

"I spent the first year of the war at an evacuation hospital in England and have been working with convalescing vets at Presbyterian Hospital two afternoons a week since I got back. Didn't see many pilots in England but there are some at Presbyterian."

When I had a minute alone with Mary Ann, I told her that David had passed the "big brother" test with flying colors. Both Cat and I liked him and looked forward to getting together in the city sometime soon. She was pleased.

Pat and Ray, as usual, seemed happy. Pat's law firm was slowly gaining clients.

Janet chimed in, "They're establishing a reputation for working hard for their clients."

"That's because we like most of our clients. It's easier to work for people when you like them. It's one of the benefits of being able to choose who we represent and the cases we work on."

Janet still enjoyed teaching in Pittsburgh as much as ever. She was also involved in an after-school program sponsored by U.S. Steel for children whose parents worked in the mills. After talking to her for a while, it became clear that she and Pat had decided not to have children and were content with the decision. What I found out later from Mom was that Janet had several miscarriages in the past two years and didn't want to go through that again.

Both Ray and Angie were doing well. They had enrolled Timmy into a private school, the Harrisburg Academy, which surprised me. "There is a direct path from the Academy to the Ivy League. Angie and I would really like Timmy to go to an Ivy League school."

I was still a little surprised. I expected Ray to send Timmy to Dickinson. Something that didn't surprise me was that with Ray in charge, the stores were doing well. I also found out that Ray had begun investing in the stock market.

"So far, I've made more than I've spent. With the economy roaring back as it did during the war, there were lots of investment opportunities out there. I even bought a little stock in Eastern Air."

"I guess that means I am sort of working for you."

"Nah, you're working for a little bit of my money. Just keep Eastern in the black. I am a little concerned about this post-war economy. There's always an economic adjustment after wars, and this was the biggest war ever fought. I expect some strange times ahead."

"I am sure you'll get it figured out. You always do."

Talking to Mom later, I found out that Ray had been investing some of her money in the market since Dad's stroke.

"He and I talked about it. He laid it all out for me and it sounded good, so we started small and now he's handling everything. He's done very well for both of us. With Ray managing my finances, I won't ever have to worry about money again even if we have another depression."

I was relieved to hear that. Even though she was over seventy years old, it seemed that Mom had a lot more years ahead of her. She was healthy and full of energy. She'd become involved in several civic organizations including the local art association. "They've asked me to be vice president next year." She had also become a movie buff. She and several friends went to a movie and dinner almost every Thursday night. When I asked her about the apartment, she made it clear that she was happy where she was.

"I love this apartment. It's all me in here. While your father was alive, I usually did what would please him. Now I can please myself. I picked out all the furniture and it is where I want it. The pictures on the walls are mine. I've got some paintings by local artists. Even the rugs are what I like. Don't get me wrong, I miss your father every day, but it is easier just satisfying myself." It was a good Christmas.

I started back at Eastern Air on Wednesday, January 2, 1946. My first stop was Gary's office.

"It's good to have you back Don. We've all missed you."

"I'm glad to be back. California was nice but this is where I belong."

"As I told you, we're planning to make several major changes. Most importantly, I want to expand Eastern into Mexico and Canada. There are a couple of wrinkles that need to be ironed out, but I expect to make the moves within the next year or so. When that happens, we're going to split your old position in two. You'll still be the general operations manager, but we'll split much of the work between a northern operations manager and a southern operations manager. You can take whichever spot you want, and, as I said, you'll have seniority regardless. Until then, you'll have an assistant. We've got a new guy doing your old job. Do you remember Ken O'Leary?"

"Yeah, I trained him just before I left. We used to call him K.O."

"Yup, that's the guy. He left about a year after you did. Joined the Army Air Corps and was shot down somewhere over Germany during the last months of the war. A sad story. We hired Ben Bennet to replace him. You'll meet Bennie later. He'll be your assistant until we go to Canada and Mexico. I've talked to him about splitting the job and he's fine with either the northern or southern job. I suspect you'll want to stay in the north."

"Yeah. Cat really missed her parents, and after three years in the Mojave Desert, we're both looking forward to green lawns, trees that change colors in the fall, and a little snow in the winter. I'll miss trips to Miami and seeing Joey every now and then, but I'm a northern guy."

"Well, you'll probably see Joey more than you think. He's back in New York. Rumor has it that he has moved up in the underworld. I don't know the specifics and don't want to know, but I've heard he is working with the unions here in the city."

After about an hour, Bennie joined us in Gary's office. He was ten years younger than me, a little shorter, and slim with long arms. He reminded me of a scaled-down version of Lindbergh. Bennie learned to fly when he was a teenager. He graduated from the University of Massachusetts, worked as a pilot, and then as a flight manager for a small company in Texas. When the company went out of business, he came to work for us in Florida and then became our operations manager after K.O. left. Bennie had missed out on the war because he was the sole support for his wife, three children, and mother-in-law.

For the rest of the day, Bennie and I figured out the best way to split up the work. We agreed that for the next couple of months we would alternate weeks working the northern and southern routes. I volunteered to take an office in the main Eastern hangar so that Bennie could stay in my old office in the terminal building until he moved south.

Gary chuckled, "You'll be close to your Haviland. It's been out there waiting for you since you left."

"Yeah, I'm looking forward to taking it up. I'll also be close to the mechanics. Maybe they'll let me get my hands dirty once in a while."

A couple of days later, I did take my Haviland up for a ride. Before the war, I considered it one of the best little planes built. That changed after the war. I still enjoyed flying it, and every now and then, once the weather got warm, Cat and I flew somewhere for a weekend, but after flying fighter planes, the Haviland seemed slow with limited maneuverability. There were times that I longed to be back in one of the Spitfires at Victorville.

From Bennie I found out that the biggest wrinkle in Gary's expansion plans was Captain Eddie. He didn't want to go international and didn't want to add bigger planes to our fleet. The war had encouraged production of a new generation of commercial planes. Now, the ones we were flying, DC-6s, carried fewer passengers and were slower than the new planes our competitors were flying. Gary and most of the board of directors wanted to upgrade, but Eddie, who was still the CEO and chairman of the board, insisted that our existing fleet was adequate for the routes we flew. As for expansion, Eddie argued that rather than compete with airlines that were going international, Eastern should further strengthen its dominance east of the Mississippi. Bennie claimed that the debate was becoming increasingly nasty.

The disagreement lasted far longer than anyone expected. We didn't begin upgrading the fleet for four years and the expansion into Canada and Mexico took another two years. During that time, Eastern remained the most profitable airline company in the country, which temporarily strengthened Eddie's position. However, once the profits began to slide in the mid-1950s, so too did Eddie's control of the company. By the end of the decade, he had agreed to step down as CEO. Several years later, he also resigned as chairman of the board and retired to Florida.

Throughout the first five of those years, Bennie remained my assistant for southern routes. Fortunately, we worked well together. Bennie was a team player interested in getting a job done. He was also very thorough and focused on details. He finally got his well-earned promotion in 1951 as we began to expand into Mexico and the Caribbean.

Among the people that Cat and I looked forward to seeing upon our return to New York were Sam and Brigitte. About a week after getting back in the city, we decided to surprise them with a visit to Le Petite Chateau. It was almost eight on a Wednesday night when we arrived at the restaurant. We expected it to be a slow time on a slow night of the week. We were wrong. The place was packed. As we waited in the foyer for a table, Brigitte saw us and rushed over with warm hugs for both of us.

"It's so good to see you. Sam and I have missed you two! Let me tell Sam you're here."

Two minutes later, Sam and Brigitte were sitting with us at a secluded table in the back of the restaurant. We spent the next couple of hours catching up. Cat and I told them about our adventures in California.

"It sounds as if you guys did pretty well out there except for Manzanar." Brigitte said.

Sam added, " After all we're hearing and seeing about the German concentration camps, it's especially disheartening to hear about our internment camps." Of course, we all agreed.

Brigitte and Sam had plenty of news for us as well. Most importantly, a year earlier they had become grandparents. Rene, who was twenty-six, married a local contractor a year after Cat and I moved, and now had a son, William George, six months before our return. Brigitte pulled several pictures out of her purse. "Billy's a real handful. Keeps Rene and Mike going from sunrise to well past sunset."

I groaned, "It's hard to believe my friends are now becoming grandparents. I think I just aged about twenty years."

"There was an adjustment period for us too. Brigitte made the transition quickly, but I'm still getting used to it."

Sam brought us up to date on their son. Charles graduated from Rutgers just before the war ended. Since he had French citizenship, he was ineligible for the draft, but, much to his parents' chagrin, he volunteered for the Army.

"He finished basic training last April and was all set to go to Europe, but after V-E Day he was reassigned to Japan. Just before he was to be shipped out, they dropped the bombs. Now he's part of the occupation force. In his letters, he's said that the Japanese people have been much more friendly than he expected. He's scheduled to be there until next October."

I asked Sam about the restaurant and he said business was booming. Even before the war ended, business had been good, but after it ended, almost every night he had a full house.

"There's been a lot of development out on Long Island. New houses going up all the time. It's amazing how quickly they go up. Dozens go on the market every day and they are very affordable. Men coming home from the war have a little money saved up. They quickly get married to the girl who has been waiting for them and head out to Long Island to buy a starter house. Rene's husband is one of the developers out there."

Sam said some investors had encouraged him to open a restaurant closer to the construction, but he decided against it, at least for the time being. I asked if Joey was one of those investors. He said he was, and that's part of the reason Sam said no. I asked if he saw much of Joey and his friends.

"Yeah, Joey's here regularly. In fact, I thought he might be here tonight. He usually comes in late so you might still see him."

I had mixed emotions about that. I liked Joey, but before we got too friendly, I wanted to know what he was doing now that he was back in New York.

We spent almost three hours with Sam and Brigitte. It was great talking with them and catching up with their kids, and now their grandchild. Cat and I were happy that things were going so well for them. We promised to stop back soon.

"Next time, we'll make a reservation."

The next time was two days before Christmas. This time Joey walked in about half an hour after we sat down. As soon as he saw us, he came over and gave us all big hugs and patted me on the back. We invited him to join the four of us. "Thanks for the offer, but I have people I'm waiting for. I can sit with you until they get here though. Sam said you guys were back in town. Figured I'd bump into you at some point. You two look great."

Joey knew I was back at Eastern but asked what Cat had planned.

"I'm going to try to get back to decorating houses."

"That's great. There's a lot of money moving to the city all the time. I've got a bunch of friends who could use your expertise. I'll put in a good word for you."

He did, and within a couple of weeks Cat was busy decorating for several of Joey's friends.

When I asked Joey what brought him back to New York, he said that he was here to help some business associates with several projects. He didn't provide any specifics about the projects or the associates, but he did mention meeting with some unnamed congressmen and other officials. Even though I was very curious to hear more, I knew that if Joey wasn't providing details, it was probably better for me not to ask about them.

The other person I wanted to see once we were back in New York was Phil. As with Sam, Phil and I occasionally wrote each other while I was in California. I knew that he was still working for the subway authority and had become president of his local union. In his last letter, he had also mentioned that he was seeing a woman he had met through his union activities. I was eager to find out more about that. I called Phil a couple of days after Cat and I got back. We agreed to get together for lunch the following week on a day when Cat was visiting her parents. It was really good to see him again. We had been friends now for almost thirty years, and even though we hadn't seen each other for several years, I felt a bond with him unlike I felt with anyone aside from Cat and my family We met at a diner near the Brooklyn Bridge. As always, I got there first. Because it was midafternoon, there were plenty of booths available. I sat in the back of the room and stood up when I saw him walk in. When he got to the booth, he reached out his hand, shook mine, then wrapped me in one of his big bear hugs.

"Hey Don, it's great to have you back!"

"The feeling is mutual, Phil."

Though he had added a few pounds and lost a little hair, Phil was still as commanding a figure as ever. For the following two hours, we got caught up with each other. I knew his mother had died two years earlier and that he had moved back home so he could take care of his father.

"I had to find him a retirement home. He has dementia, it's gotten bad. About a year ago he started wandering around and getting lost. That wasn't too bad, but one day last April he almost set the house on fire a couple of times. I was at work, and he decided to make a grilled cheese sandwich. He greased the pan, put bread and cheese in the pan, and turned on the stove, then went out for a walk. A neighbor saw the smoke and called the fire department. Two weeks later, he did it again, so I figured the time had come to find him more help than I can provide. He's been at a retirement home in Queens since the middle of May and seems to like it there. I go over and see him a couple of times a week."

I was sorry to hear about his father but was eager to find out about Phil's girlfriend.

"So, tell me about this woman you mentioned in your last letter."

"Her name is Sarah. We've known each other for about six years. After she graduated from NYU, she went to work for a union organizer. That was back in '36. She wrote pamphlets, made posters, and eventually ran a union office. She even gave a couple of speeches about the benefits my people would get by joining the subway workers union. I met her one day when she came to talk to some guys who were considering joining. We started going out shortly after you left for California. Things grew and now she's living with me at the house."

"Wow! That's great! My only question is she a Yankees fan?"

"That's part of the reason we decided to go out together. She's a big Yankees fan. Back when the Yanks won the Series in '42, I discovered she's a fan, and we went from there."

"Yeah, that makes sense. I couldn't see you with a Dodgers fan or a Giants fan. Except for the Yankees thing, she sounds great. I'm eager to meet her. If you want, I'll talk to Cat, and we can find a time to get together."

Talk about Sarah led us into talk about Phil's union work. He told me that during the war, most organized labor groups agreed to forego reforms as part of the war effort. For all New York transit workers, salaries fell, working conditions deteriorated significantly, and the work weeks got longer. The understanding was that improvements would be made after the war. To fairly negotiate those improvements, Phil's local group had joined other subway locals and formed a citywide organization. Phil was elected its first vice president. Now they were debating whether to join busing workers, ferry boat workers, taxi drivers, and railroad workers in the United Transit Workers Union of New York. Some members were also proposing that the transit workers should join one of the national unions and become part of either the Congress of Industrial Organizations or the American Federation of Labor.

"It's complicated. Of course, the government from Truman on down wants us to continue working as we did during the war, but that's not going to happen. Lots of local unions are merging into larger, more powerful organizations. Some local labor leaders are becoming more and more strident and want their members to join the CIO, which advocates confrontation. Others want to merge into the A.F. of L., which takes a more cooperative, moderate stance. Meanwhile, the Mafia has already started to bully its way into union leadership. The International Longshoremen's Association, for instance, is all but run by the Mafia. Here in New York, several gangs are fighting with each other for dominance, and when they fight, people die. Some have targeted union people who get in the way. It's really messy."

"So, where do you stand?"

"I don't like my guys losing their ability to solve our own problems. On one hand, if it's got enough members, a national labor organization would have the power to go toe to toe with anyone. I'm just not sure how much influence locals would have if that happened. I don't want to have to go on strike because plumbers in Albuquerque must work on Saturdays. Then there's the Mafia factor. I think it'd be easier for gangsters to take control of a national union. As I said, it's a dilemma. The one thing I'm sure of is that if things don't improve soon, there are going to be a whole lot of strikes all over the place. My guys are ready to walk right now."

"It sounds messy and possibly a little dangerous."

Phil was right about the labor problems. Within six months, there were thousands of shutdowns across the country. Eventually, more than four million went on strike. Everything from small, specialized locals, like film crew workers, to big, coast-to-coast unions, including the United Auto Workers and the United Steel Workers. Phil's "tubers," as they were called, were just one of many to strike in New York City. They went out in late May and with the assistance of other locals, shut down the subway system for three weeks. In the end, they won a small pay increase.

Phil was happy about the raise, but he worried about the rapidly growing tensions between labor and government and the shrinking opportunity for negotiations. Locals became evermore reliant upon a handful of increasingly powerful labor organizations. The growing polarization caught Americans in the middle and forced them to pick a side. As the strikes continued, popular support for unions began to fade. Critics of labor effectively warned about higher consumer prices and a "creeping socialism" that threatened traditional American life.

Several weeks after my lunch with Phil, Cat and I had dinner at Sam's with him and Sarah. Visually, they were a sharp contrast. She was just a little over five feet tall, thin, with thick, curly, reddish-brown hair. She also looked young enough to still be a college student even though she was in her midthirties. Phil towered over her. His broad shoulders and solid girth made him look twice her size. She wore a fashionable pale-blue dress with a floral print, and Phil came in his usual brown corduroy sportscoat, a rumpled white shirt, and no tie.

Cat and I were both impressed with Sarah. She was smart and opinionated, and it was clear that she was Phil's intellectual equal. She also shared Phil's philosophy of life and his liberal political attitudes, as well as his passion for the Yankees. They teased me several times about the plight of my Athletics compared to their Yankees success. Like Cat, she was a native New Yorker, though her family was at the other end of the socioeconomic scale. While in her teens, she began questioning her parents' staunchly probusiness political views and their lavish lifestyle. In some ways, her parents reminded me of my father. After her second year at NYU, she refused any more help from her parents, found a part-time job, moved to a walkup in Brooklyn, and paid for college on her own.

Midway through our dinner, the waiter brought us a bottle of wine. I thought it was from Sam, but the waiter nodded toward three men at a table halfway across the room. Phil gave them half a smile and a little wave. When Sarah saw who it was, she turned her back to them and frowned.

In a somewhat hushed voice Phil said: "I'm pretty sure those three are mob guys. Every couple of weeks, one or two of them comes by the office. They're trying to push our union to join a consolidated labor organization they run. So far, they haven't done anything aside from talking to our members and making promises, but they all have reputations. I'm sure they now run the taxi drivers union."

Sarah added: "I've bumped into all three at several locals throughout the city. I know the one guy threatened one of the officers in the carpenters union and I've seen another one a couple of times at the garment workers headquarters." Cat said: "Sounds as if you two may be in a little danger."

Phil chuckled. "No, we're not worried about it. At this point, they want to avoid any physical stuff, and we're just little fish in a big sea of organized labor in the city. There are lots of more important people for them to harass than us. Let's just ignore them and enjoy our dinner."

Despite Phil's assurances, Cat and I left the restaurant a bit concerned. Cat fretted: "Those three guys looked a little scary. Do you think Phil was as unconcerned about them as he seemed?"

"Phil's a pretty cool character. He knows what he's doing and he's not a big risk-taker. He told me organized labor in the city is messy, and it looks like he is right."

During the coming months, I would begin to find out how messy.

Chapter 17

AFTER THE WAR

By the time Phil's tubers went on strike, labor tensions had begun to shake the Eastern Airlines world. In fact, in some ways the Eastern problems were a spinoff from Phil's problems. During the early spring, our pilots asked for various improvements in their working conditions as well as a pay raise. Our mechanics were next to push for changes, and our flight attendants announced that they also wanted improvements. All three groups threatened to form their own unions and join the transportation workers' strikes in New York, which included Phil's subway workers.

The Eastern workers quickly discovered that they were talking to the wrong guy. Captain Eddie had for a long time been a fierce opponent of unions. He called them a communist threat to America.

"We can't let these people run the company. This isn't one of Stalin's collectives. If they want to go on strike, let them. We can find replacements. There are plenty of army pilots and mechanics looking for jobs now that the war is over, and it'd be easy to find new stewardesses. Maybe we don't even need them."

The tensions put me in a difficult position. Since my job included managing the pilots and mechanics, I was the one responsible for ensuring that they conformed to company policies. Never had that been a problem like this one. Occasionally, I had to prod a mechanic to be more careful with his tools or keep his work area cleaner, and periodically I reminded pilots about not having a drink fewer than twelve hours before a flight, but there had never been any major issues. That changed once the strikes began.

For the most part, I agreed with Phil that the American labor force deserved improved working conditions and better pay now that the war was over. I also empathized with the Eastern workers. These were the people I spent most of my time with every day. They had families, mortgages, and car payments like everyone else. While the cost of everything was climbing, they were still earning what they had before the war and working longer hours. It seemed only just that they should get a little compensation for what they had done during the war.

As relations soured, I talked to Gary about the company stand. I knew that he was bound even more tightly to company decisions than I was, but I was curious how he felt about an impending strike. He avoided taking sides.

Instead, his primary concern was about the possibility of Eddie's threat to use strikebreakers.

"Nothing good will happen if we have a strike. The company can't just shut down because people refuse to work, and the use of strikebreakers would be bad for everyone. There's a reason they call them 'scabs,' and it's not because everything is healed when they leave. Strikes like this can tear apart labor and management, which is never good. A little extra pay and a slightly shorter workweek seem worth the expense to me. Also, the thought of our workforce unionizing is very troubling. If that happens, we'll have to go through the union for everything instead of talking directly to our employees. And multiply that a couple of times if our people become part of a national union. No, in my opinion, we need to take care of this in-house regardless of who wins and who loses."

I agreed with Gary that a strike would be bad for Eastern Air. Even though I tried to be a mediator, I felt pressure from both sides. Any challenge to company policy or overt defense of our workers was met with a sharp rebuke from Eddie, and, to a lesser extent, from Gary. Trying to reconcile the workers was even more difficult. They were angry and getting angrier at management and suspicious of me. And rightfully so. Aside from cautiously defending their demands, there was little I could do.

Fortunately, amid the tubers strike, Gary had his way. The entire workforce at Eastern got small pay raises with an implied promise that more might come later. Also, pilots' and co-pilots' workweeks shrank by the equivalent of one flight per week. Meanwhile, mechanics' and flight attendants' workweeks remained unchanged. While subtle signs of the tensions remained, I thought the changes had eased relations between labor and management.

I was wrong. The problems had just begun.

About a month later, I was in my office in the hangar shortly after everyone had clocked out and I heard some chatter outside. I went to the window and saw a man about my age standing on a small platform addressing the company's mechanics. He looked like one of them, but I knew he was not. He was encouraging them to form a union. As I listened, I noticed that not far behind the semicircle of mechanics was another man in a suit watching. I was almost certain he was one of the men who had sent Sam a bottle of wine that night several months earlier when Cat and I met Sarah.

"The time has come for you to organize yourselves. This company is making profits everyday as a result of your work.

The stockholders are making money, I guarantee you that CEO Rickenbacker is making more money, and all his executives are making more money. You are the only ones not making more money. You're the ones providing the sweat and muscle that make this company successful and put cash in their pockets. You deserve more for your work. More money, better conditions, and shorter hours, and you're never going to get any of that without help. Organizing a union is the only way you'll get what you've earned.

Until then, nothing's going to improve for you here." The next day I told Gary about what I'd seen.

"Doesn't surprise me. I got a letter last week from someone asking permission to talk to our workers sometime after work. I said no, but I'm not surprised those guys showed up anyway."

I knew Gary would tell Eddie, and Eddie would inform the board, and there would be problems. This time, I was right. By the beginning of the following week, notices had been sent to all Eastern employees and lots of posters had been put up around the hangar informing everyone that Eastern was a nonunion shop and intended to stay that way. I suspected that the company notices were about the best sales pitches the union guys could hope for. I was right again.

Within a month, the mechanics were organizing. No one said anything, but the men began to avoid me, and conversations often stopped when I walked past. I had previously eaten lunch with the mechanics whenever I could, but that also stopped, and at one point, I overheard four of them talking about a planning meeting immediately after work. Twice, I saw the guy who had first spoken to the men standing outside the hangar waiting for several of the mechanics.

My suspicions were fully confirmed in early November.

Gary got a letter from one of the mechanics, John Weld, who said he was president of the Airplane Mechanics Local 553. He asked to meet with Gary. They met a few days later. Weld said that he represented about half of our mechanics throughout the company from Boston to Miami. They wanted to cut their workday from nine hours to eight hours and get a dollar-an-hour pay raise. If the requests weren't met, Weld implied that the mechanics might go on strike.

Gary took the request to Eddie and Eddie exploded.

"Threatening a strike during our busiest season, that's blackmail and they know it."

The next six months were ugly but became especially ugly after Memorial Day when an Eastern flight headed from Newark to Miami crashed into a swampy, thickly wooded area near Port Deposit, Maryland, just south of the Pennsylvania border. It happened at dusk about an hour after takeoff on a perfect day for flying. All fifty-three on board died in what was at the time the deadliest airplane crash in American history. Several witnesses claimed that the plane simply fell from the sky. A few said that they saw the tail break into pieces just before the crash. Horrific on-site newspaper descriptions of the victims distressed everyone who read them.

In the extensive Civil Aeronautics Board investigation that followed, no conclusive cause was determined. Investigators initially theorized that something had happened to the tail. Maybe a couple of bolts or pins had broken and a piece of the tail had come loose, or perhaps mechanisms that controlled the tail had failed. After an extensive search of tail-related debris and numerous tests, no flaws were found. Likewise, the engines and propellers appeared to have been functioning properly. The investigators even considered that the plane had run into a flock of birds, but there was no evidence for that.

Investigators then considered human error. I knew the pilot and co-pilot and immediately rejected pilot error. Bill Coney was the pilot. He had flown for the Navy during the war and had thousands of hours flying time. We had talked a few times and I considered him one of the best, if not the best, pilots flying for Eastern. His co-pilot was Kenny Willington who also flew during the war and had extensive experience in a DC-3 like the one that crashed. I didn't know him as well as Coney but had absolutely no doubts about his flying skills.

In the end, the case went unsolved, though some union opponents speculated that the plane had been sabotaged by a rogue mechanic. There was absolutely no evidence to support the claim, but some people stuck to it, nevertheless.

The crash added intensity to the tensions with our pilots and mechanics. John Weld, the union representative, argued that pilots and mechanics were being overworked. Coney and Willington, who were both based in Miami, had flown to New York just hours before and were attempting a return. The long workday quite possibly led to a fatal error. If it wasn't the pilots, Weld proposed that perhaps a mechanic had forgotten to tighten critical bolts or had overlooked an essential connection. He contended that like pilots, the mechanics' long workdays were bound to result in mistakes, and perhaps the Memorial Day crash was the product of one.

Despite the crash and Weld's fiery rhetoric, the strike didn't happen. However, management's relations with the mechanics and the pilots continued to deteriorate steadily. A thick wall between the two sides developed, and, of course, I was on the management side. With a few exceptions, the little interaction I had had with the mechanics and pilots became purely work-related. We no longer talked about families or sports or anything outside the hangar. I had also enjoyed talking about flying with the pilots whenever I could. That also ended. It became so uncomfortable that I considered moving my office to the terminal. Eventually, relations improved slightly, but they were never completely restored.

The strike threat ended in late June soon after Congress passed the Taft-Hartley Act. For the labor movement, the bill was a disaster. Among other restrictions, the new law made what were called "sympathy strikes" illegal. Sympathy strikes occurred when one union, often a local with nothing at stake, joined another union already on strike. For organized labor, sympathy strikes were powerful weapons. The bill also seriously cut into union recruiting.

While Eddie and the Eastern Air board as well as many Americans applauded the bill, union leaders called it the "slave labor act."

Phil was particularly incensed by the new law.

"That thing is going to kill organized labor. Do you know that it requires me to sign an affidavit stating I'm not a member of the Communist Party?"

"Yeah, I saw that."

"If local shops want anything done, they are going to have to join nationals and you watch, the mob will take over national leadership instantly. They are already taking over locals. Once they get their claws deep enough into the local leadership, it's just a matter of time before they run it all. Another thing, those mob guys are working with politicians to keep labor quiet and to keep their people in power. Mayors and congressmen dish out sweetheart contracts to mob-run national unions in return for promises of reelection and obedient workers. Ten years from now, organized labor is going to be run by the mob."

At the time, I thought Phil's prediction was a little farfetched, but within a year, events seemed to prove him at least partially right.

In early 1948, Phil was elected president of the United Transit Workers Union of New York. Immediately, people from the A.F. of L. began to hound him about bringing his union under the A.F. of L. umbrella, something Phil had staunchly opposed for years.

"There are two of them. One wears a suit, and one looks like a freshly washed dockworker. They come by separately, but both carry the same message. The suit talks about how our members will benefit by joining. He talks about health benefits and pay raises and how collectively we can negotiate better with big business. The other guy claims we're in a battle for our own survival. We need to stand up to management and we can't do it alone. He says if we all don't unite now, we're going to lose everything we've gotten since the dark days of Carnegie and Rockefeller. The bottom line for both is the same: join or suffer."

Cat got a different story from Sarah. One summer night when Phil and I went to a Dodgers game, Cat and Sarah met for dinner. During their conversation, Cat asked Sarah how she liked Phil being president of the union.

"It's a lot of work for Phil. He's out a lot talking to locals, but he enjoys that part of it. What I don't like is the pressure people outside the union put on him."

"Don told me about Phil's two regular visitors who are trying to get his union to join the A.F. of L."

"If that were all of it, I wouldn't be too worried but there's more to it. Phil regularly gets mail and phone calls at home. Someone at work even left a note on his windshield. I know he gets more stuff, but he doesn't say much. It's a little scary to me."

"I'd be nervous too."

"We're both sure that the mob is involved, and with all the gangland stuff going on in the city right now, I'm afraid Phil might be in danger. He says that he's just a little guy in a little job that isn't especially important to the mob, but that's not the way I see it. The United Transit Workers of New York City employs a lot of people and is crucially important to the city. If I were a mob guy, Phil's union would be at the top of my list."

Two years later when he ran for reelection, the pressure on Phil grew significantly.

"We're still getting letters and calls, but since he said he'd run again we've been getting packages delivered to the house almost every week. Usually there's something nice inside—oranges or apples—but there are always notes telling Phil to get the transit worker to join one of the national unions. Phil is getting notes and calls and little gifts at work that he gives away to the people he works with. Every now and then, I've also noticed a car with two men slowing way down when they pass our house. It's as if they're scouting our house for something. I think they're the ones who keep putting notes in our mailbox. Phil says not to worry, but I do."

I asked Phil about it. He claimed that he was more worried about losing the election than he was about his own safety.

"The mob has taken over some of the transit workers locals. Those are the guys who I'm running against. I'm a civilian. They don't want to hurt me. They just want me to lose the election."

"What about all those gangland hits?"

"The ones you read about are messages to their own guys. They've got less messy ways to deal with people like me. What they're doing now is infiltrating the union and stirring up opposition to me. I'd bet that the guy running against me, Michael Chavis, is already on their payroll in one way or another.

I'm sure they are helping to pay for his campaign and maybe sending him a little pocket money on the side or maybe even a mistress. They'll also probably get a couple of their political friends and a newspaper or two to say nasty things about me, but they definitely don't want to hurt me. That would be a big PR mistake for them."

A week later, I bumped into Joey at the airport. He was on his way to Miami. We talked for a few minutes, then I asked him:

"You know my friend Phil?"

"The union guy? Phil Avillo, I know who he is."

"Yeah. He's running for reelection as president of his union."

"The New York City transit workers."

"I'm worried about how some of your associates might treat him. I don't want him to get hurt. He says he's not worried, but I'm not convinced."

"So, you want me to tell you he'll be all right. OK he'll be all right. My friends don't want to hurt people like him.

He's a civilian. He doesn't owe them anything and hasn't done anything to them. He just has something they want. They've got lots of tools, they don't need the heavy stuff to get it. When you read in the papers about some of the ugly things they do, it's meant to be a message to their own guys. If they don't want to send a message, they'll just fit someone with cement shoes, and no one will ever see that person again, but that only happens to people who owe my friends something. You don't need to worry about your friend ending up like that."

I felt a bit reassured but still worried.

As Phil had predicted, the attacks moved into the newspapers but not in the way he expected. During the final two months of the campaign, Sarah became a prime target for the media. Several newspapers reported that she was a communist, and, therefore, Phil should not be able to hold office in the union. Aside from a couple of local guys, the most notable accuser was Walter Winchell who mentioned her several times on his radio program and in his newspaper column. He lumped her into a group of communist fellow travelers who he claimed were working to undermine American democracy and capitalism. After Winchell's report, media attention on Phil became intense. Reporters didn't write much about the union election. Instead, they probed the communist connection. During the last month of the campaign, Phil spent almost as much time defending Sarah as he did talking about the election.

"It's not Winchell or the papers. In this case, they're just shilling for the mob, and they probably don't even know it. The papers print what they hear, and Winchell is trying to get on the red hunt train that Nixon's running in Congress, and now there's this McCarthy guy who sees communist plots everywhere. They take a shred of evidence and blow it up into a secret conspiracy controlled by Stalin. And they do it by picking on people like Sarah who can't fight back."

There was a bit of truth that Sarah once had a connection to the American Communist Party.

"Back in the mid-1930s when I was working for the CIO, there was a bunch of card-carrying communists working there, including one of my bosses. I went to some of their meetings but never joined. Of course, that was before the war when the Soviet Union was our friend. I still see a few of those people occasionally, but we definitely aren't 'comrades,' and I doubt if they're even party members anymore."

Phil added: "Lots of New Dealers experimented with communism. Remember that Catholic priest Father Coughlin who accused FDR of taking orders from Stalin? Now with the way the House Un-American Activities Committee in Washington works, almost anyone could be labeled as a communist sympathizer. It's guilt by association."

The opposition tactics were effective. As the election approached, Phil realized that he was probably losing, and he was right. He lost by almost 10 percent of the vote. The newspaper attacks on Sarah certainly had some impact, but it was his opposition to joining the A. F. of L. that sealed his defeat.

"Chavis did a good job convincing my guys that they should go national. He had a lot more money than I did and a big team of supporters who helped him spend it. I couldn't come close to matching the ads and dinners and rallies he put together. Of course, the papers and the attacks on me and Sarah hurt, but I lost because my members were sold what I consider a bag of dishonest promises that has lots of strings attached. I wanted to win but I'm not upset about losing. I'll go back to being my local's representative, so I'll still be involved, but it's pretty clear that lots of members in other locals liked what Chavis was selling better than they liked what I was saying. Actually, I'm looking forward to having more time for myself."

Sarah chimed in: "I am too. It'll be good to spend more time together. Maybe we can at last go on a nice vacation."

Five years later, Phil had another chance to lead his union, but he passed on it. Michael Chavis, who was still the Transit Workers' president, was indicted for embezzlement and corruption. In a plea bargain, he agreed to testify against the others involved, but before he could get on the witness stand, he disappeared.

Phil spent another seven years working for the Transit Authority. During six of those years, he was president of his local, but never again sought a higher position in the union. His father died in 1954, which cut an important connection

Phil had to the city. Three years later, he and Sarah moved to Rockport, Maine.

"We'll miss you and Cat, but we're both ready to try something new and are tired of the city. I have a nice pension and things cost a whole lot less up in Maine than they do here, so we figure we can live just as comfortably up there as we do here. We both want to be in a small town near the ocean, and we don't want to go south. We also like the winter. Maine seems like a good landing spot for us even though it is full of Red Sox fans."

Cat and I visited them shortly after they moved, but we missed going to ballgames, and restaurants and movies and just being with them.

Amid Phil's union adventures, my family enjoyed a major event. In June 1948, Mary Ann married David. Mom had wanted it in Harrisburg, but Mary Ann insisted on a New York City wedding. Even by New York standards, it was a gala event. The wedding was held at the First Presbyterian Church of New York City where Mary Ann, David, and David's parents were members. The church takes up the entire block from Eleventh to Twelfth Street along Fifth Avenue and is one of the oldest churches in the city. Cat and I had walked by the church many times. Cat had been inside several times over the years.

"I bought some tables and chairs there, and once I got two pews they wanted to sell. It's a beautiful building with all the classic Gothic revival features: thick-cut stone walls, a tall spire and a tower, a high vaulted ceiling with arched wooden beams, lots of tall stained-glass windows, and a marble floor. It's not the biggest church in the city, but I think it's as attractive as any."

After the wedding rehearsal, David's parents hosted a lavish dinner for the wedding party in one of the church's reception rooms. Cat was one of Mary Ann's four attendants, and I was one of four ushers as were Pat and Ray.

The next day was not ideal for a wedding. It was hot and humid with periodic showers, but otherwise all went as planned. Almost four hundred guests watched Mary Ann and David take their vows. Mary Ann was a beautiful bride. She wore a gown that was a combination of satin and lace with a long train. She looked stunning. David matched her elegance. After the ceremony, several newspaper photographers, camped out under a light rain, clicked off shots as Mary Ann and David hustled out of the church and into an awaiting car. The next day, the pictures were part of a full description of the wedding in the *Tribune*.

Mom reserved the Starlight Roof on the eighteenth floor of the Waldorf Astoria for Mary Ann's reception. I was worried about the cost, but Ray assured me Mom could afford it.

"Mom really wanted to do this, and she's got the money."

"But a full meal for 250 guests, plus alcohol and the room rental. It's got to cost more than $50,000."

"Yeah, it'll be very expensive, but as I said, Mom has the money and wanted to do this for her only daughter."

Pat later reassured me that thanks to Ray's wise investing, Mom could pay for the reception with no problem.

"Have you checked the money you've made from the investments Ray has made for you?"

"No. Cat does all our financial stuff. She's a lot better at budgets and paying bills than I am. I figure if things aren't going well with Ray's investments, she'll tell me. Otherwise, I don't pay attention to that stuff."

"Well, you might ask her at some point. Ray's really good with investments. He's made Janet and me a ton of money."

I was happy to hear that and promised to put Pat's suggestion onto my mental to-do list but never got around to doing it.

David's parents gave the newlyweds an incredible threeweek honeymoon in Europe—one week in London, a week in Paris, and a week in Rome. When she heard about it, Cat reminded me that on our honeymoon we took a train to Victorville, California.

"That's what you get when your new father-in-law is an internationally known neurosurgeon."

The day after the wedding, Mom, my brothers and their wives, and Cat and I had lunch at Sam's restaurant. Pat and Ray had not gotten to the city until Friday afternoon and Mom was busy all week helping Mary Ann and arranging the reception, so we hadn't had much time to catch up with each other.

Sam closed off one of the dinner areas for us, and we talked until everyone had to leave to catch their rides home—Pat and Janet on an Eastern flight, and Ray, Angie, and Mom on the train. I was glad everything was going well for my brothers. Ray and the stores were as busy as ever. While they were intentionally keeping their firm small, Pat said he and his partners had a steady stream of clients.

"We're not going to get rich, but we're paying the mortgage and enjoying our work."

I was especially interested to know how things were going for Mom. Though she was clearly slowing down, I knew she was healthy, and I was curious about her life in Harrisburg.

"Donnie, I have lots of things to keep me busy, especially the Art Association, and I have some good friends who I go to the movies or dinner with at least twice a week. At home, I have a person, Margaret, come in three times a week to help with the cleaning, and sometimes she stays for dinner, which I enjoy. I've been thinking about asking if she'd like to be my full-time housekeeper. She doesn't have any family in the area, and I've got plenty of room if she'd want to move in. So, you see, I am doing very well."

Before everyone hustled home, we all promised to meet in Harrisburg for Christmas and we did.

Chapter 18

PUTTING IT ALL BEHIND ME

Two years after getting married, Mary Ann and David had a son, Paul. They asked Cat and me to be his godparents, which was an honor for both of us. After their wedding, the four of us saw each other regularly. Though David had a grueling schedule at the hospital, we often found a time to have dinner together and sometimes we'd go to a show or jazz club. Additionally, we spent some time together at David's parents' cottage on Cape Cod.

I also came to enjoy playing squash with David. We played at his club every Thursday evening. I wasn't very good, but he was patient, and after six months or so I could give him a good workout though I rarely won. He was also a mild baseball fan who, with Phil's help, I converted into a full-time fan. Turned out he was a Dodgers supporter.

"I like the Dodgers' rooters almost as much as I like the team. They are a fun bunch of spectators. There are some real whackos and of course, the Dodgers have a few of their own free spirits."

By the time Paul was born, a real friendship had developed among the four of us.

A year later, David called and asked me to have lunch with him so that we could talk. I was nervous about what he wanted to talk about. In all the time I had known him, we had only ever had lunch together once and that was to talk about the wedding.

"You know this Korean War is a mess. It's supposed to be a United Nations thing, but we are sending about 90 percent of the men. Among the problems is that there are way too few medical people. So, I'm considering volunteering for a year's service. That's why I wanted to get together. I want to know what you think about it."

The Korean War started in late June 1950 when the communist government in North Korea invaded South Korea in an attempt to reunite the two Koreas. As North Korea rapidly pushed south, the United Nations quickly came to the aid of South Korea. The U.N. forces were led by American General Douglas MacArthur and most U.N. troops were Americans. I told David that I had mixed emotions. On one hand, I admired anyone who volunteered to serve in the United States military, especially in times of war. On the other hand, David wasn't just anyone. Most importantly, he had my sister and godson to think about. Also, war changes people regardless of whether they are on the front line or patching up the wounded in a field hospital. I was concerned about how combat might affect David.

"Mary Ann and I have talked about how we would adjust. As far as money goes, there won't be a problem. We've got savings that will take care of the basics for the year I'd be away. Also, the publishing house where Mary Ann worked before having Paul wants her back. They've agreed that she can read manuscripts and do a lot of editing from home. She would probably do that even if I don't go to Korea. So, the money part is not a problem."

"What about the risk factor?"

"I'd be working behind the lines with little chance of being hurt. There was probably more chance of me getting hurt during World War II when I was working at a military hospital in England while the Germans were dropping bombs."

"You know that a lot of unplanned things happen in a war. It's dangerous wherever you are, and war can take a heavy toll on you mentally for a long time. I have friends who I served with during World War I who are still fighting demons."

"Yeah, I am treating some vets at the hospital and have seen how the war has tormented them. Who knows how it would affect me? The good thing is that I am aware of the mental traps and will be on the lookout for them."

"When would this all happen?"

"If I decide to volunteer, I'll be going to a four-week basic training program in a month and then off to Korea a week later in early April."

"Sounds as if you're going to go."

"Yeah, I think so. Mary Ann and I have talked about it a lot and I wanted to talk to you and my parents before making any commitment."

"You know, Cat and I will do whatever we can to help Mary Ann and Paul while you're away."

"Thanks. My parents have said the same thing. In fact, they want to hire a housekeeper for Mary Ann. I'm sure they'll do all they can."

David shipped out during the second week of April 1951 on the same day that Truman recalled General MacArthur. During his first two months in Korea, he was stationed in Seoul, but in June he was reassigned to a base closer to the 38th parallel where there was intense fighting. Initially, he wrote Mary Ann weekly, but after he was reassigned, his letters came less regularly. While they never talked about specific battles or the danger he might be in, we suspected from news reports that he was close to the heart of the war.

The following May, a little more than one year after he left, David returned from Korea. He looked a bit thinner but healthy and eager to return to civilian life. After a gala welcome home celebration his parents held, Cat and I didn't see him until a couple of weeks later when we had dinner with David and Mary Ann at Sam's restaurant. I was eager to hear details about David's experiences in Korea, but he gave me only general information and avoided specifics. Instead, he pushed the conversation to family and work and plans for the future. As we were leaving, David asked if I'd like to resume our squash matches. We set a time the following week.

We played almost every week for several months, then one day in late October as I walked in, he stopped me and led me to a park across the street.

"Don, do you mind if we don't play this afternoon? I thought we could talk a little bit instead."

"Sure. What's on your mind?"

"I don't know whether you've noticed it or not, but I'm having some problems readjusting to civilian life. Mary Ann thought maybe you could help me figure some things out."

"I'll do what I can."

"The problem is that I just can't seem to put Korea behind me. I have nightmares about the fighting. There are times I'll hear a car backfire or a loud noise and flash back to the artillery blasts and gunfire. I've even seen people on the street who remind me of men I treated, some who died and others who are still there. It's all left me edgy, irritable, and angry."

"Have you talked a professional about any of this?"

"No, I've been worried about how it would affect my practice and how people at the hospital would react if they found out.

You know that expression 'doctor, heal thyself.' Well, a lot of my colleagues think that since we fix other people's problems, we should be able to solve our own."

"How about the Veterans Bureau? They have people trained to help."

"Yeah, I know. I am one of them."

"The thing that helped me most to understand my World War I memories was talking to Phil. Maybe that'll work for you. So, tell me about your experiences in Korea."

"Yeah, that's the reason I wanted to see you today. I need to talk to someone who knows what war is like."

"OK, I'm here to listen."

"The first two months in Seoul weren't too bad. It was the standard hospital kind of stuff, but the ten months at the front were hell from day one. I don't know how much you know about the fighting and conditions over there because not all of it is being reported. A lot of the men are living in cold, wet, muddy trenches with rats everywhere. I was lucky. The triage people have thick canvas tents and stoves and hot showers, and we were beyond the reach of the howitzers, but we could certainly hear them and sometimes we'd hear machine gun fire around the clock."

"Sounds like World War I."

"Yeah, you're right. It's terrible. The worst part, of course, was the carnage. I got to the 38th parallel about three weeks before some of the bloodiest battles of the war, including Bloody Ridge and Heartbreak Hill. They were terrible! So many casualties. So many deaths. Sometimes I felt better for the ones who died than I did for the ones who would have to live with their injuries. It was a nightmare almost every day. There were many days that we worked eighteen or twenty hours trying to save men, got a couple of hours sleep, and then did it again.

There was still fighting every day when I left, but neither side was gaining much ground.

Our guys were just locked into their trenches blasting away." "Boy, that sounds like WWI!"

David went on to describe the people he worked with and the ways they seemed to deal with everything.

"Some of the medical staff handled their own suffering with liquor. There were even times when guys were close to drunk while they were operating. Other guys used drugs, especially marijuana, and there was a lot of wartime sex going on. Anything to ease the pain. Somehow, I managed to avoid those traps, but it all just added more misery to the full experience. It was almost surreal. And believe it or not, I felt guilty leaving. Like I was walking out on my buddies and the men who needed me."

"How does it come back to you? In a dream or a flashback or something else?"

"A lot of the time in a dream. I feel sorry for Mary Ann sometimes because she must endure it too. There are other times I'll hear some loud noise or see something or someone that looks familiar, and it triggers the fragment of a memory that quickly grows into a full-fledged flashback.

When that happens, I just try to find a private spot where I can be alone, but that's not always possible."

"How's all this affect you at work?"

"At the hospital, I often feel like I'm walking on eggs. There are so many triggers—people, sounds, experiences.

I try to anticipate things, but it doesn't always work. Now when a patient moans about petty things like noise in the hall or short visiting hours, or scratchy sheets, I often get angry. So far, I haven't barked back but I've come close. It's just a matter of time."

"And what about at home?"

"Mary Ann has been great. She talks me through things sometimes, and other times she just lets me disappear. Paul's the one I really worry about. I often don't have patience with him, so I limit my time with him. I know I'm missing things, but I don't want to be angry with him."

"David, anytime you want to talk, just let me know, but my advice is to work things out with someone trained in these things. I've seen lots of guys with problems worse than yours who were able to tame their demons with professional help. I've also seen guys who haven't gotten professional help and are still trying to figure things out. If you're worried about the ramifications of seeing someone here, maybe you could find someone near your parents or in Harrisburg. I can even give you a name or two of people in Harrisburg."

"That's a good idea. My parents are too close, but your mom would be great. We could do a weekend visit every few weeks. I like that idea. Thanks, Don, you've been a big help.

Next time we get together we can go back to playing squash."

David followed my advice and made an appointment with a Veterans Bureau counselor in Harrisburg who I recommended. He and Mary Ann began making trips to Harrisburg once every two weeks. Sometimes they took Paul with them. Sometimes they left him with David's parents. Occasionally, I flew the four of us to Harrisburg, and Cat and I visited with Mom and Ray when he was available.

The routine seemed to work well. David confided in me that his counselor was helping with the ghosts, and he felt better at work and at home. He clearly enjoyed the regular trips to Harrisburg.

"The more Mary Ann and I are there, the more we look forward to the next trip, and your mom is always so happy to see us."

About a year later, David and Mary Ann invited Cat and me to dinner at their house. I suspected they wanted to tell us something. Cat agreed. "I'll bet they're going to have another child."

Cat was partially right. Almost as soon as we arrived Mary Ann went straight to the news.

"First, we're expecting an addition next June. We had planned to have another child when David got back from Korea. Now we're both ready for it."

Cat was especially excited. "That's such great news. We are so happy for you."

"Thanks, but that's only part of the news. David and I have decided to move to Harrisburg. David's been offered a nice position at the Harrisburg Hospital, and I've decided to stay at home for a while and take care of the kids. I'm sure I could get a teaching position somewhere in the area if I wanted one, but for now I don't want one. Another reason to move is that we think Harrisburg will be good for Paul and his new brother or sister. They will have more space to play and to grow. Our place here in the city is too small for a family of four. Also, the Harrisburg Academy is a great school, and the kids could get everything they have here in the city. And then there's Mom. I don't know whether you've noticed, but Mom is slowing down and sometimes gets confused about things."

Cat and I had both noticed and were a little concerned.

David picked up the conversation. "We're worried that she is somewhere in the early stages of dementia. I've done some casual interactive tests and she fits the diagnosis. I'm not sure how rapidly it is progressing, but it is getting worse."

Mary Ann added, "If we're in Harrisburg, we can keep a close eye on her and help her with things."

David, Mary Ann, and Paul moved to Harrisburg in April 1954. They bought a charming four-bedroom house looking out on the Italian Lake in the northern part of the city. Paul was four by then, and Mary Ann immediately enrolled him in a Harrisburg Academy nursery class, which started in the fall.

Three months after the move, Jeannie was born. Mary Ann was especially happy about adding a girl to the family nest. Two years later, another child, Ellen, was also added to the family.

After Mary Ann and David moved to Harrisburg, Cat and I visited about once a month. We were happy about the move for several reasons. First, David was doing well both at the hospital and with his psychological battles. Several times he told me that the flashbacks were coming less often and were not as severe. Mary Ann spent a lot of time with Mom. Of course, seeing Mom was always a part of our visits. We usually spent at least a day and occasionally the weekend with her. She clearly enjoyed our company. I also enjoyed playing with Paul. It was almost like reliving a part of my childhood. He especially liked playing catch and having me pitch to him in his backyard. A few years later we started going to the local Little League field up the block and stepped up our ball playing. I also taught him how to play chess.

The one disturbing part of our visits was watching Mom drift further into dementia. Mary Ann was especially upset, but she was glad that she was close enough to see Mom every day. Even with a nurse during the day, the task became ever more taxing for Mary Ann, so about two years after Mary Ann and David moved to Harrisburg, Mom's nurse was hired as a live-in.

In January 1958, I got a call from Mary Ann. I could tell immediately from the somber tone of her voice that it was not good news. Through tears, she told me that Mom had died sometime during the previous night. The nurse had checked on her shortly before nine and Mom had said good night to her. The next morning Mom missed her regular breakfast time, but the nurse thought that she was just sleeping late. When the nurse finally went in to check on her, she found Mom peacefully curled up under her blankets.

Mom's death was a dark cloud that hung over me, but what followed was even darker. Not long after Mom's funeral, Cat began to have stomach pains. She wrote them off as part of growing older, but as they became more severe, she saw her doctor. The report was troubling. The doctor sent Cat for X-rays and a second round of tests. The diagnosis was pelvic cancer. After the second exam, Cat and I were ready for some bad news, but pelvic cancer was beyond what we were prepared for. The diagnosis began a long journey for us.

Shortly after we got the report, Cat was scheduled for surgery to remove several small growths and to determine the extent of her cancer. The surgery went well, and the doctor was optimistic. After the surgery Cat felt better, and we resumed our normal lives, though Cat cut back a bit on her decorating activities. For almost a year, she felt fine. Then early the next year, she began having pains again and scheduled another appointment with her doctor. This time the results were less reassuring. It appeared that the cancer had returned and begun to spread. It required yet another surgery followed by ten weeks of chemotherapy. The treatments, there were twelve of them, were tough on Cat. Though it had been around for fifty years, the use of chemotherapy to treat cancer patients was relatively new and unpredictable, and the side effects could vary significantly from person to person. During the treatments, Cat had no appetite; she was always tired, developed sores on her thighs, and by the third treatment she had lost her hair. We bought several wigs, and she joked about it— "I always wanted to be a blond"—but she became very depressed by it all.

Once the treatments were over, Cat steadily regained her strength and energy and her hair. For the next six months, she had two follow-up appointments each month, then one a month for the six months that followed. Finally, after a year, she was considered cancer-free.

After Cat's health problems were dealt with, we began to do things that we had either ignored or had been putting off for years. We both took more time off from our work to do things together. Cat became very selective about the projects she worked on and then only one at a time. I cut my workweek to four days and delegated responsibilities to others, something I wouldn't have considered before Cat got sick. We made several weeklong trips, including one to Southern California to reconnect with some friends from our years in Victorville. We spent more time in Harrisburg and visited my brothers regularly. We visited Phil and Sarah several times in Maine, and a couple of times they visited us. Cat regularly invited her friends for dinner at our Chelsey townhouse, and sometimes during the week, Cat's friends joined us for dinner at a restaurant or at a jazz club. Simply put, we enjoyed ourselves as we never had before.

Cat's days of being healthy ended in June 1962. The results of her regular six-month checkup alarmed her doctor and more tests followed. They showed that the cancer had returned, and another round of chemotherapy was scheduled. This time there was no surgery, but the ten weekly treatments were even harder on her than before. Again, she had a problem keeping food down and lost weight, she had no energy, and slept much of the day. We also had to pull the wigs out of storage. And she was depressed to the point of irritability. I tried to keep things as positive as possible, but it was painful watching what she was going through.

Unfortunately, the follow-up appointments controlled the cancer but did not eliminate it. As a result, Cat had a couple of mild treatments about every six months with hopes that things would not get worse, and they didn't for about eighteen months, but early in the summer of 1964 it was clear that Cat would not win this battle. The end came in September 1964.

The loss of Cat devastated me. Throughout her illness, I had never really considered that she would die. During her final weeks, that possibility smacked me hard. As I watched her fade away, the evolving reality swallowed a little bit of me each day. After she was gone, I was completely broken. My life had been so entwined with hers that I had a hard time functioning on my own. We had developed a daily rhythm together that completely ordered my life. We began each day at breakfast together with the *New York Times,* talking about current events. At dinners, we spent an hour or more unraveling our days and then often took an evening walk together, even during the winter, occasionally stopping in shops or galleries along the way. A glass of wine and some television time ended most of our days. That comfortable, shared routine had been shattered. Now I couldn't sleep, I couldn't eat, I had no interest in anything, even baseball, and I ached from loneliness all the time. The memories of times and adventures with Cat haunted me relentlessly. The only thing that brought me any solace was flying, but even that became a challenge.

My friends and family tried to rescue me, but for at least six months there was nothing they could do. Almost weekly, Mary Ann and David invited me to Harrisburg and though I wanted to see them and the kids, I only visited once. David tried to talk me through my grief. He called me regularly, but I hardly heard what he was saying. Sam and Brigitte made sure that I had a couple of good meals each week, and my Eastern Air colleagues unsuccessfully tried to lift my spirits.

Finally, a step at a time, I slowly began to emerge from my cave. Phil was the one who was able to begin chipping away the sadness that encased me. He visited me in New York regularly, but even more importantly, he toted me back to Maine with him half a dozen times during that terrible year. Slowly, Maine became a place of rebirth for me. Cat and I had only visited a few times, so there weren't many ghosts to upset me, and long walks in the woods and by the ocean seemed to soothe my broken soul. Phil also talked me through some of the pain and helped me begin to embrace my memories of Cat rather than mourn them.

It was a slow process.

One of Phil's suggestions was that I think about retirement. Though I had been at Eastern for almost forty years, longer than anyone in the company, I never considered retirement until Phil started to plan it for me. As he laid it out, it began to appeal to me.

During the past fifteen years, commercial flying had become all about jets, and I didn't fly jets. There was a new generation of pilots who were far more knowledgeable than me. I was still a mechanic at heart, but jet engines required specialists and I was not a specialist. I hadn't done pilot training for years. I no longer needed to oversee pilots, the Federal Aviation Authority did that. Instead, I had sunk into the administrative activities at Eastern, and I had never been excited about doing administrative stuff. I also realized that I was the last of my generation. Of course, Phil was gone. Gary had retired to Colorado five years earlier. Even Joey had somehow avoided the hazards of his avocation and moved to Southern California.

Numerous times Phil suggested: "Maybe it's time for a move. Find somewhere new where you want to live. It'll be a fresh start for you. A place where you can carry your happy memories and start to make new ones. A new adventure."

The more I thought about it, the more I liked the idea, and during the next few months I created a checklist with the things about a new home that would help me feel happy.

"I love New York City but don't think I could stay without Cat."

"I can understand that. Sarah and I loved New York too, but after Dad died, we were ready to move on. It's one of the best decisions we ever made. We love Maine!"

"Maine is a little too far for me. I want to be close enough to Mary Ann, David, and the kids so that I could visit regularly. And I don't want to go south. I hate hot, humid summers."

"Sounds like northern Pennsylvania or central New York to me."

"Yeah, and I think I'd like to have some water nearby too. Maybe a lake. Of course, I'd also need an airport. It could be a small, local airport where I can fly my Cessna."

As I began to think seriously about retiring, I checked with my financial planner, my brother Ray, and discovered that I was worth a lot more than I thought. Ray had done a very good job. Cat had always handled our finances, so I never really knew about our investments. I paid the bills while she was sick but never looked beyond our checking account and the day-to-day expenses.

When I told Phil about what a good job Ray had done for me over the years, he came up with yet another reason to retire.

"If you want, you'll be able to buy some land, build a house, and set up your own little hangar just like you had back in Middletown."

That pushed me over the edge. I decided the time had come. I was ready to start a brand-new adventure. Leaving New York behind would be emotional, but I thought about other times in my life when I had left one place to resettle in another—going off to World War I, leaving Harrisburg for New York City, the move to Victorville, and then the move back. Though each move included a degree of sadness, each one had been a positive step in my life.

The challenge now was finding the right place to go. My first thoughts were about northern Pennsylvania. There were places there that met some of my priorities, but none felt right. Phil suggested Ithaca in south central New York. It had a large lake, Lake Cayuga. I could either fly or drive to Harrisburg in several hours, it was close to New York City, and land was relatively inexpensive. It also had two colleges, which appealed to me. One Saturday I flew out to look at the area and liked what I saw. I also got in touch with a real estate agent who suggested land that was available. The more I thought about it, the more I became convinced that a move to Ithaca would be good for me.

By the end of the summer 1965, I had purchased fifty acres of land on Cayuga Lake, just west of Ithaca. In September, I contracted with a builder, and we designed a cozy three-bedroom, shake-shingle cottage about one hundred yards from the lake. The house would have a large living room with a stone fireplace and a view looking out over the lake. Each bedroom would have its own bathroom and there'd be a large screened-in porch that connected a den and kitchen with a hangar big enough for two planes. The contractor also helped me find someone to carve out and pave a runway.

Watching the house go up energized me. I had the runway and hangar done first so that I could fly to Ithaca on weekends to inspect the construction. I was excited seeing the foundation in place, then as the floors and walls and roof went up, my plans for the move became ever more tangible. The house was completed a couple of weeks before my scheduled June 1 retirement date, and by the time retirement rolled around, I was raring to at last make the move. I had already flown mementos that Cat and I had acquired over the years but decided to buy all new furniture instead of keeping what we had in New York. It meant that the first couple of weeks in my new home were a bit spartan, but it was worth it.

Appropriately, my first visitors were Phil and Sarah who came for the Fourth of July and fireworks across the lake. I wanted them both to know how appreciative I was for the attention and help they'd given me during the past two years.

"If you and Sarah hadn't convinced me to retire and build this house, tonight you'd probably be in Maine, and I'd still be wallowing in grief somewhere."

"Nah, you'd have worked your way out of those clouds.

Sarah and I just helped you figure it out."

That first summer I spent most evenings at dusk on the front porch looking out over Cayuga Lake. It became a time to conjure up warm memories and thoughts of Cat. I still missed her so much that sometimes it hurt, but I also recognized that she would always be a part of me. Her stamp was permanently on the way I looked at life. She had shown me how to see the little wonders of life that are everywhere if you're willing to look for them. She helped me understand that pain is part of life, and while it may never go away completely, it will fade if we let it. I had always been a pretty intense guy, but Cat taught me how to be more patient and to laugh at myself occasionally. I learned how to put things in perspective from her. Don't get too excited about your successes or too upset about your failures. Life is to be appreciated even when things don't go the way you expect them to. Most of all, Cat pushed me to be good to myself. Life is to be enjoyed as much as possible.

Chapter 19

LIFE ON CAYUGA

Uncle Don spent his last twenty years on Cayuga Lake. I was sixteen when he moved to the lake and still remember how worried Mom and Dad were about his transition from New York City. They were especially concerned that he would feel isolated. He had no friends in Ithaca, and while it was a busy little town, the entertainment and recreation options were limited compared to New York. Uncle Don quickly proved their concerns unfounded. He became involved in several community organizations, including the local veterans organization. He joined the local chess club and began to play in tournaments. He also sat in on history classes at Ithaca College and Cornell. He told me many times that his one big regret in life was that he never went to college.

After he moved, he visited us in Harrisburg for two weeks each summer and a week in the winter. I always liked his visits, but I enjoyed visiting him at the lake even more. I spent several days at his house a couple of times a year. When I was there, he took me flying and often let me fly the plane once we were up in the air. It was a thrill. He said that someday he'd teach me to fly, but we never got around to that.

"My runway is too short for a beginner. We'd need to use the Ithaca airport."

One of my favorite things to do with him was to paddle on the lake. He had gotten a canoe shortly after he moved to Ithaca, and we spent many hours exploring the lake. There were lots of little inlets and rocky banks to probe. He also had fishing rods but neither of us fished.

"I got those rods because my friend Phil said I'd learn to enjoy it. I tried it numerous times but never got the hang of fishing. I'd rather paddle around than sit with a pole in my hands waiting for fish to bite."

I tried it a couple of times too but agreed. For me, there were better ways to spend time on the water.

Nights at Uncle Don's were a combination of watching the news after dinner, playing chess or pool or ping pong in his basement rec room, and reading. He always set aside time to read. Whenever I talked to him, I knew that one of his questions would be, "What are you reading?" If I didn't have a good answer, he'd recommend something or tell me to find a book from his collection, and he had lots of books.

"Your Aunt Cat loved books and got me into the habit of reading every day. It opens all kinds of new worlds and there are so many good stories."

I was always a reader, so abiding by his reading edict was fine with me.

My relationship with Uncle Don grew when I went to college. Of course, I was looking for a school that was academically strong, but I also wanted to play baseball. I had made all-star and all-conference teams in high school and was being recruited by several colleges. It didn't take much for Uncle Don to convince me that Cornell would be a great spot for me.

"It's Ivy League, and you don't get better than that academically, and the baseball team plays the big guys like Syracuse and Penn State and Ohio State."

I knew he'd be happy to have me only be a few miles away and that he'd enjoy watching my home games if I made the team. My only concern was whether I had the credentials to get into Cornell. I had done well in high school and my college board exams were better than I expected. Still, Cornell would be a longshot. I applied to three other schools, but Cornell was my first choice.

On February 5, 1968, I got an acceptance letter from Cornell. I was ecstatic about getting in. When I told Uncle Don about the news, he seemed almost as happy as I was.

During my four years at Cornell, I saw my uncle a lot. We had dinner together at least once every two or three weeks. Often, he treated me at one of the restaurants in Ithaca. A couple of times each semester I spent a weekend at his house, which I always enjoyed. During my last year at Cornell, Uncle Don set up a room with a desk and bookshelves where I could work on my senior thesis without interruptions. I made the Cornell baseball team as a freshman, but for three years was the backup shortstop/ second baseman. Even though I didn't get a lot of playing time during those three seasons, my uncle came to most of my home games, including the ones on cold and ugly early spring afternoons. In my senior year, I was the starting shortstop, and he didn't miss a game. I always liked having him there. Also, the summer between my junior and senior years I played in the Cape Cod League and Uncle Don flew my parents and sisters to the Cape to watch four of my games and have a short family vacation.

My college years came during the height of the Vietnam War. Reaction to the war split the nation. Dozens of protests on college campuses included several at Cornell. There was never any doubt about where Uncle Don stood on the war. "Something I learned over the years: Nobody wins a war. The 'winner' is the one that loses the least. There are times when a war is unavoidable. World War I was unavoidable. World War II was unavoidable. Korea was avoidable and this thing in Vietnam was a giant mistake. It should never have started and now should be ended as quickly as possible. Mark my words, Vietnam will be a scar that will take the nation a couple of generations to heal. What it's doing to our troops is almost unforgivable."

After my sophomore year, I found out that my uncle's opposition to the war was not just limited to marches and protests. Several years after I graduated, I was talking to a college friend who told me that my uncle had helped six classmates I knew avoid the draft by flying them to Canada. When I asked Uncle Don about it, he admitted the story was true.

"It was in the summer of 1970. You were just about ready to go home for the summer and had some friends over to say goodbye. The war was going terribly. Every night, Walter Cronkite showed footage with piles of bodies and bloody fighting in rice paddies. Two of your friends were graduating. I got talking to them, asking what they planned to do with their Cornell diplomas. All they could talk about was being drafted. They both had low numbers in the lottery, one was in single digits and the other wasn't much higher. They were sure that Uncle Sam would soon be in touch with them. That's when one of them, Jeffery something or other, mentioned heading out for Canada. He had some friends there but was worried about getting across the border. I tried to convince them that Canada might not be the best solution. I told them that they could register as conscientious objectors, but they would have to pay the consequences. They paid no attention to what I said. Theywere set on going to Canada. Somewhere in our discussion, I told them that I had a plane and could fly them there. They both liked the idea and asked if I was serious. I said that if they were serious about running to Canada, I was serious about flying them there.

"We started planning several days later. We set a date when there would be a new moon so that it would be as dark as possible. I mapped out a route that crossed the border over a stretch of land between Lake Ontario and Lake Erie. I didn't want to fly over water because it would have been easier to spot us. Jeffrey got in touch with his friends in Canada to arrange a pickup spot and time. Ten days later, each of my two passengers filled a couple of suitcases, loaded them onto the plane, and we made our flight.

"We left about midnight and flew low to avoid radar. We crossed the border just north of Niagara Falls, then flew north to a private airfield outside Hamilton, Ontario. We had carefully mapped out the trip and had no problem finding the runway. The guys' friend was there to meet us just as we had planned. It took about fifteen minutes to land, unload, and get back in the air headed for Ithaca. I landed back home at a little after three in the morning. The trip went about as well as I could have hoped, and I felt a sense of accomplishment that I hadn't felt in a long time. I really didn't like defying the government, but I did like the idea that I had possibly helped save the lives of two young men.

"Two weeks after the flight, four friends of the guys I had flown to Canada came to my house and asked me to do the same thing for them. I told them I would, but I could only take two at a time. My plane could carry six passengers but with all the luggage they would be carrying, I didn't take a chance. The four of us planned a trip for the next new moon and then the one that followed four weeks later.

The second trip went almost as well as the first. We left a little before midnight. I flew the same route and made a little better time. In fact, we arrived a few minutes before the pick-up car. The turnaround went smoothly, and I was home again by three.

"The third trip had problems from the start. It was a blustery, rainy night in Ithaca when we left, and it got worse the closer we got to the border. It was a bumpy trip from start to finish. Normally, I would have flown above the weather but because I wanted to stay beneath radar, we flew low, which added to the danger. The wind also picked up as we approached the border. Rather than continuing to fly into the wind, I decided to fly almost one hundred miles west of the planned route, which meant we had to fly over Lake Erie. Getting back to Hamilton and finding the airfield also took a while. We finally made it to the drop-off spot about an hour and a half past our expected arrival time. Fortunately, the contact person waited for us. My flight back home was a little easier because I was flying with the wind behind me, but I didn't get home until just before dawn. I vowed that it would be my last trip and it was."

I was surprised when Uncle Don told me about his draft-dodging trips. As far as I knew, he had never so flagrantly broken the law, but he knew the risks involved and must have been very committed to helping the guys. He never did tell me who they were.

After I graduated, I didn't see Uncle Don as much. Fortunately, I got a teaching position an easy three-hour drive from Ithaca. The job gave me some time during summers for an extended stay. I was also close enough that an occasional weekend trip during the school year was possible. While I was in school, my uncle and I had gone to at least one Cornell football game each year. We continued the tradition after I left Cornell.

Three years after graduating, I married a woman who I taught with, and three years later we started a family.

Through those years, Cindy and I made a visit to Uncle Don a permanent part of our summer activities. Even as we added our two girls and a boy during the next six years, a week or two at the lake remained a part of every summer. We also usually visited him for several days during Christmas breaks until the kids were in middle school. He visited us every spring.

By the time my kids were in school, I could see that Uncle Don was slowing down a bit. He was still healthy, in good shape, and active for his age, but our canoe trips and hikes were shorter and less frequent. His daily afternoon naps got longer, and his stride became a bit less robust. The most telling sign that he was feeling his age was when he stopped flying.

"It's my eyes. I just can't see into the clouds or estimate distances the way I need to. It gets dangerous landing a plane when you're not completely sure how far it is to the runway."

He was about eighty-two at that point.

Despite becoming ever more sedentary, my uncle remained a favorite of our children. They loved his stories and liked being around him. I know he enjoyed them too. Aside from his stories, walks in the woods, and summer swims in the lake, the kids always looked forward to playing board games with him. Just about every night and many rainy afternoons when we visited, a couple of hours were spent playing board games. At first, the games were simple children's games, but as the kids got older, they played more complicated thinking games. Of course, my uncle taught them chess, though only one, Danielle, the oldest girl, ever really learned the finer points of the game. Regardless of what it was, Uncle Don always kept the kids entertained.

One of my uncle's goals was to make it to the new millennium, and I was certain that he would. I was wrong. He missed it by six years, but I'm sure he died happy even though it was still the twentieth century. I learned of his death from my mother. It happened during the early spring. She said he had been on his daily walk by the lake and had a heart attack. A neighbor saw him fall and called 911, but by the time the paramedics got to him, he was gone. Of course, I grieved his death, but in the weeks that followed, I came to realize what a rich life he had lived. I also realized that bits and pieces of him were as alive as ever. I could see it in my children, my parents, and, especially, in me. And now, after having read about my uncle's many adventures, a tiny piece of him lives with you.

Everyone should have an Uncle Don in their lives.

ABOUT THE AUTHOR

Paul Doutrich is a professor emeritus of American history at York College of Pennsylvania where he taught for thirty years. He now lives on Cape Cod in Brewster, Massachusetts.

www.ingramcontent.com/pod-product-compliance
Lightning Source LLC
Chambersburg PA
CBHW031207310726
48969CB00001B/250